ICHABOD'S CURSE ENDURES

The Headless Horseman Rides Again

Veronique Holloway

Dedication

For the real Ichabod Crane, lost to time and fiction

1

Modern Day

"DOCTOR Crane? Are you saying the *Legend of Sleepy Hollow* was a work of nonfiction and the Headless Horseman was real, riding through the countryside searching for his missing head?"

Isadora and the entire class looked towards the back of the room at the student who had asked the question. She tried to determine if it had been an attempt at a joke or if it had been asked in earnest. There had been a few snickers, but the confused looks around the room told her it was the latter. Her students seemed to think she was trying to convince them that the impossible was real.

"Of course not" she replied. "No one could survive without their head."

At this, there was laughter and noticeable relief that their professor was not crazy.

"I was referring to Washington Irving's *explanation* as to how the Headless Horseman came about, not the Horseman himself. This was based on a real incident that actually occurred during the Revolutionary War. Irving used real events along with real people and places in his story. The Brom, Van Tassel, and Ichabod Crane characters were all based on real people and Sleepy Hollow was and still is a real location. Irving spent a lot of time traveling around various parts of New York and Europe and he drew from his experiences and the people he encountered. The Village of Sleepy Hollow is a little north of New York City along the Hudson River, though it was only named that in 1996 in honor of the story. Prior to that, it had always been North Tarrytown. It has its own government and its own police and fire departments. The Old Dutch Church, the burial ground, and the mill pond from the story are all real places within the village. These landmarks are how the story was identified as having actually been set within Tarrytown, even though Irving called the location Sleepy Hollow in the story."

It was the first lecture in Doctor Isadora Crane's month-long *'Ode to Halloween'* series where every week her English Literature students had to read a different short story that had something to do with fall or horror. Of all the courses she taught, all the stories she had her students read, this month of this class was always her favorite. It often proved to be a favorite of the students as well. Isadora had always loved Halloween, and not only for the candy, either. Even as a child, she had always enjoyed the idea of dressing up as something she was not. She loved the creativity behind the costumes, the possibility that anything could happen, and the pretense that for one night, a person could be anyone or anything. People always talked about the magic of Christmas, but it was Halloween's magic that had always drawn her in.

"As for the characters," Isadora went on, "the names are those of real people to varying degrees, but this is where Irving took quite a bit of license. The area was settled primarily by Dutch families. Van Tassel was a very common name in the area as the family was large and had many holdings. However, there was no record of anyone by the name Baltus during the period referenced in the story, and Katrina Van Tassel was thought to have been named after someone called Catriena Ecker Van Tassel, though the inspiration for the character may have come from Catriena's great-niece, Eleanor Van Tassel. There's a lot of speculation surrounding the inspiration for this character as Irving apparently enjoyed telling women in town that they had each inspired the character."

This was met with more chuckles and knowing looks amongst the students. It was thought to be a ploy to get into the good graces of many a woman Irving encountered.

"When we talk about Brom," Isadora continued, "his name and character may have been an amalgamation of different people. There was no one named Van Brunt in the area, but it was a common Long Island name. During the Revolutionary War, there was a name recorded on the muster roll of Captain Gabriel Requa's company as Abraham Van Tassel, aka 'Bones,' and Brom was a common nickname of Abraham. Brom's character may also have been drawn from another real person. When Irving lived in the area, there was an Abraham Martling living there as well. He was the local blacksmith in the village and was reportedly a large man who rode a gigantic black horse. There's some speculation that Martling may have been the inspiration for the character, if not the name."

Isadora watched her students to make sure she had not lost them, or worse, put them to sleep. She glanced out the window at the trees which were beginning to change colors. She loved this time of year and wanted more than anything to be outside hiking in the surrounding mountains, taking in all the color and cool air. Instead, she continued her lecture.

"Unlike the variations Irving used in naming his other characters, Ichabod Crane was the name of a real person. Though there's no evidence that Irving and Ichabod ever met in person, he and Ichabod were both stationed at Fort Pike on the New York side of Lake Ontario during the War of 1812. It's likely that Irving saw the name somewhere and decided to use it in his story. As an aide-de-camp to the governor of New York during the war, it's entirely possible that he saw Ichabod's name in some paperwork and it stuck with him.

"Now, the real Ichabod was nothing like the mousy schoolteacher in the story. He was the son of a brigadier general and a military officer himself, having enlisted at the age of twenty-two. His grandfather was a judge and a delegate to the First Continental Congress. One of his brothers was a naval officer while the other was a judge and a congressman in Ohio. His own son was also a brigadier general and the Surgeon General of the United States, and in fact, was an attending physician to Abraham Lincoln after the president was shot. Ichabod spent forty-five years in the military, having served in the War of 1812, the Black Hawk War, and the Mexican American War, ending his own career as a colonel. Now, does this sound like someone who often shrank," Isadora referred back to her notes and quoted from the original story, "'with curdling awe at the sounds of his own steps' and dreaded 'to look over his own shoulder, lest he should behold some uncouth being tramping close behind him'?"

A round of murmurs was heard and heads bobbed in agreement around the classroom.

Someone near the front of the room declared, "He never would have run away from a fight."

Isadora Crane may have been biased but was inclined to agree. Another student raised a hand and asked, "Why didn't Ichabod just sue Washington Irving or something to get him to change the name in the story? I mean, did he ever confront Irving about it?"

Isadora considered the question briefly before answering. "Again, there was no evidence they ever met. And remember, this was two hundred years ago. It was a different time. People weren't quite as sue-happy as we are now. There were no television or movies, and it was rare to achieve such literary success in one's own time, even then. This story along with *Rip Van Winkle* were both short stories published in *The Sketch Book of Geoffrey Crayon, Gent.* At the time, the short story wasn't even a genre. These two are often thought of as the first examples of short stories. And *The Legend of Sleepy Hollow* was the first piece of

American literature to garner international acclaim. Irving was thought to be not only the father of the short story, but the first American writer to achieve international fame. It's likely he never imagined how successful and popular his story would become. Ichabod was only a captain during the War of 1812, so most likely, Irving came across the name of what would have been some random officer who wasn't even all that high-ranking yet. Fame came after publication and by then it was too late."

Another student joined in with, "Why not just use the name of another local person like he did with the Van Tassels?"

"The Ichabod in the story was an itinerant worker, which was true to the period. It was not uncommon for schoolteachers then to travel to other areas in search of employment. So, it wouldn't have made sense for Irving to use a local name for that character. Katrina, on the other hand, was a local character and Van Tassel was a common enough real name. In that area during that time, it would've been like using 'Smith' today. But, since there's no record of a Katrina, he clearly used a common local surname and made up the first name, as he did with his other local characters."

With no more questions, she pressed on, "While Irving used Ichabod's name, a fact we can easily surmise Ichabod was none too happy about, the inspiration for the character was drawn from another real person that Irving knew. Irving had met a schoolteacher in Kinderhook, New York who was, in fact, from Connecticut just as in the story. Jesse Merwin moved to Kinderhook in 1808 with his parents and brothers. Not only was he reported to have had the mannerisms and behavior of the character in the story, but apparently, he relished in his likeness having been used for the main character and often bragged about being the inspiration for it."

"Someone actually bragged about inspiring a character like that?" one of the students scoffed, causing chuckles throughout the room.

Isadora smiled but continued on. "Perhaps the most interesting background on any of the characters is that of the Headless Horseman."

This next part of the story was Isadora's favorite part to tell. Most of her students enjoyed hearing the tale of how the Hessian came to lose his head, even if the rest of the story was not always as exciting. She could see some of the students perk up at this, including the student who had asked about the realness of the Horseman.

"We know the story takes place in 1790, shortly after the Revolutionary War, and that the Horseman is 'said by some to be the ghost of a Hessian trooper, whose head had been carried away by a cannonball, in some nameless battle' during the war." She read the segment of the story directly from her notes as she had when speaking about the fragment describing Ichabod in order to make sure she did not misquote anything. She knew the story inside out, but she had never been good at memorizing things word-for-word.

"During the Revolution, that entire area of the Hudson River Valley was a sort of neutral territory between the British in the south and the Americans to the north. Because no one claimed the area, it left the population particularly vulnerable, with constant fighting and skirmishes between the two armies. The British contracted about thirty thousand German mercenaries to serve during the war. These mercenaries mostly came from the state of Hesse-Cassel, which led to them being called Hessian Jägers or Hessians. They were known for their sharpshooting and horsemanship skills along with their ruthlessness and brutality both on and off the field."

A soft knock at the door followed by it opening interrupted Isadora. She looked over to see the student aide for the department standing in front of a mailman. Denise lowered her voice as Isadora came over.

"I'm sorry for the interruption, Doctor Crane. He wouldn't leave the letter unless you signed for it in person."

"It's fine, Denise."

The mailman held out an electronic device for Isadora to sign. She did so then handed it back to him and he handed her a certified letter in exchange. She glanced down at it, not recognizing the return address in Yonkers, New York.

Closing the door behind the departing pair, Isadora walked back over to the desk and placed the envelope in her briefcase for later perusal. Turning back to her class, she tried to remember where she had left off.

"Where was I?"

"You were telling us about how a Hessian became the Headless Horseman, Doctor Crane," one of the students supplied helpfully.

"Right. It begins in 1777 with a raid on the farmhouse of a Cornelius and Elizabeth Van Tassel followed by a Hessian soldier being buried in an unmarked grave inside the Old Dutch Church burying ground at the insistence of the Van Tassels."

2

November 17, 1777

"Where's my baby?" Elizabeth Van Tassel screeched hysterically as the flames roared high into the night sky.

"Leah!"

Eleanor watched as her mother tried running back into their modest farmhouse on the Saw Mill River that was now fully engulfed in flames. Her father ran after Elizabeth while yelling at her and the British soldiers, but the soldiers reached her first. The men in their red uniforms roughly held her back from going any closer to the burning building. Elizabeth was so distraught, it took three of them to prevent her from going any further. As Eleanor looked around, she realized Leah was not the only one of her siblings missing. Her oldest brother was also unaccounted for.

When the soldiers came, they had barged into the farmhouse and taken everyone prisoner, but Cornelius

Junior had somehow managed to not be caught. He must have hidden. Was he still inside the house now? Eleanor had tried to get to Leah, but the soldiers pulled her away before she could. She had kicked and screamed as she tried to get to her sister, but one of those Hessian mercenaries that accompanied the redcoats lifted her up and threw her over his shoulder like a sack of flour.

Eleanor huddled closer to her younger brother John, pulling him into her side. They watched as the redcoats and their mercenaries stole all of their cattle. When this war first started, they had all thought they would be safe living as far away from any of the cities as they did. It quickly became apparent they would not be spared from the atrocities after all. They found themselves in neutral territory which sounded far better than the reality.

After the Battle of White Plains in October 1776, the Continental Army and the British both abandoned the area with the Americans staying to the north of the Hudson River Valley while the British remained in the south, around New York City. The entire Westchester Valley was left scorched and primed for raids from both sides. Loyalist rangers, British light infantry, Hessian Jägers, and Patriot militias all marauded as they pleased. If that was not bad enough, the door was left open for outlaws and vigilantes to engage in whatever devastation they wished as well. The area was filled with violence and the population had been left in constant danger from attacks by all manner of men.

"Cornelius, where have you been?" Eleanor asked as the boy was carried over and dropped on the ground at her feet, wet and shivering, wearing nothing but a pair of trousers.

"I tried to get help," he said between chattering teeth. "I hid in the attic at first, but when the smoke got too thick, I jumped out the window and tried to get to the picket station at Farcus Holt. I made it to the river but I broke through the ice."

"John, come over here," Eleanor ordered.

At thirteen, she was almost four years his senior and often took charge when their parents were otherwise engaged as they were now. She directed John to scoot in close to Cornelius, and together, they used their body heat to try and warm him up. Despite the darkness, she could see that his lips were blue and he did not look so good. They did their best, but Cornelius was soaking wet and it was a cold November night. The snow on the ground around them made it impossible to warm up, but Eleanor had already failed to keep her baby sister safe. She would not fail Cornelius.

Elizabeth sobbed into her hands as the British soldiers finally left her. Cornelius Senior took his wife into his arms, knowing there was little he could do to console her. Their farmhouse was past the point of being saved and anyone still inside would be long gone. All she could do was watch her home burn while her husband held her. The scene before them would have broken her heart even without Leah's death. How would they ever recover from the loss of their home and all their cattle? They had plenty of land and could rebuild, but it would take time. Without her baby, though, she was not certain she wanted to rebuild.

With the soldiers now preoccupied with taking everything they could, a Hessian mercenary approached Elizabeth and Cornelius. Was he there to finish them off and leave them for dead? She did not care.

"Come with me," he said roughly while looking around at his compatriots.

Without another word, he turned and started to walk away. Elizabeth did not want to follow him, but she did anyway. Despite the roughness to his words, there had been compassion in his eyes. She and Cornelius followed him into the dark shed and he pointed down to the ground where she could make out a small bundle in the corner. As her eyes adjusted to the darkness, she saw her baby wrapped tightly in a blanket, safe and sound. The relief on her face was instant and her tears of mourning quickly became tears of joy. She hurriedly scooped the bundle up and cradled Leah in her arms while Cornelius thanked the man profusely.

"How will we ever repay you?"

"It's not necessary. I became a soldier to fight other soldiers," he explained. "Not to harm innocent families."

ೠ ಞ

September 16, 1778

"That battle last night was close by," Eleanor said to her father as they made their way back from selling at the market.

"It was," her father agreed. "Try not to let it trouble you overly much, my dear. By the grace of God, this war shall soon be over."

The farmhouse had slowly been rebuilt and the Van Tassel family was doing their best to recover from the events of almost a year ago. Cornelius Junior battled with pneumonia for months and still struggled constantly after his fall into the icy river. Every time he had nearly recovered, he fell ill again in no time.

They were nearing the Pocantico River that ran along Philipse Manor, but before they got there, they could see the remnants of the previous night's skirmish. The guns had roared, and John had tried guessing what size they were. He was certain the balls were thirty-two pounders, arguing that because they were the biggest, they were also the loudest and that was why they could hear them all the way at their farmhouse. They had even watched some of the battle from the upstairs windows, seeing the occasional flashes of light in the distance. Eleanor had been terrified after the raid on their home the year before, but her mother had tried comforting them by saying the soldiers were too busy to stop and harass them again. Eleanor was not so easily convinced.

Looking at the bodies strewn across the field, it gave Eleanor a strange comfort to see so many dead soldiers. Most of them were either British or Continental, but there were also a few French, Indian, and Hessian soldiers amongst the dead. She did not care whose side for which they fought, only that it meant fewer soldiers to raid their farm again. They would not be safe until all of the soldiers were dead. One of the provincial soldiers moved, and she let out a little screech. Cornelius pulled the wagon to a stop and jumped down, running to see if he could render aid.

"Stay here," he ordered Eleanor, but she did not listen. Jumping down, she followed after him, staying close to his side.

No sooner had they arrived at the soldier she had seen moving than they saw him expire from his wounds. They looked around and realized there was nothing they could do for anyone on that field. Other people from the town were already there, looting the bodies, salvaging what could be saved, and cleaning up what they could.

Cornelius rested a hand on his daughter's shoulder as he turned her back in the direction of the wagon. On the way back, they saw a soldier in a Hessian uniform face down in the dirt. The poor soul was missing his head entirely.

"Afternoon Cornelius," Eleanor's uncle called out.

"Peter," her father acknowledged in greeting.

"Have you come to help with the clean up?"

"Eleanor and I were returning home from the market. Looks like you'll have plenty to keep you busy, though. What will you do with them all?"

"We certainly do. The men are digging a ditch over there," Peter said as he pointed in the direction of a group of men. "We'll throw them all in together."

Cornelius frowned. "Not much of a proper burial. They won't be in consecrated ground."

"No. But there are too many to haul up to the burial ground and dig individual graves."

"Well, I certainly don't envy you the task." He turned to walk back to the wagon as he said, "I must be getting back to Elizabeth."

The men bid each other farewell as a couple of men from the village came over to take the Hessian away to the mass grave. Cornelius watched with a frown, hesitating as he guided Eleanor into the wagon. He turned then, going back towards Peter and the other men, calling for them to stop.

"I'll take this one."

Peter's brow furled in confusion. "You'll take him where?"

"To the burial ground beside the Old Dutch Church."

"There's no one to pay for his burial. We don't even know who he is. His head is missing completely." At Cornelius's determined glare, Peter added, "Why would you do that?"

Cornelius leaned closer. "What if it's the same soldier who saved our Leah last year from the fire during the raid?"

"Surely you can't think that. There are thousands of Hessian soldiers here. There's no way to know if this is the same one that helped you last year. This could be anyone."

"It could," Cornelius replied, nodding. "But what if it's not? What if it is him? I would do this for his act of kindness to us."

Peter shook his head but relented. "Alright. He's yours to take."

While her father had been talking with her uncle, Eleanor had run over to the large iron ball she saw several feet away from the Hessian whose head was missing. She bent down and scooped it up, thinking to take it back to John. She would prove to him they were not firing thirty-two pounders after all. This thing must have only weighed twelve or eighteen pounds.

After loading it into the wagon, her father and Peter arrived carrying the Hessian soldier. Her father carried his shoulders while her uncle held his feet. She stared in awe at the gruesome sight of dried blood and tissue hanging from the man's neck, seeping into what remained of his uniform collar, turning it dark.

"Eleanor, give us a hand," her father ordered.

Climbing into the back of the wagon, she helped her father with the awkward maneuvering of the upper body. Careful not to touch what was left of the neck, she pulled on the man's arms and tried to help as best she could. When they finally got the body settled in the back of the wagon, she stared at it for a moment, studying it. She thought maybe she would be able to tell if it was the same man who had helped save Leah, but she could not determine anything. While she studied the body, she saw his top button hanging by a thread. She bent down and tore it off, leaving behind a flap of the uniform where it had been torn during the event which had taken his head. Pocketing the button in her apron, she smiled to herself. John had his souvenir and now she would have one, too.

3

Modern Day

Saturday morning, Isadora met up with her best friend, Simon Diego, for their weekly kickboxing class. They were both transplants to Utah and neither had ever felt like they particularly fit in, which was perhaps in part why they were such good friends. Years ago, she had moved there in the fall for graduate school after a bad break up with her fiancée and Simon had moved there with his wife for work that same winter. They had all been in their twenties and met while skiing, becoming fast friends. Though Isadora was immediately attracted to him, she put him firmly in the friend zone knowing that he was married. The breakup with her fiancée was caused by him cheating on her and there was no way she was going down that road as the other woman, even if Simon had been willing to do so, which he never gave any indication of being. Two years later, Simon's marriage had fallen apart and his now ex-wife moved away.

Of course, Isadora still appreciated his good looks, but now they were friends and she relied on him far too much to think of him romantically. In addition to their weekly kickboxing classes, they hiked together every chance they got when the weather held and skied all winter as soon as there was enough snow on the mountains. Regardless of their individual relationship status with other people, they always spent holidays and birthdays together. They were always there for one another when it came down to it. For every breakup or heartache, she knew she could call Simon and he would be there in minutes.

Simon walked in wearing gym shorts and a tee shirt which hugged his lean chest. His thick black hair was getting long, and he brushed it out of his eyes. Those ice blue eyes always stood out against his golden skin and dark hair and his six feet of height towered over Isadora's five foot six inches. With his looks and charm, he always seemed to have his choice of women, though none of them ever lasted long. She was certain he had given up the idea of ever being in a serious relationship again after his divorce and was content to play the field instead.

Isadora greeted him with a smile, happy to see him even though she was suddenly nervous to share her news with him. She was not sure what it all meant for her future yet and did not know how to tell him. He knew she never felt like Utah was home and she desperately wanted a sense of home. Despite having lived there for several years, she still did not have many ties to the area. Other than him and her job at the university, there was nothing keeping her from leaving, and there were plenty of other universities that she could get hired on with. She did not even have tenure yet. He always bristled at her when she spoke of possibly leaving Utah and she could see this new turn of events easily turning into an argument when she still did not even know what it was.

The class began with a warmup that was too strenuous for talk. Once it got underway, they were able to chat lightly. "How are things going with Becky?" she asked.

"I don't know. She's nice enough, but there's something missing," he replied while punching the bag in front of him.

"There's always something missing, Simon," she teased. She placed a roundhouse on the bag, hitting it exactly where she was aiming and followed it up with an uppercut and a jab. The instructor passed by at that moment and complimented her technique.

When the instructor moved on, Simon took the opportunity to turn the tables on her. "How are things with Derek?"

She groaned and rolled her eyes before replying, "We broke up." At his look of surprise, she continued, "He was way too jealous and possessive. He got mad anytime I even talked to other men. If waiters lingered too long, or if one of my male students stayed late to talk with me, he'd go nuts. It was all too much."

"Really? He must have hated me."

Jab. Side kick. Uppercut. Simon was surprised she had not called when they broke up, but it was not like she had been dating the guy for long. She never let anyone in close enough for her relationships to last.

"Oh, he did. He thought we spent far too much time together."

Of course, she would never tell Simon that he was actually the reason they broke up. When Derek told her it was him or Simon, she did not hesitate. They had not been together long, though even if they had been, she could not see herself ever choosing someone who would demand that she gave up her friendship with Simon in order to be with him. She told him to get lost and did not look back.

When class finished, they walked out to their cars together. Wisps of her deep copper hair had fallen out of her ponytail and were now plastered to her sweaty skin. She imagined how awful it must look and found herself playing with her hair while she and Simon talked before leaving. She still had to tell him her news but was hesitant.

Finally, he left her no choice when he asked, "You want to get in one more hike next weekend before it gets too cold?"

Isadora knew this was her opportunity to tell him, but she was still nervous. "I can't. I have to go to New York next week."

At this, Simon was really surprised. He wondered how he had suddenly become so uninformed about what was happening in his best friend's life. First Derek, now a trip to New York?

"Why are you going to New York? When did this even happen?"

Isadora could see the surprise on his face but there was something else there, too. Was it hurt? It had been a particularly busy week, and they had not spoken since last Saturday. She guessed she should have called him after she received the letter. However, the contents of it had not made sense to her, and she did not yet know if there was anything to tell. She told him it was an impromptu trip and filled him in on everything that had happened that week.

"I received a certified letter from an attorney in Yonkers." Isadora danced from foot to foot, playing with her necklace. "It said that I've inherited some estate. The letter wasn't very informative, so I called the number, and they told me I need to come to New York in order to sign all the paperwork and claim the estate. Apparently, it comes with some property but there's some sort of problem with it. It sounds like it's been vacant for a while, has fallen into disrepair, and the officials want to condemn it. As the owner of the property, I have to go in person and prove that I'm taking the necessary steps to fix it up. Otherwise, I forfeit my rights to any of it. I have to provide regular updates to the building inspector, showing significant progress by the end of the year or they'll declare the property abandoned. It's probably just some little hovel that will end up costing more than it's worth to repair, but at least the estate is paying for the trip, so I won't be out of pocket for all the travel costs. But the attorney said it's in Sleepy Hollow." Isadora paused to let that sink in for a moment.

It took no time for Simon to pick up the significance of it. "Is it a joke?"

"That's the first thing I asked!" she exclaimed, happy that she did not have to explain it to him. It made her feel good that he knew her so well. "The attorney didn't say much over the phone; only that they found me through my ancestry DNA profile." She nudged his shoulder with hers. "Thanks for convincing me to do that."

The previous fall, when Isadora had been feeling particularly lonely, Simon had purchased the kit for her as a Christmas present. She had been skeptical about taking the test, but he convinced her, saying that she was out nothing by taking it. If it came back showing that she had no living relatives, it was nothing she did not already know. However, there was always the possibility that it could come back saying that she did have living relatives. Was that not worth trying?

Simon nodded but was still skeptical. "So, who was this person? How are you related?"

"I have no idea. The attorney said he would explain more in person. He has some documentation to back everything up. But it had to be someone on my dad's side of the family. Probably someone who got a kick out of our connection to the story. They probably lived it up and worked it as much they could, perpetuating the image of the cowardly schoolteacher."

Isadora rolled her eyes. She ran into people like that often; people who always believed that Ichabod Crane was the man from the story whenever she said he was a real person. It was the reason she rarely told people who her famous ancestor was. Sometimes people would be curious and open to hearing about the real person, but usually, they only thought of the character as Irving described him. Simon had been one of the curious.

"That does seem likely. Why else would someone in your family live in Sleepy Hollow of all places?"

"Ichabod is the only one with ties to Sleepy Hollow that I was ever aware of and there's no evidence that he ever stepped foot there, let alone that he ever lived there. He spent most of his life in military service and died in Staten Island. His only link to the place is the story. But really, I simply cannot imagine who would leave me an estate." They had been friends for a long time, and he was her closest confidant, so she allowed herself a brief moment of vulnerability with Simon, something she never did with anyone else. "I mean, it's not like I have any family."

She had said it so flippantly that Simon was stung by the declaration. He thought of himself as Isadora's family. Despite her flippancy, he also knew it hurt her more than she let on. He knew her history well and had marveled at her telling of it, both the recent history and the ancient. Isadora's father had been in the military when she was a child, which meant they had moved around a lot. She was always attending a new school and had never put down roots anywhere. When he was sent off to fight in the War on Terror, he never came home. He had been killed in action and her mother had not known how to cope with his death. She had numbed herself with drugs and by the time Isadora was fifteen, her mother had died from an overdose, leaving her to live with the only living relative of which she was aware, her father's mother. Her Gran had cared for her until she went away to college, but she got sick and passed away when Isadora was home during a summer break. It was the following year that she had found her fiancée in bed with another woman. She had a hard time letting people in after that.

Simon knew she was always waiting for the people in her life to leave, which was why he tried so hard to be involved and be there for her. After all the years, she still kept him at a distance, too. They were best friends, but he wished she would open her heart to him. He had fallen in love with her after his divorce. She had been there for him when his world fell apart and he saw a side of her that she never showed the rest of the world. When he had finally realized he was in love with her, she had been seeing someone else. Even if she had not been, they had been friends for so long, he was sure she did not feel the same way and he was afraid to ruin their friendship by pushing the issue. He wanted to give her everything she longed for. But right now, he felt like he had not been there for her this week and now she was going off to New York. He was not even sure what this would mean. What kind of inheritance was this? Would she leave Utah permanently? Would she find a new life in New York and leave him behind?

"Do you want me to come with you?" Simon was a software engineer, which gave him a lot of flexibility in his work. He often worked from home or took his work with him when he was away. It allowed him to travel more than he would otherwise be able to.

"No. I'm sure it's just a bunch of paperwork, and the run-down hole-in-the-wall that I'll have to figure out how to dump and then I'll be done. Maybe I'll catch a show in the city while I'm there."

"I really don't mind coming with you, Iz. I'd love to help anyway I can, and you know I still have family in Brooklyn. I mean, they'd want to see me of course, but I could use you as an excuse and tell them we're too busy to stay," he joked.

Isadora warmed at the use of his nickname for her and thanked him but told him she could handle it. As much as she wanted him there, she also felt like this was something she had to do on her own. She did not want to have to rely on anyone else for anything. She always felt like she leaned on him a little too much, and knew it was only a matter of time before one of his girlfriends became more than merely a girlfriend. Then she would lose him, too. No. Whether or not there was anything more to this inheritance than the rundown residence, she needed to be able to stand on her own two feet and she could not do that if he came with her. She needed to be free to decide her future without him there distracting her.

4

November 1813

Captain Ichabod Crane sat near the rear of the gunboat, one of his lieutenants beside him, as the eight-thousand-man army wound its way along the Saint Lawrence River toward Montreal with them amongst the lead of the advance. The men commanded one of the ten batteries that made up the First Artillery Regiment. Their men crowded into the boat along with various provisions and artillery. Of the watercraft making up the expedition, over three hundred scows, bateaux, Durham boats, sloops, and schooners contained only men or supplies while twelve gunboats carried the artillery. As artillerymen, they were on these gunboats, responsible for many of the guns and howitzers used by the army. The provisions and stores had been hastily distributed amongst the flotilla, causing the boats to be arranged haphazardly, resulting in overcrowding. Many of the gunboats had even been used to carry hospital stores, against the arguments of Major Abraham Eustis, the artillery commander.

Two eighteen-pounder guns were swivel-mounted at either end of their gunboat, but they also transported a lighter howitzer and a twelve-pound cannon while the thirty-two-pounders on traversing carriages were transported in other vessels by the heavy artillery corps. Once the army engaged the enemy, they were responsible for maintaining and firing these lighter weapons, while keeping them from falling into enemy hands. Each man also carried their own personal arms as well. As artillery officers were usually on horseback, they each had a brace of pistols and a saber which they could use for one-on-one combat. In addition to weapons, each man in the army carried a leather cartridge box containing one hundred twenty-five grains of gunpowder and projectiles, extra pieces of flint, a cloth, and a musket tool to keep the pistols clean along with a knapsack containing all of his own personal belongings, though this was not much. Most knapsacks were filled with a blanket, linen shirts, trousers, extra socks, fatigue blouses, shaving tools, button repair kits, quill pen and ink, a comb, and playing cards. It was not much, but when they traveled twenty-five miles a day, any extra weight quickly became burdensome. Now, the knapsacks only served to contribute to the overcrowding on the small boats.

Ichabod was grateful he was normally on horseback, rather than on foot like the infantrymen. He did not have to carry all of his belongings on his back but instead was able to pack it on his horse. Though he was in the artillery corps, he had initially acted as infantry due to the lack of men when he had first joined, so he knew how burdensome it was to be on foot. It had taken some time to build up the army for the war, but now he was finally serving in the capacity for which he had enlisted. Yet, now he found himself aboard watercraft once again instead of on horseback. At least it was only for transportation and not as a permanent duty station, which had been the case during his service with the marine corps. He had left the corps at the start of the war, not liking the close quarters and conditions of the ships and joined the army as an artilleryman. He would leave naval service to his older brother; the artillery was where he felt he needed to be. Though the majority of this war had been fought on the water, he was only aboard watercraft long enough to be transported to the next location. He did not mind that as much.

"We should be making plans to go into winter quarters right now, not starting an expedition to invade Montreal," Lieutenant Samuel Van Tassel shivered as he pulled his wool coat tighter around himself, trying to block the relentless wind and rain.

It was still early morning, and the air was cold and wet. They had begun planning this expedition in the summer and should have left Lake Ontario much sooner than they had, but the weather had not cooperated. It had pushed their departure back until mid-October and now they had only entered the Saint Lawrence River three days ago, on the first of November. They were almost to French Creek now but still had a long way to go.

"Yes, but if we can take Montreal, it will go a long way towards ending this war. The British supply lines would be cut off to Upper Canada. Right now, there are only six thousand British troops in Montreal. When we join with General Hampton's forces, we'll outnumber the British by two to one. If we wait, they may get reinforcements. They have another eight thousand militia in reserve. If they're allowed to reach Montreal, we'll lose our advantage." Ichabod blew on his fingers, trying to chase away the numbness setting in.

General Wade Hampton was coming from Lake Champlain by way of the Chateauguay River with four thousand men. They were to meet up on the Saint Lawrence River before invading Montreal.

"I heard General Hampton tried to resign when he found out General Wilkinson was to be in charge of this expedition," Samuel said conspiratorially. "They say he refuses to take orders from Wilkinson."

Ichabod frowned. He did not wish to encourage gossip amongst the ranks, but if there was discontent amid the command, it could affect their lives. And Samuel was not simply his lieutenant; they had become friends during the course of the war. They had served together in many battles thus far, during which they had formed a tight bond. Ichabod was well aware of the events of which his friend spoke. General James Wilkinson was rumored to be a scoundrel and a drunkard. As far as he knew, many of the issues were based on General Wilkinson's character and past indiscretions rather than any personal grievances between him and General Hampton. Still, their issues could affect the entire army.

Ichabod lowered his voice, trying not to be heard by the other men under his command, and told his lieutenant, "The rift goes back before the war. General Wilkinson was an agent of the Spanish government and was also somehow involved in the conspiracy that led to Vice President Burr being charged with treason, though I know not the details of that."

Samuel's eyes got wide. "It's little wonder General Hampton refuses to take orders from him."

"Indeed. Because of the conflict between them, the Secretary of War decided that all orders would pass through the War Department instead of being sent directly between the two generals. I admit that I do worry how this will affect us. We need both forces in order to take Montreal. Yet, if the generals cannot communicate directly with each other, or worse, if there's conflict between them once we arrive, how shall we ever defeat the British? It will be up to us to work together despite their differences. We must do what we can to lead by example."

The young lieutenant nodded his head. He knew his captain was concerned over the unwieldy command structure under which they found themselves, but they could still run their company with integrity and do what they came to do. Though, it felt as if everything on this expedition had gone against them thus far. They should have left months ago, but Major General Dearborn had wasted time on campaigns against York and the Niagara Peninsula instead of this expedition, leading to him being relieved of his command and replaced by General Wilkinson only last August. The preparations for this expedition had finally begun in earnest after that.

"In truth, Lieutenant, I'm more concerned with the disease running rampant through the men and the lack of experienced officers," Ichabod continued with his concerns. Now that he had given voice to some, the rest wanted to come out as well. "I'm thankful to have you by my side after having spent the better part of this war with you, but we are an exception. Most of these officers do not have the experience that you and I do. Our men are poorly trained and ill-supplied. We have the superior numbers, but the British have the superior training and experience."

The men watched the banks of the river, keeping an eye out for attackers. Ichabod also watched the fifty men inside the shallow boat they were in as a handful of the men worked the sails at the same time thirty of them manned the sweeps, rowing the boat with the long oars for additional speed. With any luck, they could make up some time on the water, reaching Montreal sooner rather than later.

"Thank you, sir. I —"

Samuel stopped talking as both he and Ichabod leapt to their feet and began looking around while they passed French Creek and suddenly heard shots ring out. Everyone else aboard the vessel began searching as well. All of the men were on alert, and it did not take long to see from where the shots were coming. The flotilla was being pursued and the rear line had come under fire.

"Ground oars," Ichabod ordered his men.

The men responded, pulling their sweeps from the water and holding them out horizontally while they awaited additional orders. He could hear the shouts from the captains in the other boats surrounding them as well. Major Eustis commanded the eight gunboats leading the flotilla, but he never gave the order to assist the rear. They had it well under control. Some of the boats furthest back were heading toward the rear of line while others further up the line held their position. It appeared as though their attackers were few in number. The rear was fighting them off and the four artillery boats bringing up the rear let their guns loose on them. Ichabod itched to join the fighting. It went against his nature to simply sit and wait while others were being attacked, but he had orders. Being at the head of the advance, he was not in a position to assist. If the British made it any farther up their line, then he could engage. Until then, he had only to wait and watch.

The men watched as the gunboat loaded its eighteen-pounders, swiveling them to aim at the enemy, and fired away. One of their pursuers was hit directly with the men inside the boat jumping into the frigid water before it sank. The artillery exchange continued another several minutes and eventually began to ebb. When the enemy boats retreated and the gunfire ceased, the flotilla continued on its way.

The plan had been for the flotilla to sail in rows of four boats across according to regiments in order of battle. Eight of the twelve gunboats were to take the lead, followed by the light artillery and elite corps. The First Brigade would follow next, then the Third Brigade, Ordnance, the Hospital Department, Commissary and Contractors, the Second Brigade, and the Fourth Brigade. Bringing up the rear would be the last four gunboats. At a minimum, each of the gunboats carried a twelve-pounder or a four-pounder. It was a great plan on paper, but with the winds assaulting them, it was much harder to execute. The boats had been so heavily loaded, they became difficult to row. Coupled with the severe winds, it became nearly impossible to stay in formation, but they did the best they could.

As the convoy made its way farther along the river, they heard the occasional pop of a musket or rifle coming from the shore, but they only heard small arms for the first day or so. Intelligence informed them that the British had sent a Lieutenant Colonel Joseph W. Morrison to command a detachment of six hundred thirty men from the Forty-ninth and Eighty-ninth Regiments to harass the American Army. It was this group that had begun firing on the rear of their flotilla. The lieutenant colonel picked up additional men along the way as they absorbed them from the local garrisons they passed. They also picked up two schooners and seven gunboats. It did not take long before the guns on those boats started firing upon their rear guard as well.

The British were not doing major damage to the expedition, but they were a nuisance, causing as much damage as they could. Several men were injured, and a few boats were damaged or sunk. The sutler's boat named *Nighthawk* that had been heavily loaded with beef and bread would prove to be a great loss to them. If they could not refill their stores in Montreal, it would be a lean winter. Still, the expedition pressed on.

Storms continued to assail them. Winds, waves, and rain battered them, and many soldiers became sick. One hundred and ninety-six men had to be returned to Sackets Harbor on Lake Ontario. As the flotilla pressed on, they often had to stop at night and go ashore to wait for a violent storm to pass before continuing again the next day.

When the flotilla reached Fort Lawrence at Prescott on the seventh of November, they knew they would have to change their approach. This would be the first fort they would have to pass along the river and its guns controlled the water. The fort was in a position to do a lot of damage. When they were close, the men disembarked on the American side of the river, marching past the fort. Under the cover of darkness that night, the empty boats were floated past in order for the men to resume their journey the following day. As they traveled on, they continued coming under attack from Lieutenant Colonel Morrison on the water, but also from the Canadian militia who fired at them from the shore whenever the river was narrow enough. Morrison's detachment had now increased to nearly one thousand men. It was quickly becoming apparent that the army would have to stop and face Morrison soon if they wanted to reach Montreal.

On November ninth, they reached the Long Sault Rapids where General Wilkinson split his army into two forces. The general would continue towards Cornwall with an advanced guard while Brigadier General John Parke Boyd would take two thousand men and form a rearguard, land on the Canadian bank, and clear away the detachment following them. Once he took care of Morrison, Boyd was to continue forward to Montreal. Between the rain pelting down on them and the constant menace from Morrison and the militia, the army was ready to act instead of sitting in the boats continuing downriver. With double

Morrison's numbers, Ichabod was confident this would be a quick task and they would soon be underway to Montreal.

5

Modern Day

"It's a pleasure to meet you, Doctor Crane," the attorney said when Isadora was shown into his office. "I'm George Bachman."

Isadora arrived in New York City and picked up her rental car at LaGuardia before leaving the airport and heading north to Yonkers. She had booked a hotel in Yonkers for two nights, unsure what to expect. Her plan was to check in, then go straight to the attorney before making any further plans. Depending on what she needed to do and what the commute looked like, she could extend her hotel stay longer or find something closer to Sleepy Hollow. As she drove north, the city seemed to stretch on and on as she paralleled the Harlem River. The trees began to become more prevalent the farther north she went. It was her first time in New York, and she was eager to take in everything she could. Though the buildings did not extend as far up into the clouds as they had in

Manhattan, they were still huge. There were large commercial buildings and giant apartment complexes that stretched over entire city blocks. She could not even fathom the number of people they would house. She craned her neck to see better as she drove past Yankee stadium. Though she was not a sports fan, she could appreciate the architecture that went into a building that size. No sooner had she passed the stadium than she was craning her neck once again at the bridge over the river that seemed to soar above everything else in the area. It was a beautiful brick bridge with multiple arches underneath. It was obvious the bridge was quite old, and she wondered when it was built. If she had time, she would have to come back and get a closer look at it.

Isadora shook George's hand while taking in the slightly overweight short man with his receding grey hair, glasses, and warm smile. She immediately felt at ease with him, which she had been worried about. Attorneys had always given her the creeps, making her wonder if they could be trusted every time she had interacted with one. This man had a charming demeanor that reminded her of someone's grandfather.

With introductions out of the way, they got down to business. George had a file in front of him and began rattling off assets, but Isadora interrupted him. "I'm sorry, I know we'll probably get to this, but before you tell me about the estate, can you tell me who left it to me?"

"Oh yes, I do apologize my dear. I'm used to people knowing who their benefactors are. The estate belonged to a Mary Crosby. Does that name mean anything to you?"

Isadora shook her head. "I'm afraid not. Can you tell me how we were related or even how you found me? You mentioned something about ancestry DNA over the phone."

"Yes. You see, Mrs. Crosby did not have any living relatives that she was aware of. Her husband died years ago, and everything was supposed to be passed down to her daughter, but she passed away unexpectedly a few years ago, leaving Mary alone. She never changed her will, so we were left trying to find the nearest living relative. Mary's daughter had taken an ancestry DNA test before she passed, but we were unaware of it. My partner, Ernie Lemkowitz, was assigned to handle the trust, but he ran into some medical issues and ended up retiring on short notice. I'm afraid everything got lost in the transition. When the village officials tracked me down this last summer, I was left trying to piece everything together and find the beneficiary. I managed to find the DNA profiles and was able to track you down." George opened a website on his computer and turned the screen to face her.

"You share a common ancestor, here," he said, pointing at the screen. "It's about seven generations back on your side and eight on Miss Crosby's line."

Isadora studied the profile, surprised at how far back the connection was. Her own profile would show the same results George showed her now. When she had first received her results, she did a cursory glance to see that she had no living relatives, and did not look any further than that. She would pull it up later to study it more closely now.

"Is there really no one closer to claim the estate? I would hate to claim something that should rightfully go to someone else."

George shook his head, turning the screen back towards himself. "No. I'm afraid you're the closest we could find. That's why it took us so long to find you at all. Had it not been for that profile, we likely never would have found you."

Isadora nodded, letting his words sink in. She had hoped to find more living family members when she had done the test, but instead, she only found more dead ones. Even Mary had already passed by the time Isadora had done it. She really was alone in the world.

"Now, the estate has been passed down through several generations," George continued. "The property has been in the family since before the Revolutionary War. I have the deeds here, showing each owner. It has been passed down through the eldest daughter of each generation. Of course, it's odd that it was not passed down through the male heirs, but apparently, family lore has it that as long as the family lives there, they will be protected but it must always be passed to the daughters."

George lifted a piece of paper, showing her something to emphasize the point he had just made, but Isadora found she had not been listening. She was too busy feeling sorry for herself again, knowing with a certain finality that there was no one else out there in her family tree. She shook herself and made a concerted effort to focus on what he was saying.

Placing the paper back into a folder, he continued, "Along with the house and property, there is a trust containing all of the funds left behind. It is a substantial amount."

Isadora listened as he went on to tell her about the trust fund that held enough money that she would never have to work again if she chose not to. The house would need repairs, but it sounded like the trust would easily cover the costs, whatever they amounted to. At least she would not be out-of-pocket for the repairs herself, like she had worried would be the case. Though, it was hard to get excited about her sudden windfall knowing that it only came to her because she had absolutely no relatives anywhere.

George finished telling her about everything in the estate and placed each of the papers back into the folder from which he pulled them, then placed the folder inside an envelope which he handed to her. He stood then, asking, "Shall we go see your property, Doctor Crane?"

Nodding, Isadora stood as well. He offered to drive them, and she let him, wanting to be free to look out the windows at the scenery instead of focusing on the drive like she had on the way there. She had already discovered there were too many distractions. This would give her the opportunity to take it all in.

"This is a wonderful time of year to be here. There's so much to do what with Halloween and the ties to Washington Irving's story of the Headless Horseman. Are you familiar with the story, dear?"

Izzy bit back a bark of laughter and the sarcastic comment with which she wanted to reply and instead simply said, "I'm familiar."

"Well," George continued with an informative guide to the area, "The village used to be part of Tarrytown. Now it's separate but it's all part of

Westchester County. They took a small chunk off the northern part of Tarrytown and made it Sleepy Hollow. You'll find the Old Dutch Reformed church and burial ground that Washington Irving wrote about in the story along with Philipsburg Manor and a lighthouse on the Hudson River. Sunnyside and Lyndhurst Mansion are both in Tarrytown if you're interested in some of the history here. The village always has many events going on this time of year. I'm sure you could find something every weekend. I believe this week there's a block party downtown."

Allowing George to drive had not been a mistake. He told her about the area while he drove, sounding like a tour guide. She took in the scenery, noticing how many more trees there were. They drove up the Saw Mill River Parkway and she could see the river and towns occasionally poking through the trees. There were no more skyscrapers, only houses, apartments, and small commercial buildings. Neighborhoods were tucked into the trees lining the road. As the sunlight peeked through the tree branches that were covered in leaves beginning to change their colors, Isadora noted how many trees there were. Utah had trees, but nothing like this. This entire area seemed as though it was carved out of the forest. In some places, she could barely see any man-made structures through the trees, though she knew they were there. She missed being around such dense foliage.

The winding road continued through the colorful landscape. Among the orange, yellow, brown, green, and occasional spot of red on the trees and ground were grayish-black aged brick and stone retaining walls, arched bridges, and overpasses. The same grayish-black rock peaked out through the leaves along the hills and gullies. It looked as though the naturally occurring rock was collected from the hillside and made into bricks to make the overpasses and walls that were so prevalent. It was far more beautiful than the standard concrete infrastructure that seemed to dominate in every other city in the country.

"Do you what kind of rock this is?" she asked, thinking it was likely a longshot that he would know. Most people did not know geology. "It's so beautiful and it's everywhere."

To her surprise, he answered, "It's called gneiss."

"Did you say 'nice'?"

"Yes. G-N-E-I-S-S. It's actually Yonkers gneiss. It's a metamorphic rock. The granite from Yonkers has made its way as far as Canada and Chicago and has been used for centuries to make buildings, monuments, roads, and walls. As you can see, it holds up quite well."

Isadora could hear the pride in his voice over the rock from his hometown. With a legacy such as that, she could understand why he felt that way. It was not only strong, but beautiful as well.

They continued past the Tarrytown Reservoir and into Sleepy Hollow. It was such an odd feeling to finally be there after having spent so much time researching the area and the history. Isadora had always had a picture in her mind of what it would look like, but the reality was so much more than she had ever imagined.

George slowed as they came to a private dirt lane through a gated stone entry. More of the old stone walls bordered the property along the roadway low to the ground as they approached. Isadora could only see walls and trees. Turning onto the private lane, they drove through a large grassy lot covered with more trees and lush vegetation.

"The house was built in 1859 and still sits on slightly over seven acres," George offered. "It used to be farmland but has since been mostly sold off. This is all that remains. As you can see, the landscapers have continued maintaining the grounds. Unfortunately, when my partner retired, no one realized the house was not being maintained properly as well. In truth, no one realized any of this was still in our custody. I do regret that oversight. Apparently, the local teenagers have made it a place to hang out. The neighbors had to call in the authorities after hearing the loud parties on occasion. When a storm came through a few months ago and part of the roof collapsed, they called it in to the village officials. They came out to inspect it and also found the damage from the kids. That's when they finally tracked us down." George was remorseful. "We really do pride ourselves in taking better care of our responsibilities. I cannot express to you how deeply sorry I am that this happened on our watch."

"It's not a problem, really. I didn't even know any of this existed, let alone that it might one day be mine. These things happen."

She was beginning to think that he was worried she might take some sort of retaliatory action against him and his firm and wanted to put his mind at ease. George parked the car, and they got out, exploring the property.

The house that stood before them was a four-story Victorian with a porch that extended across the front of the house and another extending across the back. The double doors at the front opened into a wide foyer with stairs going up in the hallway directly ahead. A parlor was to their left and a drawing room to their right, with a kitchen and formal dining room taking up the back corners of the first floor. A bathroom was between the kitchen and dining room and Isadora found stairs leading down into a partially finished basement beside the bathroom. There were three bedrooms and two bathrooms on the second floor with the master bedroom having an attached vanity walkthrough separating it from the bathroom, which was bigger than her bedroom at home. It contained a claw foot tub in the middle of the room, directly across from a fireplace. The third floor contained three more bedrooms, another bathroom, and a family room. There was wide plaster molding throughout the house and several window seats. The first two levels had floor to ceiling windows and Isadora counted nine fireplaces throughout the house, many of which had marble mantles.

George informed her that the house was four thousand square feet. Isadora immediately wondered what she would ever do with that much space. The thought made her question whether she was even planning on living there. It was a beautiful house, but considerably larger and far more opulent than she was used to. She would have to put some real thought into what to do with it all. Under any other circumstances, she would probably consider selling without a second thought but seeing as how the property had remained in the family for so long, she was hesitant to do so. Not only would it break that legacy, but it was the only tie she had left to a family that she wished she had, even if she had not known them.

The roof had collapsed over the family room upstairs and there was water damage in that room. The house had been decorated in a fashion to resemble the original period in which it was built with busy, loud wallpaper that was now peeling off throughout the house. Several of the rooms had severely damaged plaster on the walls, showing the lath underneath, likely from the kids that had partied there. The water and electricity had understandably been turned off. It was probably a good thing considering the vandals had not only punched holes in the walls but had caused quite a bit of other damage as well. Light fixtures were torn out, pipes were broken, and belongings were thrown into disarray. Copper thieves had even struck, cutting into the lath which covered the plumbing and electrical behind the walls. Most of the furniture had been damaged and there was debris everywhere. In addition to the repairs, the house would need some serious cleaning.

Isadora and George continued their tour outside and found the detached three-car garage, a workshop, and a shed. The entire property was overwhelming in the enormity of it all. How could this all be hers? What was she going to do with it? Isadora took a deep breath and decided to face one decision at a time.

"I can recommend a few general contractors, if you'd like?" George offered.

Isadora nodded. "I'd appreciate that. I have no idea where to even begin right now."

George gave her a sympathetic look. "Contact the building inspector for the Village of Sleepy Hollow and let him know that you've taken custody of the property and find a contractor to come out and give you an estimate. The building inspector will want a timeline as to when the work will be done, and the contractor can help you hire anyone else you might need." George patted her shoulder. "It'll be alright, dear."

They returned to the car and George drove them back to his office where Isadora picked up her own rental car and went back to her hotel for the night. It was getting late, and she was exhausted. She would tackle the insurmountable project ahead of her the next day.

6

November 1813

"Captain, behind you!" Samuel shouted.

Ichabod fired his pistol at the Voltigeur trying to pull him from his horse and spun to face another one approaching him from the rear. The British forces were everywhere, the Regulars holding their lines and the Canadian Voltigeur and Mohawk skirmishers trying to prevent the American artillerymen from lobbing the large iron balls through their ranks. Ichabod sat atop his horse behind a line of guns and howitzers while his men tried to load them and fire at their enemy. The Voltigeurs and Mohawks did what they could to draw out the artillerymen from behind their guns while also attempting to take out the officers on horseback. If the officers fell, it would increase the confusion amongst their soldiers or possibly cause them to retreat. Ichabod and Samuel did what they could to protect their gunners while the men loaded and reloaded the large guns in front of them.

The army had made their stand at a narrow strip of farmland belonging to John Crysler. The land was bordered by the Saint Lawrence River to the right and a swamp and woodland to the left. Lieutenant Colonel Morrison had arrived the night before, camped out overnight, then placed four hundred and fifty British Regulars behind a heavy cedar log fence bordering the farmer's fields that morning. Another force of Regulars was placed ahead and to the right in a gully and in buildings near the river while a smaller force of Voltigeurs and Mohawks stayed in a ravine in front of the British line, acting as skirmishers to draw the Americans out. An additional thirty Native Americans were in the woods.

The battle was well underway by two o'clock on the afternoon of November eleventh. Brigadier General Boyd attacked in three columns with one sent to manage the skirmishers; another sent left, extending north from the river; and the third going right, into the woods. The column sent to take out the skirmishers came under fire from the line of British Regulars posted at the cedar fence and quickly fell back. The column to the right tried to force the British to turn left, but with no success due to the narrowness of the battlefield. The forces in the woods decimated the

American infantry with the accuracy of their fire. The infantry finally drove back the British skirmishers, but another brigade under Brigadier General Covington struggled. They were stopped by a ravine in front of them, preventing them from effectively deploying. This led to them coming under heavy fire from Morrison's troops, giving Morrison time to reorganize his line for a second attack. Ichabod watched as Brigadier General Covington and his second-in-command were both mortally wounded in this attack. With no command on that part of the field, organization amongst the American forces broke down.

The same ravine, along with ruts and other unevenness from the rain-soaked ground hampered the artillery as well. Ichabod and the other captains had struggled to get the artillery in place and form a line. The six-pounder guns were attached to carriages which were placed about forty feet apart from one another while the smaller howitzers in their wooden field chests were interspersed amongst the larger guns. The heavier thirty-two-pounders were placed sporadically along the line, bordering each battery. The commanders had made a strategy before the battle to determine where the line would be, then it was up to each captain to determine the layout of his own line and the position of each gun, while making corrections to the trajectory as needed. Each captain oversaw a battery consisting of six guns, and about fifty-four men, nine of which were required to fire each gun and seven for each howitzer. Each detachment assigned to a gun had two trained gunners who aimed, loaded, and fired the guns while their matrosses assisted by bringing the ammunition or moving the heavy gun around. A sergeant supervised the whole affair, setting up the gun into the correct position, watching the trajectory of the heavy iron ball, and making any necessary corrections.

The distance between each gun allowed the captains and lieutenants to easily oversee each crew while maintaining enough space that each gun could easily be moved if necessary and also being far enough away from its neighbor to not cause damage to another gun if it exploded. With the artillery finally in place, the guns in the battery were fired on a rotation, with every other gun being fired simultaneously. This allowed for a constant rate of fire while reducing the amount of smoke present and allowing for guns to be loaded at all times. While one set of guns was being fired, the ones to either side of it were being loaded and readied.

Ichabod had watched his gunners as they fired upon their enemy. He assisted the sergeants in making appropriate adjustments to the trajectories of each gun as the heavy iron balls fell amongst the large numbers of British infantry approaching their lines. As the battle commenced, he watched to determine whether any of the guns needed to be moved and stayed in communication with his lieutenants, other captains, and his commanding officers, all while performing all of his other duties as a captain and trying to stave off the skirmishers. His lieutenants made sure the gunners were not firing too quickly while also protecting them from skirmishers.

Brigadier General Boyd continued to try pushing his troops across the field and around the British left. Unfortunately, they were met with heavy fire from the British Regulars, causing their efforts to fail. Across the field, Boyd's men began to fall back as their force lost momentum. The artillery finally came to be fully in place right as the infantry was beginning to retreat across the river to Saint Regis. However, they opened fire as soon as they were able, inflicting losses on the British wherever they could.

Lieutenant Colonel Morrison began his counterattack, pushing the American forces even further back. Ichabod saw that they were making their way in large numbers towards him and the artillery.

"They are hoping to capture our guns, men," Ichabod shouted. "Do not let them."

The artillerymen began fighting off the British soldiers who were now beginning to surround them. Ichabod dispatched the man who had been approaching him from behind and moved onto another one. He only had two pistols which now needed to be reloaded, but there was no time. With his sword drawn, he faced down another skirmisher, trying to still maintain awareness of his command. He and his lieutenants fought off whom they could while the gun squads began the process of packing up the guns and ammunition. Any men who were not actively engaged in removing the guns faced off with the British.

Lieutenant Samuel Van Tassel was fighting two skirmishers but held his ground. From atop his horse, he stabbed one in the shoulder and kicked the other in the face, his boot at eye level to the man on the ground. He looked up to see more men surrounding Ichabod. Samuel had moved farther away from him and with the noise of the battle raging around them, there was no way he could yell loudly enough to warn him. There were no more soldiers in his immediate vicinity, so he spurred his horse forward in Ichabod's direction, shoving people aside as he did so. He remained by his friend's side for a time, holding off as many soldiers as they could together while their men began retreating.

The US Dragoons arrived then, engaging in a series of charges as they urged their horses into the fray. The American Army was not done yet. This was the opportunity that the artillery needed to withdraw.

The Dragoons managed to push back much of the British Regulars, but there were still a few skirmishers close to Ichabod and Samuel and several Regulars still volleying musket balls across the field. The men continued to fight. As Ichabod was busy with a Mohawk warrior, he looked up in time to see his lieutenant guiding his horse in next to Ichabod when they were peppered with another volley of gunfire from the British. He heard a splat and immediately saw red slowly seeping through Samuel's coat, spreading outward from a spot on his breast. More blood trickled down his chin as the man slumped forward. Ichabod's eyes went wide with horror and with an extra surge of energy, he kicked his attacker in the face, slamming his sword down into the man's neck. The attacker fell to the ground and Ichabod immediately turned his attention to his friend. Ichabod dropped to the ground to help Samuel, but it was obvious his wound was fatal. He pulled the man off his horse and into his arms and held him.

With shaking hands, Samuel pulled a small book from his pocket, placing it in Ichabod's hand. "See that this gets back to my mother."

"I will," he promised.

"It's been an honor, sir."

Ichabod nodded, trying to hold back the tears in his eyes. "The honor has been mine, Samuel."

Before he could say more, Samuel was gone. Ichabod wanted nothing more than to stay there, holding his friend, but there was no time. He placed the book into his own pocket, cleared his eyes, and quickly mounted his horse to face the enemy once again. His anger fueled him and he took it out on any Native warriors or anyone wearing a red coat, thrusting, slashing, and stabbing anyone in his path.

As artillerymen began to retreat around him, Ichabod held his ground, ordering his men to take the guns with them. Many of the other batteries had abandoned their guns, but Ichabod directed his men to assist in retrieving them. The Dragoons had bought them time and he intended to take full advantage of it.

The battle climaxed by four o'clock in the afternoon and the American line collapsed, resulting in men running in panic to their boats. Ichabod worked his way toward the river behind his men, bringing up the rear. As he looked back to the field behind him, he saw only one of their guns still on the field. This was a rare thing as guns were often sabotaged and rendered inoperable when left behind during retreat. They may not have won the day, but at least he had been able to save as many of their guns from falling into the enemy's hands as possible. This was little consolation, though. He desperately wished he had not had to leave his friend behind.

The following afternoon and evening were spent ferrying the horses used by the Dragoons and artillerymen back to the New York side of the river. Ichabod assisted with the operation, wanting to stay busy and feeling a personal responsibility to the horses used by his battery. Despite having the resources to retrieve them, many of the horses were left behind. The army headed back towards French Mills the following morning, staying to the safer American side of the shore, where the winter weather iced them in almost immediately.

Despite outnumbering the British two-to-one, the American force had taken a heavy loss at the battle on Crysler's Farm. With 102 dead, 237 wounded, and one hundred men taken prisoner, it had affected the morale of the entire expedition. While they sustained 148 wounded, the British had only lost twenty-two men. It did not help morale that General Wilkinson had reportedly been drinking heavily and dosing himself with opium the night before the battle.

The day after the battle, General Wilkinson received a letter from General Hampton, informing him that the other man's forces had made it to the Chateauguay River in late October, but had immediately met with a force of Canadian militia. Hampton's men had been forced to retreat back to American territory and were now in winter quarters in Plattsburgh. The four thousand additional men under General Hampton would not be meeting General Wilkinson in Montreal.

Wilkinson called a council of war where it was decided that they, too, would go into winter quarters on the American bank of the Saint Lawrence River. His army spent the winter at French Mills before they dispersed in February 1814.

7

Modern Day

Isadora felt better after a good night's sleep. After waking refreshed, she showered and called Simon to update him on her meeting with the attorney. He had gotten called in to do some work on a system that had been having problems and they only spoke briefly, but it had been good to hear his voice. She would try him again later. While eating breakfast, she made a plan. Pulling out the hotel's notepad and pen, she made a list of all the major repairs that needed to be done on the property to the best of recollection. She then added a separate list at the bottom of the page of the life decisions she now needed to make. Her life had been on a set trajectory for so long, she had not even questioned it. Though she always prided herself on being flexible and going wherever the wind took her, she was not sure where it was trying to take her now. This was the first time she had to consider her career when making a decision like this. Not to mention Simon. It would be easy to leave everything else in Utah behind, but how could she leave Simon?

Considering it briefly, she quickly pushed it aside. That would be a decision for another day. First things first, Isadora needed to hire a contractor, take inventory of the house and property, figure out what to do with everything inside the house, and begin the clean-up and repairs. That was going to take time and she needed to be there to oversee the workers and make sure everything was done properly without any further damage or costs. Being there would allow her to do the clean-up work on the house as well. The dean was not going to be happy with her, but she gathered her courage and sent an email, letting her know what happened and that she would call on Monday to discuss it.

Isadora had originally asked for a week off, but she knew now that she needed to stay at least until the end of the semester. A grad student was already covering her classes for her this week. He could continue covering some of them and anything he could not handle could be divided up between other grad students and faculty. People left mid-semester for other emergencies and while it did not happen often, life sometimes interrupted routine. The university would cope without her. Within an hour of sending the email, the dean called, despite it being Saturday.

After spending several hours on the phone talking with the dean, scheduling appointments, and making arrangements to stay in the area longer, Isadora was more than ready to venture out and explore. She drove up towards Sleepy Hollow, following the same route she had taken with George the day before, noting the multitude of banners advertising the events that were scheduled over the next few weeks. There was a block party and haunted hayride later that night on Beekman Avenue that sounded intriguing. Parking her car down the street from the Old Dutch Reformed Church, she got out and made her way to the north entrance of the Sleepy Hollow Cemetery while it was still light out. The days were still getting shorter, and the sun would set early, but she loved old cemeteries. She was eager to see the infamous burying ground.

Rock bridges, retaining walls, and steps built into the hillside and reclaimed by nature over time gave the grounds an appearance of being part of the natural environment. The Pocantico River ran along the eastern side of the cemetery, bordering most of the grounds and wrapping around to cross Broadway and continue past Philipsburg Manor before eventually emptying into the Hudson River a few blocks away. A section of the cemetery continued in the northeast corner past the river which was connected by a wooden bridge. Rocks jutted out from the ground all around the riverbank and the soft ground was covered with leaves like everywhere else she had been. Isadora took a deep breath, taking it all in. The air was crisp and clear with a slightly cool breeze lending to a comfortable temperature. Birds were singing while a raven cawed nearby. Wind rustled through the trees, stirring the leaves as they fell. A train whistled in the distance and the light sounds of auto and air traffic added to the ambient sounds. The landscape was breathtaking. Isadora thought this would be perfect without the sounds of the traffic. She never imagined a place in New York could look like this. She had always associated New York with the city and the five boroughs. It never occurred to her that most of the state did not look like that.

The graveyard was quiet even though there were a lot of people milling about. Old headstones mingled with new, and she wound her way south and east along the hills, taking it all in. The leaves crunched under her feet, raising up an earthy scent. The mausoleums were impressive, with some of them being massive structures. Many of them were built right into the hillsides with the brick being covered with ivy. Isadora had stopped at the office and picked up a map of the grounds before getting started. Given the size of the place, she was glad she did. She was surprised to see how many other famous people had been buried there. She knew Washington Irving had been, but she had not known about Andrew Carnegie, William Rockefeller, Walter Chrysler, Elizabeth Arden, and Harry and Leona Helmsley.

As she walked, she noted that most of the older graves were at the south end, nearest the church while most of the newer ones were at the north end, nearer the office and chapel, though there were old and new intermingled throughout. The Van Tassel family had indeed been a large presence in the area as there were numerous graves bearing the name. Isadora found several different sections around the grounds with a number of Van Tassels buried within each.

Winding her way towards the Old Dutch Church at the south end, Isadora walked alongside the river to get there. She could feel her batteries recharging with every step, despite the people surrounding her. Many were on tours of the grounds and others milled about. There were even a few portable shade canopies set up randomly throughout the grounds where vendors were selling their wares, which Isadora found odd. She would not have expected to find such a thing in a cemetery. After walking past a few of them, she saw that they were manned by people selling their artwork or books, the subjects of which all somehow related to the area.

Once she got to the church, she wound through the countless headstones, trying to find one that might say it belonged to an unknown Hessian soldier, but she never saw anything of the like. Of course, many of the oldest headstones had long since been eroded of any words that were once there. The sun was beginning to go down and as she roamed the stones, she briefly got a chill and the hair rose on the back of her neck. The ground almost seemed to tremble beneath her, and she chided herself for letting her imagination get away from her. Cemeteries were a regular haunt for her, and they had never spooked her before. She laughed at herself with the thought that she was allowing herself to get caught up in her connection to the story. After walking around the church, she noted the time, seeing that the grounds would be closing soon.

Isadora made her way back out onto the street, heading back towards Beekman Avenue. It was almost dark now and as she got closer, Isadora could already hear the music from the bands playing for the block party that was about to get underway. Ready for food, she decided to try getting a seat in one of the restaurants along the way, but with the block party, they all had extraordinarily long waits. She opted for one of the food vendors there for the party instead.

There were several other vendors along both sides of the street before she reached the food vendors and she strolled along slowly, taking it all in. The street had been closed to vehicular traffic and there were already people filling every corner of the street, despite it all having just gotten underway.

The building housing the fire department and police station was at the end of the street closest to Broadway and both had tables set up, selling tee shirts and other souvenirs. She stopped and picked up a tee shirt from each of them. The building behind the table had been decorated for the holiday with hay bales, pumpkins, and corn stalks lined up along the exterior walls. On one of the hay bales between the bay doors, a skeleton sat beside a firefighter's turnout suit that had been stuffed to look as though it was filled by a person without a head. The firefighters were giving some sort of showing inside the bays and Isadora followed a group of people inside. Someone turned off the overhead lights and another firefighter used a flashlight on the rear of the truck revealing a glowing pumpkin surrounded by flames with the words 'Sleepy Hollow' above it. The logo on the side of the truck door had an illustration of a Headless Horseman holding a flaming pumpkin in the air. She quickly noticed that all of the emergency response vehicles for the village had some sort of illustration related to the Headless Horseman. Others may have thought it tacky or corny, but she thought it brilliant that the village had adopted the story and made it a part of their town. It was obvious throughout the streets she had been on that the entire village had embraced it.

There was a heavy police presence which filled Isadora with comfort as she wandered the street. With this many people, it would be easy for trouble to break out. After looking around at her options, Isadora settled on a vendor who sold sandwich wraps. It seemed to be her best bet for attempting to stay as healthy as possible. She ordered, waited for her food, then continued on her way, opting to eat while she wandered. She stopped and watched a local dance troupe perform a dance for a few minutes, then kept going down the street. A table was set up by a local bookshop and she decided to head towards it. Focusing on it while trying to maneuver through the crowd, carry her souvenirs, and manage her food was a feat.

As she tried navigating the crowded street, a couple directly in front of her veered left, opening her view, allowing her to see the police officer facing away from her. He was close enough that she could reach out and touch him and she had very little room to maneuver. She started to go around the sandy-haired officer when he suddenly turned and started walking forward, running directly into her. Her plate was knocked from her hands and the contents fell to the ground at their feet. He cursed as he watched the food spill down the front of his uniform. She was apologizing before he could look up to see who he ran into.

"I'm so sorry Officer," she read the name plate above his breast pocket before adding, "Kaderson."

Alex was fuming but the annoyance immediately left his face when he looked up to see a beautiful young woman with long copper-colored hair standing before him. She was several inches shorter than him but not so much that he would have to bend far to kiss her. He liked his women on the taller side and though the one which stood before him now was average height, she had an incredible body. He could see her shape even through the light sweater she wore. And if the jeans hugging her hips were any indication of what was underneath, he knew he would enjoy taking them off of her. She was clearly athletic but retained her curves in all the right places. He had never been a fan of redheads, but he would make an exception for one with a body like that. The images that immediately played through his mind curled his lips up into a smile which he directed at her as he put on his charm.

"No, I'm sorry," he said smoothly. "I should have been watching where I was going. I'm Alex. You have to let me buy you a new plate."

His intense stare moved down her body and Isadora felt as though she was completely naked. His directness unnerved her, but the obvious interest also excited her a little. She agreed and they walked over to the vendor she had come from and stood in line.

Alex looked around, scanning the area as if looking for someone. "Is there someone waiting for you? A boyfriend, or...?"

The man doesn't waste any time, Isadora thought as she tried to suppress a smile at his brazenness.

"No. I'm here by myself." She knew he was asking about more than just that night, but she did not want to make it too easy for him. "I'm Isadora. My friends call me Izzy."

Alex took the hand she held out and shook it. They chatted amiably while moving through the line. Isadora could see the confidence rolling off of him while they talked. She knew he was flirting with her and to her surprise, she flirted back. She enjoyed the attention and found she had been even more lonely there than she normally was. At least at home, she had Simon. The thought made her wonder what Simon was doing right then. It was Saturday night, so he was probably on a date with Becky. Her heart pinched at the thought, and she brought herself back to the conversation with Alex.

"Are you doing the haunted hayride?" he asked.

Isadora shook her head. "The tickets were sold out by the time I looked at it. I'm only here for the block party."

"Yeah, things sell out quickly this time of year. People come here from all over for Halloween."

"I would imagine."

"Most of the events are actually pretty fun."

"What's your favorite?" she asked while they made their way forward in the line.

"I like the parade. And the Great Jack O'lantern Blaze up at Van Cortlandt Manor. They do a really good job on that one."

"I saw the signs for that. It's worth seeing then? I was debating whether to go."

"Absolutely worth seeing. Are you free Tuesday or Wednesday? I could take you."

Nope. Did not waste any time at all. Isadora considered the offer and found herself agreeing to go with him. He was pleasant and attractive enough after all; maybe she would enjoy herself. Though she did not know if she would be staying long-term, it did not mean she could not have fun while she was there.

The vendor handed her a new plate as another officer approached them. Alex introduced him as his partner, Cory Greene. Cory informed Alex that the chief was watching him, and he needed to move on before he was reprimanded. They were encouraged to interact with people during these events, but only for so long. Alex had spent far too much time in one place with one person.

They exchanged phone numbers and before leaving, Alex turned to Isadora. "It was a pleasure meeting you. I'll text you and we can figure out the details."

She gave him a smile and watched as he strutted off with his partner.

Isadora continued down the street, taking in not only the vendors, but the permanent businesses that were there. If she was going to be there a while, she may as well get to know the area. When she reached the end of the street, she turned around and made her way back. Dodging the kids in costume, trick-or-treating at the vendors, she wove in and out of the crowd. It had been a full day, and though she had enjoyed it, she was more than ready for sleep.

8

June 1815

"Have you received your orders yet, brother?" The men sat on the edge of Lake Ontario, enjoying a rare sunny spring afternoon with nowhere to be.

"I still await them, William," Ichabod replied. "Have you received yours?"

They had spent the previous three years at war, engaging in battles, expeditions, and raids. They had built ships and a fort and trained soldiers. With the war at an end and all of the war men having gone home, the five years men sat and awaited their orders. Some would stay there while others were sent to other duty stations.

Ichabod had spent the winter after the battle at Crysler's farm in winter quarters with the rest of what remained of their expedition. It had been long, cold, and miserable. They were short of medicine and food, and they did not have the proper winter clothing. Ichabod had been grateful they had canceled the invasion of Montreal. After losing Samuel, his heart was no longer in it. They had fought side-by-side for nearly two years, surviving four separate battles that year alone.

After getting back to Fort Pike at Sackets Harbor the following spring, the war resumed. Several more battles came close to Ichabod on Lake Ontario near Niagara and on Lakes Erie and Champlain, though there were more battles farther away from him than there were nearby. Finally, on Christmas Eve 1814, the Treaty of Ghent was signed. It was ratified by congress on the seventeenth of February 1815, marking the end of the war.

The army had begun the slow process of reducing its size. In March, the Corps of Engineers, Regiment of Light Artillery, and Corps of Artillery were all retained, allowing the five years men, or those who had enlisted for five years, to stay on. However, by the first of May, all war men, or supernumerary officers and soldiers, were discharged immediately.

"I am to go to Boston to take command of the *Independence*."

Ichabod whistled in appreciation. "That's the flagship of Commodore Bainbridge's squadron. You're off to fight the new war in Algiers, then?"

"I am." William nodded. "She has seventy-four guns, Ichabod. Can you imagine? Even the *Constitution* only has forty-four guns. She's the largest ship in the navy's fleet; the first seventy-four in the US. If we'd had her ready these last few years, we would have been better prepared to take on the Royal Navy with her giant ships, each of which carry more than a hundred guns."

"Congratulations on your new command, brother. I do not think it likely that I will go as well, now that I am no longer with the marine corps."

"Wherever you end up, I know you will continue to serve with honor and courage, as you have always done."

It had been good to get back to Sackets Harbor and see his brother again. He had missed him terribly. Waiting out that winter without William or Samuel had been nearly unbearable. His thoughts often drifted back to that battle, wondering what he could have done differently to keep Samuel alive.

Once he had returned to the gunboat after the battle, he found their knapsacks waiting for them. He kept Samuel's with him. He knew the man wrote to his family every week and Ichabod wanted to make sure any unsent letters reached the family along with the bible Samuel had entrusted to him. Ichabod also wanted to make sure any other personal items were returned to Samuel's family as well.

Ichabod nodded at the compliment. "When do you depart from here?"

"We are to set sail at the beginning of July. I shall leave here in a few weeks."

"I have some leave coming to me. I have business to attend in Tarrytown, along the Hudson River. Perhaps you shall allow me to accompany you as far as Albany?"

William clapped his hand on Ichabod's shoulder, giving him a squeeze. "I would like that very much brother."

The brothers spent the first half of the month preparing for their journey. While William was departing the area for good, Ichabod was only going for a short time. He would spend a couple of days in Tarrytown, then return to Sackets Harbor to await word of his next duty station. It was possible that he could stay there at Fort Pike, though he knew it was not likely. With the war over, troops were moved to more strategic locations. Once his orders came through, he knew he would be assigned elsewhere.

§ ♋

It took five days to reach Albany by horseback. The brothers spent the night in the city then parted ways in the morning, saying their goodbyes and wishing each other luck. Though they had different assignments, it had been nice spending the war so near each other. Despite William being nine years older than Ichabod, they were still close. Ichabod looked up to his older brother and had been comforted by serving in proximity to him during the war. If anything had happened to either of them, they would know far more quickly than the rest of the family, who were still in Elizabethtown, New Jersey. When their father had passed the previous year, it had taken months for word to reach them.

After parting ways in Albany, Ichabod began his journey down the Hudson River to Tarrytown. He had promised Samuel that he would personally deliver a letter to his family if anything had happened to him and he intended to do exactly that. It would not be an easy task, but he had to honor his friend. Ichabod rode another three days before reaching Tarrytown.

Not really believing it would ever actually come to a need for Ichabod to know, Samuel had not left word on where to find his family, only that they were in Tarrytown. Ichabod knew from Samuel's descriptions, however, that the town was full of Van Tassels. As he rode into town, he stopped at a tavern near a port that sloops were pulling in and out of in order to fill his belly while beginning his search for Samuel's family. He hitched his horse to the post out front and made his way inside, taking a seat. When the proprietor came to wait on him, he placed his order. When his food arrived, he asked if the man knew Samuel's family.

"If you go back out onto the Albany Post Road and head north about two miles, you'll come by the Old Dutch Reformed Church. You'll find all the Van Tassels you could ever want there tomorrow. They shall all be at the service. If you can't find the family you're looking for there, you won't find them anywhere."

"That's the church near a small river with the graveyard beside it?" Ichabod remembered passing the small stone church on his journey.

"The Pocantico River, yes. That's the one."

He hated having to go backward and retracing his steps, but at least it was not far. He thanked the man for the information and got a room for two nights. He was lucky to get a room at all, as they were filling quickly and were expected to be full as soon as he left. He hoped he could find Samuel's family in that time.

9

Modern Day

Isadora checked out of her hotel on Sunday, opting instead for a vacation rental home. Since she was staying longer, she decided she needed something slightly more than a hotel room. Due to the holiday season, the nearest she could find was in Hawthorne, but it was only a few minutes away, so she took it. Once she got settled, she went to the Victorian manor that now belonged to her and began making a plan for cleaning it up. She made more lists, noting the supplies she would need. As she worked on cleaning it up, she would decide how she wanted to redo each room. She may even hire a decorator for that part. The thought made her giggle. Isadora Crane had never been in a position to hire a decorator for anything. This was certainly a luxury for her, but she wanted to keep the home authentic to the period if she could and that was not something she knew enough about to do herself.

Each room would be worked one at a time. Starting in the parlor and working her way around the first floor, then upstairs, she would clean and inventory each room, writing down the contents and photographing them. Then she would decide what would stay and what would go. If she could salvage any of the furniture, she would in order to try and keep with maintaining the authenticity. To her untrained eye, it looked like many of the pieces had either been originals or quality replicas of period pieces. Anything she did not want to keep would be donated. She knew she could sell some of it, but with the size of the trust that was left behind, she did not need the money. She would rather donate everything she could.

Isadora made slow progress, but it was progress, nonetheless. The two front rooms were the least damaged and therefore the easiest. She had them both finished by the end of the day.

By Monday, the potential contractors arrived, and she met with them one by one. She did a walkthrough of the house with each of them in turn and they provided her with an estimate and a timeline. One of them stood out from the rest by having specific knowledge and extensive experience in restoring older homes. With so many homes in the region being as old or nearly as old as hers, she would have thought they all would have had the same experience, but two of them only had limited experience with it. She opted for the one that had the most.

The manor was going to need more work than she had initially thought, though she was thankful it was not worse than it was. Along with the new roof, electrical work, and plumbing, she would need mold remediation in the attic and several other places in the house, new flooring, and some minor siding done. Most of the major repairs would need to be done in the attic and third floor. All of the contractors had agreed that asbestos removal and lead paint removal had been done within the last twenty years along with the pipes all having been changed over from lead to copper, so she did not have to worry about any of those. Isadora was particularly grateful for that as each would have been a much bigger undertaking than she would have wanted to tackle at that point.

"I'll begin reaching out to my subcontractors and get them scheduled, but I'll be able to get started on the construction and repairs next week. I should be able to get the necessary work permits by then," Neil Lowry said as they walked out of the house.

"I appreciate it," Isadora said. "I'll be staying in town and will be working on the rest of the house while you do your thing, so I'll be available whenever you need me. If I'm not at the house, give me a call if you need anything."

"I'll send over a contract, lien waiver, and a copy of my liability insurance to you tomorrow. Keep an eye on your email. Once we get that done, I can have a crew out here on Wednesday to begin prep work while we wait for permits. We'll work Saturday this week to get a jump on things, but after that, we'll go Monday through Friday unless we fall behind. We can reevaluate the schedule later and add weekends if we need to. I know you're in a hurry to complete everything."

"Sounds good," she said while they shook hands. "I need to show that I'm making progress towards getting it done before the village officials take action."

Isadora shifted her focus to the upstairs. She needed to clear out a space for the contractors to begin working before they arrived in a couple of days. Starting in the attic, she began hauling everything down to the basement for future inspection. Since the attic was exposed to the elements, she wanted to protect and preserve the items that were there before moving on to the other areas of the house. It was tedious work, going up and down three flights of stairs carrying heavy boxes and she had to take regular breaks. She was in decent shape, but that was a lot of stairs and some of the boxes were quite heavy. It was going to take her a few days to finish this section of the house and she was going to need to get help carrying some of the boxes. Between flights of stairs, she slid furniture across the most heavily affected rooms into a corner where it would be out of the way. A tarp would be put over it all before the work began.

By Tuesday afternoon, Isadora was more than ready to take a break and go see the Great Jack O'lantern Blaze in Croton. She finished up early, going back to her rental to shower and get ready for her date. The days had been sunny and mild, perfect for a light sweater and jeans with boots while the nights cooled down enough to add a jacket. By the time Alex arrived to pick her up, she was ready to go. She took a moment to admire his good looks, much as he did to her. His broad shoulders and chest filled out his sweater nicely while his jeans did nothing to hide the muscles in his legs. Despite his sandy-blonde hair, he had a bit of a rough and tumble exterior that gave him an air of authority which likely served him well as a police officer.

Van Courtlandt Manor was about fifteen minutes away and he took her to dinner at a nice Italian restaurant on the way north, where they spent some time getting to know one another.

"I'm new to the area," she said without further explanation after he mentioned he had lived in the area his whole life.

"Yeah? Where'd you move from?"

"Oh, I haven't moved here. I'm only here for a little while."

"So, you're just visiting? One of the Halloween tourists?" he accused with a snicker.

Isadora was a little put off by his condescending tone but opted to ignore it. Maybe it was simply part of his bravado for women he dated. "No. The timing was not my idea. I actually had to take a leave of absence in the middle of the semester in order to be here. I had some business that brought me here."

Alex looked her up and down briefly, as if he was taking stock. The server brought them their dinners and they each took a bite. Alex finished chewing and asked, "Mid-semester? You're a student?"

"I'm a professor."

His chocolate eyes sparkled at that as he said with a grin, "Ooh, a sexy teacher. Every boy's fantasy."

When she did not respond to the comment, he added, "What do you teach?"

"English Lit." Isadora took a drink of her water. "Including the works of Washington Irving, incidentally," she added.

"I see. So, you're here visiting Sunnyside." It was a statement, not a question.

"It's not what brought me, but I have every intention of taking full advantage of my time here. I actually did my dissertation on Irving and Ichabod Crane."

"You've been here before, then?"

Isadora shook her head. "I never made it while I was in school. I would've loved it but couldn't ever make it work." The stereotype of the starving college student existed for a reason. She did not have the money at that time to have been able to come for a visit then, though she would have loved to have seen Irving's home and the inspiration for the story in person while she was in the middle of her research.

"So how long are you here?"

"I'm not sure yet. I wasn't planning on being here long, but it's starting to look like it's going to take me longer to finish everything I need to do."

Alex lifted his glass to his mouth. "And what's that?" he asked before taking a drink.

Isadora sighed thinking of the task ahead of her. "I inherited a house. I have to figure out what I'm doing with it."

Alex leaned back in his seat, placing an arm along the back side of the booth after finishing his dinner.

He gave off an appearance of confidence and a little bit of cockiness. "That shouldn't take that long. Just empty it out and put it on the market if you don't want to keep it." He shrugged. "Empty it and move in if you do."

"Why didn't I think of that?" she asked sarcastically. He made it sound so simple. "Unfortunately, there's a lot of damage to the house. And it's really old. I'd hate to destroy the history of it, so I want to make sure the repairs are done right. I have a contractor that specializes in historical buildings, but it's going to take a while to complete everything. Apparently local teenagers decided to use it for a party house while it sat empty."

Alex leaned forward, putting his hands on the table in front of him. "Wait. Are we talking about the old Victorian off Bedford Road?"

"You know it?" Isadora asked, surprised.

Alex chuckled. "I'm a police officer. Of course I know it. I chase kids out of there all the time. It's been empty a long time. We all thought it was abandoned."

"Not abandoned," she said between bites. "The previous owner passed, and it took the executor a while to find me. I didn't even know I still had any family."

Alex looked thoughtful. "You did your dissertation on Washington Irving, then inherited a house in Sleepy Hollow from a relative you didn't know existed? That can't be a coincidence, Izzy."

Isadora set her fork down, finished with her meal. "It's not. I'm actually descended from Ichabod Crane. As far as I know, he never lived here, but someone else obviously did."

He barked out a laugh. "You're descended from Ichabod Crane?" he asked incredulously as he leaned back again. "You do know it's just a story, right?"

Isadora shook her head, letting out an exasperated sigh. "Except that Irving used the names of real people. The story may have been made up, but the people weren't."

"Sure. Except that the character was based on some schoolteacher named Jesse Merwin," he said matter-of-factly. "Ichabod Crane was just a name he made up."

She shook her head, once again. "The mannerisms were based on Jesse Merwin, but he got the name Ichabod Crane from a real person. Ichabod was actually a military officer."

He scoffed. "I'm sure that was only a coincidence."

"No. We can't say they ever actually met, but they were both at Fort Pike during the War of 1812. If they didn't meet, it was likely Irving at least saw his name on paperwork."

"Is that why you did your dissertation on Ichabod Crane? Because you're related to him."

"Probably. It was always just lore passed down through my family. My grandmother and her mother were part of the Daughters of the American Revolution and did the genealogy, but all I ever knew was that we were related to him. I've always been a big fan of Halloween and wanted to know more, so I started doing research. I guess it always bothered me that his name was used in a manner so contradictory to his character. I can only imagine how pissed it must have made him and I guess teaching the true story behind the story is my way of giving back, if only a little."

The server came, dropping off their check. They finished everything up and headed to the Jack O'lantern Blaze. Isadora was in awe of the sheer number of pumpkins that had all been meticulously carved and put on display. When the banners had said there were over seven thousand hand-carved pumpkins, she was expecting each pumpkin to have its own individual design and that they would all be lined up along a road or in front of the manor. What lay before her was nothing like what she had imagined.

There were some individually carved pumpkins on display on their own, but the majority of the pumpkins told a story or came together to form a picture or a structure. Pumpkins were stacked together to create a larger image like a mosaic. Some replicated famous paintings while others were made to look like stained glass windows. There was a canopy overhead with blue and white lights shining through stars carved into rows of pumpkins that led them to a spinning carousel, a working windmill, a field of giant spiders and a spiderweb, a New York City street scene, a field of sunflowers with green lights shining through the carvings made to look like stems, another field of scarecrows, and another canopy with bats carved into the pumpkins, these ones filled with green lights. Every scene was something new, created completely out of carved pumpkins filled with different colored lights. Music played in the background while they strolled through the display. It was dark enough that the lights really stood out.

By the end of the evening, Alex knew he had made the right decision in bringing Isadora there. She had been in awe of the creativity and the artistry of the displays. He watched her all night while she took everything in and was certain she had not stopped smiling since they arrived.

"That was incredible. Thank you for taking me, Alex," she beamed from the passenger seat while he drove back to her place.

Alex turned his head briefly to flash a smile at her. "I had a great time tonight. I'm glad you enjoyed it."

"I really did." She was still smiling.

"What are you doing tomorrow? Maybe we can get together again?"

Isadora's smile finally fell. "I can't. I have to work at the house. I have a ton to get done before the contractor starts."

"Do you need help? I could swing by and give you a hand." The words were out of his mouth before he had even thought about what he was saying. The last thing he wanted to do on his day off was manual labor, but he really liked her. He would do it if it meant spending more time with her.

Her head resting on the back of the seat, she turned her neck to look at him while keeping her body facing forward. The smile had returned, though it was gentler this time, not beaming like it had been. "Thanks for offering, but I can't ask you to do that."

"You didn't ask. I offered."

"That's only because you have no idea what I need help with," she teased. "If you did, you wouldn't be so quick to offer."

"Try me," he challenged.

Her head came off the seat as she said, "Okay, I have about two dozen heavy boxes that need to be hauled down three flights of stairs. I also have furniture that needs moving, a lot of debris that needs to be cleaned up, and at some point, walls to be cleared of peeling wallpaper and painted." The last would be done by the decorator that she had finally made up her mind about hiring, but she wanted to give him an idea about the level of work that would be required at the house.

Alex did not hesitate. "Okay. What time should I be there?"

Isadora studied him, trying to find the teasing in his statement. There was none. He had been serious. "It's okay, you really don't have to."

"What time, Izzy?" he repeated, turning his head to look at her again.

Isadora heaved out a breath. "I'll be getting started at seven. You're welcome to show up whatever time works for you."

Alex nodded as he pulled into her driveway. They got out and he walked her to her door. She unlocked and opened it, then turned to him.

"Thanks again, Alex. This was exactly what I needed tonight."

His deep brown eyes bore into her, and his hand went to her hip before she could turn around and go back inside, not that she was trying to. She had enjoyed his company, even if he sometimes came across as arrogant. The corner of her mouth curved up in a smile, relishing the feel of his hand on her hip. Her last boyfriend had not lasted long, and it had been a while since she had enjoyed dating. She thought she could enjoy dating Alex.

When she lingered on the porch, Alex took it as a cue. He leaned in, sliding his hand from her hip to the small of her back, pulling her into him. His other hand went to her neck, and he lowered his mouth to hers as she went up on her tiptoes to meet him halfway. Alex wanted to take her inside the house and rip their clothes off. He wanted to know how she tasted, sounded, and felt. The thought was getting him excited, though he knew she was not ready for that yet. However, it would not stop him from trying. When his hands began to roam, she pulled back, breaking the kiss. Breathlessly, she wished him goodnight, said she would see him in the morning, and slipped inside the house.

With the door closed and locked, Isadora leaned against it. Her fingers went to her swollen lips, reliving the kiss Alex had planted on her. He was so intense. He went after what he wanted without hesitation.

Isadora appreciated the assertiveness, but also worried that it would become overbearing as time went on. She tried to dismiss the negative thoughts from her mind as she straightened from the door and readied herself for bed.

10

June 1815

After a good night's rest and cleaning the grime from the road off his body, Ichabod donned a fresh uniform and headed to the church. He had not traveled in uniform but wanted to honor his friend when he notified Samuel Van Tassel's family. It was the least amount of respect he could show both Samuel and his family. He thought it may also help make the family more likely to speak with him, though he was not certain about that. Many had not wanted this war and had openly argued against it. The uniform may have the opposite effect than what he wanted. He decided to take the chance. It was for his friend, not the people, that he wore it now.

Ichabod arrived at the church half an hour before the service was scheduled to start. He spoke to many people, asking after Samuel's family. Immediately prior to the start of the service, he was pointed toward a family who had just arrived. The young woman being accompanied by whom he assumed were her parents immediately caught Ichabod's eye. Even with her blonde hair pulled up and secured under a bonnet, she was stunning. The blue dress she wore brought out the color in her eyes while her smile made them sparkle. Her dress was in the latest fashion with a high waistline, tubular skirt, and short, puffed sleeves. A few curls peaked out from under the bonnet, framing her beautiful face. Ichabod's breath caught for a moment before he gathered himself and made his way over to them.

"Good morning. I'm Major Ichabod Crane of the Third Artillery. I understand you are Mr. Caleb Brush?" Ichabod removed his hat and extended his hand to the man before him.

Caleb Brush took the offered hand and shook it slowly, wondering what this man could possibly want with him.

"I served with Lieutenant Samuel Van Tassel and am trying to find his family. He said he was from the area, and I was told you might know how to find them."

"Ah, yes. Samuel. He was my nephew. His loss has been difficult." Caleb's face darkened with sadness. "His family should be here shortly. Samuel's father is my wife's brother. I'll be happy to introduce you."

"Thank you."

"In the meantime, may I present my own family? This is Mrs. Eleanor Brush and two of our children, Katrina and Jacob." The man gestured to each in turn and they each nodded at the mention of their names.

Ichabod was trying to not stare at the beautiful Katrina, but it was difficult not to. He took each woman's hand in turn, kissing their knuckles lightly, then shaking the hand of Caleb's son.

Katrina smiled sweetly at Ichabod, a slow blush creeping across her face when he took her hand. Caleb began to ask about Samuel, but the service was getting underway. They made their way inside the small church and found seats, with Caleb inviting Ichabod to sit with them.

"I'm certain my brother-in-law and his family will be here soon. I shall introduce you after the service."

Ichabod sat beside Katrina throughout the service, trying to pay attention to the pastor instead of focusing on how close she was and how good she smelled. She sat so primly, with her small hands folded together in her lap. He wanted to reach over and take one of them in his own hand. Ichabod had focused on his career for so long, he had not had much opportunity to meet women, but he was twenty-eight now and thought he should probably start considering doing so. Perhaps once he received his orders and got to his next duty station, he would be able to find a woman suitable for marriage. He would only be there for another day, which was nowhere near enough time to get to know the young lady next to him, but he could not help wondering about her.

After the service, Ichabod followed the Brush family out of the church. Once outside, they met up with another family whom Caleb introduced as Samuel's parents, John and Weintie, and his younger siblings to include a younger brother and three younger sisters. Harmon was now the eldest, followed by the three sisters. It was not lost on Ichabod that though the oldest daughter was likely the same age as Katrina, she did not catch his attention the same way the other girl had. Rebecca also had blonde hair and fair skin, but her smile simply did not compare to Katrina's. Betsey and Margaret both favored their brothers with light brown hair.

"Your son was assigned to my command." Ichabod addressed John and Weintie while Caleb and Eleanor looked on. "He was a great soldier and a good man. He saved my life before he was cut down. I wanted you to know that he died a hero."

Weintie and Eleanor both had tears in their eyes. They were holding each other while Ichabod spoke.

"I have some of his personal effects and wished to return them to you."

With a shaky voice, John said, "We thank you for that. Please, join us for dinner this afternoon. You can bring his things then."

Ichabod returned to the inn where he had left Samuel's things. Uncertain whether he would be able to find the family, he wanted to leave the items somewhere safe while he searched for them. When he arrived at the farm later that afternoon, he saw that there were other people arriving as well. One group of newcomers appeared to be the Brush family, and Ichabod's heart sped up a little at the thought of seeing Katrina again.

Ichabod met with Weintie and John, giving them the bible and the letter he had taken from Samuel's things. There were a few other personal items, but these carried the most significance. Both of their eyes were moist after scanning the letter. Weintie hugged Ichabod, thanking him for returning a small part of her son to her while John shook his hand, taking it in both of his.

"The bible was my father's," Weintie said on a sniffle. She had a faraway look in her eyes, as if she was remembering better days. "He carried it with him all through the war for independence. He always said it brought him comfort, even through the worst of days. I wanted Samuel to have that comfort."

"He read it often," Ichabod replied in an attempt to give the woman some reassurance.

Afterward, Ichabod was escorted into the parlor where he was introduced to the other guests that he had not yet met. He met Cornelius and Elizabeth Van Tassel, parents of Eleanor Brush and John Van Tassel, followed by the single men in attendance.

"This is Abraham Martling," Caleb said. "He's our blacksmith here in Tarrytown."

"They call me Brom Bones," the large man said while shaking Ichabod's hand. His chest was wide and his forearms were strong and muscled, shaped by years in the shop. He had dark hair that fell over his forehead. Ichabod was a tall man, but Brom rivaled him in height. Between them, they stood over most of the other men present.

Weintie Van Tassel handed Ichabod a drink while Caleb Brush continued the introductions.

"And this is Mr. Washington Irving. He's a lawyer and a writer."

"Ichabod Crane? Now, why does that name sound familiar?" Washington asked after shaking hands with Ichabod. He held a drink in one hand and his other hand went to his jaw while he thought for a moment. "Where were you stationed?" he asked, taking note of the uniform Ichabod was still wearing.

"Sackets Harbor," he replied.

"Fort Pike. Yes, that's it. I was aide-de-camp for Governor Daniel Tompkins there. I saw your name come through after the Battle of Crysler's farm. Your efforts during the retreat did not go unnoticed. Congratulations on your meritorious service award and promotion."

"Thank you." Ichabod inclined his head in acknowledgment.

Eleanor asked, "Crysler's farm? Is that not where Samuel was killed?"

"It was," Ichabod replied without further embellishment.

"So, our Samuel died and you came out with an award and a promotion?" she asked with a little bit of a bite to her words.

"It was at Crysler's farm that Samuel saved my life." Ichabod spoke with every bit of reverence in his voice that he could muster. The man had been his friend and he missed him. Even had they not been friends, Ichabod had every respect for him after what he did. He looked into his glass while he spoke. "He was cut down in my stead. I did what I could to save him, but his injuries were too severe."

Instead of answering the question, Ichabod deliberately left out any mention of his own actions that led to his recognition of meritorious service and his being conferred with a rank of brevet major. He was not there to brag about himself, and he did not want to take away from Samuel's bravery.

Ichabod looked up, making eye contact with Samuel's parents. He raised his glass then, saying, "Here's to Samuel. He died bravely, with honor."

Everyone raised their glasses, toasting to the son, brother, grandson, nephew, and cousin that they had all lost. Most of the women were seen wiping a tear from their eyes, as was John. Even those with dry eyes had a somber countenance to them. Ichabod had not meant to bring down the mood of the gathering, but it was inevitable, given his presence there. It would have happened sooner or later.

"Will you be returning to the military after you leave here?" Katrina asked, blushing slightly when he turned his attention to her.

Ichabod preened under Katrina's attention. "Yes. We've yet to receive our orders, but I shall return to Sackets Harbor until we know our next duty station."

"When will you head back there?" she asked.

"I shall leave here tomorrow. I came only to return Samuel's things."

A wave of disappointment flowed through Katrina. She had hoped the soldier would stay a little longer. Her mother probably saw the disappointment on her face, because she came over then and slipped her arm through hers, guiding her out of the room while singing the praises of Brom Bones.

"You could have sent Samuel's things along in the post. Surely it was not incumbent upon a major to personally deliver the items in question?" Washington asked.

"Samuel was my friend. I wanted to make sure the items made it."

"Thank you for that," Weintie said. "You will not stay there at Fort Pike?"

"It's possible, but doubtful," Ichabod replied. "With the war at an end, most of the remaining soldiers shall likely be reassigned." Turning his attention back towards Washington, he asked, "Will you be returning as well, Mr. Irving?" He had wanted to continue speaking with Katrina but was unable to do so after she was pulled away by her mother.

"Heavens, no. I've had my fill of war. I shall be sailing for Liverpool soon. I merely wanted to get in some more time in my beloved Tarrytown before I leave."

"Is this your home, then?" Ichabod asked.

Washington sighed. "I hope it will be one day, but alas, no. I grew up in New York City. Though, I've been coming here since I was a child. I fell in love with this sleepy little hollow as a boy avoiding the yellow fever spreading through the city."

"Will you be practicing the law in Liverpool, Mr. Irving?" John asked.

"I shall be assisting my brothers in the family business. We import hardware and I am to assist in any way I can, though I'd much rather spend my time writing. Perhaps they will have need of my talents with the written word."

"What have you written?" Ichabod asked.

"I wrote essays for the *Morning Chronicle* and prior to the war, I published the *History of New York*," Washington said with a flair of the hand.

Ichabod's brows drew together in thought. "*History of New York? From the Beginning of the World to the End of the Dutch Dynasty?*"

"You're familiar with it?"

"I've read it. I thought it was written by a Diedrich Knickerbocker?"

"A pen name. One of several I've used thus far. What did you think of it?"

While they discussed Washington's book, Ichabod's attention was again drawn to the fair

Katrina who returned with her mother. The woman guided the girl toward Brom where they chatted. Or rather, Eleanor and Brom chatted while Katrina looked around the room. Her eyes met with Ichabod's often, where she would blush and quickly look away. This only served to draw him in even more.

Katrina could not stop blushing every time Ichabod Crane looked at her. His gaze was so intense, it felt as though he was looking right through her. He was a handsome man. Tall, with dark hair and eyes, he cut a dashing figure in his uniform. She wanted to talk with him and ask him about his experience during the war, but instead, she was stuck there, talking with Brom. He was such a bore, only talking about himself. Katrina noticed that Ichabod always diverted attention away from himself, making sure to ask about others every chance he got. Brom would never think to do that. Everything he did only served to bring attention to himself. She had no idea how she would ever survive a marriage to this man. If her mother got her way, the marriage would happen soon. Katrina had been delaying it, trying to find an alternative, but there were few options open to her. She was related to most of the eligible bachelors in town. Brom was thought to be a catch with a successful blacksmith shop and his good looks that made most of the girls there swoon. Most young ladies would be eager to wed him, but Katrina was not one of them.

Dinner was served while the conversation flowed. Ichabod was seated at the far end of the table from Katrina, who was seated between her mother and Brom. He sat between Washington and Samuel's mother, both of whom kept him engaged with questions about his service and Samuel. He was happy to discuss Weinte's son with her and answer every question she threw at him. By the end of the evening, Ichabod not only had a full belly, but a full heart after visiting with this family. He would have liked to stay longer and get to know them better, but he had to get back to Lake Ontario. His furlough was only so long, and he had duties to which he needed to return. He reluctantly climbed onto his horse after saying his goodbyes and headed back to the inn. He could get an early start in the morning and with any luck, he could make it back to the fort in a week.

11

Modern Day

With help from Alex and the contractors, Isadora got the attic cleared out and all of the boxes down to the basement. Alex helped move furniture and clean up debris, doing whatever she asked without complaint. She had begun thinking she would likely get rid of all of the furniture and replace it with newer things in the same style, even if the existing ones were all authentic. As much as she had wanted to keep as many of the original pieces as she could, she simply did not like the look of any of it. The styles were fine, but the fabrics were rather gaudy. Perhaps she could simply reupholster it all. It was something she would have to think about.

Isadora was enjoying spending time with Alex. With all of the events, he worked every weekend in October, so she usually only saw him during the week. When he could, he tried to come by in the mornings before his afternoon shift started and texted her when he could not. If his shift was slow, he and his partner would occasionally stop by the house for a few minutes between calls.

The cleanup went more quickly than she anticipated, which gave her more time to enjoy the area. She ran every morning, trying to go to different places when she could. One morning, she ran in the cemetery; another, she went to the Rockefeller State Park Preserve; and on another, she tried the Old Croton Aqueduct Trail. She loved each of them and tried to rotate between them as much as she could. With more than seven acres, she wanted to run over her own land, but there was no trail, and the ground was rather uneven and interrupted with landscaping. If she stayed, she thought she might try adding a trail to the property.

With the cleanup moving along, Isadora tried to get out and explore the town as well. She would work at the house during daylight hours since the power had not yet been turned back on, then find someplace new to see. Many of the places in which she was interested required tickets which were all sold out, but she decided those could wait until after Halloween. Instead, she went to places that she could get into or those which did not require tickets. Everyday seemed to bring something new. She visited Lyndhurst

Mansion, the town center, the farmer's market in Patriots Park every Saturday, and the mill and Philipsburg Manor.

Near the top of her list of places to go see had been Sunnyside Manor, the home in which Washington Irving had lived for decades. Isadora toured the grounds before it got dark, taking her time exploring the pond and waterfall and walking along the stream, across the bridge over it, and up the leaf-covered stone steps beside it into the trees. Like everywhere else in the Hudson River Valley, the retaining walls and steps were made from the Yonkers gneiss, and it had all been there so long that it looked as though the earth had tried to reclaim it, giving the man-made landscape a more natural feel, as if mother nature herself had placed the stones in such a manner.

After spending time wandering the grounds, Isadora finally made her way to the house, waiting in line for the next tour. The costumed tour guide told everyone in the line that the house was originally a Dutch stone house but had been remodeled and expanded after Irving purchased it with Tudor-style chimneys, stepped gables, gothic windows, and a Spanish tower. He had taken his favorite parts of his time in Europe and used them to influence the home he purchased upon his return to America. He had even planted wisteria by the front door and Scottish ivy in other places. It was exciting to finally get to go inside the house where Irving had lived and died.

The tour started with the study directly inside the front door. Inside the study was Irving's personal library including all of his previously published works. Most of his original works had been given away by his family who had continued living in the house for one hundred years after Irving died, but his journals and collections of letters were there. Standing in Washington Irving's study gave Isadora goosebumps.

The small group continued into the dining room where dinner would have always been served before dark. Each room had its own costumed tour guide and in the dining room, they were informed that in 1809, the term 'donut' was used for the first time when it was coined by Irving in *A History of New York*, written under the pen name of Deidrich Knickerbocker. Despite the grandeur of the home compared to modern houses, the manor was an example of a middle-class home from the period. Irving had servants, but that was also common for the middle class at that time. Servants were typically immigrants trying to establish a foothold in America.

They made their way through the house, up the narrow stairs and back down into the kitchen at the back of the house. There had been running water in the kitchen when Irving resided there, though it did not reach the upstairs. He even had an early refrigerator in the pantry, which was a simple ice box. The property had fruit trees and once housed poultry, cows, and pigs. The tour guides informed them about Irving as well as his home. He had been an ambassador minister to Spain; spoke five languages: English, Spanish, French, Italian, and German; and when he died at age seventy-six, he was mourned widely. Irving never married after losing his fiancé to tuberculosis in 1808. For years, he would not even mention her name and he was said to have dreamt of her 'incessantly.'

Isadora listened intently to the guides, asking questions, but not so much as to bore the others attending the tour. Much of the information that was imparted she had already known. It was new insights that she craved. At the end of the tour, she asked her guide about the history of the property.

"I thought I remembered seeing somewhere that this was the site of the Van Tassel farm from the story?" She had wanted to verify the information so she could add it to her lecture.

"I don't know about that," the guide replied. "What I do know is that it was bought by Irving in 1835. It was formerly a tenet farm owned by Woolfert Eckert, attached to Philipsburg Manor. But if you have more specific questions like that you can contact our historian. Just stop by the gift shop on your way out and pick up her card."

Upon the end of the tour, Isadora roamed the other side of the property, viewing the ice house which she had been informed would typically keep ice until September. After seeing everything she could, Isadora finally made her way to the gift shop where she looked at the books on offer. The shop was busy with several people shopping and a few employees working. Isadora asked the cashier for a business card for their historian, explaining she was a professor of English Literature at a university and had some questions she would like to ask. Before the cashier could respond, a buxom woman with velvety mocha skin turned around and grabbed a card from the counter, holding it out to Isadora.

"I'm the librarian here," she said. "Tamara Petit-Blanc."

Isadora took the offered card and extended a hand. "I'm Isadora Crane. It's nice to meet you."

The other woman scoffed. "Crane? Really? You pulling my leg?"

"I wouldn't dream of it." Tamara may have been small, but Isadora could see she was not someone to mess with. She imagined the woman taking on men twice her size and getting them to back down. "And it's not a coincidence, either. I'm actually a descendant of Ichabod."

Tamara shook her long scarlet and black braids out of her face, assessing Isadora through shrewd eyes. "Are you now? I do believe this is a first for us. What kind of questions you have that we could possibly answer here, Chil'?" Isadora noted the southern accent. She had always loved that accent. The 'child' without the 'D' annunciated was something she had heard a lot growing up. Hearing it now reminded her of her childhood and happier days, before her father went off to war.

"I was asking your tour guide about the history of the property. Was this the site that the Van Tassel farm in the story was based on?"

"That's your question? That's all you want to know?"

"I actually did my dissertation on Washington Irving. There's not much I haven't been able to gather from my own research. But that was one of the few pieces of information I could not find an answer to, though it was brought up as a possibility. If I had an answer, I could incorporate it into my lecture on *The Legend of Sleepy Hollow*, but I don't want to misinform my students."

Instead of answering the question, Tamara asked one of her own. "How 'bout I buy you lunch and ask you questions, Sugar?"

Isadora's brow creased in confusion and her head cocked slightly to the side. "What would you want to ask me?"

"That depends. How much do you know about your family history?"

ॐ   ॐ

Alex went with Isadora to the Lyndhurst Mansion before his shift Friday morning and as he drove, he explained, "This road we're on is Broadway, but it's the road in the story that Irving called Albany Post Road."

Isadora appreciated his knowledge of the story, but he had a way of bringing up basic aspects of it that she already knew through her research. He would explain things to her as if she was completely unfamiliar with the story. She tried not to get upset, and instead, responded with, "I remember seeing that when I did my dissertation. It's interesting to see it in person."

After visiting Lyndhurst Mansion, Isadora met Tamara for lunch. They hit it off immediately and shared their personal stories with one another. Tamara was a few years older than Isadora and had grown up on the coast of Georgia. After her daughter left for college, she took the job at Sunnyside, moving away from her family. It took her no time after getting settled to begin singing in her new church choir. She was boisterous and outgoing to Isadora's reserved quietness.

The women discussed Washington Irving and their respective research on him, and Tamara asked questions about Isadora's ancestry. She told her what she could, but there was not a lot she could tell her that was not already in the public domain.

"It's some of the subsequent ancestors I wish I knew more about," she said as she proceeded to tell Tamara about the house she had inherited and why she was there in Sleepy Hollow.

"Have you cleansed the manor?" Tamara asked. "Or the place you're staying in, for that matter?"

"That's what I'm doing now, cleaning. I spend all my time clearing out the old furniture and belongings at the manor to get it fixed up and emptied before I decide what I'm doing with it. But the rental place was already clean when I arrived. The owners keep it quite tidy."

"I'm not talking about *cleaning*, Sugar. I meant a *cleansing*. To rid the space of negative energies."

How did Isadora politely say she did not believe in that stuff? She took a sip from her glass to buy herself a moment. "I've never done that anywhere."

"Honey Child! That's the first thing you should do whenever you arrive in a new space. You don't want other people's energies hanging around. Being in a rental, you know that place has had a number of people there and for as old as that house of yours is, I'm sure it's in desperate need of a cleansing."

Isadora nodded. "Want to come by the manor sometime and see it?"

Tamara finished chewing the bite she had placed in her mouth. "You know I do. I love all that historical stuff."

After occupying the table at the restaurant far longer than they should have, Isadora recommended they walk while they finished their conversation. Tamara took her down to the Scenic Hudson Riverwalk Park where they could see the Tappan Zee Bridge to the south and the Sleepy Hollow Lighthouse to the north. When they finished, Isadora gave Tamara the address of her new manor and they arranged a time for her to come get a tour of the property.

While she explored her acres the next morning, Isadora was thinking about Alex's habit of mansplaining things to her. She really liked him, but he also drove her nuts sometimes. She felt like he was using the story to try to connect with her when he had nothing else to talk about. Unfortunately, it showed a complete disregard for her own knowledge and research when he explained the most basic concepts. He was also starting to show the overbearing side she had been worried about on their first date. She told herself it was still early, and they were still feeling each other out, but she was not sure. People talking down to her or over her were some of her biggest pet peeves, and he did both. She did not think he was trying to be condescending, but he often was. Still, he had helped her immensely at the manor and he often made her laugh.

Isadora knew Alex wanted to take things further than they had, but it had only been a few days. His hands roamed as often as she would let them. Sometimes she did not mind it, enjoying that he appreciated her body and was that attracted to her. Other times, it annoyed her that it seemed like that was all he was after. She did not think that was the case, but she worried that was the only reason he was helping her out at the manor. If she gave in and slept with him, would he lose interest and stop coming around? She hated thinking that she was stringing him along or worse, using him for manual labor, but she was not ready to have a physical relationship with him yet. It was too soon for her. She needed to know he was not going to leave as soon as he got what he wanted.

12

June 1815

As soon as he hit the road, Ichabod noticed the limp. He had barely made it back to the church when he dismounted from his horse and began checking her hind quarters for an injury. Holding her reins, he watched as Athena walked in a slow circle, then as he picked up her pace a little. He narrowed the injury down to her left hind leg and began to run his hands along the leg, looking for any visible injuries. As he did so, a man approached on horseback. Ichabod remembered Athena stepping into a hole in the dirt road on his way back to the inn the previous night and began to wonder if she twisted her ankle. When he did not see any visible injuries, he checked her ankle, which did not seem to bother her much. He curled his finger and ran the knuckle along the length of the leg, finally finding the soreness.

"Is everything all right there, Major Crane?" Caleb Brush asked.

Ichabod looked up as the other man pulled his horse to a stop and dismounted.

"You have a lame horse?" he asked.

"She seems to have some soreness. I can't find any visible injuries. I'm afraid she may have pulled a muscle."

Caleb leaned down and examined the horse as well, agreeing with Ichabod's assessment.

"I guess I won't be departing today after all. She'll need to rest before I can travel."

He could potentially book passage aboard a boat to take him as far as Albany but most of the remaining journey would have to be on horseback. Either way, his horse needed time to heal before he attempted the journey back. With a sigh, he turned back to Caleb and asked if he knew of any other inns nearby.

"We only have the one. Will they still have your room available?"

"That's what I was afraid of. They said they were all booked up. In fact, they were grateful I checked out as early as I did. How far is the nearest town with an inn?"

Caleb gave Ichabod a look of pity. "She'll never make it that far on that leg."

Ichabod lifted his top hat and ran a hand through his hair. It was an old habit that he thought he had broken himself of after years of wearing the uniform, but it still showed up periodically.

"Why don't you follow me? You may stay with my family while she heals."

Ichabod shook his head. "I don't wish to put you out. If it's as bad as I suspect, she will need to rest for several weeks."

Even as he said it, Ichabod began thinking about the repercussions of his horse's injury. He could not simply leave her there or easily replace her, but traveling as far as he needed to go on a pulled muscle could make it much worse, turning it into a permanent injury. If that happened, he would have to put Athena down. He did not take chances with his horse and wanted to allow her the appropriate time to heal. As a soldier, he never knew when he would need her in top condition in order to save his life. He would have to send word to his commander and let him know he needed to extend his furlough.

"Nonsense. It's no bother. As a friend to Samuel, John would allow you to stay with him as well, but he already has Mr. Irving staying there. It's the least I can do in his stead."

"I thank you, Mr. Brush. Hopefully she recovers quickly, and I may be on my way again."

Ichabod led Athena behind Caleb as they moved away from Albany Post Road toward farmland. He was grateful for the man's offer of boarding, but also that he maintained a slow enough pace that it did not put undue stress on the impaired horse.

When they arrived at the homestead, Eleanor came out to greet her husband.

"Major Crane will be staying for a while, Mrs. Brush. See to it that he gets settled in with Jacob. He can take Joshua or Caleb's bed."

She frowned at Ichabod but went inside and did as she was told, twirling the blue and silver ring on her finger in annoyance. Their oldest sons had recently moved out and their beds were free. Ichabod would share a room with Jacob, the youngest, but he did not mind. He had grown up with two brothers of his own, then became accustomed to being quartered in the homes of families or in barracks with several other officers during the war. Jacob was slightly younger than the other officers he typically bunked with, but not by much. The boy was fifteen and excited to hear all about life as a soldier. He had asked Ichabod several questions at dinner the night before and Ichabod suspected the boy would be thrilled to share his room with him.

The home was a modest two-stories with chimneys at each end. The downstairs consisted of the kitchen, dining room, and parlor while the upstairs held a handful of bedrooms. A set of benches lined the covered front porch. It stood on a large property with a weeping willow tree slightly off from the house, a chicken coop, barn, and other outbuildings. A garden was off the kitchen in the backyard and the crop-filled fields and orchards extended all around them.

After getting settled, Ichabod headed back downstairs to see what he could help with. He was not an idle man and if he was going to be there for an extended period of time, the least he could do was assist with the chores. There was always plenty to do on a farm and never enough hands to do everything. If he was assisting, he would feel like he was at least earning his room and board from these generous people. He had offered to pay Caleb, but the man would not hear of it.

Instead, he had said, "You may help bring in the hay in a few days and we'll call the matter settled."

Ichabod agreed and Caleb had dropped him at the farm and headed back out again, off to tend to whatever business Ichabod had interrupted.

As he reached the bottom of the stairs, he could hear someone in the kitchen. Expecting Eleanor, he headed that way but found Katrina instead. Or rather, she found him, when she ran right into him.

"Oh. Excuse me. I'm so sorry. I was –"

Katrina stopped when she looked up to see who she had run into. For a moment, all she could do was stare into Ichabod's handsome face. She had never been shy, but something about this man made her go speechless. Or perhaps it was his proximity. She took in his scent and realized he had his hands on her waist. They had gone up to steady her when she bounced off his sturdy frame, but he had yet to drop them. She suddenly looked away and took a step back, a slow blush spreading across her face.

"What brings you here, Major Crane?"

"I was looking for your mother. I'm to stay here for a time and I wish to be helpful. I thought perhaps she might have some chores to which I could tend."

"Mother went to see a neighbor. She'll be back shortly. Perhaps I could keep you company until she returns," she offered hopefully.

Ichabod's blood warmed at the thought. However, he knew the girl was not simply being polite. He could sense her attraction and though it was mutual, he had no intention of dishonoring this family who had agreed to help him by acting on said attraction. He could see the mischief in her eyes and decided he would do well to keep a distance from her while he was there.

"Thank you. I'd hate to pull you away from your tasks. I'll find something with which to occupy myself until her return."

Ichabod quickly walked away and went outside. He checked on his horse, massaging her sore leg. Then he looked around until he found an axe and a pile of wood which he began to chop into smaller pieces to keep himself occupied until Caleb and Eleanor returned. In this part of the world, winters were always long and hard and there never seemed to be enough fuel for fires. He knew the help would be appreciated.

13

Modern Day

The early morning fog was beginning to lift, but it still blanketed the area. The rain had come down hard the night before, but it had stopped sometime early in the morning. Walking through a portion of her land dense with trees, Isadora pushed further on. There was a creek along the edge of the trees where she stopped and listened for a while before continuing. Knowing the water was there on her property filled her heart. This may be her new favorite place on earth. She loved being amongst all the trees but loved the water even more. Her and Simon always tried to find trails that were covered in trees when they went hiking and if they could find a trail near water, it was even better. She thought of him now and how much she missed him. She had not even been able to talk to him much since she had been in New York. With a two-hour time difference, it would be too early to call him in Utah now, but she would call him later when she knew he was awake.

The fall colors poking through the fog were like something out of a dream. Isadora realized how much she had missed the abundance of trees along the east coast. She had grown up on the east coast, primarily in the south, but with her father being military, they moved around a lot. She never stayed in one place for very long, even as an adult. Everywhere she went now, leaves fell from the trees and littered the ground along with the largest acorns she had ever seen. She had lived in the desert for far too long. Utah had some beautiful mountains with plenty of its own trees, but when compared with the Hudson River Valley, it looked downright sparse. This place was already getting under her skin and into her heart. She was beginning to understand Washington Irving's love for it.

Isadora ducked to miss a low branch and as she did so, she tripped on a gnarled root sticking up from the ground. The tree was old and thick, making its roots massive. She lost her balance, catching her ankle on a rock jutting up at the base of the tree. She felt a sharp pain as it ripped through her leggings, cutting open her flesh and she dropped to the ground. The outside of her ankle was spewing blood and she tried to stem the flow with her hand. Unfortunately, there was too much pouring out. It flowed down while she sat on the ground, dripping down her foot and shoe into the dirt beneath her. In her pain, she thought she felt the earth tremble beneath her. Remembering the same sensation at the cemetery, she made a mental note to research whether there were any fault lines in the area. She ripped at her leggings where they had torn from catching on the rock and tried to use the scrap to catch some of the blood. Isadora applied as much pressure as she could, sitting there in pain while thinking about the long walk back to the house.

After wrapping her ankle the best she could, she gathered the strength to stand, clutching the rough bark of the tree for support. Isadora hobbled her way back to the house, dripping a trail of blood behind her as she went. When she got to the house, Neil Lowry was there, directing contractors and deliveries where they needed to go.

"Are you alright, Izzy? What happened?" he asked as he rushed over to help her. The older man had a concerned look on his face as he wrapped an arm around her back, giving her support.

"I'm okay," she replied. It still hurt immensely, but the pain had become a dull throb instead of the sharp stab that it had been. "I'm pretty sure I'm going to need stitches though."

"Have a seat. I'll go get my truck and drive you to the hospital." Neil guided her towards a bench nearby. She had not yet made it to the house, though she was close.

Isadora shook her head. "I'll be fine, Mr. Lowry. I can drive myself."

He was not having it. "Call me Neil," he said before adding, "Stay here."

He left before she could say anything more and was back in a minute with his truck. He got out and helped her into the passenger seat, then proceeded to drive her to the nearest hospital.

"And how will you get home when they give you pain meds?" he asked when she was still protesting.

"I don't need pain meds. It's not that bad," she lied.

"It doesn't matter. It's done. We're already on the way."

Acquiescing, she said in a quiet voice, "Thank you."

When Isadora was finally released from the hospital, Neil offered to drive her back to the rental. She considered it momentarily but decided against it. "My car is still at the house. And I really do feel better now." He began to argue, but she added, "I don't want to lose an entire day. There's too much that needs to get done. I know what the doctor said and I'll take it easy. But I can at least start going through some of the boxes while I elevate my foot and rest."

This appeased him and he drove back to the manor. Once they arrived, he helped her set up a workspace in the large drawing room on the first floor at the front of the house and brought her a couple of boxes with which to start. He went about his day and came back to check on her every hour, bringing her new boxes when she finished with the ones she was working on.

As she slowly emptied an old trunk that had been mixed in with the boxes, writing down and photographing everything inside it, she came across a small pouch with the initials 'EB' embroidered on the outside. The trunk had been filled with old clothing that looked as though it was from the civil war. She wanted to have it all professionally examined in order to confirm the age and learn how to properly store and preserve them. They were an incredible find. When she lifted a large skirt from the trunk, the small pouch had fallen to the floor with a thunk. She picked it up, opened it, and turned it upside down. A gold button and a heavy silver and blue ring fell into her hand. The silver filigree was laid over a flat sapphire circular stone and extended partway down the sides of the ring. It was ornate, but not overly so. It was beautiful. She wondered why the button was in the pouch with the ring. It had obviously been important enough to someone to save it, but what was the significance and how did it end up with the ornate ring?

"I'm heading out. Is there anything else you need?" Neil asked while she was examining the ring.

Isadora looked up from the pile of old heirlooms surrounding her. She absently slipped the ring onto her finger. "I didn't realize it was so late. Thank you, no. You go home. Have a good night."

Neil hesitated. "Are you sure? I can stay a little longer if you need me to."

Isadora smiled. She knew his family would be waiting for him, but he had a strong sense of responsibility. Apparently, she had become one of the things toward which he felt a duty. He treated her as he would a daughter. "I appreciate the offer, but I'm fine. Really. Go home. I'm almost done here, then I'll be heading home myself. I don't have much daylight left anyways."

Neil nodded. "Okay. But call me if you need anything."

"Thank you. And thanks for your help today."

Neil nodded, said goodnight, and went on his way, leaving Isadora alone in the quiet manor house. She added the ring and the button to her inventory, photographing them both and adding them to the notebook, then she put the button back in the pouch to go back into the trunk. This was her favorite time of day, when all the workers left, and it was quiet again. There was always so much noise when they started working. There were power tools which were connected to a noisy generator, hammering, and men talking over it all. Isadora stretched her neck and resumed the task in front of her. She did not even notice how quickly she was losing the light. When it finally got too dark to see, she set aside the new box on which she was working and stood. She grabbed her keys, locked up, and limped out to her car, planning on picking up a quick dinner and taking it home with her.

It was darker than she had thought, and she wondered how she had been able to see anything inside the house. They had been using shop lights, but it only put out a small swath of light in the large room where she had been working. Now that she was outside, she saw that the sky was almost black. A gust of cold air hit her skin, causing her to shiver. Isadora had not yet been there at night, and it felt eerie. It was quieter than it should have been. She could not hear any insects or birds. There were no sounds from nature, nor man. Even the train and traffic seemed to have been silenced. The lack of any sound had her imagination running wild and her heart rate kicking up a notch. For a moment, she even imagined that she heard the whinny of a horse. She shook off the thought, laughing at herself for being ridiculous and climbed into her car a little more quickly than was probably necessary. Turning the keys in the ignition, she tried to suppress the shakiness that was arising and started heading back to Hawthorne for the night.

As she began her turn onto the main street from the private lane, Isadora heard a loud thump and the car jerked. Had she hit something? Her heart immediately started racing and she slowed. It had sounded like the noise came from behind her and she looked up into the rearview mirror. She saw a dark shadow in all black atop a giant black horse. Isadora could not make out a face or anything at all where the head should be, and the figure was holding a sword raised in his hand. It was difficult to see the figure in the darkness, but the sword glowed as bright as day. The air seemed to have shifted, suddenly becoming oppressive and heavy. Her palms were beginning to sweat. The feeling of hostility radiated through her.

Turning in her seat to try to see the figure more clearly, there was nothing but darkness. She told herself again that she was being ridiculous and pulled out onto the main road with a squeal of the tires. Speeding off as fast as she could, she checked her rearview mirror constantly, her speed matching the racing beat of her heart. She thought she saw the figure again, but after speeding away, she seemed to have lost it. Isadora briefly thought that even a ghostly horse could not keep up with a car. Dismissing the thought as quickly as it came, she vowed not to make her anxiety worse by imagining something that was not possible. It was likely either her imagination or just a prank. Regardless, it had rattled her more than she cared to admit and she could not seem to shake the malicious feeling that was hanging over her.

She pulled into the driveway of her rental and looked around for several minutes before unlocking her car door and getting out. Isadora did not see anyone, so she got out and hobbled as quickly as she could on her sore ankle to the house. Her hands shaking, she fumbled at the lock, but managed to get the door open, get inside, and lock the door behind her. Unable to explain it, the animosity she felt was not consistent with a simple prank. Had she only imagined it? She forgot about food or anything else and stayed in her room all night, trying to will her heartrate to come down.

14

June 1815

Ichabod quickly fell into a routine. He checked on his horse every morning and night, massaging her leg and looking for signs of improvement. He spent his days assisting Caleb and Jacob with some of the chores around the farm. He chopped wood for hours at a time and waited until it was time to cut and harvest the hay. The Brushes would still need to hire more hands to help, but with him there, it would be one less they would have to hire. The labor was hard, but it felt good. Much of the woodwork reminded him a little bit of the construction of Fort Pike. The soldiers had been responsible for building it, and among other things, he had chopped a lot of the wood used in the construction.

Ichabod also assisted wherever else Caleb needed the help. With his two eldest sons gone, there was much to do. Eleanor eyed him often, always glaring or frowning at him. At dinner, she would study him, then turn her attention to Katrina, then back to him. Whatever she saw there, it was nothing that he would feel guilty about. He kept his distance from Katrina as much as he could.

Despite his best efforts, she continued trying to get close to him at first. Katrina would seek him out whenever she had a spare moment. She especially loved watching him chop wood. He would remove his shirt and the hot summer sun would blaze down on him. He usually chopped early in the morning, but it was already warm enough that he would glisten with sweat within minutes. She could hardly take her eyes off of him while she tended to the chickens and gathered the eggs.

The men gathered together one morning to cut the hay. They all went out with their scythes, cutting the knee-high grass. They tried to cut as quickly as they could, taking advantage of the dry weather while it lasted. They took a break for lunch, which was served by Eleanor, Katrina, and her cousins and aunt. This was a communal event they did every year. Caleb and John alternated their crops every year, and next year, the hay would be planted on John's land. They had worked out the system in order to maximize their labor when it was most needed. The family all came on harvest days, and if additional people were needed, they often pulled them from neighbors where they could.

Katrina brought Ichabod a lemonade, which he savored. He happily accepted the glass from her, but did not linger, much to her disappointment. There was still much work to do. After lunch, the cut hay was raked. The next day, pitchforks were used to pile the hay into stacks that measured four feet wide and four feet high, being constructed carefully in order to stave off any rain and wind that might come along. After a couple of days, once these stacks were dry, they would be loaded into a wagon and moved to the barn where they would be unloaded and stored on the second floor.

Ichabod's inattentiveness began to frustrate Katrina. No matter what she did, the major was aloof. At first, she had thought her interest in him was mutual, but after the first two days, he had barely spoken a word to her. It felt like he was avoiding her, though she would still catch him looking at her sometimes. She would turn her head just in time to see him watching her, then turn away quickly when she caught him. She did not understand it. He had seemed so confident, and he had a commanding presence, yet he shied away from her.

In the evenings, the family would gather around in the parlor where the women would do needlework or some other endeavor while they all talked. They would tell stories, someone would sing, or the men would discuss politics and current events.

"My oldest brother is a judge in Ohio," Ichabod explained. "He took after our grandfather who was also a judge and a delegate in the First Continental Congress. My other brother is a naval captain. He's heading to Algiers even as we speak. He and I followed our father's footsteps in the military."

Caleb had been telling him that his family had always been farmers, leading Ichabod to share his own family history.

"The stories you must have," Caleb said in wonder. "Am I to assume your father served in the war for independence?"

Ichabod nodded. "He did. He was a brigadier general. I hope I can live up to his legacy."

"Well, you are certainly well on your way. You speak of your father in the past tense. Did he pass in the war?"

"He passed last year. Though it was from an injury sustained during the war. He was never quite the same." Ichabod had been looking down into his glass, but then a smile spread across his face. "He never let it slow him down, though. He served all the way to the end. He was deputy mayor of Elizabethtown in New

Jersey and still continued his military service. He remained a major general of the militia even during the latest war. Despite my grandfather, father, and brother, I have no desire to become entrenched in politics. I would be happy to remain in service to the military."

"Do you enjoy being a soldier, then?" Jacob asked.

"I do." Ichabod nodded, turning his attention to the boy. "It gives me purpose."

"Is it not dangerous? Are you ever afraid?" Katrina joined the conversation, questioning him with concern in her eyes.

"It is dangerous and sometimes I do get scared," he acknowledged. "But I have a duty. I do what I must."

"You're so brave." She had stars in her eyes now.

Ichabod was uncomfortable with the adoration he saw, though he did enjoy her appreciation of him and he stood a little taller. "I simply do what is expected of me."

"As soldiers do," Brom said. "Though, I dare say, it did not serve Major André well, did it?"

"Major André?" Ichabod asked, trying to place the familiar name or why Brom mentioned him now.

"The treasonous accomplice to Benedict Arnold during the war for independence. The one who was captured right here in Tarrytown and hanged for his role in the plot, while Arnold not only went free, but was rewarded with the rank of general in the British Army. I dare say the major was only doing what was expected of him."

Eleanor scowled at the mentioned of Major André but did not interject her opinion. She let Brom and Ichabod discuss the man while she absently played with the heavy ring on her index finger, recalling the day the man was hung with perfect clarity. After all these years, her opinion on soldiers had not changed and it was bad enough to be housing one; the last thing she wanted was to have to listen to talk of them.

"Ah yes," Ichabod replied. As soon as Brom mentioned Benedict Arnold, he recognized the reference to the major. "Well, Major André was abandoned by the British. General Washington wanted to trade him for Arnold, but they would not have it."

"They say his ghost still haunts these parts. In the early mornings, he can be seen wandering near the tulip tree under which he was found, asking, 'Why me? Why not Arnold?'" Brom was suppressing the smirk he felt bubbling, while trying to convince Ichabod of the truth to his allegations. "But do not fret, good sir." He leaned in, conspiratorially. "If you encounter him, you simply need ask 'What party are you from?' to make the ghost disappear. It confuses the poor man to have to answer to which side his loyalties lay."

Ichabod was not taking his bait. "Old wives' tales, I'm sure."

"Have a care, Major," Washington interjected. "Folks around here are rather superstitious."

Ichabod shook his head and let the men have their tales. He did not believe in such things and would not let Brom get to him.

The family alternated Sunday dinners between the Brush and the Van Tassel households. This week was at the Brush house. Ichabod quickly saw how close the two families were. If he had not known better, he would have thought the women were sisters or the men brothers; not that John and Eleanor had been the siblings. He enjoyed spending time with them. They were good people and despite his eagerness to be back at the fort, he delighted in getting to know them all. He even had fun talking with Washington Irving who stayed with the Van Tassels. Ichabod learned that he was an old family friend. They had met when he first came to the town as a child and had spent his summers with the Van Tassel children. He was a few years younger than John and Eleanor, but he had known them well. They had looked after him often.

Brom Bones was often an addition to Sunday dinners as well. Ichabod initially wondered how the blacksmith was related to the family, but it did not take long to find out.

"You look lovely today, Katrina," Brom said as he sidled up closer to her.

She had been sitting on a bench on the front porch, escaping her parents while she could. Her cousin had been with her for a little while, but Rebecca left to go chase after her youngest sister, who was trying to climb a tree.

"That is unbecoming, Margaret," she yelled after the young girl. Not quite into her teenage years, she was on the cusp between childhood and adulthood, and she was still clinging onto her childhood with everything she had. "You'll ruin your dress. Or fall and break your neck. Come down from there at once."

Katrina could not stifle the giggle at her cousins' expense. That was when Brom found her. He had sat on the bench beside her, a little too close for her liking.

"Thank you, Mr. Martling," she said, trying not to be familiar with him, despite having known him her whole life. He was only a few years older than her, and they had practically grown up together. He may as well be a brother to her; a thought that made her shudder given how much her mother wanted her to marry the man.

"Really Katrina, you may call me Brom. I love hearing my name roll off your tongue." Brom moved even closer, taking her hand in his. It was rough and calloused, and she hated the feel of it on hers.

Katrina tried to slide further away, but there was nowhere for her to go. She pulled her hand from his, clasping it together with her other hand in her lap. This did not deter Brom who brushed the fine hairs off her neck that had come loose from her bonnet. She shrugged his hand away and turned to look at him, prepared to tell him how she felt about his proximity, but he was so close, it threw her off balance.

Gathering herself, she said, "You are far too forward, Mr. Martling. I would beg you to have a care and give me a little room."

Brom laughed. "I've given you room, Katrina. Yet, you've not come to me. It appears I must make my intentions clearer."

With that, he leaned in, kissing her neck. Katrina tried to push him away, but he was so much stronger than her that her efforts were futile. He pulled back only enough to look at her, then he pulled her into him, wrapping his big arms around her waist and kissed her fully on the mouth. Katrina pushed as hard as she could. When he did not budge, she began hitting his shoulders. He moved one hand to the back of her neck to hold her in place and she squealed, while still trying to get away. Suddenly he was no longer there, leaving nothing but air behind as he was ripped away from her. When she looked around, she saw Brom being hauled back by Ichabod. He had pulled the big man off of her and off the bench entirely. The men were now both standing, facing each other.

"The lady said she wanted a little room," Ichabod said angrily.

Katrina looked between the men facing off against one another and Washington standing between them, apparently trying to decide whether or not to intervene. They must have heard her struggle and come to investigate.

Brom merely laughed again. "The lady does not know what she wants, as most women don't. It is up to us as men to tell them what is best for them."

"It might be best if you leave now, Mr. Martling," Ichabod demanded.

Without giving Brom a chance to reply, Ichabod pulled Katrina to her feet and escorted her off the porch. He held his arm out for her and walked her down the steps, away from the house. With a hand on his arm, Washington was trying to calm Brom down as the pair walked away. Ichabod fully expected Brom to follow them or get physical with him, but he did not. Instead, he glared at Ichabod and Katrina as he watched them leave, though Ichabod felt this was not the end of the matter. He knew Brom would not simply let go of the slight.

The sun had set, and the sky was growing darker. Katrina was shaking visibly. Ichabod led her over to the weeping willow near the house where a bench sat underneath the hanging branches. He guided her down, sitting down beside her and placed his hands on her bare arms, rubbing them up and down.

"Would you like me to fetch you a shawl?" he asked softly.

Katrina shook her head. She had been fighting back tears, but the kindness in his voice had them falling now. Her hands went to her face, giving her something to hide behind as she cried while leaning into him. Ichabod gently pulled her to him, loosely placing his arms around her, rubbing her back. After what she had just gone through with Brom, he did not want to put her in the same position of having to fight off unwelcome advances. He wanted to give her comfort, but he also made sure that she knew she could leave if she chose, even though he did not want her to.

Katrina gathered herself and sat up straight. Ichabod dropped his hands as she sat up and she immediately missed them. She liked the feel of him touching her. She wiped her eyes before looking at Ichabod.

"Thank you," she said.

"I'm sorry you had to experience that. Has that happened before?"

"No," she sniffled. "Brom has always made his interest known, but he's never acted on it quite like that before."

"I'm sure he won't do it again." Ichabod was not sure of that at all. In fact, he thought it likely that the man would double his efforts to do so again, but he did not want to scare the girl. "I hope you know there are men who are more honorable than that and would not put you in a position of discomfort."

Katrina nodded. "I know. I'm ever so grateful you and Mr. Irving were there."

She gave him a small smile and his heart leapt. "I wish I could always be there," he whispered.

Had he really just said that? After successfully managing to avoid her for the last two weeks, there he was alone with her in the semi-seclusion of the tree, saying things he should not be saying. The words had slipped out before he had even thought to censor them. When her eyes searched his, he thought she would see right into the heart of him. He turned away, standing.

"I should get back to the house."

Katrina put her hand in his and tugged, encouraging him to sit back down. He turned to look at her and she said, "Please don't go. I don't wish to go back yet and I'm afraid Brom will find me again if I'm alone."

Ichabod sighed, running his free hand through his hair and sat back down beside her. She had not let go of his hand, and for a moment, they merely looked at one another. Her breathing quickened and he could see the longing in her eyes. He wanted to kiss her, but he thought of her parents inside the house only yards away. How would they react if he took advantage of their hospitality?

"Brom has pursued me for some time. He used to pull my hair when we were children. He would call me names and laugh at me as I followed my brothers around. They were all good friends growing up. At some point, the name calling turned into something else. He's made his intentions clear, and my mother approves of him, but he's not what I want in a husband. I wish she would stop encouraging his affections."

"What does your father think?"

"He thinks I'm still too young to think of marriage." She smiled sardonically. "I wish he could see that I'm not, but it protects me from having to wed Brom just yet. I'm sure it won't last forever, but I have hope it will last long enough for me to find an alternative."

"Is that why you look at me the way you do? Am I an alternative, Miss Brush?" Ichabod was torn between being angry at her for seeing him as a means of escape while simultaneously wanting to fulfill that need for her.

Katrina shook her head emphatically. "Not at all, Major Crane. I found myself drawn to you from the moment we met. I can see that you're a good man, a noble man, strong and brave. You came all the way here to deliver Samuel's things in person when you could have sent them along through a courier. You knew how difficult it would be to face his parents, yet you did so anyway. When my parents opened their home to you, you jumped right in and helped with the chores when you did not have to. I know you are a soldier, yet I do not believe you would ever harm a thing unless it was necessary."

Katrina had not released Ichabod's hand and she was moving closer to him now. His gaze landed on her lips and her tongue darted out to lick them. His free hand went up to her face and he ran a finger lightly from her temple to her jaw. She closed her eyes and leaned into his touch. He leaned in and touched his lips to hers; only a light brush at first. Her arm came around his neck as he did so, pulling him into her. With that, he deepened the kiss.

When he pulled back, her heart was racing. She reluctantly opened her eyes when she realized he was not going to kiss her more.

"Katrina," he said breathily, "I do not wish to take advantage of you or your parents' hospitality. Your mother would not approve of this."

"Is that why you've avoided me all this time?" she asked.

He nodded while barking out a laugh. "Yes. Apparently, I am not so brave after all. Avoiding you was easier than telling you no."

Katrina snickered but shook her head. "You are no coward, Ichabod."

He searched her face, seeing the truth of her words. She felt safe with him, and she admired him. He kissed her again, showing his appreciation. He wanted to live up to everything she saw in him. They stayed under the tree, talking, all the while never letting go of each other. Katrina held his hand the entire time. When they heard voices as the guests all said their goodbyes for the night, Ichabod escorted Katrina back to the house. When they left the privacy of the tree, he released her hand and put some distance between them. She balked at first but did not push for more. She knew he was right; her mother would not approve. Eleanor Brush had already made her decision. Katrina needed to find a way to convince her mother that Brom was not the man for her. Ichabod may be what she needed to help convince her. If her mother saw how much she liked Ichabod, perhaps she would let Katrina make her own decision.

15

Modern Day

Isadora finally dozed fitfully in the early hours of the morning, waking often with disturbing dreams of being chased. The dreams featured flaming pumpkins flying through the air at her and a horse with a headless rider who was trying to cut her head off with his gleaming sword. When she finally woke for good the next morning, she decided she had been spending too much time in the village being bombarded with the story. Most likely, the pain meds coupled with the constant reminders combined to cause her to have a hallucination. Her mind was playing tricks on her. She needed a break.

Deciding to take the day off from working on the house, Isadora stayed home all morning, taking her time getting ready for the day. She needed to rest her ankle anyway and with Neil and the other workers being off, there would be no one to help her carry boxes up the stairs. After a late breakfast, she sat down and pulled out her phone, needing to hear Simon's voice.

Hey, Iz. How's everything going out there? You get the house all cleaned up yet?" His voice was rough with sleep.

"I'm sorry Simon. I didn't mean to wake you. I can call you back later."

"Don't be ridiculous," he said. "I'm glad you called. I miss you."

Isadora blinked back the tears that sprang into her eyes unexpectedly. "I miss you, too," she said quietly.

"What's wrong Izzy?" he asked, suddenly alert. "Did something happen?"

She laughed, but there was no mirth in it. "What makes you think that?"

"I know you, Iz. I can hear it in your voice. Tell me what happened."

Simon hated that something was bothering her and he was on the other side of the country, unable to help. Whatever it was, he wanted to fix it for her.

Isadora did not know what had happened last night. She could not tell Simon she was having hallucinations and nightmares and that she had freaked out over a figment of her imagination. Trying to make her voice sound as normal as possible, she said, "I just miss you. I haven't even been able to talk to you in forever."

Simon sighed through the receiver. "I know. I miss you, too. I hate not seeing you and I really hate going so long without talking to you."

With the time difference and their schedules, they kept missing each other when either tried to call. They still texted regularly, but it was not the same. They were always brief and not as personal.

"How's everything going? When are you coming home?" he asked.

"It's going well. There's so much to do, though. It's really been a lot of work. I'm not sure how much longer I'll be here, but I won't be back before the end of the semester. I talked to the dean and requested a leave of absence."

Simon was quiet for a minute. Feeling a need to justify her decision to stay, she quickly added, "I need to be here to take care of everything."

"Oh." Simon could not hide the disappointment in his voice when he finally managed to speak. "Are you going to stay then? Keep the house and move in?" Was this what had her so upset? Had she decided to stay and was having a hard time telling him?

"I still haven't decided what I'm going to do with the house yet. I do like it here, though. The city is close enough to visit but it's far enough away that I don't have to deal with all the traffic and people everywhere."

As much as he did not want to encourage her, he still wanted to be supportive. He also wanted to feel out where she was and how possible it was that she might stay. "Have you looked at campuses nearby where you could teach?"

"I'm sure I could find one. But honestly, the inheritance was more than I ever imagined. I don't need to work anymore. I could take some time off and write or do some traveling. It could be a really big change for me. I need to take my time and really think it through."

Simon's heart dropped into his stomach and his throat felt like it was closing. What would he do if she did not come back? "That's a good idea. Don't rush into anything."

"That's why I took off the rest of the semester. I think spending time here will help me make the decision."

They chatted for a while, Isadora listening to what was going on in Simon's life. She told him all about the village and the manor, but not much else. By the end of the call, he felt like they had both spoken a lot about nothing at all. Whatever had been bothering her, she had decided to keep to herself. Maybe it was as simple as her missing him like she said, but his gut told him there was more that she was not telling him.

After hanging up with Simon, Isadora hugged her knees to her chest and allowed herself a brief moment to wallow in her loneliness. Finally, she decided she needed to spend some time with another human being. Whatever had happened last night had shaken her and she was still a little raw from it. Needing to take her mind off of it, she called Tamara and invited her out. They decided to rent some kayaks and take them out on the Hudson River for a few hours. It was exactly what Isadora needed to get her mind off last night's incident and recharge her batteries.

After getting dressed and ready to go, Isadora headed out to her car and drove to meet Tamara. When she arrived, she got out and greeted her newest friend with a hug.

"Just what did you do to your car, Sugar?" she asked with wide eyes glued to the trunk.

Isadora rounded the car and looked where Tamara was staring. On the passenger side of the trunk was a slash several inches long. Seeing it brought everything racing forward again. Her eyes went wide, and she started trembling. This was from whatever had caused the thunk she had felt and heard while leaving the house the night before. Tamara saw her face and immediately wrapped her arms around

Isadora. As she rubbed her back, Isadora could not fight back the tears that had sprung into her eyes. She was struggling enough to keep breathing without hyperventilating.

"Whatever it is, I'm sure it'll be okay," she tried to soothe. "That's what we have insurance for."

Isadora pulled herself out of Tamara's embrace, wiping the tears from her eyes as she regained control over herself. She could not look at the gash without the tears threatening again, and she kept her eyes averted. Shaking her head, she said, "I'm not sure what happened. I think I might be going mad."

Tamara barked out a laugh, "Chil' I've seen mad and you ain't mad. Come sit and tell me what's going on."

Tamara guided her over to a bench outside the kayak rental company and they sat overlooking the river. Isadora folded her hands together, twisting her fingers as she described her injury to her ankle. "They gave me some pain meds at the hospital, and I think it caused me to hallucinate, but then that gash is actually there and if it was just a hallucination, then where did it come from?" Isadora was talking fast, running her sentences together as she tried to make sense of it all.

"What medication did they give you?"

"Tylenol with codeine."

"That shouldn't cause hallucinations." Tamara's eyes narrowed. "What exactly did you hallucinate?"

Isadora looked away. "It's ridiculous. I can't…"

"Honey, what did you hallucinate?" Tamara asked again, more firmly. She tilted Isadora's face to hers, so she had to look her in the eye.

Isadora looked down. "The Horseman, what else?"

Tamara released her and nodded her head. She turned to look out over the water and was quiet for a moment. Isadora had been waiting for the woman to laugh at her, but Tamara's silence was worse. The seriousness with which Tamara was taking this had Isadora concerned.

"Tell me exactly what happened."

Isadora recounted what happened the night before as best as she could remember beginning with leaving the manor and ending with the nightmares that had plagued her all night.

"This is the first time this happened?"

She nodded.

"When you cut your ankle, how much blood was there?"

"A lot," she shrugged, unsure how to answer.

"You were outside? Did the blood go into the ground?"

Isadora nodded again, not sure what difference that made.

"Okay," she said, nodding her head. "Alright. You're going to tell your cop so he can investigate it from his side. I'm going to do a little digging around and see what I can find out. We'll figure this out. In the meantime, don't stay at the property after dark."

"I don't understand. Are you saying this wasn't a hallucination? And what does the cut on my ankle have to do with anything?"

"It's too early to tell. I'll let you know when I have more." Tamara stood. "Come on now, let's go kayak."

Isadora was confused at the abrupt change of topic and she stared after the woman momentarily before standing up and following her into the shop. She had so many questions, but Tamara was not answering anything else. They went out on the water and Isadora worked out her fear and frustration by paddling as hard as she could. The exertion felt good, particularly since she would not be able to run for a while. By the time they returned, they were both sweating despite the cooler temperature. Isadora had even managed to laugh some. It had been a perfect Sunday afternoon.

As they headed back to their cars, Tamara asked Isadora, "Do you have any personal belongings of Ichabod Crane?"

Thinking she wanted something for Sunnyside, she said, "I don't think I do. I have a box of old family keepsakes that might have a birth certificate or something, but I doubt there's anything else in there."

"No letters, journals, or anything written by him? A personal photo maybe? I know photography was in it's infancy, but maybe there's one floating around somewhere?"

"I really don't know what's in the box. I found it in my gran's stuff when she passed, but I never had the heart to look through it. I know there's a lot of books and paperwork in there, but I couldn't tell you more than that."

Tamara nodded, lost in the distance somewhere. After a moment of quiet, she said, "You need to go through the box and see if any of it is his. Even if it there's nothing there from him, maybe there's something else we can use. We also need to find out who originally owned the house." She got in her car and rolled down her window. Before pulling out, she said, "Let me know what you find."

When she got home, Isadora called Simon again.

"Twice in one day, wow! I must really be on your mind," he teased.

Isadora chuckled. "You always are."

Simon could hear the smile in her voice, and it warmed him as much as the words did. "So, when are you coming home?" He could not resist asking again, even though she had made it clear that morning that she was nowhere near ready to come home yet.

Isadora laughed. Simon sounded so eager to have her home. Despite their conversation that morning, she decided he was probably missing his kickboxing partner. It was good to laugh and take her mind off the incident from last night.

"Listen, I actually need to ask you a favor," she began hesitantly.

Her hesitance made him smile sadly. She hated relying on other people for anything. He loved that she knew she could ask him for anything but hated that she still felt bad doing so. He did not hesitate in his answer. "Anything."

"There's a box full of paperwork and books in my bedroom closet. Would you mind grabbing it for me and shipping it out here? I'll text you the address and transfer you the cost of the shipping." Simon had always held onto a spare key to her apartment in case of emergencies.

"In your bedroom closet? Isn't that something you'd rather ask a girlfriend?"

She snorted. "What girlfriend? You know you're the only friend I have," she said disparagingly. "Besides, you're the one that has my spare key, and I wouldn't trust anyone else."

"Are you sure? You're not afraid I'm going to rifle through your underwear or something?" The banter had been a welcome change from the seriousness of the morning's phone call.

Isadora knew he was teasing and her voice took on a matching tone. "You've never tried getting into my panties before. I'm pretty sure I can trust you."

Simon was glad she could not see the frown that broke out on his face. He appreciated her trust, but her words hurt. They were yet another reminder that he was only a friend. Perhaps the time had come for him to remedy that. He had missed her more than he imagined he would have and now this inheritance meant that she may not be coming back. The last two weeks had made him realize that his feelings for her ran deeper than he had ever admitted, even to himself. The thought of losing her made his chest hurt. If he did not want that to happen, he would have to tell her how he felt and hope that it did not destroy the friendship they had.

Now was not the time for that conversation, though. That was something he needed to tell her in person.

"Send me the address. I'll get it to you."
"You're the best. Thanks, Simon."
"Anything for you, Iz."

16

July 1815

After their night under the willow tree, Ichabod found it difficult to avoid Katrina. Nor did he want to. He tried to be respectful of her parents while still engaging with her every chance he got. It was a fine line to walk. She spent the following week seeking him out whenever she could, and they took advantage of every opportunity they had to talk. They shared their interests and their family histories and spoke of books and new technologies and discoveries. He tried to make sure they had a chaperone whenever possible. If she approached him while no one was around, he would gently turn her away.

"It's not proper, Katrina," he would say. He knew even addressing her so informally was improper, but he could not help himself from doing so. It was always difficult to remember to do so when others were around.

Katrina replied by asking her cousin along with them as they went on walks around the property. Their farm bordered her own and the young women had grown up almost as sisters. Her cousin would hang back enough to give them privacy while still giving the appearance of propriety.

"Your mother is not fooled by this," Ichabod said, gesturing toward Rebecca following at a distance behind them.

"My mother watches my every move," Katrina said on a sigh. "I don't think she will be happy until I'm wed to Brom with a child on the way."

"Is she so set on Brom for you?"

"She has been for a time. His mother and her have been close friends for years and he has been a friend to my brothers their whole lives. He's a successful blacksmith, respected by everyone in town. She thinks he could provide for me better than anyone else. Admittedly, there are not many prospects nearby. She's afraid I shall leave, and she'll not see me again."

Ichabod walked with his hands clasped behind his back. "Which is what would happen were I to ask for your hand. She would never agree to a match with me, Katrina."

Katrina cocked her head and looked at him with a smirk. "That's rather presumptuous of you to assume I would accept a proposal from you, Major."

Ichabod's eyes got big as his brows raised up on his forehead, wondering if he had misread her intentions. When she started laughing, he relaxed, knowing she had only been teasing him. He joined in her laughter for a moment before asking, "What would you accept from me, Katrina?" he asked. "What is it you want from me?"

He stopped walking and Katrina stopped beside him. Placing a hand on his wrist, she pulled his hands apart and slid her small hand into his. She entwined their fingers, staring down at them as she asked, "Is it not obvious, Ichabod?"

Ichabod placed a finger under her chin, gently raising her face to look at him. "Do you want me, Katrina?" He loved saying her name.

Katrina melted at the smoldering look in Ichabod's eyes. All that heat was directed at her. She knew he wanted her and it turned her insides all aflutter when he looked at her like that. She nodded, barely able to speak. "Yes."

He kissed her then, slow and sweet. Katrina grasped his hand as if she was holding on for dear life. Maybe she was. She felt as though she could lose herself in Ichabod's kiss. His other arm went around her waist as he pulled her closer. When he broke the kiss, she immediately mourned the loss of his lips on hers. He stroked her face while looking into her eyes.

"You are absolutely stunning, Katrina. Not only are you beautiful, but you have a mind like few other women I've known."

Katrina smiled at the compliment. It warmed her to hear it. Her intellect was one of the things that drove a wedge between her and Brom, who believed intellect to be wasted on a woman.

Ichabod reluctantly separated himself from Katrina and continued their walk. If they stood there much longer, he would surely break down and do more than just kiss the fair lady.

ജ   ഇ

When they returned to the farmhouse, Katrina's parents were waiting inside. Rebecca went home and Ichabod went to the barn to check on his horse, sending Katrina in alone. He thought it best they did not enter the house together. Her father was reading in the parlor while her mother was waiting for her at the door.

"Just where have you been?" Eleanor demanded.

"I was out walking with Rebecca and Major Crane."

"You are not to spend time with him Katrina."

"Rebecca was with us the entire time." Katrina turned to face the direction of her cousin's home. "You could ask her if anything untoward happened."

"He will be gone soon. You will not associate with him. Do you understand me?"

"Mother, we merely talk. I don't understand what the harm is."

"I'll not repeat myself. You'll not speak to our guest while he is here. Brom shall be by tomorrow. You shall accompany him to church."

Katrina huffed. "I really wish you would not encourage Brom, mother. I do not like him."

"You may learn to like him. He shall make a fine husband for you, but he will not have you if you continue to behave this way and make yourself a harlot."

Katrina gasped, "Mother –"

"Katrina, go to your room." Eleanor cut off Katrina's protests as she saw Ichabod coming towards the house.

Katrina knew better than to argue with her mother. She had already gone too far, and her mother was not someone to cross. She knew how far she could push her and had reached that limit. Turning to go up the stairs, she heard the door open behind her.

Eleanor stood with her arms folded in front of her and a sour look on her face as Ichabod entered the house.

"Is everything alright madam?"

"You would take advantage of our generosity and ruin my only daughter?"

Ichabod recoiled as if struck. "Not at all Mrs. Brush. I care deeply for your daughter. I would never do anything to see her hurt."

"Then you ought to leave her alone. She has been promised to another."

"With all due respect, madam, Katrina does not wish to wed Brom. If you wish her to be happy, you shall not force her to marry him."

"You overstep, sir. Katrina is not your concern."

"I'd like her to be. As I said, I care for Katrina. If you are looking to have her wed, I would urge you to consider me."

Eleanor scoffed. She unfolded her arms, only to place them on her hips. "You will take her away from us," she accused. "What shall become of Katrina when you die in battle? She'll be left on her own with small children to feed and care for. How will she do that on her own?"

"The war has ended, Mrs. Brush. I shall not die in battle if there are no battles. Wherever I am assigned next, I can see to it that Katrina visits here often."

"This war has ended, but there is always another. Even now, your own brother is off to fight across the sea."

Eleanor continued to glower at Ichabod. He had faced down enemy soldiers trying to kill him in battle, but this woman managed to curdle his blood. She had an air about her that almost made him want to retreat. But he held his ground.

"Yes, but I am not in the naval service. I shall not be sent to fight in that war."

"Stay away from my daughter," she said menacingly while walking away.

Ichabod was not certain what it was about the way she said it, but he could feel the underlying threat in her tone. His concern was for Katrina more than for himself. He did not know what Eleanor Brush could possibly do, but she made it clear that whatever it was, he would not like it. With a shiver, he shook himself then headed up to bed.

"Is anything amiss, dear?" Caleb asked when Eleanor went back to the parlor.

"I should say so. I beg of you to send that man you let into our home away. He is no good."

Caleb barely glanced up from the book he was reading. "Nonsense. He's been of great help to me around here. I never would have gotten half the things done that needed doing this summer. Now that Joshua and Caleb are gone, I may need to hire more help."

"He will take Katrina away from us, too. If he doesn't simply defile her then discard her first."

Aghast, Caleb looked up from his book now. "He'll do no such thing. He's an honorable man."

"You are a blind fool. He would take advantage of her under your own roof given the chance."

"Would you have me turn him out? For something he's not done. And something I'm not convinced he shall do, I might add."

"Yes. I would have you turn him out. He is a scoundrel, even if you cannot see it. He shall take what he wishes and leave us disgraced, with nothing."

"Enough. I will not have this. Major Crane would not do such a thing. You shall stop this and treat our guest with respect."

Eleanor was irate. Why was she the only one who could see what was happening here? She was tired of waiting around for Ichabod to leave or for her husband to step up and take care of the matter. If Caleb would not help her, she would have to take matters into her own hands. Realizing she was playing with the blue and silver ring on her index finger once again, she looked down at it as a thought came to her. Perhaps it was time to call upon her past for help. She had work to do before the next full moon.

17

Modern Day

"Good morning, Izzy. How's the ankle?"

"It's starting to feel much better, Neil. Thank you." Isadora looked up from her box of remembrances to see Neil carrying an armload of two by fours.

"Glad to hear it. You'll be happy to know we're almost ready to turn the power and water back on. Should only be a few more days now."

"Now that is good news." Isadora smiled, happy at the progress they were making.

She had thrown herself back into cleaning out the house, carefully looking through all the boxes for anything that would indicate the history of the property. She thought she remembered George Bachman saying something regarding it, but she could not remember what it was. Still convinced that it was not real, she was determined to figure out what she had seen the other night and who was responsible for it. Since she did not believe in ghosts, what other option did that leave? The hoof prints she found along her private lane that morning and the slash in her rental car had certainly been real enough. Someone had to have been either playing a prank on her or threatening her. The property damage to the car certainly did not feel like a simple prank.

Isadora had called her insurance the first thing that morning and started a claim on the damage to the car. When they asked what had happened, she said she did not know. She told them that she had come out in the morning to find it there. It was not even entirely a lie, either.

With the car taken care of, Isadora was trying to forget about the incident, but when she arrived at the property that morning, there had been hoof prints along the private lane. She had almost missed them and was surprised to have even seen them with so many people going in and out all morning. But she had glanced over at movement in the corner of her eye and saw a squirrel in the grass. When she turned her head back to the dirt road in front of her, she caught a handful of small round impressions along the edge of the road where the dirt lane met the grass. Slamming on her breaks, she had stopped the car abruptly, not even pulling out of the lane and got out to get a closer look. When she bent down, there was no mistaking that the impressions were from a large horse. The ground must have still been soft from the rains that had come the night before the incident.

Isadora had not been at the house long when Tamara showed up, carrying a large handbag. Despite Isadora's invitation to set it down, she carried it with her throughout the large manor house while Isadora gave her a tour of it. They dodged workers going in and out of rooms while Isadora showed her around each floor. When they finished inside, they walked around the property a little bit.

Afterwards, Tamara looked back at the house, then turned to her new friend. "Well, there's nothing I can do about this place just yet. There are far too many people going in and out of there right now, but I'll come back when the renovations are finished. In the meantime, let's go take a look at where you're staying."

When Isadora stared back at her blankly, Tamara said, "So I can cleanse the space, of course." She patted her handbag, "I brought everything I need with me. You'll notice a difference right away and you'll sleep better tonight."

The skepticism must have shown on her face, because Tamara added, "I have my sage and whether you believe in this or not, there's actually a lot of science to back up the benefits we've already known about for centuries. 'Cause I know how you like your science. There's a long history of smudging being used to cleanse spaces. Sage in particular helps reduce stress and insomnia, but it also has antimicrobial properties. It'll clear out pathogens and bacteria in the air and people been using it for centuries to help stop the spread of disease. So, you see, Sugar, it's not just about the energies. That's simply one element. If it helps you feel better, just think of the antimicrobial properties."

Though skeptical, Isadora agreed, thinking it would not hurt anything to let her friend try it. Maybe people did leave negative energies behind. If that was the case, perhaps Tamara's ritual would do something to clear them out. She had always been of the belief that other people's beliefs had power if they believed it, even if she did not. If it had been a priest asking, she would likely have done the same thing. If it helped her sleep, it would be worth it. She did not have to believe in the outcome herself to allow her friend to try it.

They got to the rental and walked through the small house, opening windows in each room. They went back to the kitchen where Tamara began pulling a tied-up bundle of sage, matches, and a small ceramic bowl out of her handbag. Holding the sage at a slight angle over the bowl, she lit one end of it and allowed it to burn for a few seconds, then blew out the flame. The sage emitted orange embers as it continued to smoke, reminding Isadora of an incense stick. It had a sweet, earthy aroma that she found surprisingly calming.

Beginning at the front door, they slowly walked around with the smoke wafting through the room while Tamara guided it toward the open window. All the while, Tamara repeatedly chanted, "I release any negative energy that may linger here. I cleanse this space, driving away any harm or fear."

After making their way slowly through each room, Tamara pressed the smoldering end of the sage into her small ceramic bowl, extinguishing the embers. Smiling at Isadora, she said, "You should sleep well tonight."

Finding herself curious about everything Tamara was doing, Isadora had wanted to ask questions. Since she had not wanted to interrupt her, she waited until they had finished going through the house. She was partially afraid her energy might somehow interject into the ritual and make it less effective. Either that, or her questions would distract Tamara, preventing it from working. Though she was skeptical that it would work at all, she decided that if she was interrupting and distracting Tamara, it could only lessen the possibility of it doing so. Now that they were finished, she tried to remember everything she had wanted to ask.

"Why open the windows and push the smoke out? Is that to lessen the scent and prevent the smoke detectors from going off?"

"The negative energy attaches itself to the smoke and leaves through the open windows." Tamara rested the now extinguished smudge stick in the bowl while it cooled.

"Where did you learn about this?"

"Child, I've been performing cleansings since before you was born." Tamara's accent became exaggerated when she talked about herself or got excited. "It's all part of Hoodoo."

Isadora's brows rose. "Hoodoo? Is that the same as Voodoo?"

Tamara tsked while giving her an expression of derision. "No, it ain't the same thing. They're similar, but Voodoo is a religion. Hoodoo is not. It's based in rootwork. We use roots and herbs to heal, protect, or show devotion to our ancestors, who used it to defend enslaved people from bodily harm and suffering."

"But they're both folk magic?"

"Folk magic and medicine," she corrected. "We use both the practical and the mystical aspects of herbs and natural elements to combat illness and promote healing. But it's also a way to respect our ancestors and watch over our descendants. You see, Sugar, the dead are a link to the spirit world and can bring us protection and wisdom. Or, in your case, can cause disruption and chaos. When a person passes on, their soul returns to God, but their spirit remains to protect their descendants."

Isadora scoffed. "Or continue attacking descendants."

Ignoring the sarcasm in Isadora's voice, Tamara said, "Exactly. Magical attacks can target a person's mental as well as physical well-being. They typically start at the surface, which is the physical, then move onto deeper levels of the mind, hence your nightmares. We're more vulnerable when we sleep, so it's easiest to attack in dreams, which is why distance does nothing to stop the nightmares. But if an attack is not ended, it'll stay active until it's reached its goal. It can go on for an extremely long time, no matter where you are in the world."

"Great. So, I guess I'll just have nightmares forever?"

Tamara gathered her things and the women headed for the door. She put a hand on Isadora's shoulder. "We'll sort it out. You'll be good as new in no time."

Isadora hoped she was right.

18

July 1815

Katrina barely looked at Ichabod over breakfast the next morning. He could feel the chill in the air despite the warm summer weather. When he saw Eleanor's face, he understood. She must have spoken with Katrina before speaking with him the night before. He did not wish to make things more difficult for Katrina, so he did not push the issue. He was polite and as cordial as he could be without singling Katrina out. When breakfast was over, she promptly cleared the dishes away and left before he could speak to her.

Katrina met her cousin on the road while waiting for Brom to accompany her to church. "Oh Rebecca, mother is forcing me to spend the service in Brom's company. Please tell me you will not leave my side," she begged.

Rebecca took her cousin's hands in her own. "I shall stay with you all day, Katrina. Or at least, I shall try to. Brom may not like it. I'm afraid he may pull you away and there will be nothing I can do about it."

Katrina sighed. "I worry that, too."

A smile spread across Rebecca's face. "But your Ichabod… Did you enjoy your walk with him last eve?"

Katrina could not stop her lips from curling up at the memory. "He's so remarkable. I do adore him so."

"By the looks of it, he adores you as well."

The ladies giggled at that. Washington approached while the girls were still giggling together. "You ladies look like you're enjoying this fine morning."

"We are," Katrina replied, straightening up. "And how are you this morn, Mr. Irving?

"I'm looking forward to another wonderful sermon from the pastor. He is a wonderful orator."

Rebecca suddenly looked inspired. "Mr. Irving, I shall be accompanying my cousin and Mr. Martling today. Would you care to join us? It shall be a grand time, the four of us spending the day together."

"I would be pleased."

Katrina gave her cousin a look of gratitude while they both thanked him. Brom arrived shortly after, and Washington held out his arm for Rebecca while

Katrina reluctantly took Brom's. They all walked thus to the Old Dutch Reformed Church.

"Mrs. Martling, how lovely you look this morning," Eleanor called to her friend when she and Caleb arrived at the church.

"Thank you, Mrs. Brush. I might say the same of you."

The men exchanged pleasantries as well and their conversation quickly turned to politics, leaving the women to excuse themselves.

"I was glad to see Katrina accompanying Abraham today," Mrs. Martling said. "I was beginning to wonder if we would ever get them together."

"Katrina has always been such a willful child. I'm afraid as the only girl, her father has spoiled her and encouraged her to maintain strong opinions on everything. He has done her a great disservice." Eleanor frowned.

The women walked around the church grounds, arm-in-arm, watching as people arrived for the service. Ichabod was across the yard from them, talking with Jacob. "I always knew she would come around. Though I must say, I'm surprised. I see your guest is still with us. I thought Katrina was beginning to favor him?"

Eleanor shook her head, blowing out an exaggerated sigh. "He has been nothing but trouble. I have had to take matters into my own hands. I shall put an end to it, mark my words."

"I know you have things well in hand, but if you need me or any of the other ladies to assist, all you need do is say the word."

"Thank you, my friend. I can always count on you."

"As long as we can count on you. My Abraham deserves only the best and your Katrina is the fairest young lady in the village. They'll make a wonderful couple."

Not to mention the riches your Abraham would inherit if he marries my Katrina, Eleanor thought. She wisely held her tongue and did not say that to her friend. While Brom would become even wealthier if he were to marry Katrina, it was a small price to pay for her daughter's security and her family's standing in the community. Brom would never take her riches and leave her like a soldier would. Brom would take care of Katrina, even if she did not like him. Eleanor knew her daughter would grow to like him, in time. If only she would give him a chance.

After the service, Eleanor pulled Brom aside while Katrina was distracted with Rebecca and Washington. "You must not give up on Katrina. Put yourself between her and Major Crane. Show her that you mean to fight for her hand. I know she appears distant, but she only wishes to make sure that you are willing to fight for her."

"I thought things between Katrina and the major had grown more serious?" he asked.

"Not at all." Eleanor shook her head while pasting a smile on her face. "She is merely trying to see how far you are willing to go to win her over."

Brom watched Katrina as she and her cousin laughed at something Washington had said. She certainly was beautiful. Though, he wished she was not quite so spirited and opinionated. He would much rather have a meek wife. However, her beauty was unsurpassed, and he would have only the best. If she wanted him to prove himself, then he would.

When everyone else was preoccupied, Eleanor found her way to a corner of the burial ground to sit beside an unmarked grave. She used to come visit more regularly when she was young but found it difficult to make it out there often now. In her upset at the recent turn of events with her daughter, she felt a need to visit her old friend and unburden her soul. Sitting on the ground, she brought him up to date, then proceeded to tell him her plan for preventing Katrina from running away with the major, telling him she would need his assistance once again. The experience reminded her of all the times she would sit there as a teenager, sharing her thoughts and desires with the unknown Hessian soldier.

19

October 2, 1780

“ “There's to be a hanging today.”

Sixteen-year-old Eleanor Van Tassel sat beside an unmarked grave in the burial ground beside the Old Dutch Church. It was a sunny afternoon with a bit of a chill in the air, but she never missed her weekly visits to the Hessian whom she helped her father bury two years before. Though the grave was unmarked, she knew where to find it. She felt that she could confide anything to the Hessian. Today, she updated him on the traitorous British officer, Major John André. She wished all of the soldiers would be hanged and they could finally be done with this infernal war.

“A few weeks ago, three Patriots stopped a man named John André while heading south on the Post Road near an enormous tulip tree right here in town. The Patriots had been dressed in uniforms of the British Army, causing the stranger to believe them to be Loyalists. Major André had been dressed as a soldier of the Continental Army but told them he was headed to New York City, which as you know, is the headquarters of the British Army. This led the Patriots to inform the man that they were, in fact, American Patriots, and they detained him. Upon hearing they were not British, the major then informed them that he was on business for the American General, Benedict Arnold, which resulted in him being arrested for espionage and strip-searched. The Patriots found several papers stuffed in Major André's stockings including plans for General Arnold to surrender our fortress at West Point to the British. Alas, Major André is to be hanged while Benedict Arnold has made his escape and is free to flee to England."

Eleanor tsked and shook her head at this. Most wanted to see Benedict Arnold hanged. He was an American which made his betrayal feel all that much worse. John André was not only a major, but he was an adjunct general as well. No one believed he would be hanged because of this. Generals were typically taken as prisoners, not executed, but General George Washington had to remain firm in his decision.

Eleanor picked at the grass around her while she spoke. "The hanging is to be across the Hudson River, in Tappan, even though André was caught here in

Tarrytown. Father will not allow me attend the hanging, though I begged him to let me."

Eleanor had envisioned it for days. In her imaginings, the major's head popped clean off his body much like that of the Hessian with whom she now spoke, though she did not share that with him.

"If it would bring Cornelius back, I would see all of the soldiers hanged. It was because of the soldiers that my brother died."

Cornelius had finally succumbed to illness on January third of that year, and Eleanor had cried to the Hessian when it happened, pouring out all of the emotion that she could not share with anyone else. He had become her confidant in a way that no living person could be.

She stopped picking at the grass and stared out across the graveyard for a moment. Seeing no movements to catch her attention, she looked back at her hand in her lap, playing with the heavy ring on her index finger. Her mother had passed it down to her on her last birthday and she imagined one day passing it down to her own daughter. The silver filigree that laid over the top of a flat round sapphire extended down the sides of the ring, hiding the compartment inside, but she had known it was there. The first thing she did when she received it, was to open the top of the ring and anoint it with a drop of her blood. It would now forever be linked to her.

"But I don't blame you," she continued. "You only ever helped my family, protected us. I'm so grateful to you. My sister would not be alive were it not for you and I know I may always rely on you. But had the British never raided our farm, brother never would have died. I am sick of this war and all of the violence that follows soldiers wherever they go. I want no part in war ever again. I wish all of the soldiers would kill one another and be done with it all."

20

Modern Day

The antique dealer arrived shortly after Isadora got back to the manor. She escorted Annette through the house, going from room to room as she carefully and thoroughly examined each piece. The older woman took notes and photos to refer back to later. Isadora asked questions, but mostly, she listened. This was not her area of expertise, and she did not even know enough about it to ask many questions.

They talked as they went through the manor. Annette asked her what she had planned for the house and Isadora told her she was still working that out.

"For now, I'm inventorying everything that's here, so I can make a more informed decision about what to do with it all. There's so much more here than what's out."

That caught Annette's attention. "Where's the rest of it?"

"It's all boxed up. There were dozens of boxes and trunks in the attic and basement that I've been going through."

"What have you found so far?" Annette picked up a golden vase in the drawing room to examine it more closely.

"Most of it is similar to the contents that are out on display, but I've also found books, old clothes, jewelry, and a button tucked away for safekeeping."

Annette turned to look at Isadora. "A button? As in, just one, not a container full of miscellaneous buttons in a sewing kit to replace missing ones?"

Isadora shook her head. "Just one. It was in a pouch with this ring as if it had some significance."

She held her hand out for the woman to see the ring. When Annette turned Isadora's hand to look at it more closely, Isadora pulled it from her finger and handed it to her.

"This is gorgeous," she said, turning it over in her hand.

She slid the top of the ring, exposing a compartment underneath. Isadora gasped, not knowing it was there.

"It's a poison ring," Annette explained. "They were popular in the sixteenth century. They're called poison rings because people like to imagine the intrigue of someone using it to slip poison into their enemy's food or drink, but most of the time, they were used to carry perfume, locks of hair, messages, or other important keepsakes. Jewelry isn't my specialty, but I'd guess this one is Victorian. You might want to have it appraised by a jeweler."

"I might do that."

"I'm curious about the button that was with it, though." She handed the ring back to Isadora who slid it back onto her finger. "It sounds like there might have been some significance to it."

"That was the impression I got as well." Isadora pulled out her phone, showing her a picture of it. She scrolled through the different angles of it and accidentally went past it, revealing other pieces she had inventoried.

"Are you photographing everything as you inventory it?"

"I am. I wasn't going to at first, but when I looked back on what I had written down for the first box, I couldn't remember half of the items I wrote down. I wanted to be able to have a visual of each item as well. Plus, there were several things I couldn't identify, so the pictures help with those as well."

"That's smart. I'd be happy to take a look through your photos and see what I can identify."

"That'd be great. I'll send you copies of everything."

They continued chatting as they worked their way through the house. Some of the pieces were authentic Victorian pieces of furniture or décor, while some were more modern replicas. The bedframes on the second floor were all authentic while the ones on the third were not. Most of the sofas and some of the chairs were also authentic. The rugs and some of the other decorative pieces were mixed as well, with some being authentic and some being modern.

"What would it do to the pieces if I had them reupholstered?" Isadora asked.

"Well, with the damage to some of them, you'll have to get them reupholstered regardless, so it doesn't really matter for those. However, reupholstering can actually increase the value. Of course, you'll want to make sure it's done by someone who'll be careful with the piece and keep it as close to the original as possible."

"Do you have any recommendations?" Isadora always tried to use referrals whenever she could. She believed in word-of-mouth and supporting local businesses wherever she was.

"I can connect you with someone," the woman said.

The more that she thought about it, the more Isadora liked the idea of reupholstering the pieces already inside the home. The frames were still in good condition on most of the pieces and she wanted to try and salvage as much as she could. There was far too much history in the house to simply discard it.

"I'll do a more thorough write-up on everything and send you my report as soon I get it finished. You have some wonderful pieces here that you should be proud of," Annette said, smiling.

"I am," Isadora agreed. "Thank you."

With one more thing checked off her list, Isadora also crossed off the lines regarding discarding the damaged furniture, donating furniture, and selling furniture. Instead, she added *'reupholster furniture.'*

While Isadora sat on the floor surrounded by knickknacks as she got back into her work, people moved past the drawing room. She had become accustomed to the constant noise, though she still did not like it. After a while, she could almost block out most of it. When she heard another knock at the front door, it surprised her. With all the people going in and out, the door was always left open, and people rarely knocked. The antique dealer had already been through, and she was not expecting anyone else. She began standing but before she could get up, officers

Alex Kaderson and Cory Greene walked in fully dressed in their uniforms.

"We were in the neighborhood and thought we'd stop by to say hi," Alex said as he bent down to greet her with a kiss.

Isadora smiled at the thoughtful gesture. "Been busy today?" she asked.

"Not too bad today," Alex said.

Cory added with a huff, "Not like yesterday."

"Not like yesterday, thankfully," Alex agreed. "We were running around all over the place yesterday. But we're only now coming on duty, so it could change."

That explained why she had not heard from him all day yesterday. Surprisingly, she had not even realized it until she saw him walk through the door. Other than when her and Tamara had spoken about him, she had not even thought about him all day. Speaking of which....

"Do you have a few minutes, then? There's something I need to talk to you about."

The men exchanged a look and Cory shrugged. "Sure," Alex replied.

Cory began backing away out of the room, but she stopped him. "No, you can stay, Cory. It might be something you should hear, too."

Another look passed between the men; this time it was confusion. Isadora stood up off the floor, moving over to a tufted Victorian-style sofa, gesturing for the men to do the same. She had not yet begun clearing out the furniture downstairs, though she had tried to consolidate the damaged pieces into one room with Alex's help. Once she knew exactly which pieces were going, she would hire a moving company to help haul them all away.

With Alex seated beside her and Cory across the room, Isadora was suddenly nervous to share her story with these men. She sat, wringing her hands, trying to figure out where to begin. With Tamara, everything had just come out. This time, she had time to think about what she wanted to say. Alex reached over and put his big hand over hers, trying to comfort her and still her fidgeting. Instead of being a comfort, she felt stifled by the gesture. She was anxious and needed to fidget. She pulled her hands out from under his and rubbed them on her pants.

"Something happened here the other night," she began slowly. "Someone came after me as I was leaving."

Alex and Cory both jumped to their feet. "What?" Alex exploded. "Why the hell didn't you call me when it happened? You should've at least called 911, which

I know you didn't, otherwise I would have known about it."

Isadora looked up at him calmly, even though her insides were twisting and turning. She was not going to let him make her feel any worse about this. With a stern look on her face, she asked, "Are you going to let me continue?"

The men both sat down again.

"I'm fine, by the way," she said sarcastically, seeing as how neither of them had asked yet. Chastised, they both mumbled their apologies and she continued. "I wasn't entirely sure anything had actually happened until yesterday. I heard and felt something while I was driving away and when I looked in the mirror, I saw someone following me on a horse. I didn't think too much of it, but then yesterday, I saw the gash in the trunk of my car and this morning, I saw hoof prints in the roadway." She deliberately downplayed the severity of the encounter and how much it had freaked her out, as well as the fact that the person on the horse looked as though he had no head.

The more she had thought about it, the more she decided it had been someone in a costume trying to scare her away. Was it someone who felt the property should have been left to them? She had been reluctant to share this with them, but now that she had time to think about it, Isadora knew Tamara had been right to tell her she needed to let Alex know. What if this person came back and actually tried to hurt her the next time?

Alex took her hand in his again and smiled at her like he would a confused child. "A man on a horse? Really? Are you sure someone wasn't just pranking you, Izzy?"

Isadora pulled her hand away angrily, folding her arms across her chest. It was one thing for her to not believe what had happened, but for him to dismiss it outright or even mock her made her mad, particularly after the way she had presented it to him as the encounter having been a real person trying to attack her. Why would he simply dismiss it so easily?

"Prank or not, Alex, the man had a sword which did real damage to my rental car that I'm going to have to pay for. At a minimum, that's vandalism and property damage. At worst, someone was trying to attack me."

"She's right," Cory said. "We should take a report. If it happens again or if it escalates, at least we'll have a paper trail. Do you have security cameras here?"

"You're not serious?" Alex asked his partner. "You want to write up a report on a prank?"

Cory raised a single brow in challenge. "Yes."

Alex shook his head. "Fine. But you're writing it up."

Cory turned his attention back to Isadora. "So. Cameras?"

Isadora shook her head. "No, we haven't even had any electricity. But it's supposed to be back on again soon. I'll look into getting some installed."

Cory nodded. "Good. Can you show us the car and the hoof prints?"

They trio stood and went outside. Isadora showed them the car, then they walked down the lane, and she showed them the hoof prints.

"Who even has horses around here?" Alex asked, still skeptical. "And how would they be able to ride through town without anyone taking notice?"

Cory and Isadora both scowled at him. "You're right," Cory said. "Someone probably did notice. We'll check in with your neighbors and ask around."

Alex threw his hands up. "Are you that bored today, Cory?"

Cory ignored his partner and looked back down at the impressions in the ground. "By the size of the prints, I'd say the horse was rather large. You said it was black?"

"It was quite dark, so I could be wrong, but it looked black." When Cory asked for a description of the rider, she hesitated. She told them the person appeared to be male and was dressed all in black.

"Did you get a look at his face? Was he wearing a mask or a hat?"

Isadora shook her head and chose her next words carefully. "I couldn't see anything."

"It was probably just one of the teenagers who have been using this place as a party house," Alex said. "Likely, someone heard about your ancestry and decided to have some fun with it."

Cory looked between the two, momentarily confused. "What about your ancestry?" he asked Isadora.

She shot Alex a look, letting him know she was irritated with him. She had been trying to stay away from any connection to the story this whole time, but now she had to share more than she had intended.

"I'm descended from Ichabod Crane," she said through a clenched jaw.

Cory's eyebrows shot up. "How is that possible?"

Isadora shook her head, exasperated, "You know, for a town whose identity comes entirely from a story, its inhabitants are woefully lacking in knowledge of the facts surrounding that story." She was met with blank stares and continued. "Ichabod Crane was a real person. Yes, the character was based on a man named

Jesse Merwin, but the name came from a real person. I'm descended from that person."

"Oh." Momentarily at a loss for words, it was all Cory managed to reply. Catching himself, he added, "We'll look into that angle."

As they walked back to the house, no one spoke. Finally, Alex looked over at Isadora. "You're limping."

There was a question there, but she refused to answer unless he specifically asked her. She was upset with him and did not want to give him more than he gave her. She had been limping all morning and he had only just noticed? This did not help with her anger at him. "Yes. I am."

Alex breathed out a heavy sigh. "Why are you limping?"

"I cut my ankle."

His brows drew in. "When?"

"Day before yesterday." She kept her answers clipped.

"The same day the–" he cut himself off and rephrased his question. "The same day of the incident?"

"Yes."

Alex stopped walking, putting a hand on her arm to stop her as well. "Did this happen during the incident?" Cory had heard the exchange and was now waiting for more information, too.

"No." Isadora turned and began walking again. So did Cory.

Alex stayed in place a moment longer, then followed. When they got to the house, Cory went to their patrol car and Alex followed her inside. They stood in the drawing room, Isadora looking around her at the explosion of things from the latest box she had emptied. He ran a hand over his jaw, knowing he had messed up with her, but not knowing how to fix it. How could either she or Cory be taking this seriously? He got that it was vandalism, but they had nothing to go on, and they would never catch the person responsible for it. Whoever it had been was most likely long gone, laughing it up. It was a one-time prank that would not happen again.

"I'm sorry you cut your ankle. How did it happen?"

"I tripped over a tree root and clipped myself on a rock."

"Did you make sure you cleaned it out thoroughly? Who knows what kind of stuff could've been on the rock. You don't want to get an infection."

Isadora stared at him, incredulous. Was he implying that the cut was nothing more than a small scrape that she could simply slap a bandage on? Or was he really telling her that she needed to clean a cut? How dumb and incompetent did he think she was?

"Actually, I went to the hospital and let them do it. I would've done it myself, but I didn't have my sewing needle and thread for the eight stitches I needed to close it up." She could not help the sarcasm that dripped from her words.

Alex had the grace to look surprised and a little ashamed. "Sorry. I didn't realize it was that bad."

"Well, it was."

He nodded. Why was this suddenly so awkward and difficult? He had asked after her well-being, and she was mad at him for it? Alex would never understand women. "I guess I better get back to work. Cory will be waiting for me."

Alex left without even trying to kiss her, for which she was grateful. Isadora had been too upset with him to deal with that, but it had still surprised her seeing as how he always got handsy with her any chance he got. He had upset her by not believing her, but then everything he said afterwards had driven the nail in deeper. He had to *get back* to work? Cory seemed to have taken her seriously, taking notes in order to file a report. Was that not work? It was merely one more indication that he had not taken her concerns seriously at all. Isadora sat down on the floor with a thump and threw herself back into her work again.

21

July 1815

At the Van Tassel house after church that evening, Ichabod watched Katrina stand beside Brom. She had spent the entire day with him, Rebecca, and Washington, conversing with Brom and even laughing at his jokes. Ichabod had thought she had despised the man, but her actions today made that hard to believe. She may claim that she did not wish to marry him, but her behavior proved at the very least that she did not dislike him. Every so often, Katrina would look up to see him watching her and she would quickly look away, a guilty look on her face. Had she only been playing with him? Was she simply using him to make Brom jealous? Had this been her goal the whole time? And what of their time together? He knew she was not faking the way she melted into him when he kissed her. Perhaps it was only physical attraction she felt for him? Ichabod felt as though he was going mad trying to understand what she wanted. He turned from the parlor and headed to the porch outside for some air. It was not long before the door opened behind him.

"Is everything alright, Major Crane?" Washington asked, handing him a drink. "You appear troubled."

"I'm thinking on my horse. I really must be returning to Lake Ontario. I fear I've dallied here far longer than what is wise." Ichabod accepted the offered drink and took a sip.

Washington watched Ichabod for a moment. "I believe there is more on your mind than merely your horse, if I may be so bold. I dare say you have few friends here, Major. I'm happy to lend an ear if you are in need."

Ichabod turned away, looking out over the farmland stretched out in front of them. He was quiet for a time. The silence stretched so long between them, Washington was beginning to think Ichabod had no intention of sharing anything. But the soldier surprised him.

"Perhaps I should leave and forget about Miss Brush," he said quietly.

"Is that what you wish? Or is it her wishes you are taking into account?"

Ichabod went quiet again. When he did not say anything else, Washington said, "I've seen you together. She is quite taken with you, and I dare say, you are with her. Do you love her?"

"Does it matter?" he asked in reply. "Her mother will never approve. I do not wish to make her life difficult nor take her away from her family."

Washington scoffed. "I envy you such a difficulty, Major. I would give anything for another chance with my beloved. If it meant taking her from her family, I would not hesitate."

"What happened to her?"

"My love died from consumption some seven years ago. We were engaged to be married, but she passed before we could wed." It was Washington's turn to look deeply into his glass.

"I'm so sorry. I would love to hear about her." Ichabod placed a comforting hand on Washington's shoulder.

Washington looked up at the other man and took a drink, shaking himself off. "It is far too painful to speak of her. Alas, though the image of her is always with me, I find I'm unable to even speak her name. I would give anything to be with her again."

Ichabod nodded in understanding. "I do not wish to diminish your time with her, but have you thought to take a new wife?"

Washington shook his head. "I have loved more deeply than I ever imagined possible, Major Crane. That kind of love only comes to a man once. If you find it, you must hold onto it at any cost. There shall never be another for me. Tell me, is this how you feel towards Miss Brush?"

Ichabod turned away again. He pulled a drink from the golden liquid inside his glass. Avoiding the question once again, he answered, "I'm not certain it matters. Her parents would never agree to the match. Her mother dislikes me immensely."

Washington chuckled. "She really does, doesn't she?"

Ichabod turned and looked at Washington, laughing along with him. The levity was welcome after the intensity of the previous topic of conversation.

Washington added, "You must understand, it's not about you. She has a plan for her daughter that she does not want to admit does not take into account what Katrina wants. But even that is not the whole story. Mrs. Brush was born shortly before the war for independence. She and John had an older brother and a younger sister. This entire area was rife with raids from soldiers on both sides. When her sister was but a babe, her family's farm was raided by British and Hessian soldiers. Their farmhouse was burned down, and the entire household was taken hostage. Her oldest brother jumped out the window on the second floor and ran towards the Saw Mill River, trying to get help but fell through the ice. Mrs. Brush's sister Leah was missing; she was only a babe. Her mother tried to go back into the house for the baby, but the soldiers would not let her. The soldiers stole their cattle and their crops, destroying anything they could not take with them. As they finally began to leave, the baby was found wrapped in a blanket in a shed. Her brother was also found, and tended to, but he never healed. His time in the icy water ended up killing him. Her sister died some years later, though it was not from that. Her and John are the only two siblings remaining. So, you see, Ichabod, it was never about you. This experience has affected how she feels about soldiers despite only being a child at the time."

Ichabod was speechless. He personally knew the atrocities that were committed during wartime. The war for independence had been particularly brutal for those who lived through it. He did not begrudge Eleanor her feelings towards soldiers after hearing her story. Still, he wished she would not hold him responsible for the atrocities committed by soldiers some forty years prior.

It was apparent to Ichabod that he had a lot to think about. He cared a great deal for Katrina, but did he love her? Did he want to fight for her and keep her by his side forever? The thought of her being a part of his life made him warm inside. He did want her, but how could he convince her mother that he was worthy of her hand? If he did somehow manage that, how could he ask her to leave her family and live the life of a soldier's wife? It was not an easy life. He spent long periods of time away from his family. Katrina would be on her own, likely with children to look after for months at a time. Was this the best life for her? Or would she be better off staying there, close to her family, and marrying Brom who could give her a stable life and who would be there for her and her children?

22

Modern Day

How'd you sleep? Tamara asked via text Tuesday morning.

Not well. More nightmares.

Isadora had fallen asleep quickly but was almost immediately plagued by more dreams of the Horseman. She got up and made herself a tea and fell asleep on the couch, but the nightmares continued there as well. After waking several times, she went back to bed, deciding if she was only going to get sporadic sleep, she could at least be more comfortable. Leaving the light on seemed to help, but only a little. The nightmares still came, but at least it took less time to recover from them when she woke as it did in the dark.

Sorry to hear it. I'll bring you something else to try. Have you made any progress on finding anything of Ichabod's or about the history of the house?

Not yet. Still waiting for my box of family history to arrive. Been going through boxes here, but so far haven't found anything.

Keep looking.

Isadora laughed. Like she was going to stop?

I will. Any luck with your research?

I'm not sure yet. I have a few leads, but I'm waiting to find out more.

Okay. Well, keep looking. Isadora could not help throwing Tamara's words back at her.

Still smiling from the exchange, it reminded Isadora that she was going to call George and see if he had any information on the history of the manor. After another fitful night, she was ready to renew her search. She was tired of not sleeping well and wanted answers. Not wanting to admit to him that she had not been paying attention, she would have to be careful in how she worded things.

Checking her phone for any other new messages before calling the attorney, she saw that there was still nothing from Alex, which infuriated her even more than the original offenses. Was he avoiding her now? She had hoped if nothing else, that maybe he would let her know if he and Cory had found anything, but there had been no word from him at all. She supposed she should not have been surprised considering he did not believe her to begin with and had not wanted to take a report on the incident. Isadora tried putting it out of her mind while she focused on making her phone call.

"Is everything going alright, dear? Have you decided what you're going to do with that big house?"

George was always so polite; it was hard to reconcile him with being a lawyer. "Not yet. I've had the contractor here working away, but I wanted to get it fixed up before I make a final decision."

Happy to have been able to make the connection for her, he asked if the contractors were working out as she had hoped.

"Mr. Bachman, I thought I remembered you saying something about the history of the house? That maybe it had been in the family the whole time?"

"Oh yes. The house was built in the nineteenth century, but Mrs. Crosby said the property was owned by the family dating back to the Revolution. I put the list of owners in the file I gave you."

Isadora remembered him handing her the file now but could not remember what she had done with it. He had given it to her before leaving his office, but was that before they toured the property or after? It had to have been before because she had not gone back inside his office when they returned. She had climbed into her car and drove away. Had the envelope been in her hands when she climbed into her car? She did not remember having it. That meant she either left it in his car or there at the manor somewhere. She checked the kitchen counters at the rental, just in case, but it was not there.

Isadora looked around as soon as she got to the manor but could not even begin to guess where the file might be. With all the cleaning and moving around of everything, there was no telling where it would be if she had left it there. Throughout the house, everything was now covered with tarps. Furniture was shoved into corners and covered, rugs had been removed or rolled up and shoved into a corner. When not unboxing the things she had found in the attic, Isadora had spent her time boxing up all of the various décor around the house. These boxes were now piled up along with everything else. It was a good thing she had a moving company coming out that morning to help her put everything into the garage temporarily. If she cleared out the excess furnishings, maybe she would find the envelope underneath a tarp somewhere. She hoped she had not accidentally boxed it up. The items were all inventoried as she boxed them, so she checked her list, but did not see anything on there about an envelope. This was not surprising since it was not something she would have boxed had she known what it was. If it was in a box, it had gotten in there on accident and therefore would not be on her list.

The movers made quick work of emptying each room, moving all the large pieces to the garage and some of the boxes down to the basement. It all barely fit, but they got it all stowed away. She had them pile all the furniture into two categories. The pile further back was to be left as it was while the other would be reupholstered. Those were left nearer the front for easy access. She already had an appointment with an upholsterer scheduled for the following week. The decorator was supposed to be there tomorrow afternoon.

The boxes were likewise arranged into piles. The newly filled boxes went into one portion of the basement towards the back while the old boxes that had been brought down from the attic were placed in another part of the basement. She continued to bring those back upstairs to sort through. Not only was it was too cold and dark to work in the basement, the drawing room and dining room were the only rooms that still contained any furniture. She had left the kitchen table and a couple of sofas and a coffee table in the drawing room where she worked. Though she spent a lot of time on the floor while she inventoried and sorted, she needed a place to sit when she had people come to the house or when she needed a break.

With the rooms mostly empty now, everything felt less cluttered, but Isadora still had not found the file from George. Sighing, she went back to her inventory. Pulling another box up from the basement, she set it down on the floor in the drawing room. No sooner had she sat down beside it than she heard the knock. She looked up before standing and saw Alex entering the room. He looked sheepish and held out a cup and a bag to her.

"I brought you an apple cider and a cider donut. They're local staples around here."

Isadora sighed. She was touched by the gesture, but it was yet another indication that he did not listen to anything she said. She never ate donuts. Apparently all the times they had gone out to eat, he had not heard her say that she preferred to eat healthy. She stood and took the offering anyways.

"Thanks."

"Still upset with me?" he asked.

She was, but she had enough other things on her mind that she decided to let it go. "Did you guys find anything?" she asked instead of answering him.

"No. We asked around, but no one saw or heard anything. It's not surprising, though, given how secluded you are here."

The corner of Isadora's mouth lifted. "Right? It's amazing that all this is hiding right in the middle of such a populated area. It's like a little oasis."

He smiled back at her, relaxing slightly. "It is."

Sitting, she gestured for him to join her, and they got comfortable on the sofa. She set the bag and the drink on the coffee table while he asked how she had been progressing on the house. She updated him about the movers and the appraisal of the household goods. "Now I'm digging through all the old boxes from the attic."

"Are you looking for anything in particular?" Alex leaned back, putting his arm across the back of the sofa behind her.

"Sort of. I mean, not really. Well…" she stopped and regrouped, trying to figure out how to describe what she was looking for. He had not believed her story and thought she had been overreacting and she did not want to bring that up again. "I'm mostly just looking to see what's in the boxes, adding it all to my inventory so I can decide what to do with all. But I'm also trying to find anything that talks about the family history. I still don't know anything about the people who lived in this house, even though I was apparently related to them. I guess I'm trying to find some sort of connection to them."

"Have you found anything yet?"

She let out a breath. "Unfortunately, no. Not yet."

"Well, let's see what's in this box." Alex reached down and began pulling things out and photographing them for her while she added them to her inventory.

With his help, they got through several boxes by lunchtime. They stopped to eat, and things between them had started to improve. They had been laughing and joking as they unpacked and repacked the boxes. There were several items that neither of them had recognized. They tried to guess what the items were, each one trying to outdo the other with each guess becoming more and more outlandish. This was the side of Alex that had drawn her in. She enjoyed spending time with him when he was like this. He made her laugh and by the time they took a break for lunch, he was back to being physical with her. When they stood up, he pulled her into his arms, placing a slow kiss on her lips.

"I'm sorry I was a jackass," he said.

Isadora put a hand on his cheek. "Just don't let it happen again," she teased with a playful slap.

He pulled her in for another kiss, his hands moving lower down her back. When they traveled down even lower, she enjoyed it for a moment, then broke away. "The house is full of people," she reminded him.

As if on cue, Neil stopped in to check on her. He had been helping her bring boxes up, but with Alex there, he had left her alone that day. Now, he wanted to make sure she was doing okay. He was very protective of her, and she imagined that if she had told him Alex was bothering her, Neil probably would have thrown him out, not caring that he was a cop. The thought brought a smile to her mouth.

23

July 1815

Ichabod was up early the next morning, checking on his horse. He massaged her leg again, measuring her progress. Athena was healing slowly, though it was still too soon to ride her across the vast distance he needed to travel. He had begun taking her out daily for short distances, trying to stretch the muscle so she would be ready to leave when it was time to go. Based on her progress, it would be at least another week, possibly two before he could travel with her. He spent the day in his usual routine, chopping wood for the first several hours, then tending to chores around the farm. He was mending a fence late in the day when Katrina approached. She held out the glass in her hand to him without saying anything. He looked at the light-yellow liquid and appreciated it on this hot day. He had worked up quite a sweat and the lemonade went down easily. He handed back the empty glass, nodding.

"Thank you."

There was so much more he wanted to say but was not certain any of it was worth saying. When he did not say anything more, she finally spoke.

"I'm sorry for the way I behaved yesterday."

Ichabod continued sawing the wood he needed to replace the broken beam in the fence. "You owe me no apologies, Miss Brush."

The brusque response and the more formal use of her name caused a ripple of pain to slice through her heart. Katrina knew she should have tried to explain herself to him yesterday instead of going along with her mother's wishes. At the very least, she could have sent Rebecca to tell him that while she was being forced to spend time with Brom, it was Ichabod she wanted to be with. He deserved at least that much. Instead, she had merely assumed that he would understand and forgive her. She saw now that she was wrong.

"Ichabod, please. I must explain."

Ichabod stopped sawing long enough to look at her. He could see the pain in her eyes, and wished he could take it away. But her mother was right; he needed to stay away from Katrina and leave as soon as he could.

"There is no need to explain anything. I know you were only doing what was asked of you. All is well, Katrina. This is your life; you must live it. I am merely an inconvenient detour, though I'll be gone soon enough. Your life will still be here long after I leave. You owe me nothing." When Katrina was unable to respond, he added, "You should go back inside now. If your mother sees you out here, she will not be pleased."

Katrina could not stop the tears that pooled in her eyes. He had said her name yet somehow had managed to say it as though she were a small child, unable to make her own decisions about her life, despite his words to the contrary. She wanted to run back inside the house, fleeing from the humiliation she felt. She wanted to scream. She wanted to hit the stubborn man in front of her.

"I don't care if she sees," she yelled. "You're right, though; this is my life. I shall live it how I see fit with whom I wish to spend my time."

Ichabod admired her tenacity. He could see how upset she was, and he hated that the tears falling down her cheeks were because of him.

"Katrina, I'm trying to tell you that I shall not stand in the way of your happiness." He sighed. "You should accept Brom's proposal."

"Is that what would make you happy, Ichabod? Do you wish to rid yourself of me? Was I only a dalliance to keep you entertained while you were awaiting your horse to heal?"

Ichabod growled. "That's not it at all, Katrina. I would never think of you in such a way. I only wish for your happiness."

"Then why do you push me away now?"

Ichabod threw the saw to the ground and yelled, "Because you'd not be happy with me. You would spend countless months by yourself while I'm sent off elsewhere. Your mother is right. We never know when the next war will be. I could be killed in battle in a month's time. Then where would you be?"

"I could be killed from yellow fever in a month's time. Where would *you* be?" she countered. In a softer voice, she added, "We can't know what our future has in store for us, but we have to hold on to what we have while we can. I spent all day yesterday wishing I was by your side. Every time I heard something funny, I wanted to see the laughter in your eyes as your smile lit up your face. One day of that was quite enough, Ichabod. I don't want to spend a lifetime wishing I could hear your voice or know your thoughts or see your smile."

Ichabod searched her face for the truth of her words. He knew Katrina was right. He had tried to push her away, thinking it best, but he could see now that she was not going anywhere. She wanted to be with him as much as he wanted to be with her. Pulling her into his arms, he kissed her deeply, urgently. She answered with her own urgency, their tongues seeking out one another, arms searching. Ichabod slowed the pace of the kiss, wanting to continue, but needing to stop. He somehow dragged his lips away from hers and rested his forehead against hers. For a moment, they held each other, breathing in one another.

"Nor do I, Katrina. We shall find a way to make this work."

24

Modern Day

After lunch, Isadora and Alex resumed the inventory. The process had been incredibly slow with Isadora working on it by herself the last few days. There were a lot of boxes, and she was often pulled away for other things. Constantly being called on to make decisions regularly, she often had to meet with Neil or his subcontractors, or with other people there to do other tasks. It made her glad she had decided to stay. There was no way she could have done this from Utah. She would have spent her days on the phone and without seeing things in person would not have been able to make appropriate decisions. Thinking of Utah inevitably made her think of Simon. What was she going to do with this house and how was it going to affect her relationship with Simon? The longer she stayed there, the more she wanted to stay even longer. But the thought of moving so far away from Simon pulled at her. How could she move there? If she did, he would no longer be a part of her life. They would stay friends for a while, of course. But she had moved enough times in her life to know that long-distance relationships never worked. The friendship would continue for a time, but it would not be the same. Eventually, they would drift further and further apart. Could she live with that?

Isadora shook the thoughts of Simon from her mind and added the vase Alex was holding to her list. With the box now empty, she set the notebook and pen down on the floor beside her and stretched. Alex sat up, then leaned forward onto his hands and knees, crawling seductively toward her. He had a predatorial look on his face as he trapped her between him and the sofa behind her, placing his arms to either side of her. The movement caused her to laugh as she tried to playfully push him away. He leaned in to kiss her, but she did not want to make it easy for him. Pretending to try getting away, she turned her head away from him while laughter spilled from her. Her head tilted back while she laughed, and he leaned in to nibble at her neck. This caused her to squirm while squeezing her head to her shoulder in an attempt to block him. His hand moved around her waist, and he pulled her in closer to him. Without the support of the sofa behind her, she fell back onto the floor, and he was now on top of her. Still laughing, she wrestled with him until

he grabbed her hands into one of his, lifting them above her head. Bending down, he took her mouth with his. She squirmed at first, but as he deepened the kiss, she slowly stilled, melting into it. Isadora could feel how excited he was as he pressed against her, and a small moan escaped from her lips. Alex's hands slid down her body and hers went around his neck, up into his short blonde hair.

They heard voices in the hallway right outside the drawing room and it pulled them back to the present. Alex pulled back reluctantly with a wide, smug grin across his face. Isadora smiled back at him, holding him in place above her a little longer. He dropped another chaste kiss on her lips and slowly stood, holding out a hand to help her up.

"I'll go grab another box," he said.

They had gotten into a rhythm wherein he retrieved a box or two while she packed the one they had just inventoried. By the time he came back, she was usually finishing up repacking and he would then take the full box back downstairs.

Isadora began repacking the latest box as he left the room. He took his time in the basement, making Isadora laugh inwardly at the thought that he was probably trying to calm himself down, removing the visible evidence of his arousal. Before she finished repacking, there was an unexpected knock at the door, and she stood to go answer it, wondering if she had forgotten an appointment. Alex always knocked then entered without waiting for her, but he was already there. Everyone else who knocked always waited for an answer, despite the open door.

Brushing off the debris from the contents of her last package, Isadora made her way to the front door. She looked up as she turned the corner and immediately stopped in her tracks as her eyebrows soared up on her forehead.

"What are you doing here?" This was the last person Isadora expected to see standing on the porch in front of her.

Simon Diego was suddenly self-conscious and unsure about his decision to come in person. He held his arms forward, gesturing to the large box he held. "I brought the paperwork you were looking for."

It took a moment for Isadora's brain to kick in, and she simply stared at him before shaking herself and stepping back, allowing him entry. Isadora felt as though she had not seen her friend in years. She found herself staring at him, appreciating the way his arms flexed around the bulky box, his tee shirt clinging to him, showing the muscles in his back. Reminding herself that he was not interested in her that way and they would only ever be friends, she suddenly

remembered what she had been doing with Alex only moments ago and felt guilty. She decided she only noticed Simon in that way now *because* of what she had just been doing with Alex. He had turned her on and right now she would appreciate any attractive male standing in front of her. And Simon was nothing if he was not attractive.

"You didn't have to come all the way out here. Why didn't you just mail it?"

She escorted him into the drawing room where Simon set the box down on the coffee table in the middle of the room.

"I missed you," he shrugged.

With his arms free, Simon came closer to Isadora and pulled her in for a hug. She wrapped her arms around him, putting her head on his chest, taking in his warmth and breathing in his familiar scent.

"It's good to see you," she sighed. "I missed you, too."

Neither was eager to end the hug, and they stood there for several minutes, breathing in each other.

"I found this old photo album..."

The voice startled both Isadora and Simon, causing them to part as Alex came into the room holding a book in his hand. He looked at the scene before him, taking measure of Simon.

"This is my best friend, Simon," Isadora said while absent-mindedly resting her hand on his bicep. She addressed Simon then, saying, "And this is my new friend, Alex."

Alex bristled at being introduced as her 'friend,' but held out his hand regardless. The men grasped hands tightly and shook while locking eyes with each other, sizing one another up. When they released, Alex stood beside Isadora, wrapping an arm around her shoulder, pulling her in possessively.

"What brings you all the way out here? I assume you came from Utah?" he asked with a smug smile on his face.

Simon nodded while looking between the pair in front of him. He knew that Isadora had never liked men who were possessive and wondered what the story was with this guy. She had not been there long, yet she had already managed to find someone to date? He thought she had come to take care of this estate she had inherited; yet she had the time to meet people and form relationships? A pang of sorrow and jealousy hit Simon square in the gut. She already had relationships at home; she did not need to go clear across the country to find a new one. Is this really why she had extended her trip? Just how serious were things with this guy?

"I did. I brought some things Izzy was looking for."

"How long are you staying?" Isadora asked.

"The box was full of paperwork that I thought might be useful and I figured it would be easiest to bring it all and go through it here," he said, ignoring her question. "You said you found an old photo album?" he asked, turning his attention to Alex.

Simon already did not like the guy, but it did not mean he could not be polite. It also drew the attention away from himself, which he desperately needed at that point. Isadora had not said anything about dating anyone, so he had not been expecting this new development. He needed a moment to regroup before he answered any questions about why he was there.

"Oh. Yeah." Alex held up the forgotten book that had hung down by his side while the men were introduced and sizing each other up. He released Isadora and set the album on top of the box Simon had set down only moments before. When he opened the cover, they all gathered around to see old black and white tintype photographs from the 1800s. Some of them had names underneath the pictures, and Isadora could not wait to do research on them to see what she could find.

"They're probably old relatives," she said in awe.

She flipped through the book, noting the names that were written in it. "I thought you were going to grab another box?"

Alex shrugged. "You said you were looking for anything to connect you to the house and the family, so I've been trying to look through the boxes a little to pull up the ones that might be useful."

Isadora smiled. "That's a good idea. Thanks. Was there anything else in this box that might be useful?"

Shrugging again, he said, "There might be. I just saw this on top and thought you'd want to see it right away."

"You weren't wrong."

"I'll go get the box." Alex looked hesitantly at Simon, kissed Isadora quickly on the lips in a display of possessiveness, and added, "I'll be right back."

With Alex gone, Isadora smiled back at Simon again. "I'm really glad you're here."

"Are you?" he questioned. He was not so certain.

"Are you kidding? Yeah. I am." Isadora put her hand in his, pulling him towards the sofa. He sat down next to her enjoying the contact. She was not usually this physical and she rarely ever held hands. But she kept her hand in his now as they sat side-by-side.

"I have so much to tell you," she began. "I feel like I haven't seen you in years."

He nodded his agreement. "I was thinking the same thing."

Before they could start talking, Alex was back with the box. He placed it on the floor, turning his attention back to Isadora and Simon. He took in the two of them sitting on the couch together, holding hands. Isadora saw where Alex was looking and realized she was still holding Simon's hand. It had been so natural; she had not even realized it. Letting him go, she stood to look inside the box. It was full of books. She began pulling them out, one by one. After getting about halfway through the box, she realized that the whole thing was likely full of nothing but books. Grabbing her notebook, she started writing down the titles and authors.

The trio talked while they worked, but it was strained. Alex and Simon seemed to be trying to outdo each other and Isadora wanted to catch up with Simon and ask why he was there, but he had clammed up in front of Alex. He was not sharing anything personal with her as long as the other man was there. Isadora did not understand what was happening. She had boyfriends in the past who acted like this, but Simon never had. Why was he doing so now?

As they got to the bottom of the box, Alex pulled out a large brown book that looked quite old and handed it to her. It had been wrapped in linen and when she pulled it off, they saw that it was a bible. Carefully flipping through the pages, they discovered that it was ornately illustrated.

Alex whistled. "I wonder how old that is."

"Should we even be handling it?" Simon asked.

"Probably not," Isadora said. "At least, not without gloves on."

She set it down carefully, closing it as she brought it closer to the coffee table. As she did so, the pages all flipped down, leaving only the front cover open. Isadora looked at the handwriting inside the cover. It had been done in neat hands and looked as though it was likely done by several people. Each line contained names and dates and were written very legibly. The names at the top of the page were Eleanor and Caleb Brush with a date of 1782. The next line of names were Katrina Brush and Abraham Martling with a date of 1815.

"Abraham Martling!" Isadora exclaimed.

The two men looked at her, confused. "He's Brom Bones." When the faces remained blank, not understanding the connection, she explained. "From the story. That's one of the people thought to have been an inspiration for the blacksmith. Abraham Martling actually was a blacksmith, and he was said to be very large and rode a large black horse. Abraham was a common name at the time, but it was also common to shorten it to Brom."

"That's incredible," Simon said.

"Sure, but what does that mean to you?" Alex asked. "I thought this was supposed to be your family history. Does this mean you're somehow related to both Ichabod *and* Brom?"

Isadora paused to think about that for a moment. It did not make sense. She had been excited to find the familiar name, but now she was more confused than ever. None of the other names were familiar to her.

"I'm not sure," she said sadly.

"Maybe your friend at Sunnyside can help you figure it out," Alex said, putting an arm around her shoulder.

She nodded. "Maybe."

"What's Sunnyside?" Simon asked.

Isadora explained that Sunnyside was Irving's home and then she told him about her new friendship with Tamara Petit-Blanc. She pulled out her phone, snapping some pictures of the bible's cover, then the names and dates written inside the cover before closing it and wrapping it back up in the linen. She sent a couple of the photos to Tamara with the caption, *Guess what I just found.*

Isadora left the bible and the photo album out and repacked the other books back inside the box. She wanted a closer look at both books and also wanted to preserve them. She stood and took them over to the kitchen, where she placed them inside a cupboard for safe keeping while Alex took the box back down to the basement. When she glanced out the window, she saw that it was starting to get dark. Panicked, she spun back around, going back to the drawing room quickly.

"We should be going," she said, gathering up her things.

"What's the rush?" Simon asked. "You haven't even shown me around the place yet."

"It's getting dark and we still don't have electricity. You won't be able to see much. I'll show you tomorrow." She tried hurrying the men along, but they were being obstinate.

"It's still early," Alex said. "Neil and some of the workers are even still here."

"That's fine. Neil will lock up behind himself."

"Are you okay?" Simon asked, placing a hand on her arm to stop her frantic rush to leave.

"I'm fine. I just need to leave. I need to get back to my rental and take care of some things." She was probably worrying over nothing, but she did not want to be on the property after dark.

The men slowly followed her out the door.

"Where are you staying?" she asked Simon as they walked. She looked around but did not see any unfamiliar cars.

"My mom will have a conniption if she doesn't get to see me while I'm here, so I'll head down to Brooklyn and stay at her place."

"That's over an hour away."

Simon nodded. "It is."

"Where'd you park?" she asked.

"I didn't drive. I took an Uber from the airport so I didn't have to navigate the train with that box. But I'll take the train back to town. The station isn't far from here."

Isadora frowned. She had been so surprised to see him when he arrived and now in such a panic to leave that she had not noticed the suitcase he grabbed after having left it by the door upon his arrival.

"Stay at the rental with me. I have two rooms. You can go see your mom anytime."

"I don't want to impose."

"Stop it. You know you're not imposing." She pressed the unlock button on her key fob and he went over and placed his luggage in the trunk.

Alex had kept a possessive arm around her waist the entire time as they walked out and pulled her into him on the porch as Simon went to the car. He kissed her hard, sliding one hand down to her butt and placing the other on her jaw. He wanted to make sure this Simon knew who she belonged to. He did not like that Isadora had invited him to stay with her at all.

Isadora pulled back a little, feeling self-conscious in front of Simon, even though she had never done so before.

"Should I come over with you?" Alex asked, his voice a deep rumble that she felt in her chest.

She shook her head slowly. "I don't think so. Not tonight."

Isadora tried pulling away again while watching the darkening sky, but he held her tight, kissing her again. "Are you sure? We could continue what we started at lunch."

She smiled up at him. "Tempting, but no. I really do have to go."

Prying herself out of his arms, she started down the steps to the car where Simon was waiting inside. One look at his face told her he had been trying not to watch them.

Isadora said goodnight to Alex while she quickly walked to the car. Without hesitating, she hurriedly buckled her seatbelt, started the ignition, and pulled out from the lane. Alex had still been standing on the porch. Isadora kept an eye on her mirrors while she drove, but did not see anything. The sky darkened as she drove down Bedford Road towards Tower Hill Road. Glancing in her rearview mirror, she saw the horse with its rider behind her once again. Her heart rate sped up instantly and her palms went clammy. She gripped the steering wheel tighter. Spinning around to get a better view of the specter, the car swerved into the oncoming lane of traffic. Thankfully, there were no cars there at the time. She quickly corrected it while Simon grasped the dashboard in front of him.

"What the hell, Iz? What's wrong?"

She shook her head and mumbled out an apology while looking in the mirror again. The horse had stopped in the road and was now pacing there, watching, as if blocked by an invisible fence, unable to go further. It reared up on its hind legs, surging forward then suddenly disappeared in a flash of fire and smoke. Isadora was not sure what was more disconcerting: the appearance of the Horseman or the fact the entire apparition disappeared into thin air. She felt the sweat trickle down her back as she tried to focus on the road ahead of her. Thankfully, the rental was only about six miles away. They had already passed into Hawthorne and only had a few more minutes to go until they were there. She was shaking far too much to drive any further than that.

Simon saw Isadora looking in her rearview mirror and spun to look behind them, but there was nothing there. What had she been looking at and what had her so spooked that she had almost driven into oncoming traffic?

25

July 1815

It was much harder to sneak away after the events of the previous weekend. Eleanor kept an even closer watch on her daughter and Ichabod. Brom came around every evening and Eleanor encouraged Katrina to entertain him. Katrina tried to make sure she was never alone with him and also brought Ichabod into the conversation whenever she could. When he suggested they go for a walk, she insisted that Jacob come along to chaperone them. She did not trust Brom enough to have Rebecca chaperone. He could easily slip away from Rebecca, but he would think twice about doing so with Jacob. Her brother may have only been fifteen, but he was a male. He would make sure Katrina's honor was protected; it was his duty as her brother.

Whenever Katrina was stuck in conversation with Brom, she would glance across the room to find Ichabod watching her. Instead of turning away as she did that previous Sunday, she flashed him a smile that told him that she would rather be with him. He would wink back at her and she would flush with excitement.

"Are you alright, Katrina? You've gone quite red. Did I say something that upset you?" Brom had asked the last time it happened.

He was so engrossed in himself, he usually did not notice, but he had this time. Unfortunately, Katrina had not been paying attention to what he had been saying and was at a loss as to how to respond. Washington had been watching the exchange between her and Ichabod and came to her rescue.

"I believe it has become rather warm in here. Perhaps the lady is merely tired after a long day?"

"Oh. Yes. Thank you, Mr. Irving. I believe I am rather exhausted. Perhaps I shall retire."

She was not yet ready to sleep and wished she could stay longer and visit with Ichabod or at least watch him across the room if they could not converse, but going to her room was preferable to standing there with Brom even a moment longer.

"Are you well, Katrina?" her father asked as she bid everyone a good night to leave for her room.

Her mother scrutinized her while she responded. "All is well, father. It has merely been a long day. I fear the heat this day has worn me out."

Giving him a smile, she kissed him on the cheek. As she left the room, the last person she saw was Ichabod. She gave him a warm smile and a nod. When he nodded back to her, she left.

"I see you have come to a decision regarding the fair Katrina," Washington said as he crossed the room to speak with Ichabod. He kept his voice low, so as to not be overheard by others.

Ichabod glanced back at the man standing slightly behind him. He turned around to face him when he saw there was no one else standing there with him. "I'm still trying to decide how, but I would like to try and win her hand.

Washington clapped him on the shoulder. "It's never a mistake to give in to love, my friend," he said.

Ichabod found himself looking toward the doorway as if expecting to see Katrina still standing there. He made his way back over to Caleb where they spoke at length about the latest innovations described in the paper. Eventually, everyone else began to retire for the night and Ichabod went outside to check on his horse once again. He had already administered her nightly massage, but he wanted to see to her. He was not yet ready to retire and needed the fresh air and comfort of another soul, even if that soul was not human.

Ichabod stroked Athena's neck while brushing her out. He considered his situation and tried to puzzle out what he needed to do about Katrina. He did want her in his life. There was no question about that. The thought of leaving her tore him apart. However, he was not sure how to do it. How could he ask her to leave her family? He knew her mother disapproved, but what of her father? Would they have to steal away in the night like thieves? The thought left a bad taste in his mouth. He preferred to face his adversaries. Though, would that make it harder for Katrina? Would it be easier for her to silently steal away?

He heard a noise behind him, and he turned to see Katrina standing in the doorway, as if summoned by his thoughts of her.

"I was not yet ready to sleep," she confessed. "I was looking out my window and saw you come out here. I waited for you to return, but you didn't."

"What if your mother finds you here, Katrina?" Ichabod looked behind her as if her mother was waiting there, ready to pull Katrina by the arm back to her room.

Katrina stepped further into the barn. "The household is quiet. Everyone sleeps."

Ichabod took a step closer to her. "Why do you not sleep as well?" he asked softly.

"I was not tired."

Katrina still wore her coral-colored dress from the day. She had not yet changed into her bedclothes, suggesting either she had changed back into her dress to come outside, or she had never readied herself for bed to begin with. He was betting on the latter as she took another step closer.

His feet moved forward on their own accord, bringing him even closer to her. He could reach out and touch her now. "It's not proper for you to be out here at this hour with me."

"I don't care," she responded. "I'm tired of doing what's proper. I want to feel, Ichabod. I want to follow my heart for once, not my head."

Unable to resist any longer, he reached out and touched a curl that fell loose over her forehead that was not obscured by a bonnet for a change.

"And what does your heart tell you, Katrina?" he asked on a whisper.

She looked up at him with her eyes big and innocent and his heart melted, but it was her words that stole his breath away.

"That I'm in love with you, Ichabod. And if I can't have you, I shall surely not survive from the heartache."

Ichabod closed his eyes for a moment, overcome by the joy in his heart. He had no idea he could feel this strongly about someone. Opening his eyes, he pulled her into his arms.

"I love you, too Katrina. More than I ever thought possible."

When she leaned into him, he pressed his lips to hers. Katrina was the one who broke the kiss this time. Pulling back from him, she took his hand in hers.

"Come with me," she said as she pulled him along behind her.

They left the barn and walked past the orchard into the woods nearby. "Where are you taking me?" he asked on a laugh.

"You'll see," she smiled.

They walked through the woods for a few minutes, crunching on leaves and twigs until finally they came upon a clearing. The grass led down to a small stream, trickling over rocks. The air was clean and crisp with a slight chill, the scent of the stream lifting into his nostrils. Katrina stopped beside the stream, pulled Ichabod into her arms, and lifted her face to his. He took the opportunity to kiss her thoroughly.

"What are we doing here, Katrina?" he asked when he pulled back from her.

"I wanted some privacy. It's been difficult to stay away from you. I thought it would be nice to sit by the water, lean back in the grass, and look up at the stars."

Ichabod smiled. "What a lovely idea."

He removed his overcoat and laid it on the ground for her to sit on. Following suit, he sat beside her and pulled her close. They watched the water for a while as they talked.

"What shall we do about our situation, my dear? I would have you with me if you'll have me."

"I do want you, Ichabod. I would leave my home and follow you anywhere. I don't want to be without you."

"That fills my heart with joy. Marry me, Katrina." It was not a question, but she answered anyways.

Nodding her head emphatically, she threw her arms around Ichabod's neck saying, "Yes," a smile splitting her face. She kissed him while his hands roamed her back.

"I know this is not proper, but I would have your consent before I discuss it with your parents."

Katrina sagged. "Must we ask them? Can we not simply run away together?"

Ichabod lifted her chin, saying, "We must. I would not skulk away from this. I would have their blessing if they'll give it. If they won't, then we shall consider an alternate solution. Though we may need to do precisely that. I have doubts that your mother will ever agree."

"It's father we must convince. He shall not be happy at the thought of me leaving, but he will want for me to be happy."

"Then it's decided. I shall speak to your father on the morrow."

The smile returned to Katrina's face. "Oh Ichabod, you've made me so happy. I shall begin packing my things in preparation to leave with you as soon as your horse is ready to travel."

"You may need to stay here a little while. We can wed before I leave, but there is nowhere for you to live with me in Sackets Harbor. I won't be there much longer regardless. I can return for you as soon as I get my orders. This will give you time to say your goodbyes and spend a little more time with your parents before I whisk you away."

Katrina pouted a little. "It's not ideal, but I can wait for you, if I must. I do think we should wed before you leave, though. If we don't, mother will try to undo it all."

"I agree."

The couple continued discussing plans and logistics. Katrina was excited to see all the new places they would go. Ichabod promised to ask for a duty station close to Katrina's home so she could easily travel to visit her parents.

Soon, they were lying on the grass, talking while they looked up into the night sky. There was enough of a clearing from the forest around them that they were able to see the stars twinkling like pinpricks in the darkness. Katrina curled into Ichabod while he wrapped his arm around her. He looked down at her and kissed her every chance he got.

Katrina pushed herself up, resting her arms on Ichabod's broad chest. He moved his arms behind his head and smiled up at her. She leaned forward enough to kiss him, but it was not the brief kisses they had been swapping since lying down on the grass. This time, she kissed him slowly, passionately. His arm came from behind his head to rest on her waist. Katrina deepened the kiss, her hand moving across his chest. His arm moved up her back as their desire became palpable between them.

Ichabod gently pushed her back slightly, his voice gruff. "Katrina, we must stop."

"I don't want to stop, Ichabod," she said breathlessly.

He tried to sit up, but she pushed all of her slight weight against him. He easily could have moved her, but he did not want to. He kissed her again, briefly, only enough to lessen the blow of his words.

"I do not wish to stop either, my darling, but we must. Before it gets out of hand and goes too far."

"What's too far? I've pledged my love to you, Ichabod; and you to me. We plan to be wed. I want to give myself to you."

Ichabod searched her face and saw the truth in her eyes. This was not some impulsive decision that she was making in the heat of the moment. "This is why you brought me here to this place?"

She nodded her head. "I've thought of little else since Sunday. I realized how much I love you, and I want to show you how I feel."

"I know how you feel, Katrina. You don't have to do this now. We can wait until we're wed."

"I don't wish to wait."

Katrina sat up and pushed her sleeves off her shoulders. The bodice of the dress would only go so far without being unbuttoned in the back, but it was a symbolic gesture to show Ichabod that she was ready.

"Oh Katrina," he breathed. Ichabod rubbed her arms, moving his hands along her bare shoulders. His hands made their way around to her back where they slowly started working the buttons he found there. "Tell me to stop anytime you wish, and I shall stop and see you home."

Katrina shook her head. "I won't say it."

Ichabod continued working her dress while she worked the buttons on his vest, sliding it down his arms. He continued kissing her, pulling away from her lips to move down along her neck. Taking his time with her, he gave her every chance to change her mind. He slowly removed her dress, setting it gently on the ground nearby, his own clothes in a pile beside hers.

"This may hurt, Katrina."

She nodded, biting her lip. "I've heard such things said."

The slight fear in her eyes tore at Ichabod's heart. He did not want her to be afraid of this and the thought that it would be painful for her caused him pain as well. Wishing there was another way, he did what he could to go slow and ensured her comfort as much as possible. He continued his kisses along her neck, moving down her breasts, trying to erase the fear from her eyes. His hands and tongue working her body into a frenzy, he ensured she was as ready for him as she could be. Continuing his ministration until he could no longer wait, he poised himself above her and slowly pushed himself inside her. She let out a small gasp and clenched her eyes closed tightly. Holding still for a moment, he allowed her to adjust to the invasion. She clutched his strong back and urged him on. He slowly began to move, still taking his time with her. It took all of his control to go as slow as he was. She felt so good, he wanted to loose himself inside her. Soon, their movements began to speed up as the pain subsided and Katrina was able to start enjoying herself.

The couple gave themselves to one another there in the grass beside the stream, pledging their love to each other forever. It was the start of a new life that they were both eager to meet. When they finished, they cuddled together as long as they could before they had to go back to the farmhouse, holding on to each other as if neither would ever let go. It was everything Katrina could have ever hoped for her first time with a man.

26

Modern Day

Isadora was even more glad that Simon was with her than she had been before. Coming home to an empty house the last time had only added to her anxiety and terror. Having him there with her now helped alleviate some of that, though she was still shaken up. They went inside and Isadora showed Simon to the extra room where he dropped off his suitcase. She quickly went back towards the kitchen, needing to stay busy while she tried to stop shaking. She opened cupboard doors then closed them, moving onto the fridge next. Not knowing what she was looking for, it was more for something to do than any particular need for food or a drink.

Simon was right behind her. He saw her pacing in the kitchen and stepped closer to her, putting his hands on her arms, stilling her search. He rubbed up and down and she collapsed into him. His arms went around her and he held her close.

Kissing the top of her head, he quietly asked, "What happened, Iz?"

Isadora stood in the kitchen and shook her head against Simon's chest. She did not want to explain to him what had happened. He would think she had gone crazy. She let him comfort her for a moment, but the need to stay busy returned. If she stayed in his arms, she would start crying and that was the last thing she wanted. Pulling away, she quickly turned back towards the fridge again so he could not see her face.

"Damnit. Talk to me, Iz."

"Are you hungry? I could make something for dinner."

Simon closed the refrigerator door, took her by the hand, and pulled her into the living room, sitting her down on the couch. She was wringing her hands again and looking towards the kitchen.

"Izzy, you're white as a ghost and you're shaking like a leaf. Tell me what's going on. What spooked you?"

Isadora finally turned to look at him, albeit briefly. The intensity in his eyes was too much for her. It was as though he would see right through her if she let him look too long. Knowing him, he probably would. He knew her better than anyone else ever had. Sometimes she thought he knew her better than she knew herself.

"Why are you here?" she asked, turning the attention onto him in an attempt to distract him.

Simon frowned. "What do you mean? I came to see you."

"No. I know. But why?" Isadora's phone notified her of an incoming text, but she ignored it. She wanted an answer.

He scoffed. "Jesus, Iz. I thought we were friends. I didn't realize I needed a reason."

She shook her head. "That's not what I meant. I just… I'm surprised to see you. Why did you fly more than halfway across the country just to visit me? Without even telling me you were coming."

It was Simon's turn to look away. "I told you; I missed you."

Isadora glared at him without saying anything. There was something he was not telling her. Another text message came in. Again, she ignored it. Most likely it was Tamara answering her previous text about the bible. She would get back to her when she and Simon finished talking.

Simon let out a breath. "Fine. I was worried about you. You sounded spooked when we spoke the other morning, then you wanted that box of paperwork. You weren't saying anything on the phone, so I wanted to come out and see for myself that you were okay. I'm glad I did because there's clearly something going on that you're not telling me."

Isadora turned away and stood up. She looked around, looking for an escape, then sat back down again. "I think someone is trying to scare me away from the manor house."

"What? Who?"

"I don't know."

"What makes you think that, then?"

Isadora let out a breath and looked down at her hands in her lap. "I've seen the Headless Horseman. Twice now."

Simon's brow furrowed. "What do you mean you've seen the Headless Horseman? I mean, this is Sleepy Hollow and Halloween is next week. I'm sure there are statues and images of him everywhere."

Shaking her head, she said, "No. Not a *likeness* of him. I've seen *him*. He was at the house one night as I was leaving. I only caught a glimpse of him, and I thought I was imagining it, but then there was a gash in my car and hoof prints in the drive."

"A gash in your car?"

Isadora told Simon everything that had happened that night and that she had filed a report with the police. She left out any mention of the nightmares.

"That's when you called me? The morning after this happened?"

She nodded. Two more text messages came in.

Simon was quiet for a moment, processing it all. "You said twice. You saw him again tonight?"

She nodded again, looking down.

He took her hand in his. "Okay. So why would someone do this? Do you think it's a prank or do you feel threatened?"

"I keep trying to tell myself it's just a prank, but it feels threatening. I don't know how to explain it, but I can feel the malice rolling off the thing."

"Both times you've seen him were at night? At the house?"

She began to nod, then remembered, "No. Tonight it was after we left the house."

"But it had only just gotten dark. He hasn't shown up during daylight?"

"No. But why didn't he follow us tonight? Why doesn't he show up here?"

"Maybe he doesn't know where you've been staying and it's not like a horse can travel as fast as you drive."

Isadora barked out a nervous laugh. He always teased her about her driving. She had a bad habit of speeding that she could not seem to shake. It looked like this time it was working to her advantage. The brief moment of levity felt good in light of the conversation they were having.

It was good to see her laugh. Simon could see how scared she had been, and it had gutted him. "We'll figure it out, okay?" She nodded. "And Iz?" He waited for her to look at him. "I'll be right here with you. I won't let anything happen to you."

Isadora gave him a smile and patted his knee. "Thank you. That reminds me. How long are you staying?"

Simon looked sheepish. He rubbed his hands on his thighs. "My return flight is a month from now."

Isadora's eyebrows rose. "A month? Wow. Nice extended vacation?"

He chuckled. "I wish. I cut my hours, but I'll be working while I'm here. It's nice to have the flexibility to work from anywhere. It's been a while since I've visited my mother, so I figured I may as well make it count while I'm here."

"Well, I'm sure she will certainly appreciate it."

"She better," he joked. When she laughed again, his heart lightened a little. When her phone went off again for what was probably the tenth time, he said, "Someone is trying really hard to reach you. You should probably answer it."

Isadora went to the kitchen and grabbed her phone to check it. Alex had been sending her texts 'checking in.' "As if he didn't just see me ten minutes ago," she said, exasperated.

"You're *friend?*" Simon asked.

Isadora dropped her hand holding the phone down to her side, giving her attention back to Simon. "Okay, let's hear it."

"Hear what?" he asked innocently.

"You don't like him, do you?"

"I'm not the one dating him. It doesn't matter if I like him."

She came back over and sat down on the couch again. They were turned sideways, facing each other, his arm resting on the back of the couch. Isadora wondered why it looked so natural when he did it, yet so forced and full of bravado when Alex did it.

"It does matter. I value your opinion."

Simon sighed. He reached out his hand and brushed a coppery strand of hair off her forehead. "I —" he began as her phone pinged again.

She looked down, lifting the phone to see it. "Oh. It's Tamara. Sorry. I should answer this one."

Tamara wanted to meet up to discuss what they had both found out and was asking when they could get together. After several texts back and forth, they worked out their schedules and arranged to meet Friday afternoon.

While she texted Tamara, Simon pulled out his own phone, arranging for delivery from a nearby restaurant that he found online. He had not realized how hungry he had gotten. He ordered for both of them, then put his phone away as she was finishing up.

"Sorry. We're going to meet Friday. You'll like Tamara. She's full of personality. I can't wait for you to meet her."

Simon nodded at her. "So, what are we doing tomorrow? Working at the house?"

"You don't have to spend your vacation working with me cleaning up an old house."

"Because I have anything better to do?" he joked.

Before she could answer, her phone went off again. Checking to see if Tamara had forgotten anything, she saw that it was Alex. Again. "I guess I better answer him or he's just going to keep texting."

She replied back to him that she had made it home and was fine. Simon got settled, and they were in for the night. No, she did not want to go back out again. No, she did not want him to come over.

"He's a little threatened by you," she told Simon.

"Why would he be threatened by me?" While Simon was not a small man, and he was rather muscular, he was not generally intimidating. He could be if he chose to be, but he did not go around trying to be threatening. If anything, people often underestimated him.

Isadora tilted her head. "Really? You intimidate all my boyfriends."

Simon shrugged, trying to be nonchalant when he felt anything but. "I don't know why. It's not like you and I are together or that I have any say in who you date." As much as he wished otherwise.

"I think men can't handle women having friends of the opposite sex. They're always afraid they're going to lose their girlfriends and wives to them."

"Maybe if those men treated their women better, they wouldn't lose them."

Isadora smirked. He always had such an easy answer for everything. At least it did not sound patronizing like it did when Alex spoke.

"Is he good to you, Iz?"

He was trying to be supportive, even though he would have preferred to tell her to get rid of Alex and give him a chance. That would only backfire, though. If he wanted to win her over, he would have to be patient.

She shrugged. "He can be kind of condescending and arrogant sometimes but he's also sweet. I like him, but it's early."

The doorbell rang, and Isadora tensed. Simon stood, going to the door. When he came back, he had a bag full of something that smelled delicious. He pulled her up from the couch and into the dining room where he set down the bag, then began pulling out all of the small boxes. Isadora pulled out a couple of plates and utensils and sat down at the table to see that he had ordered all of their favorites. They often went to Chinese, or had it delivered at home, but it had been a while since they had done so. She could hardly believe that he had done this now. Food had been the last thing on her mind, but once the aroma hit her, her stomach let her know it would be welcome.

Simon started piling up her plate, and Isadora sat there, staring at him, thinking about how thoughtful he was. She suddenly felt as though she had never seen him before. He noticed her staring and stopped with a spoonful of orange chicken hovering above her plate.

"What's wrong?"

A half-smile lifted the corner of her mouth. "Nothing. I just really missed you."

His shoulders relaxed and he said, "I missed you, too."

"I don't just mean since I've been here. I feel like we never have time to get together anymore."

"Me too. I know the school year is always busy for you, but my schedule has been crazy lately, too. I'm sorry I haven't made more time for us."

The way he said that made her stomach do flips. She tried not to read anything into it, and said, "Thank you for being here."

As they ate, her phone pinged several more times. She ignored them all and enjoyed her time with Simon. When they finished, she checked the phone and asked, "What do you want to do tomorrow? We never did decide on anything and it's your vacation."

"We can do whatever you want to do. You've had a lot going on and it's been stressful for you. Why don't we do something fun?"

"I've been out seeing as much of the area as I can already. I can take you to see all the places I've found," she offered. She checked her phone again. Her and Alex started texting back and forth now while she talked with Simon.

"We can do that if you want to see them again. Otherwise, we can see them later. I've probably seen several of them already when I was a kid anyways."

He began washing the plates and utensils they used while she stood next to him. When she did not answer right away, he knew she did not want to redo everything she had already done in the last couple of weeks. She wanted to do something new, but without knowing what that was, she did not know what to suggest. He smiled to himself at how transparent she was.

"Alex said there's a game tomorrow."

"Sports? You? Have you told him how you feel about sports?"

She laughed while wrinkling her nose. "I did. I guess he doesn't believe me?"

"Or he wasn't listening," he grumbled.

"I was trying to give him the benefit of the doubt." Isadora dried the clean plates and utensils, putting them away while Simon wiped down the counter.

"I have an idea." Simon stopped, put the sponge in the sink and leaned against the counter. "There's a museum in Yonkers that you'll love. Why don't we do that?"

"You know I love a good museum."

"I do."

She texted Alex and it did not take long before he replied. She laughed at the response before sharing. "He's not thrilled about going to a museum, but he said he's down if that's what I really want to spend my time doing."

Simon rolled his eyes. He wanted to ask her what she saw in this guy but was almost afraid to hear the answer. Instead, he asked something else he had been wondering about. Lifting her hand for a better look, he asked, "Where did you get the ring?"

Isadora looked at her hand, holding it out for his examination. "Isn't it incredible? I found it in one of the boxes. It's weird, but I kind of felt like I was stealing it when I first took it. Is that strange?"

Simon chuckled. "Not at all." He released her hand. "What else have I missed?"

Isadora filled him in on everything that had happened since she arrived. She told him how she met Alex and Tamara and all the places she had visited since being there. She described all the places she had gone running and spoke of her Victorian manor house and property. They talked late into the night like they used to do before life got in the way.

"How's everything with Becky? Any better than the last time we talked?"

"We broke up." And was that not the way of it? Every time Simon was ready to tell her how he felt, Isadora was in a relationship with someone else.

"What happened?"

"She just wasn't–" he stopped himself before he could say 'she wasn't you.' "She wasn't right for me."

Isadora put her hand over his. "I'm sorry, Simon."

He only nodded. What else could he do?

As they were getting ready for bed, Simon watched as Isadora went over and double-checked the lock on the door again, making sure it was latched. He tried to reassure her, but she simply smiled and said goodnight.

Simon tried to sleep, but he could not get there. Though it was late in New York, and it had been a long day, he was still on Utah time where it was still early, and he was too wound up to sleep. He kept thinking about everything Isadora had told him. If someone was trying to scare her away from the property, it had to be someone that had something to gain from it. She said the attorney had exhausted the possibility of there being any other family members with a claim to it. Could it be a neighbor or someone else who wanted the land? Simon would see what he could find out. He hated seeing her scared and wanted to make it better for her.

Simon pulled a book from his luggage and settled in to read for a while in the hopes it would help him get to sleep. A couple hours later when he was still awake, he got up to get a drink. When he went out into the hall, he noticed the little sliver of light coming from the bottom of Isadora's door. He tapped lightly on her door to check on her, but he did not get an answer. Worried, he popped his head in slowly, calling her name softly in an attempt to not startle her. She was asleep in bed and must have fallen asleep before she could turn her light off. He smiled, then shut it off for her, backing slowly out of the room.

27

July 1815

"Did you not sleep well, my dear?" Caleb asked when Katrina yawned at breakfast the next morning.

"After going to bed so early, I would not expect you to be so tired," her mother added, eyeing her suspiciously.

"I did not sleep as well as I would have liked," she replied carefully.

Katrina had been too happy and excited over the events of the night to have been able to sleep. Once she returned to her room, she laid awake replaying the stolen moments of sharing her love with Ichabod. Katrina was proud of herself for not blushing deeply when Ichabod entered the room. His eyes immediately met hers and she smiled briefly before looking away. She wanted him to kiss her and hold her in his strong arms, but with her mother watching so closely, she barely dared look at him for fear of giving anything away.

Ichabod's heart stuttered at the sight of Katrina. It had been torture to separate from her the night before. They had snuck back into the house as quietly as possible, her going before him in case anyone was awake. Before going inside, they had stopped at the barn first to say their goodnights from there. It was all he could do to let her go. Seeing her now, he wanted to pull her close and redo everything they had done the night before. He wondered how long it would be before he could have her again. He desperately wanted her in his bed, and he wanted her there to stay. Not wanting her to have to sneak off to her own room after they made love, he vowed he would speak to her father that day.

At the end of breakfast, Ichabod followed Caleb outside where Katrina's father made his way to the fields near the house. As they made it outside, Ichabod said, "Sir, I wonder if I might have a word with you later? About Katrina."

Caleb was in a rush, mumbling something about the cows having gotten loose from the pasture again. He was bringing them into the barn before the rains came. Ichabod looked up and saw the clouds for the first time. He had been so preoccupied, he had not even noticed the approaching storm. With his attention diverted, he followed Caleb to assist instead of the task of going to the barn to check on his horse. She could wait a few hours. He wanted to make sure it was not the repair in the fence that he had done that allowed the cows to break free.

With only six cows, it did not take long to round them back up and bring them in. Much to Ichabod's relief, it was a different section of fence that had broken, not the section he had repaired. The men worked together to get the cows back to the barn quickly before the clouds broke. The fence would have to wait until the storm passed. The winds had already picked up and it looked like this would be a bad one. As much as Ichabod wanted to discuss Katrina with Caleb, this was not the time for it. The sky would open up any minute and they needed to focus on the task at hand.

The men spent the afternoon dealing with the storm, ensuring everything was tied down securely and the newly harvested hay remained dry. The winds had picked up greatly with this storm, wreaking havoc across the farm. The women had been as busy at the house, covering the garden as much as they could, in an attempt to protect the fragile fruits and vegetables from the damaging winds. By the end of the day, everyone was exhausted and on edge. This was no time to ask for Katrina's hand. Ichabod would have to wait until the following day.

Although the winds had died down, the rain lingered through the night and into the next day. It was a much lighter rain, coming in stops and starts. By the afternoon, Ichabod went out to the barn to check on his horse, for lack of anything else to do. She had greatly improved, and he knew he would be able to leave soon. The thought of his imminent departure was bittersweet. While he was excited to begin the next journey of life, he hated the thought of leaving Katrina behind, even if it was only for a short time. He wanted to take her with him. He had not been able to sneak away with her the night before and he had missed holding her. When she came into the barn, he was delighted to see her. He immediately went to her and gathered her to him.

"I missed you last night," she whispered between kisses.

"I missed you, too."

"I want to feel you inside me again."

Ichabod's eyes flared with heat at her brazenness. "I want that, too."

Katrina took his words to mean right then and there, and she began pushing off his overcoat. His own hands roamed her body, only moving away long enough to remove his arms from his sleeves.

"We should not be doing this," he said while making no effort to stop. "Not here. Not now. We shall meet later tonight in our spot beside the stream."

Katrina nodded but continued groping him and relishing in his touch.

They both froze when they heard a noise behind them. Before they could even turn, Eleanor's voice rang out, echoing in the barn.

"Katrina Brush! Just what do you think you're doing?"

Ichabod stepped in front of Katrina, shielding her with his big body. He was thankful they had not had the chance to get any further undressed, though the situation was precarious enough. Eleanor stormed over, grasping at Katrina while Ichabod did his best to continue shielding her. This only proved to further enrage the woman. His focus had been so consumed by Eleanor, Ichabod had not seen Brom enter the barn behind her. It was not until the man's beefy fist struck across Ichabod's jaw that he realized he was even there.

Ichabod would berate himself later for not noticing the man's presence, when he had time. Now, he had to focus on the brute in front of him who was trying to hit him once again. His jaw ached, but he squared off with the man, dodging his jabs while trying to get in his own. Ichabod was a trained soldier, but Brom had brute strength on his side. Still, he only managed to land one blow to every three or four of Ichabod's.

Katrina watched as the two large men fought over her. She wanted to help Ichabod but knew there was nothing she could do. Before she could see what was happening, her mother pulled her by her hair out of the barn, across the yard, and into the farmhouse where she marched her right up to her room and shoved her inside. Eleanor pulled the door closed behind her, then pulled a key from her pocket, locking her in. She had not done that since Katrina was a child, when she used to run off into the night in search of an adventure. Having been wild as a child, her mother had installed a lock on her door to keep her safely inside. Katrina banged on the door with her fists, screaming and crying to be let out. She heard her mother's footsteps as she furiously stomped away from her door. She ran to her window but could not see inside the barn and no one was coming out of it.

28

Modern Day

Isadora woke with a start as the flaming sword was about to make contact with her neck, sitting up as her eyes flew open. When all she could see was darkness, she thought for a moment that she was still in the dream and cried out. When she tried getting up, she got tangled in the sheets which made her panic even more, feeling like she was being held down. A distressed noise that was not quite a scream escaped her mouth while she struggled. Before she could break free, the overhead light came on and Simon came running into the room. He sat down on the bed beside her, staring into her big blue eyes. He could see the fear there and he pulled her into his arms, rubbing her back. She wrapped her arms around him and sobbed into his shoulder. Simon petted her hair and kissed the top of her head, trying to soothe her the best he could.

They sat that way for some time before Isadora finally pulled back slowly. "Sorry I woke you."

"Don't you dare apologize," he said sternly.

Simon went to get a glass of water and came back and handed it to her. She took a long pull from it, then handed it back to him. She was still shaking a little and did not trust herself to hold it.

Wiping her eyes, she said self-consciously, "How ridiculous am I to have a nightmare?"

Simon shook his head. "Not ridiculous at all." He lifted her chin so she would meet his gaze, knowing she did not believe him. "Do you hear me? It's perfectly natural."

Isadora nodded. He knew she was merely placating him, but it was probably the best he would get. He stood and went to his room to get his phone. When he came back, he plugged it in and turned on a nightlight app that he kept for when his niece visited, then turned off the overhead light. Going around to the other side of bed, he climbed in beside her, pulling her to him. Wrapping her in his strong arms, her head rested on his shoulder. He rubbed her arm with one hand, her hair with the other.

Simon had not asked if Isadora wanted him to stay. He had seen she needed the companionship and did not hesitate to crawl into bed with her. There was no conversation about it, no expectations or awkwardness, only comfort. She felt safe for the first time in days. Isadora was embarrassed about having a nightmare at her age, but he had not laughed or made her feel bad about it at all. Instead, Simon did everything he could to take care of her and make her feel better. She tried not to overthink it. This was what friends did for each other. She finally felt her breathing slow and her heartrate calm down. It was not long before she was asleep again.

Simon slowly came awake with Isadora's vanilla scent filling his nostrils. He breathed it in deeply, the smell making him feel as though he had come home. It had taken him an eternity to fall asleep with her curled up around him. His heart raced, as did the images in his head. Somehow, he managed to sleep, but now that he was awake, it was best if he got up and let her sleep on. Feeling her steady breath on his chest, he wondered if he could extricate himself from her before she woke. It was still early, but the sun was up now. He did not want her waking up while he had no control of the issue currently tenting the sheet below his waist. Normally, he would blame it on being morning, but today, it was all her. He slowly lifted his arm and started to slide but felt her stir before he made it even a couple of inches. Stopping and freezing in place, it was too late.

"Where are you going?" she asked in a froggy voice, her eyes still shut.

"Shh. It's early. Go back to sleep." He kissed her forehead and rubbed her hair.

"Don't go," she said while squeezing him tighter.

Simon groaned. "Iz," he growled.

Isadora slid a heavy hand up his chest and chin, resting her fingers over his mouth. "Shh. It's early. Go back to sleep," she parroted.

Simon closed his eyes, trying to gather all of his willpower and self-control. If he was going to spend one more second in this bed with her like this, he was going to need it. He kissed her fingers, then scrubbed a hand over his stubbly face when her hand fell heavily to his chest. He held her until she fell back to sleep again. Getting back to sleep himself at that point was out of the question. Waiting a while longer to make sure she was fully asleep, he tried extricating himself again, this time successfully. After taking a cold shower and getting ready for the day, he settled on the couch with his laptop, getting some work done while he waited for her to wake up.

ℂ ℂ

Simon plugged in the address of the Hudson River Museum into the GPS on his phone and drove Isadora's rental car to the museum in Yonkers. Alex had offered to drive them, but Simon did not trust him. He could see the man throwing a fit over something petty and leaving them there. They could always pick up a train if that happened, but this was easier. If Alex ended up wanting to leave, he could do so without leaving them stranded.

They started in the planetarium, taking in the *Dark Side of the Moon* show, then wandered around the exhibitions. There was a variety of paintings, sculptures, photographs, and costumes and other textiles. Isadora took in everything, taking her time while Alex grumbled and tried to hurry her along. Simon saw her annoyance and tried to come to her rescue, distracting Alex.

"So, what do you do, Alex?"

"Izzy didn't tell you?" Simon shook his head and Alex puffed out his chest. "I'm a cop. I'm surprised she didn't say anything."

Clearly, he wore it as a badge of honor. Simon certainly agreed that it was a noble profession, but this guy used it as something to brag about. It gave Simon the impression that it provided Alex Kaderson with a feeling of superiority.

"How about you? What is it you do?"

"I work in IT."

Alex scoffed. "So, you're a computer geek? People just call you with their computer issues and you fix them?"

Simon smiled knowingly. "That's part of what I do."

It was only one very small part, but if that was what this guy wanted to think, Simon was not going to correct him. He was actually a software developer, spending his days working with complex algorithms and things that Alex would never understand. Simon had met plenty of guys like him before, though. It was pointless to argue with them or try to explain what he did. They already had their minds made up and nothing he could say or do would ever change that.

"I guess Utah doesn't really have much else to do than sit around playing with computers or going to church. You probably didn't have many other career options there. Being this close to New York City, I had all the options in the world. I had my pick of things to do. I always knew I wanted to be a cop, though."

"You grew up here?" Simon asked as they moved on to the next exhibit hall, leaving out the fact that he grew up in Brooklyn. He was trying to make things easier for Isadora, not have a pissing contest with her boyfriend.

"Lived here my whole life," he bragged. "My family's from here. Though, it was still North Tarrytown back then. It didn't become Sleepy Hollow until 1996."

Simon nodded. "So you've spent your whole life in this little town. That's cute."

Isadora stopped in front of a photograph with trees alongside the edge of the Hudson River and stared at it for a while.

"We could always just go outside if that's what you want to see," Alex said more loudly than was warranted for the space they were in.

She turned to glare at him, then went back to looking at the photo without saying a word. Simon came over and looked at the image. After a moment, he said softly, "That reminds me of the place we went hiking up in Idaho a few years back."

She turned to him and flashed a smile. "That's what I was thinking."

Alex put an arm around her, pulling her in close as they moved on to the next hall.

After seeing all of the exhibits, they made their way to the attached Glenview Historic Home, which was built in 1877 and had been restored. Though it was almost twenty years newer than Isadora's manor home, they were contemporaries.

"This was the biggest reason I wanted to bring you here today," Simon said as they walked in. "I knew you'd love the planetarium, but I thought you could get some ideas for your place."

"It certainly does give me some," she said. "Whoever did my place last made it a little gaudy. I know a lot of that is the period, but this place is done up nicely. It's nowhere near as busy as my house. I really like how the walls are a solid color, but the ceiling and rugs are done up with the busy patterns of the period."

Isadora began taking photos and notes on her phone to discuss with the decorator she was meeting later that afternoon. She was definitely going to need to redo everything, including the rooms which had not been vandalized.

☙ ☘

Once they were back in Sleepy Hollow, they went to the house to meet with the decorator. Isadora gave her a tour of the house and grounds with Simon joining them so he could see it all as well. They stopped in each room, most of which were now empty, and discussed the possibilities.

"I'll do a few mock-ups to show you what each room will look like, and you can chose from there. We'll do one floor at a time," she said.

Isadora got more excited with each new idea they had. Her excitement was contagious, at least to Simon. He became more excited along with her, while Alex only grumbled. The rest of them did not even notice Alex's comments as they were stuck in their own little world.

"So, are you thinking about staying?" Simon asked hesitantly when the decorator left. It was obvious to him how much she had been enjoying her time there, even with the threat hanging over her head.

"I don't know. I really like it here."

They made it outside and she was showing him around the grounds. Alex had stayed with them the entire time, despite his grumblings. He had walked with his arm around Isadora's waist at first, but it was awkward, particularly with their height differences, and the ground was rather uneven. She quickly stepped out of his grasp.

Simon nodded and looked around. "I forget how beautiful it is here. I don't blame you."

"You've been here before?" Alex asked.

"I grew up in Brooklyn."

Alex jerked back in surprise. "I thought you were from Utah?"

"That's just where I live now. I moved there almost ten years ago, but I always lived in Brooklyn before that. I used to come up here a lot as a kid."

Simon turned his attention back to Isadora. "Well, it's not like you have to decide soon. Take your time. See what the winter is like," he said with a smirk. She loved skiing, but she hated having to deal with traffic and getting places in the snow.

"If I can handle Utah winters, I think I'll be fine." She smiled back at him. "But honestly, even if I do stay, what am I going to do with this giant monstrosity of a house?" *Not to mention my own personal stalker that comes with it*, she thought.

"I'm sure you'll think of something," Alex said.

She gave Simon a doubtful look that said she was not so sure.

ജ   ൫

They left the house before it got dark this time. Alex tried dragging out their departure, but Simon did not let him. He was not taking any chances and he made sure Isadora was in the car before the sun set. Alex had tried coming home with Isadora again and she had turned him down again. She was beginning to wonder how much longer he would put up with her. In the grand scheme of things, they really had not known each other long. But they had spent a lot of time together since they had met. Alex had spent most of his free time with her on his days off. *But*, she thought, *if he can't accept her pace, then he's not worth keeping around.*

Isadora and Simon made dinner when they got back to the rental. After eating and cleaning up, they got to work. They had loaded the box Simon had brought with him from Utah into the car before leaving the manor tonight since it had been left behind in Isadora's haste to leave the day before. It was still early enough that they opened it up and started going through the contents.

Working from the top of the pile, they each grabbed a book or a stack of papers and started scanning to see if it might hold anything pertinent. It was a large box and there was a lot to go through, so it was slow going.

Simon grabbed a stack and instantly recognized a page as a genealogy chart. He knew it would not give them anything new, but he found it interesting, so he took his time studying it. The names and dates on it went back to the Revolutionary War and included Ichabod's father and grandfather. There were additional pages with brief descriptions about the lives of the first few generations on the chart.

"Why does this only go back to the seventeen hundreds? Could they not find anything before then?"

Isadora lowered the pages she had been scanning and leaned over to see what he was looking at. "My gran and her mother were both in the Daughters of the American Revolution. They were only interested in linking themselves to someone who served in the war. Ichabod's father would have sufficed, but they found the information on his grandfather easily enough, so they included it as well. Gran was always proud of the history in our family. Every generation served in the military in some capacity." She had said the last with pride, but then her face darkened as a thought occurred to her. "Except mine."

Simon reached a hand toward her, patting her knee. "You had a different calling. You're not obligated to serve just because your ancestors did."

"I know," she huffed. "But sometimes I wonder if my dad would have been proud of me."

"Of course he would have been. Are you kidding? You have a doctorate. Not everyone can say that."

"Thanks," she said with a small smile.

Isadora returned to her pile of letters, then set it down, pulling out her phone. "Let me see that chart again."

Simon opened the folded pages and laid it out on her lap while she pulled up an application on her phone. She searched the app for a moment, then said, "I just remembered looking at this with the attorney. Mary Crosby's DNA profile was linked with mine and I was able to see where we connected." She counted to herself for a moment; then, "Yes. Our common ancestor is seven generations back for me." She pulled the chart closer, and Simon leaned in to count with her. As they reached the same line, they looked at each other.

"Ichabod," they both said at the same time.

"It keeps coming back to the story," Simon said.

"I can't imagine in two hundred years that I'm the only one who ever had an interest in our family connection to it all. Maybe someone else further back studied history. Or studied Washington Irving, like me."

Simon agreed. "It is likely." He looked down at the chart again. "So, if your common ancestor was Ichabod, that means you're descended from one of his children and Mary was descended from another."

She smiled. "That's exactly what it means. And we know I came from Charles Henry Crane and Sarah Payne Nicoll, which means Mary must have come from William M. Crane. Those were Ichabod's only children." Isadora pointed at the names on the chart as she spoke.

Simon looked through the pages attached to the chart, searching for the description of Charles Henry Crane. "Charles was a brigadier general, Surgeon General of the United States, and one of the attending physicians to Lincoln after he was shot." He whistled. "That is a rather impressive career."

"It is," she agreed. "But with the family history at that time, I can't imagine the pressure on the male children. They must have been driven to succeed."

Simon squeezed her hand and they both returned to their search. They spent hours looking through the box and had only gotten halfway through it when Isadora yawned. "I'm going cross-eyed. I don't think I can read anything else tonight."

"I hear that. I feel like I'm cramming for an exam. Remind me not to take any of your classes. You're a slave driver."

Isadora laughed. They said goodnight, agreeing to resume in the morning.

After managing to stave off the worst of the nightmares, Isadora got a little bit of sleep between the remaining dreams of the Horseman that continued to disturb her. She missed having Simon in her bed to cuddle with, but she knew it was for the best. There was no way she would ask him to stay with her again. If she did, she would probably make a fool of herself. He had been gone when she had woken that morning, and she had felt his absence deeply. Though she had tried to get him to stay, he had made it abundantly clear that he was not interested in doing so. She had to stop thinking of him that way.

Maybe that was why she had not been physical with Alex yet? Though, it had never stopped her before. Isadora had dated plenty of men over the years. While she had not engaged with all of them sexually, she was not a prude, either. She took her time and made sure it was really what she wanted. Relationships were not something she was impulsive with. Her time with Alex was following the same path she had always followed with her boyfriends. It had nothing to do with Simon. She only had to keep telling herself that.

The next morning, they continued working their way through the box. Soon, they began to see the bottom. There had been a few things that had referenced Ichabod, but nothing helpful in regard to the manor. There was nothing indicating ownership, no matter how far back they went. Isadora had even taken the genealogy chart and compared the names on it to those in the bible they had discovered at the house. None of them matched. What did that mean for Mary Crosby? Her name was not in the bible, nor on Isadora's genealogy chart. Of course, the last date written in the bible had been before Mary would have been born. It probably had nothing to do with the family but was something that someone had found and purchased as a collector's item since it appeared to possibly be related to the story.

Frustrated, they dug out the last remaining items. Isadora looked through one stack while Simon looked through another. Lying on his side on the floor, he pulled a book from the pile and quickly scanned a few pages. He darted upright, his eyes wide. Isadora looked over at him from her perch on the floor with her legs crossed in front of her.

"What is it?"

Simon turned back to the cover and the first few pages. "This is Ichabod's," he said excitedly.

"No, it's not?" she challenged, disbelieving.

Simon slid across to her, holding the book so she could see what he was looking at.

"Oh, my gods," she exclaimed.

She looked up at him with her blue eyes sparkling. Even if there was nothing in there about the house and the property, this was a firsthand account from the person she had studied for so long. Simon handed the precious book over to her and she flipped through it eagerly.

"It's dated 1850. This was written shortly before he died in 1857." She scanned the pages, stopping here and there. "It looks like a memoir of some sort. It seems to cover his entire career. I can't wait to read it. Maybe once the house is further along, I'll have more time."

Simon's chest filled with joy at seeing her so happy. He wanted to pull her into his arms and celebrate the find with her. Instead, he smiled, soaking in her happiness.

29

July 1815

Eleanor tried to calm herself as much as that was possible before heading back out to the barn. She had watched Katrina go in there after Ichabod and had sent Jacob to go fetch Brom, on the pretense that Caleb needed his assistance fixing a wagon. She knew Brom would challenge Ichabod if he saw him and Katrina together. He had performed admirably. What she had not expected, was her own rage at seeing her daughter throw herself at a man to whom she was not wed, and him taking full advantage of it. When Caleb first brought Ichabod to their home, Eleanor had wanted to believe him when he said that Ichabod was honorable and would not do such a thing, but she had watched him and Katrina for weeks now. She knew how persuasive her daughter could be. Eleanor needed to calm herself enough to face Ichabod now in order to accomplish what she needed for the next part of her plan. Initially reluctant to invoke this part, after witnessing what she just had, she now knew that it was necessary. Even if Brom were to beat him senseless, Ichabod and Katrina would not stop. She needed to guarantee that he would leave there and not come back.

Eleanor took several deep breaths and composed herself before going outside, back to the barn. Walking in, she was not sure what to expect. She had almost hoped that Brom had beaten Ichabod to a pulp, and he would be withering in the corner. Instead, to her surprise, it was Brom she saw curled in a ball on the ground and a bloody Ichabod standing over him.

Ichabod looked up when he heard Eleanor reenter the barn. Katrina was nowhere in sight, which was not a surprise to him. He was furious with her mother for the way she had pulled her by the hair out of the barn, but he understood her rage. He tried to keep his tone as even as possible.

"Where is Katrina?"

"She's safe."

Eleanor looked down at Brom and helped him to his feet. "Come now, Brom. You must stand up and go home. Let your mother tend your wounds."

Eleanor had to almost pull the big man to his feet, struggling to keep her balance as he stumbled more than once. Ichabod was more adept than she had given him credit for. No matter. He would not be adept enough to handle her next challenge. Once she rid herself of the sniveling Brom, she turned her attention back to Ichabod once again.

"I underestimated you," she said as calmly as she could.

"As I did you," he replied, knowing full well that she had been the one to bring Brom there.

She looked him up and down for a moment, taking stock of his injuries. He may have been victorious, but he had not come out of the bout unscathed. In as neutral a voice as she could muster, she said, "Come inside. You need to be tended as well."

Eleanor turned her back on him and began walking back to the house. Ichabod's brows shot up and his eyes went wide. That was the last thing he had expected from this woman. He was prepared for her rage, expecting her to yell at him, scream, accuse him of all manner of things, and throw him out. This calmness, this almost maternal side of her to rear its head was entirely unexpected.

Ichabod stood in shock for a moment, unmoving. Eleanor turned her head back to look at him when she did not hear any movement behind her.

"Are you too injured to walk? Do you need assistance?" she asked with a curt edge to her voice.

"I am well enough, madam."

Ichabod found his feet and warily followed her from the barn, maintaining a distance between them. When they got inside, she pointed at a chair in the kitchen, directing him to sit. She put a kettle of water on the stove, then pulled out a linen cloth and began wiping the blood away from the cuts on his face. Without looking at his eyes, she focused instead on the individual cuts and the blood dripping down his temples, cheeks, lips, and chin. It had fallen onto his clothes, and she marveled that he had none in his eyes. It had been exactly what she needed, however; and she tried not to be giddy at how well this part of her plan had worked.

She worked his injuries quietly for a time. When the first cloth was covered in blood, Eleanor carefully folded it up and placed it inside her apron pocket, then pulled a clean one out from a drawer. Getting that one wet, she started cleaning the wounds more carefully now, adding salve once she got them all sufficiently cleaned. When she finished, she moved back to the stove and busied herself with making tea. Ichabod watched her in silence the entire time, uncertain as to what was happening. Had Eleanor finally come around to him? Did she finally see how much he and Katrina meant to each other? He could not begin to guess at what was happening and did not want to misread the situation, so he remained quiet and let her tend to him. He would wait until she spoke.

When the tea was ready, Eleanor brought two cups over to the table and sat down across from Ichabod. She looked down at her tea while she spoke in a calm, even voice which was more unnerving than had she been yelling.

"I know you and Katrina believe you have feelings for one another, but you have betrayed our trust and taken advantage of my daughter. I shall never allow you to wed."

"Mrs. Brush–"

Eleanor held up a hand to stop him from saying anything further. "You will leave this house. I am a good Christian woman and would not throw you out this late in the day despite what you have done. You shall stay in your room with Jacob tonight and not leave it. Tomorrow morning, you will climb on your horse and leave here. You shall not see or speak to Katrina before you leave. You will never return."

Eleanor lifted her gaze to his now, and her glare could cut glass. "You will not speak of this with Mr. Brush."

Ichabod lifted his chin and met her icy stare. There was nothing but coldness there. He nodded his assent and did not try to dissuade her from her decision. He knew his efforts would be futile. Even if she were in a mood to hear him out, Eleanor would not change her mind. There was nothing more he could do now. Standing from the chair, he went back to the barn to check on his horse one more time. Then he would go back to Jacob's room and pack his things. He would leave the farm at first light as Eleanor wanted.

30

Modern Day

Simon and Isadora spent the next few days at the house, continuing with the inventory and the search for any further information that might be helpful. Simon did some research on the internet, trying to see if anyone else would benefit from Isadora not owning the property. She had called Cory and asked him to look into it as well to see if he could find anything. On Friday, they met with Tamara Petit-Blanc.

"I remembered seeing this when I first got to Sunnyside, but it didn't mean anything then. It still might not, but we can't rule it out. It took me a while to find it again. I couldn't remember exactly where I saw it." She handed Isadora a piece of paper that appeared to have been photocopied from a notebook or journal of some sort.

Isadora read aloud:

Hear me my Hessian hero.
Rise with the moon and serve me once again.
Protect my lineage like you once protected my sister.
Keep those inside my home safe.
Recognize the blood of my blood and protect it always.
Taste the blood of my enemy and destroy it forever.
So mote it be.

At the confused looks on Simon's and Isadora's faces, Tamara explained, "It sounds like a blood curse." When that did not clarify anything, she continued. "Blood magic is the most powerful kind of magic someone can do. It's associated with death and pain, but also with life and passion. People typically use it for protection or health and wellness. There are limits on it, though. When it's used as a curse, it has to follow specific instructions. There's usually a limit on time and distance. If the curse specifically says forever like this one does, then there's likely a limit on the distance it can travel. Though, I'm more convinced than ever that this curse is the cause of your nightmares, Izzy. I believe it's attacking you in your sleep. There may be a limit to the physical distance in which it can reach you, but there's no limit to how far away it can reach into your dreams. It may be possible that it can follow you around the world while you sleep. Which reminds me..."

Tamara reached into her handbag and pulled out a couple of items which she handed to Isadora. A black beaded bracelet and a bundle of some sort of plant with purple flowers rested in her palm. At her questioning stare, Tamara explained, "Fresh hyssop. Put it under your mattress and wear that onyx. They'll protect you."

"Is this more Hoodoo?"

Isadora did not believe the cause of her nightmares was some supposed curse. She knew them to be caused by a very real threat; one which was still unknown. Regardless of the cause, the continued nightmares were starting to grate on her. She was beginning to feel unnerved all the time, as if she was afraid of her own shadow. Every noise and every dark corner had her crawling out of her skin. Even with her doubts about Hoodoo and curses, she would do as Tamara instructed if only to see if it helped.

"Those are," Tamara said, pointing at the plant Isadora was now putting on top of her purse after slipping on the bracelet. "But I don't know what kind of magic the curse is, aside from it being blood magic."

"You said there's a limit to the distance?" Simon asked. Isadora had explained Tamara's history to him and her thoughts on the situation when they talked that first night.

"It's possible the curse only works on the property," she replied. "And where it says, 'rise with the moon' likely means that the Horseman can only come out at night."

"But I've seen him on the road away from the house. He almost came into Hawthorne with us that one night." Isadora saw where Simon was going with the question and added these details.

Tamara thought about this for a minute. "Have you ever seen him outside of Sleepy Hollow?"

Isadora shook her head.

"Maybe he's bound to the village," she offered.

Isadora considered this. Then she immediately questioned *why* she was considering it. She still did not want to believe the possibility that it was anything other than a flesh and blood human.

"I don't understand what this has to do with any of this," she said, holding the paper up and waving it around. "These are notes from Washington Irving. He probably just had an idea for a story and wrote it down. Maybe he was going to put it into the *Legend of Sleepy Hollow* and it didn't make the final cut."

"Maybe," Tamara replied. "But Sugar, it doesn't sound like Irving's work. It doesn't have his style. And did you read the passage below it?" When Isadora shook her head, Tamara continued, "It's a description of a woman, whom he calls Eleanor by the way, lighting candles and performing some sort of ritual with a cloth covered in blood."

Isadora shrugged. "Again, it's probably just notes for the story. It doesn't mean anything."

Tamara pulled out her phone and opened the picture Isadora sent her of the names inside the bible they found. "Look at the names at the top. Caleb and *Eleanor* Brush," she said, emphasizing the name Eleanor. "Below them is Katrina Brush and Abraham Martling, but look at the date, Sugar. 1815. That would have been right before Irving went to Europe. And I'm sure you know as well as I do the significance of Abraham Martling."

Isadora nodded. "Brom Bones."

Tamara echoed while nodding, "Brom Bones."

"I'm not saying the notes are not connected to the story," Isadora argued. "Obviously they are. I'm only saying that we can't make any assumptions that it's an account of an actual event. Or that it has any connection to Ichabod or me or this house. There's never been any evidence that Ichabod was ever in Sleepy Hollow or even met Washington Irving. He would've been fighting in the War of 1812 around this time."

Tamara leaned back in her seat. "No, we can't make any assumptions. But we also can't know for certain that it's not an actual account of something Irving witnessed."

Simon had been listening to the exchange quietly but jumped into the conversation now. "Say that it is an account of an actual event. What does that even mean? Are you saying that the whole story was based on actual facts and a Hessian with no head really rose from the dead to do the bidding of this Eleanor Brush based on some blood magic curse she conjured?"

Isadora had a moment of déjà vu, remembering her student who had asked almost the same question. She could not stop the bark of laughter that erupted from her. Simon joined in her laughter, thinking about the absurdity of it while Tamara turned her mouth down and frowned at them both.

One look at Tamara and Isadora sobered. "I'm sorry," she said. "I had almost this exact conversation with one of my classes right before I came here, and I told them how ridiculous it was. Can you imagine if they could hear this conversation now?" She shook her head. "I'm sorry Tamara. I don't believe in the supernatural. The person I've been seeing is simply a *mortal* being who's trying to scare me from the property. We just need to figure out who it is and why they want me to leave."

Tamara shook her head. "Fine. If you want to pretend these things don't exist, then you do that." She stood and gathered her things. "Don't say I didn't warn you."

"Come on, Tamara. Don't leave. Stay and visit a while." Isadora entwined her arm with her friend's and started guiding her over to a sofa. Tamara set her things back down begrudgingly while Isadora went and grabbed the family bible and the photo album from the kitchen cupboard. "I thought you might be interested in taking a look at these."

∮ ∯

The next morning, Simon and Isadora started their day at the Farmer's Market. They went down to Patriot's Park and strolled through the vendors, purchasing fresh meat, cheese, produce, preserves, and bread, and looking at the various wares on display all while listening to the live music playing nearby. Isadora had been visiting the market each week and some of the vendors remembered her.

"Everyone is so friendly here," Simon commented.

Isadora chuckled. "I thought the same thing. It's been like this since I arrived. It's one more thing I like about this place."

Simon let the comment go. He knew she was considering staying, but he was not yet ready to talk about it. He did not know how to convince her not to.

They took their finds back to the rental, then headed back to the manor to continue the inventory. They had made a great deal of progress and were almost finished. Once they were, they would begin removing the old, peeling wallpaper from each of the rooms before moving onto the next project.

They finished up early that afternoon so they could get cleaned up and head to the Tarrytown Halloween Parade. Isadora had always loved Halloween and under other circumstances, she would have been excited to go see the parade. However, with the threat hanging over her, she was reluctant to go. She had not left her rental after dark since the Horseman first appeared. Tamara and Simon had talked her into going, with Tamara arguing that the parade started on the south edge of the village and continued into Tarrytown, so if the curse had bound the Horseman to the village, she would be safe. Isadora was not convinced. When Simon pointed out that they would be on a crowded street filled with law enforcement and hundreds, possibly thousands, of other people, she had to admit he was likely right. No one would take any chances under those circumstances.

The parade would begin at Patriots Park, then move south on Broadway, and finally turn to go west on Main Street. They arrived early, meeting up with Tamara and walking down the street to find a good location. It was still early but people were already getting into place, finding spots to watch the parade. They made it to the corner of Broadway and Main Street where Isadora saw Alex, looking sharp in his uniform. Cory was standing beside him. She bounced over and said hello, placing a quick peck on Alex's lips. She did not want to do more than that in such a public venue while he was working. He pulled her in close but did not escalate the kiss.

Simon and Tamara went to get seats for dinner at a local restaurant while she visited with Alex. She asked him and Cory if they wanted anything, but they both declined. Heading to the Greek restaurant on the corner, she saw Simon and Tamara already walking away from the door.

"What's wrong? Are we not eating there?" she asked.

"It's over an hour wait," Simon informed her.

"Wow. I figured it would be a long wait, but an hour?"

"We ordered takeout instead," Tamara said. "We can sit here on the curb in front of the restaurant and eat while we wait for the parade to start. It'll be like a picnic."

The trio ended up sitting right in the street while they ate, the sidewalks filling up around them. People crowded in, many wearing costumes. DJs played music from somewhere Isadora could not see. The cool air was starting to feel festive, and Isadora was glad she let them convince her to come. She was still nervous but was trying to stay calm. The sun was starting to get low, and the parade would be starting soon.

As people made their way into any place they could still squeeze, the music changed. The DJ could no longer be heard, and a marching band was beginning to sound in the distance. The excitement was palpable as the parade finally got underway. Isadora stood between Tamara and Simon as they all waited with anticipation. They finally saw the beginning of the parade making its way down the road. At the lead were two police motorcycles. As Isadora leaned forward to see around the people beside them, she saw two riders on horseback following the motorcycles. Her heartrate immediately sped up, but when she saw one of the riders wearing all black with no head visible, she began shaking and her knees went weak.

Simon saw the riders on the horses and immediately looked over at Isadora. She was pale and clutching the metal street barrier in front of her so hard her knuckles were going white. He stepped closer to her side and put his arm around her, his hand on her waist. She startled at his touch, but when she looked up at him, he saw the moment she recognized him through her fog of fear. He tried to keep her focused on him, maintaining eye contact with her.

"It's just a costume," he said. "It's not the same person."

She nodded, but her gaze kept going back to the man on horseback. Her logical brain knew that it was only part of the parade, but the emotional part of her brain kept insisting she was in danger. When the man riding the horse guided it closer to the crowd, she tensed. As the horse reached where they were standing, it suddenly lunged forward. It was so close; she could have reached out and touched it.

Isadora jerked back in fear, trying to get away. It was all she could do not to scream. Simon held her tight and encircled his arms around her, putting himself between her and the parade. She buried her face into his chest. He cursed inwardly that they ever thought this would be a good idea. It had not occurred to him that there would be a Headless Horseman character in the parade, but of course there would be. This was Sleepy Hollow. How could they *not* have the character in their parade?

Simon continued holding Isadora, watching as the horses moved on. He waited until they were fully out of view before whispering to her that they were gone. He did not mind at all if she wanted to stay in his arms; he would be happy to oblige if she did. Isadora made no attempt to leave the comfort of Simon's arms, but she did turn her head, looking out to see for herself that it was safe. She saw Edward Scissorhands, Beetlejuice, and the Witcher walking down the parade route. It took some time, but she slowly began to relax. The Sleepy Hollow Firefighters went by next, with several firefighters on foot and a few vehicles going past. One of the passengers inside an engine truck even had a jack o'lantern on his head. Isadora finally relaxed enough to stand on her own, much to Simon's disappointment at the loss of her touch. He stayed close in case she needed him again.

The parade continued for over an hour with various characters, businesses, clubs or groups, and teams going past them. Several Ghost Riders went past on their motorcycles, followed by a zombie baseball team, cheer teams, dance troupes, aliens and spacemen, zombie school girls, a roller derby team, the *Incredibles* family, several classic hearses, and clowns inside a car decorated with blood. An ambulance went by with its rear doors open, showing a 'dead' patient inside. There were elaborate floats as well, one of which was a replica of a church and a windmill on a trailer created by the Reformed Church of Tarrytown's Old Dutch Church of Sleepy Hollow. Interspersed with it all were marching bands from local schools, academies, or other organizations.

It was thoroughly dark by the time the parade ended and Isadora ended up having a good time, much to her surprise. As they walked back to the car parked a few blocks away, she realized how tired she was. The last several weeks of hard work and not sleeping well were beginning to catch up with her. They arrived at the car, only to see they would not be getting out of their parking spot anytime soon. Isadora sat down on the curb next to the car. Simon and Tamara sat down on either side of her while they all watched the traffic, waiting for it to thin out. It was late and they were all quiet. Isadora enjoyed the relative quiet with only the ambient sounds of the parade-goers leaving. She stared over at the old-fashioned street lamp across the street as the leaves fluttered down from the tree above it. In the light breeze, they danced down around the base of the lamp. The longer she stared, the more she thought she saw the light flickering as if it had still been powered by a flame. She decided it was time to go if her eyes were so tired the lights were beginning to flicker. They piled into the car and tried making their way out of Tarrytown, giving up on the idea of waiting. It took them twenty-five minutes to go three miles in the mass exodus. Despite how tired she was, Isadora was so relieved that she had been able to go out after dark and not have any threats, that she did not even mind the traffic. The day felt like a success.

31

Modern Day

The days had been getting cooler, but Sunday morning after the parade it was downright cold. A storm had moved in sometime overnight and the rain was pouring down. When they got to the manor, Isadora made a fire in the drawing room fireplace before doing anything else. With the sky overcast and cloudy, she was glad to finally have electricity so she could turn the lights on, but they were still waiting on a part for the furnace to get it working. Still, it was nice and quiet without all the contractors and construction going on and she was happy to spend the quiet day working with Simon after sleeping in late, as much as that was possible between nightmares.

Sometime after lunch, Tamara arrived to help as well. They ended up talking and laughing more than they worked, but the trio was on no deadline, and they enjoyed each other's company. When one of Tamara's long fingernails broke, she went to grab a nail file from her purse and paused.

"Oh lordy. I completely forgot. I found this the other day while I was scouring Irving's notes and personal papers again. It's a letter from Brom to Irving." She pulled a paper from her purse and handed it to Isadora. "Of course this is a photocopy." She laughed. "No way would I be carrying the original around in my purse."

Isadora began opening the folded paper when she heard a car pull up outside. She went to the window and saw Alex and Cory pull up in their patrol car. While they came to the door, running to stay dry, she set the letter down on the counter.

"Did everyone have fun at the parade last night?" Cory asked as they came into the room.

Alex greeted Isadora with a kiss, and they all talked about the parade, each sharing their favorite parts or costumes and the quality of the floats.

Finally, Cory got down to business. "We still haven't been able to find anything, Izzy. No one knows of anyone who wants to see you lose the property. I'm sorry. We'll keep looking, though."

Isadora nodded while Simon asked her, "Didn't you say the village was going to declare the property abandoned and take possession of it if you didn't get it fixed up soon?"

"Yes. You think a village official is behind this?"

"I don't know, but couldn't it be possible?" Simon replied. "I mean, what will the village do with it if they take custody? They're not going to keep it. Most likely, they'd sell it, probably at a significantly reduced price from what it's worth."

Cory saw where Simon was going. "If it means someone has inside knowledge of the property possibly being sold for really cheap, I could see that being pretty motivating."

Isadora thought about it for a moment, then shook her head. "That doesn't make sense. If someone wanted the village to take possession of the property, they would be doing more to stop the work, not targeting me, personally. The work would continue even without me. They should be targeting the workers or the equipment if that was the case. This feels more personal."

"Maybe it just seems more personal, because it's your property and you're the one that stands to lose it," Alex suggested dismissively.

They discussed possibilities, trying to brainstorm places to look and where to go with the investigation from there. Unfortunately, they were all coming up empty. After a couple of hours, they realized they were all going around in circles, getting more and more frustrated.

"I think we should call it a night," Isadora finally declared. "I'm exhausted. And you two," she pointed at Alex and Cory, "should probably get back to work before someone realizes you're gone."

Cory looked down at his watch. "Oh shit. I didn't even realize we'd been here so long."

Alex shrugged, "Yeah, but the radios have been on this whole time. No one's called for us, so we're good."

They all stood to leave, the women grabbing their purses and Simon dousing the fire. They walked out of the house together. As soon as Isadora looked outside, she saw that the rain had stopped but the darkness immediately filled her with dread. Her heart started pounding. She tried to calm herself down by reasoning that they had been inside the house this long and nothing had happened, so they must be fine. Reasoning did not stop her hands from shaking.

Once outside, the air turned heavy, and they could all feel the malice heading toward them. As they headed down the porch steps to their respective cars, they heard it and turned at the sound of a horse barreling down on them. It was the largest horse any of them had ever seen. Atop the black horse sat a man in all black with no head on his shoulders. The image seemed to draw all of the warmth from the air, only to be expelled from the horse's nostrils in a swirling ribbon of steam.

Cory and Alex were immediately on alert and Cory used his radio to call in a disturbance to dispatch. They stood at the ready and as soon as the Horseman was in range, they both began ordering him to stop. The rider ignored the orders as if they had not even spoken, going right past them toward Isadora. Her eyes became large saucers in her head as she realized he was coming directly for her. Time slowed and the blood rushed to her ears, drowning out all sound. His arm was raised and in his fist a gleaming sword was at the ready. The officers both drew their service weapons and ordered him to stop again. He did not stop.

As he was almost upon Isadora, they opened fire upon the man atop the horse. They both hit their target multiple times, causing the body to jerk.

"Shots fired," Alex yelled into his radio along with his call sign and the address. "Send backup."

They all watched, waiting for the body to fall off the horse, but it never did. Instead, there was a slight pause where it slowed, but then it picked up speed again. It straightened in the saddle, turned, and sped toward Isadora once again.

"He must be wearing body armor," Alex suggested.

Simon pulled Isadora back towards the porch. Tamara was right behind them. He was going to take her inside the house, but the door was locked.

"Where are the keys?" he yelled.

"I don't know. I think I dropped them," Isadora replied.

They looked back to where they had been standing near the cars and Simon spotted them. "Stay here," he ordered as he ran back down the steps to retrieve them. Tamara and Isadora huddled together, watching the scene play out in front of them.

Alex and Cory were trying to keep the rider occupied until their backup arrived. To their surprise, he was completely ignoring them, even though they were the threat. He seemed to be single-mindedly focused on Isadora.

As the rider raised his sword again, charging towards the porch, the officers opened fire yet again, this time trying to target his limbs or the horse. As much as they did not want to put the large animal down, they knew it might be the only way to stop the duo. Several of the bullets impacted the horse, causing it to slow to a stop. It stood, black goo oozing from the holes, and it shook its head as if shaking off an annoying fly. Alex and Cory ran forward, trying to get between the rider and the porch, each taking a side of the horse.

"Drop the sword," Alex screamed.

The horse danced in a circle at the foot of the porch. It seemed as though the rider was watching Isadora, even though he had no head. Isadora kept telling herself it was just a costume. His head was merely tucked inside his shirt.

The enormous black horse suddenly reared up on his hind legs, letting out a whinny and snorting breaths of air that looked like he was exhaling smoke. Alex and Cory tried to grab at the horse's reins and the rider spun the beast to prevent them from gaining control of the reins. Alex was now within range of the rider who brought his sword down, slashing Alex across the neck and chest with a spray of blood that reached Isadora on the porch only feet away.

"NOOO!" Isadora screamed in terror.

Tamara tried to hold her back but Isadora pulled out of her reach and ran to get to Alex as he fell to the ground at the bottom of the steps. Isadora sat on the bottom step, cradling him in her arms as a deep red liquid pooled and immediately began to flow down his uniform. Tears streaked down her face as the life bled out of him.

Cory opened fire again from the other side of the horse, hitting the rider repeatedly in the upper thigh and belly. Again, his shots did not appear to be effective.

With everyone intently focused on the rider and his horse, they did not hear Simon starting the car. He drove it forward, yelling at Cory to move out of the way. He sped up as fast as he could in the small space until the car made contact with the horse. It went down, taking the rider to the ground with it and Simon yelled for Isadora to get in. He had stopped with the passenger door right in front of the steps and Tamara grabbed her arm, forcefully pulling Isadora away from Alex's lifeless body. Despite the threat waiting for her, she was not yet ready to leave Alex behind.

Tamara shoved her into the car and closed the door then turned around and went back up the steps. Simon yelled at her to get in.

"He's not after me. Just go. I'll be fine."

Simon hesitated, but when the horse stood again, the rider climbed back into the saddle and turned towards the car. Simon stepped on the gas hard, lunging them forward down the muddy private lane that led to the street. The Horseman followed. They heard sirens in the distance as Simon pulled the car onto the street with a squeal and sped away. The horse continued to follow, keeping up with them for a couple of miles, but when they reached the edge of Hawthorne, the entity disappeared in a flash of fire.

32

July 1815

Ichabod kept his word and left the farm the next morning. He had not seen nor spoken to Katrina, nor had he tried. After seeing to his horse, he spent the remainder of the night in his room. He said a brief goodbye to both Jacob and Caleb in the morning before setting out.

They were confused as to his hasty departure and his injuries, but he did not explain either other than to say, "I've stayed far too long. I must be getting back to my post. Thank you for your hospitality and your generosity."

"Did you not wish to say goodbye to Katrina. She's not yet come down from her room but I'm sure she'll be along soon. I know you two have become amiable during your stay. I dare say the girl has even grown fond of you," Caleb chuckled.

Ichabod wanted to laugh at the irony of Caleb's words, but he kept silent. He did not need to look at

Eleanor to know the icy stare she was throwing his way, daring him to anger her by speaking out of turn. He was not afraid of her wrath for himself but had already decided not to make the situation any worse for Katrina.

Instead, he simply said, "Please give her my regards. Tell her I was sorry to have missed her."

Katrina watched from her window as Ichabod walked his horse out of the barn, speaking with her father and brother. It looked as though all of his things were packed and loaded onto the horse. After shaking hands with her father and brother, he mounted his horse, riding away from the farmhouse without sparing a backward glance. Katrina wanted to open the window and scream at him to stop, but she knew that would only further enrage her mother. Instead, she threw her fists against the window and screamed as tears streamed down her cheeks. How could he simply leave her? And he left without a word; no goodbye; no anything. What had happened in the barn after her mother pulled her away? Katrina leaned her forehead against the window, crying as her heart broke in two.

33

Modern Day

Isadora sat on the sofa in her rental, covered in Alex's blood. She sobbed while Simon held her, stroking her hair. It did not take long before Tamara was there, with police officers right behind her. Tamara informed her that the Horseman never came back after he followed them down the lane. The officers separated them all to question them individually.

"How's Alex?" Isadora asked the first officer that had arrived. "Is he at the hospital? Can I go see him?"

She knew the answers to her questions before she asked, but denial filled her. She would not believe it until she heard the words from someone else's mouth. It did not take long to get confirmation.

"I'm sorry, Miss Crane," the officer said. "Alex did not make it. He was killed in the… confrontation."

The officer had paused, unsure what to call the incident. None of them seemed to believe the story, but with Cory as a witness, it was harder to ignore.

The police finally left, but Tamara stayed. "Is there anything I can do, Sugar?"

Isadora shook her aching head. She had been crying for hours and her head was pounding, but the rest of her felt numb.

Tamara nodded. Simon changed the sheets on the bed in his room for Tamara to stay the night. None of them wanted to be alone. He took Isadora into the bathroom, stripped her blood-soaked clothes off of her, and set her into the shower in her bra and panties. She undressed the rest of the way from there and let the water spray over her. Sitting at the bottom of the tub, she watched the red water pool around her until it finally ran clear. If it had not been for Simon taking charge, she did not know what she would have done. Showering off all the blood had never even crossed her mind. She felt incapable of making any decisions. When the water ran cold, she finally turned it off and she heard the door open again slowly after a soft knock announcing Simon's presence. He handed her a towel through the curtain.

"I put some clean pajamas on the counter. Can you dress or do you need help?"

She wanted to laugh at how absurd it sounded that she might be incapable of something as simple as dressing herself, but there was no humor in it. Unfortunately, it was an entirely accurate description of how she felt.

Wanted to ask him to help her, she resisted the urge and instead, she said, "I can manage." Her voice was small and weak, and she did not recognize it.

Simon left her to dress and when she came out, Tamara had already gone to bed. Simon led Isadora down the hall to her bedroom and put her to bed. He went out and shut off all the lights in the rest of the house, leaving only the hallway light on. It was for the benefit of them all. He did not want Tamara to wake to the darkness any more than he wanted Isadora to. Climbing into bed next to her, he pulled Isadora close, much as he had when she had woken from her nightmare all those nights ago. He had not bothered with the nightlight app on his phone this time, instead leaving the overhead light on. Isadora needed the extra security tonight. He held her tightly for hours, neither of them really sleeping until they both finally passed out from exhaustion in the early hours of the morning.

℥   ℤ

"I'm going to take Izzy to Brooklyn for a few days," Simon informed Tamara in the morning while Isadora brushed her teeth and hair. "My family is there, and she needs to get away from here."

Tamara nodded. "That's probably a good idea. I'll call my mom and my aunties and see what they recommend."

"Your mom and your aunties?" Simon asked in confusion.

Tamara took a sip of her coffee. "Mm-hmm. They know their way around blood magic."

"Who knows their way around blood magic?" Isadora asked as she came into the kitchen.

"My mom and her sisters."

"I thought you said you only do rootwork?" Isadora asked.

"You really think magic is the answer here?" Simon asked in frustration. He wanted real answers, not make-believe.

"If anyone will know how to stop this thing, they will. I've been doing divination in an attempt to see the circumstances surrounding the original curse, but I've not had much luck. I believe that's because the original curse was not performed using Hoodoo magic. Sometimes, there's a barrier between different types of magic that can be difficult to cross. But until we know the circumstances, we can't know the correct way to break the curse. My mom and her sisters may be able to point me in the right direction."

Simon was skeptical. "I can't believe this is what we're talking about."

Tamara's hand went to her hip as she cocked her head. "You saw that thing, Chil'. It took every bullet Alex and Cory fired at him, and so did the horse. None of the bullets did anything to stop it."

"Because the guy was obviously wearing body armor," he shrugged.

"No sir," she snapped. "I saw it up close while you were trying to get the car. That horse took as many hits as the rider did. The only thing those bullets did was cause a black goo to seep out. Even if the rider was wearing body armor, the horse wasn't. No mortal horse would have survived those shots. And the rider took several bullets in the thigh with the same result. Not a one of those bullets slowed either creature down."

Tamara pulled out her phone then, opening up an app. She handed the phone to Isadora who leaned in to share it with Simon. It displayed an image of the headless rider with black sludge running down his leg. Isadora immediately pushed the phone into Simon's hands and moved away, filling up a cup with coffee.

She did not even want to be that close to an image of the Horseman.

"I'm still not convinced there's anything supernatural going on here," Simon reiterated.

"How do you explain what happened then," Tamara challenged. When Simon did not respond, she continued, "That's what I thought. Until we know otherwise, I'm working under the assumption that Washington Irving got his story from something that really happened. And that something involves a curse that Eleanor Brush placed on Ichabod Crane. I come from a long line of Hoodoo practitioners. If they can't help us, ain't no one who can."

"Thank you, Tamara. I appreciate you looking into it," Isadora said in an attempt to stop any further arguments from Simon.

He looked at her questioningly, but she shook her head slightly. She had been quiet this morning, not adding much to the conversation. When she did, she sounded hollow. He knew she was hurting and he wanted to take it away for her, but he knew he could not.

Tamara went home and Simon and Isadora headed down to Brooklyn. Isadora leaned her head back on the headrest, looking out the window while Simon drove.

"Why did you encourage Tamara to pursue this blood magic idea of hers?" he asked.

"It can't hurt. And I'm sorry, but she was right. Bullets did nothing to stop that thing. We have to try something. The alternative is for me to leave here and never come back. And as tempting as that is right now, it doesn't bring justice to Alex. Not to mention it probably won't do anything to stop my nightmares. And what if I ever have kids? They'll never be able to set foot in this town. Who knows how many more people will suffer or die if we don't stop this thing?"

Isadora's voice cracked as she said Alex's name. She had lain awake most of the night reliving the events of the past few weeks. At first, she kept replaying the night over and over again. Eventually, she started thinking only about Alex and she replayed every moment they had spent together. She had thought about how they met, then their first date and how it felt when he had kissed her that first time. She remembered the conversations and the way he prowled towards her on the floor in the drawing room, as if they were the only people in the world despite being surrounded by boxes and people. He had made her laugh and she had cared about him. Now he was gone. Just like everyone else in her life. And this time, it was her fault.

When the tears had come, she rolled over off of Simon's chest, curling into a ball. He had rolled over immediately, curling around her. She knew that it was obvious she was crying, but he had not tried to get her to stop. Instead, he held her while she cried. Something inside her kept telling her that she should not get used to his comforting touch, because it would not last. Eventually, he would leave her, too. Even if it was not his choice, something else would pull him away from her. Now she had this creature after her and she did not want to put Simon in the Horseman's path. She let him comfort her last night, but it was better if there was some distance between them. He would be safer without her. Isadora had eventually come to reconcile herself with the prospect that everything would be better if she were on her own.

When Simon told her that morning that he was taking her to Brooklyn, she did not argue. She would spend the next few days with him, knowing they were the last they would have together. As she thought about it now, the tears started sliding down her cheek. Isadora had thought she was all cried out after last night, yet there she was with more. She kept her head turned toward the window until the tears finally stopped.

℘   ℘

Simon's mother was an emergency room nurse and was about to head into work when they arrived. Simon had told her he would be in the area and was initially going to stay with her, but then Isadora had invited him to stay with her and there was no way he was turning that down. He had kept his mother informed of the change, letting her know he would come see her when he could. Things had gotten away from him, and he was regretful that he had not come to see her yet. She did not hold it against him and was happy that he was there now. She pulled them both in for hugs, making a fuss over them when they finally arrived.

"Is everything alright?" she asked when they finally sat at the table for a few minutes.

Laura Diego had pulled out a bunch of items for brunch, even though they had tried eating before leaving Hawthorne an hour ago. Neither had much appetite either time and they ended up putting most of the food away, untouched. Laura could see the wariness in both sets of eyes in front of her.

"Everything's fine, mom," Simon said while squeezing her hand. He did not want to worry her.

Laura did not believe her son for a minute, but she nodded and let it go. They visited for a while longer before she finally had to leave for work.

Simon showed Isadora around the small apartment, putting their bags into the spare bedroom. When he saw her standing still, looking at the only bed in the room, he said, "You can have the bed. I can make up the couch."

Despite having shared a bed before, it had always been her choice and he would have left any of those times if she had told him to. He did not want to presume anything. Disappointment flooded him when she nodded.

They stayed in, Isadora not wanting to go out anywhere. She was quiet all day, but Simon left her to her thoughts. Needing time to mourn, he did not push her, instead trying to be there for her. His heart broke for her.

He immediately knew where her mind had gone; this was simply more proof for her that people always left. She probably even thought it was her fault. Simon wanted to take away all of her pain and the guilt he knew she felt. Simon may not have liked Alex, but he had not deserved what had happened to him. If it meant saving Isadora from this pain, he would bring Alex back in a heartbeat. He did what he could to take care of her and started dinner when his mother texted to say she was on her way home.

"We had a bad traffic accident come in today," Laura began. "The cops escorted the drivers into the emergency room, but while they waited, they were talking about that cop who was killed last night up there in Tarrytown." When no one responded, she continued, "Sounds like it was close to where you two were staying. Did you see or hear anything about it?"

Laura did not miss anything. She knew something had happened to her son and Isadora, but neither was talking about it. Judging by the state Isadora was in, it had been something truly awful. She was not certain she wanted to know, but how could she not try to find out? If she could share the burden with her son, she would.

Isadora set her fork down, suddenly unable to eat. She still had not had much of an appetite to begin with, but she knew she needed to eat and had been making an effort to do so. Now, the thought of it made her throat close up and her stomach churn.

"We –" Simon began, but Isadora cut him off.

"He and I were dating," she said.

Laura gasped. "Oh my."

She looked between the two and Isadora turned her gaze away. Unable to sit still, Isadora stood and left the room. Laura watched her go, then turned to Simon with surprise in her eyes. His own fork clattered onto his plate, and he scrubbed a hand over his face.

He had considered following her, briefly, but knew she needed some space.

"That's horrible, Simon. I can't even imagine what that poor girl is going through. Is that why you came here, now?"

"She needed to get away from it for a few days."

"I'm so sorry. You both stay as long as you need to."

Laura took her son's hand in hers. Simon and his mother had always had a good relationship. Because she came to Utah to visit as often as she could, she had met Isadora years before and had spent a lot of time with her over the years.

They ate in silence for a while. When Simon stood to clear the dishes, Laura asked, "So why have you never laid a claim on that girl?"

"We've always just been friends, mom. You know that."

"What I know is that you love her. Why do you keep sitting back on the sidelines, watching her date these other men that never work out. I'm sorry to hear that her latest boyfriend has met with such a horrible end, but if she had been with you, maybe she could have avoided this heartbreak."

"Mom," he warned. Then he sighed. "She doesn't want me."

He carried the dishes to the sink and began rinsing them before putting them in the dishwasher.

"Nonsense. I've seen the way she looks at you. She's always had stars in her eyes when you're around. Now, I've sat back all these years and kept my mouth shut, waiting for you to figure things out on your own, but none of us are getting any younger. And that girl is in desperate need of a family to care for her."

"I'm working on it. Now isn't the right time."

Laura stood, moved to the counter, and placed a hand on her son's shoulder. "It never is. Before you know it, there's no time left."

Simon turned to face her. "I know." He pulled her in for a hug. "Thanks for being family to her."

He knew his mother had always thought they would end up together. It had annoyed him at first, but eventually, he came to hope that she may be right. Despite it taking him years, she had seen it the first time she met Isadora and had welcomed her with open arms. She had always treated Isadora as if she was part of their family and he loved her for it.

34

July 1815

Ichabod made it into the middle of town, back to the tavern he had visited the first night of his arrival. He spent the morning there, waiting and writing a letter. He would have to go back to the Van Tassel farm and hope he could get to Rebecca and convince her to deliver it for him. Eleanor would be meeting with some of the other women in town later and he would wait to go until she was away from the farm. Though he was not going to their farm, he did not want to take the chance of running into her. So, he continued to wait.

After a couple of hours, Ichabod was surprised to see Washington walk through the door. He was with a couple of men that Ichabod did not recognize, but when Washington saw him, he immediately made his way over to him.

"You look a fright, Major Crane. What happened?"

"I shook up a bag of bones," he replied, recalling that Brom's friends had always called him 'Brom Bones.'

Washington nodded. "You'll likely be pleased to know then, that the bag of bones appears to have fared much worse as it has been unable to be pulled from bed this morning."

It was Ichabod's turn to nod. He did not take delight in the other man's injuries, but he was pleased to hear that Brom would not be in any condition to retaliate today. He was not sure he was ready for a second round with the big man that soon.

"I'm not sure what happened last night, my friend. No one is talking and it seems only you and Brom know the details; you and possibly Mrs. Brush."

Ichabod had kept his gaze down at the table and the drink in front of him. At the mention of Mrs. Brush and the question in Washington's words, he raised his eyes to meet Washington's.

"What did she say?"

"She's not said anything. In truth, I've not even seen her today. But I did see something rather strange last night. She was outside, in the dead of night, performing what I could only describe as some sort of ritual. I could only just see her from my window. I had been up writing and when I finally decided to turn in, I took a last glance out the window and saw several small flames. Upon closer inspection, I could barely make out a woman's form. Had it not been a full moon, I would not have been able to see that much. I knew it had to be either her or Katrina and went outside to render assistance. I cannot begin to describe what I saw, but I am certain whatever evil she was conjuring, it was likely directed towards you. She was right angry."

Ichabod scoffed. "I do not believe in rituals and spells. She can conjure any evil she wishes; it shall not deter me from my path."

"No. I'm sure it was all childish nonsense but do have a care my friend. It seems you have severely crossed her. You might consider taking your leave of this place soon."

Ichabod took a drink from his glass as the tavern keeper came over to take Washington's order. When he left, Ichabod said, "I am leaving. I'll be departing in the morning. I have a little unfinished business to attend first." After a moment's thought, he pulled the letter in front of him. "In fact, I wonder if you might help me with it?"

Washington was hesitant. He held up his hands as if in surrender. "I do not wish to get between you and Mrs. Brush."

"It is nothing like that. I only need this letter delivered to Katrina. Would you take it back with you and ask Rebecca to deliver it for me? I did not get a chance to say goodbye to her before I left, and I have written it down instead. Would you see to it that she gets it tonight?"

"If you're not leaving until the morn, why not say goodbye in person? I thought you had feelings for her? How could you simply abandon her?"

Ichabod almost laughed at the simplicity of the description. It was a vast understatement of how he felt. "I find myself unwelcome at the Brush home this morning. This is why I am sitting in a tavern, licking my wounds rather than beginning my journey. But I am not abandoning her. Please, Mr. Irving, I can't leave until I know this letter has been delivered. I shall leave as soon as I know it is. I give my word."

Washington sighed, shaking his head and holding out his hand. "I shall make sure it is delivered."

"Thank you. Please make sure Mrs. Brush does not know of it. You must be discreet. As must Rebecca."

"You have my word."

છ ৫

Katrina's mother had kept her locked in her room all day, only opening the door to bring her food, then promptly locking it behind her. She had tried asking her how long she was to stay in there, but her mother did not say one word to her. Katrina had become a prisoner in her own bedroom.

Surprise and anticipation filled Katrina when she thought she heard someone approach her door not an hour after having a meal delivered. When it became apparent that the noise was in fact at her door, she rushed over, thinking her mother had come and would maybe release her this time. Instead, she heard soft footsteps receding down the hall and when she looked down, she saw a folded piece of paper on the floor. She bent to pick it up and when she turned it over, she saw a seal on the other side. Who would be writing her a letter? Could it be from Ichabod?

Taking the letter over to her bed, Katrina sat down and excitedly opened it. Scanning the page, she quickly saw that it was, indeed, from her beloved. He apologized for leaving without being able to say goodbye, but then he said that he had not yet left town, only the farmhouse. He would wait for her. If she could get away that night, he would wait for her in their clearing by the stream and he would take her with him. Ichabod apologized for having to flee in this manner, but he did not wish to see any harm come to her from her mother. He said he could only wait until morning, but if she did not come by sunrise, he would leave her in peace. He would understand her not wanting to leave her home and he would wish her well.

Tears fell from her eyes as Katrina clutched the letter to her breast. She was overjoyed to know he had not left her. He still wanted her to leave with him. They would flee tonight and figure everything else out later. The important thing now was getting away. Her eyes immediately went to the locked door. She stood up and tried the handle once again, knowing it would still be locked, but needing to try anyway. Katrina went over to her window and looked out. Opening it as far as it would go, she stuck her head out, leaning out as far as she could. Her room was over the front porch, and she could easily climb out onto the porch roof, but how would she get down to the ground from there? She thought about the columns holding up the corners of the porch roof and considered sliding down them but was not sure how she could do that. They were tucked under the roof by at least two feet. Would she be able to reach them? She supposed she could always try hanging as low as she could from the roof, then letting herself drop. It would be several feet, but surely it was not enough to break anything?

While she pondered her escape, Katrina began to throw a few personal items into a sack. She would not be able to take much, but she did not need much. As long as she had Ichabod, the rest could be replaced. Though she would miss her brother and father terribly, she hoped in time she would be able to come back and visit. It would be difficult to leave without saying goodbye. Trying not to think about that, she instead focused on the task ahead of her. Moving quietly around the room, she tried not to draw attention to herself. The last thing she wanted was for her mother to come investigate. With the bag full, she stuffed it inside her wardrobe and waited. It was best if she did not try to leave until well after the rest of the household was asleep. This was going to be the longest night of her life.

35

Modern Day

The days seemed to drag on. The rain continued, matching Isadora's gloomy emotional state. Simon tried to give her the time and space that she needed, but she seemed to be walking around in a daze. He understood and tried to be patient, but he also felt her pulling away from him. Her walls had gone up and there was a distance between them that had never been there before. Her lack of sleep was not helping matters. Simon's brother and sister came to visit while they were there. Unlike Simon, they had both stayed nearby, with his sister still in Brooklyn and his brother in Queens.

Simon watched Isadora every minute. She went through the motions with his siblings, but the laughter never filled her eyes when she did laugh and she only responded to conversation, never initiating or contributing more than was necessary to be polite. He hated that the first time they met her was under these circumstances, but when he told them about Alex, they understood. He never talked about what had happened that night or the fact that they had been there. His mother did not need to know that.

An email came in from Annette but Isadora did not want to open the attachment. It was her report on the items she had appraised in the house. Isadora did not care what any of it was worth. Her ownership of it all had cost a good man his life. She could not bring herself to look at it.

After two days staying in, Simon took Isadora out. The rain had finally ceased, and he knew that she had never been to New York City before. They drove around, seeing the city without doing touristy things. He knew she was not up for that. They rode the Staten Island Ferry and the one to Governor's Island, then rode each of them back, if only for the sake of being on the water. Isadora had always loved the water and became recharged when she spent time near it, so he tried to find things to do that kept them as close to the water as they could get. It seemed to work as she slowly started coming out of herself a little bit. She was still reserved, but she was no longer walking around like a zombie.

Isadora had ignored the email from Annette for a couple of days, but eventually, her curiosity got the better of her. If she knew, she could at least decide what to do with it all. Opening the report, she saw that Annette had separated everything into categories and listed them all individually. Each piece had a write-up describing the item including the approximate date or era from which it came and the estimated value of it beside a photo of the item. The furniture was listed first, then artwork, followed by smaller pieces. Light fixtures, clocks, urns, plates, vases, statues, figurines, books, and other trinkets were listed last. She had even included many of the pieces from Isadora's photo inventory with the caveat that the items were only an approximate guess as they had not been seen in person.

Isadora flipped through the enormous volume. Annette must not have worked on anything else for days to get it done. She glanced through it, looking at individual pieces as they caught her eye. There was little information on her ring as Annette had recommend she take it to a jeweler. However, it did say that it was likely from the late 1700s. On the last page, an item stood out from the rest. The button Isadora had mentioned was listed in the report beside one of the photos she had provided for it. She had been curious about the piece and the write-up on it said that it had come from a Hessian soldier's uniform, dating back to the Revolutionary War.

Isadora set her phone down, taking in the information. It was one more thing that was too close to the story to be a coincidence. But what did it mean? Where did it come from? Did someone collect it years after the story was written in an attempt to claim it had belonged to the headless Hessian in the story? The Hessians were brought in as mercenaries for the British during the war. Thousands of them would have roamed this valley. Likely, someone found a button in an antique store or buried in their yard, learned that it was Hessian from the period of the war and kept it in an attempt to fool people. Though, she had found it with the ring. They had been kept together in the pouch with the initials 'EB' on the outside and both were from the same era. Could 'EB' have been Eleanor Brush? There were no other names with those initials in the family bible she had found. Did the ring belong to her once as well? Was she the one who had been fascinated by the story or even helped Irving with the ideas to write it?

Isadora thought about that last one for a moment. There had been no birth or death dates beside her name, but it had looked as if she was the mother to a Katrina Brush, the woman who married Abraham Martling in 1815. If she was Katrina's mother, it was possible that she had been alive when the story was published. Katrina had still been young then, only married for five years. Perhaps Eleanor had found the button as a child during the war and kept it as a souvenir? The items had been buried deep. It all sounded reasonable enough, but then Isadora reminded herself that the house had belonged to one of *her* relations. That meant Ichabod's family; not Eleanor and Katrina. Thinking back to the names on her genealogy chart, she was certain there were none that went by the initials 'EB.' Once again, she was at a dead end. She gave up trying to puzzle it out and decided to put it aside for another time.

On Wednesday night, Isadora heard from Tamara. Her mother and aunts had a lot to say about their situation and she was certain she could do something to lift the curse and rid Isadora of the Horseman. Isadora agreed to give it a try, if only in an attempt to stave off the nightmares. After hanging up with Tamara, she informed Simon that she wanted to go back. They agreed to stay one more day and leave Friday morning.

For their last day in the city, Simon had bought tickets for a schooner that sailed around the harbor. Isadora sat on the edge of the boat with her eyes closed, enjoying the cold wind and the spray of water hitting her face. The chill cut her to the bone, but it was exactly what she needed. She wanted to feel something other than the emotional pain with which she was consumed.

By the time they disembarked, a small smile was starting to grow on Isadora's face. It warmed Simon to see it. They went to Central Park afterwards where they walked amongst the trees and sat on a bench near one of the ponds.

"Thank you for this."

"I'm happy to do it," he smiled.

Isadora put her head on Simon's shoulder, and he put his arm over hers. She wanted to enjoy these last days with him. Once they got back to Sleepy Hollow, she would tell him he should go home. She would stay there, at least long enough to finish the house, then she would sell it and move somewhere new; somewhere she could get a fresh start by herself. Knowing she would be lonely, she tried to take in every moment she had with Simon now.

They sat on the bench for some time, then as if on the same page, they looked at each other and both stood, ready to go. They started to leave, but then Simon stopped. He reached for her hand, stopping her as well. When she turned to face him, he pulled her in close. Sliding a hand along her jaw, he searched her face. Then, he leaned in and kissed her. It was soft and hesitant at first as he gave her an opportunity to push him away. When she did not, he deepened the kiss. She melted into it, her hands going up around his neck, running her fingers through his long dark hair.

Isadora pulled back, finally breaking the kiss. She looked at him, memorizing every detail of this moment, then she stepped out of the warmth of his arms. Her eyes down, she turned around and began walking away.

"Izzy?" he called after her.

Simon was confused. She had welcomed his kiss; he had not imagined that. But now, she was turning away again. Her pace had picked up and she was looking down at the ground. He caught up to her easily, putting a hand on her shoulder. Gently stopping her, he turned her to face him. She continued looking away, but he could see the tears she was fighting to hold back.

"What's wrong? Are you upset with me?"

Simon searched her face, trying to discern what she was thinking or feeling, but there was so much going on behind her eyes, he could not interpret it. This was not a good sign. He looked away a moment, his hand scrubbing his face as he collected himself. She still had not spoken.

"Iz, say something. Tell me what you're thinking."

Still looking away, she shook her head. "I don't know what to say." She finally turned to look at him.

"Where did that come from? I don't want your pity, Simon."

He scoffed. "That was anything but pity." He put his hands on her arms, rubbing them. "I'm sorry. I know my timing sucks, but our timing never seems to be right. I can't hold back any longer. I love you, Izzy. I always have."

She put a hand on his jaw and gave him a sad smile. "I love you, too, Simon. You're the best friend I've ever had."

He dropped his hands and turned away again. "Damnit, Iz. That's not what I meant." He turned back to face her, desperation, longing, and a little sadness in his eyes. "I meant that I'm *in* love with you. I've been in love with you for a very long time."

Isadora's heart broke and the tears she had been fighting back fell from her eyes. It was everything she had always wanted to hear. Yet, she could not let herself enjoy it. Not now. Love did not last. It inevitably ended and if they went down that path, it would end for them, too. She would only put him in danger and get him killed, too. If not, then he would eventually leave her some other way. Everyone in her life had left her, either willingly or through death. If he somehow managed to survive her, he would eventually just leave.

When she remained quiet, he said, "I thought... Tell me you've never thought about us."

Still, she did not answer. Isadora focused her gaze on a tree in the distance, using it to try to keep from breaking down and telling him that she felt the same way. She did not trust herself to speak, so she remained quiet.

"Say something," he demanded. "Do you feel the same way? Tell me we can make this work."

She shook her head. "I don't want to lose you," she finally said on a whisper.

His brow furrowed. "Why would you lose me? I'm not trying to stop being your friend, Iz. I'm letting you know I want more."

Isadora grabbed onto his mention of their friendship and looked at him. "But if it doesn't work out, then I not only lose a boyfriend, I lose my best friend. I can't lose that, Simon. I can't lose you." She forced the words out, knowing she was already going to lose him.

"Who says it wouldn't work out? You haven't even given it a chance." His voice was starting to rise a little.

"It never works out. People always leave. One way or another." She looked away again.

"Not everyone leaves, Izzy." Simon threw his hands up. "It never works out because you always chase guys who don't see you or who don't value you. You choose guys like Alex who treat you like a piece of meat. I'm sorry. I know you're still mourning him, but it doesn't make it any less true. He thought you were a possession that he could own."

Isadora looked at Simon incredulously, but he was not finished. "You know, I never understood it before, but I get it now. You choose guys who treat you like that, so you don't have to let them in. Because if you don't let anyone in, you won't get hurt."

"That's not fair. I let people in." She hated how well he knew her.

"Who? Who have you let in since your grandmother passed?"

In a small voice, she said, "I let you in."

He scoffed. "You only let me in the door, Izzy. You barred me from going any further."

Isadora's arms went around her middle protectively. She had always told herself they were never more than friends because *he* was not interested. Now he was the one pushing for more and she was the one putting on the brakes. There was a time when she would have jumped at the chance to be with him. Was he right? Was she incapable of letting anyone in? Was it not better to keep everyone out? Her eyes wet, she looked away while trying to keep the tears from worsening.

He had never seen her look so vulnerable. Simon sighed and shook his head. Wanting to be angry, he reminded himself she was still in pain. Rubbing his eyes, he pinched the bridge of his nose in an attempt to rein in his emotions. He hated seeing her like this but hated even more that he was the reason for it. He should not have pushed her the way he did. Simon pulled her into his arms for a tight embrace.

Kissing the top of her head, he said softly, "Forget it, Iz. If you don't want me that way, I understand. I don't want to lose your friendship, either. Forget I said anything."

He did not want her to forget anything. Simon wanted to make her understand, make her see how good they would be together. But it obviously was not what she wanted. If he had to settle for her friendship over nothing at all, he would take her friendship. He only hoped he had not just screwed that up beyond repair.

Isadora let him hold her for a minute. It felt so right. Why could she not forget about the danger and let him love her? Surely he was strong enough to survive it. And maybe he would leave, but maybe they could have a few years together first. Was that worth the heartache and pain that would come when he finally did leave? She enjoyed the feel of his strong hands rubbing her back and the comfort of his presence. She took in his spicy scent and wanted to lose herself in him. Why could she not take their relationship further? Of all the men she had ever known, Simon had scared her the most. He was the one person who stood the biggest chance of breaking her heart. If he left her, she would never recover from it. She had to make sure he never had that chance.

"Let's just go home," she said in a small voice.

Isadora had no idea what that simple statement did to him. The idea of home was nothing without her in it. Simon wanted to tell her that she was his home. Instead, he put an arm around her shoulder and walked her out of the park.

36

July 1815

Ichabod was impatient as he waited for Washington to return with word that the letter had been delivered. When he finally returned, he had insisted that not only had it been delivered, but Eleanor had been none the wiser. Ichabod smiled with relief and thanked his friend.

Washington held out his hand. "I wish you safe travels, Ichabod. Godspeed."

They shook hands, Ichabod taking both of Washington's into his. "Thank you, sir. To you as well. Enjoy your time in Europe."

Washington was leaving in the coming days himself to begin his time exploring Europe and work with his brothers. He would not be in Tarrytown much longer.

As the sky began to darken, Ichabod made his way toward the clearing in the forest. He did not expect Katrina to meet him so early, but he had nowhere else to be and he preferred to wait there rather than anywhere else. He had no idea if she would even come. Washington had assured him that the letter had been delivered, but he had not wanted to risk anyone else knowing their plan or being caught up any further than they already had been. Therefore, Ichabod had not instructed Washington to await a reply. He would have to wait and see what Katrina had decided. While he knew that this was originally her idea, he was not certain it was what Katrina truly wanted. It was one thing to desire to leave home, but doing it was something entirely different.

Ichabod settled in, tethering his horse to a nearby tree and making her as comfortable as possible. He found a spot to sit and leaned against a tree while he waited. Having pulled a book from his saddlebags, he tried reading but could not focus. He found himself reading the same paragraphs over and over again. Finally, he gave up and set the book down. It was futile anyways as it was beginning to get too dark to see the words on the pages. The moon provided a lot of extra light, but not enough by which to read. He did not wish to light a fire, so he leaned into the tree and watched the water in the stream rushing by.

As he sat there, he listened to the noises of the night. The crickets chirped, the cicadas buzzed, and the frogs croaked. Despite the impatience he felt and the urgent need to get away, he felt calm in this place. Perhaps it was the memory of making love to Katrina for the first time, but it felt like a place of reverence. He let the calm wash over him. In all his years as a soldier, he had always been able to keep a level head in battle. Having a plan helped him feel prepared even when everything around him felt chaotic. Knowing he had a plan helped him find this same calm now.

Ichabod had drifted off into a light sleep when he heard a twig snap. He jolted upright and quickly got to his feet. He would have hidden, but with his horse sitting out in the open, it was obvious he was there. A fog had rolled in while he dozed, which helped keep him concealed. He did make himself smaller behind a tree, taking cover rather than hiding, but when he saw Katrina's form step out from the woods, he immediately dropped his guard and rushed over to greet her, pulling her into a tight embrace.

"I wasn't sure if you'd come," he said, relief filling his words.

"Nothing could have kept me away," she replied, choking on a sob. "I love you, Ichabod."

"I love you, Katrina," he replied before kissing her quickly.

He wanted to hold her and not let her go, but he knew they needed to hurry and make their escape.

Once she left her house, the clock had started ticking and it was only a matter of time before it ran out and they were discovered. They needed to put as much distance between them and Tarrytown as they could. He kissed the top of her head and let her go, escorting her to the horse. Taking her bag, he helped her up onto the saddle. Tucking her bag into his saddlebags, he pulled out his sword and brace of pistols, strapping them on.

"Do you think we'll need those?" she asked, surprised.

"It's late, and we don't know who we'll run into. It's better to be prepared."

Ichabod climbed up and settled in the saddle behind her and urged the horse forward. They wound their way back into town, avoiding going nearer the farm than was necessary. While they had to skirt the edge of it to make their way out of town, they would not be near the house. Once they were away from the farm, they would have to avoid main roads as much as possible as well. Katrina had lived there her whole life. The hour was late, but if anyone was out and about, that would only serve to make their presence there even worse.

They planned on riding the Albany Post Road as far as they could get past the village then stopping further north along the river where they could book passage on a sloop into Albany. After reaching Albany, they would ride the remainder of the way. Once they left the village, they would only encounter farms dotting the road past the church. If they could not get a boat, the road would take them all the way into Albany. It was a much slower option, but one they could rely on if needed.

As they made their way toward the river and the road that would take them north, Ichabod was on alert. His ears strained to pick up every noise and his eyes scanned the area around them. Visibility was low because of the darkness and the fog, making every noise seem amplified and stretched out into the night. The wind whipped, trees shook, leaves rattled. All the while, his horse's hooves beat a steady rhythm on the dirt beneath them. Katrina leaned back into Ichabod, feeling safe in his embrace, even if she did not know how vigilant he was. He would do anything to make sure she stayed safe.

Ichabod's ears perked up when he heard a noise. It was not lost on him that his horse had also perked her ears. Ichabod scanned the area but could see nothing but fog and trees. He knew the road well by now, after having spent nearly a month there. Though he could see very little, he knew he was nearing the bridge between Philipse Manor and the Old Dutch

Church. If they could make it across the bridge, they would be nearly out of the village. His eyes strained to see what was waiting for him, while every little noise echoed inside his head.

As they reached the bridge, Ichabod could make out a form on a horse at the other end of it. The person seemed to have stopped there as if waiting for them, blocking the roadway. Ichabod cautiously slowed his horse. Had Eleanor already discovered her daughter missing and sent someone after them? Was it Brom? Had Washington read the letter for Katrina and told his friend Brom what Ichabod was planning?

"Who is that?" Katrina whispered. "Is he here for us?"

"Shhh. Don't say anything," he whispered back quietly, his mouth to her ear.

His hand reached for one of his pistols as he slowly urged his horse forward. They had to cross the bridge in order to get out of town, so he could not turn back. As they got close enough to see more than an outline through the fog, the other horse suddenly reared up on his hind legs, letting out a low roar and a snort. The rider deftly stayed upright on the horse's back and then suddenly lunged forward.

They could see the specter in front of them clearly now. The horse was bigger than any Ichabod had ever seen, and it was black as night. The very air coming from its nostrils was thick as smoke that appeared as though it would catch on fire any minute. The rider atop the beast was dressed in a uniform of some sort. It almost looked like an old Hessian uniform from forty years ago but was void of color. It, too, was all black as if charred in fire. The uniform covered the rider from shoulders to his feet, but above the shoulders, where a head should be, there was only empty space. The fog swirled around the body as if even it did not want to touch this wraith. For a moment, Ichabod considered that the lifeless body of a poor soul had managed to stay atop the horse, but on closer inspection, he saw that the body was as alive as he and Katrina. A sword was held in one hand, the reins in the other as the rider charged them.

Katrina screeched, "Is that rider missing its head?"

"He couldn't possibly," Ichabod replied, though he was seeing the same thing she was.

Ichabod turned his horse away from the phantom and fled through the houses neighboring Philipse Manor. Had it only been him, he would have stayed and fought the being, but he had to keep Katrina safe. He opted to try and outrun the beast instead. They were heading towards the river, navigating through the narrow streets, trying to lose their unwanted shadow.

The otherworldly horse was bearing down upon them with seemingly little effort while Ichabod's own steed struggled to go any faster. Ichabod thought he could feel the hot breath of the beast on his neck. He turned around and stretched out his arm, firing on the rider behind him. He watched as his bullet struck the being in the middle of the chest, resulting in a puff of dirt rising off the coat, but still, the rider continued. He replaced the pistol in its holster and pulled the other one. He turned, aimed, and fired. Once again, he watched as he hit his mark, dead center this time, but with no effect on the headless body.

Katrina watched the ball hit the ghostly rider in the chest, but it did not stop the creature. She could not help the scream that escaped from her mouth. Turning back to face forward again, she held tight to Athena's neck while trying not to strangle the poor beast.

Ichabod hurried his horse onward, turning into the trees, hoping to disorient their shadow in the thick woods. He replaced the second pistol and focused on navigating through the tightly spaced trees. It was difficult to go fast through the thick forest, and they had to slow down slightly, though the pounding of their hearts did not reflect their slower pace. Ichabod could hear the rush of blood drumming in his ears.

When he next turned to look behind them, the phantom was nowhere to be seen. Not relaxing his guard, he tried to carefully navigate their way back out to a roadway.

As they exited the trees, they found themselves on the banks of the Hudson River. Ichabod turned Athena north, and they rode along the bank for a time, trying to catch their breaths. The trees ran alongside them, keeping them bordered between the water and the woods. He tried to comfort Katrina as best he could. She was trembling, but there was little he could do for her then. He held her closer, lending her his warmth, and enveloping her with his body. They did not speak as he did not want to create any more noise than they were already making.

As they picked their way along the riverbank, they began to make some progress toward their goal when the specter suddenly charged forward out from the trees in front of them. Ichabod had not believed he had lost the phantom, but he had hoped. Its appearance startled them both and Katrina screamed again. Ichabod drew his sword, and the wraith drew down on them, his own sword raised once again. As the gap between them closed, the arm holding the sword swung down, causing Ichabod to raise his own in defense. The swords clanged beside their heads and Ichabod's horse whinnied, shaking her head. Katrina shifted in her seat as she tried to make herself small and Ichabod could feel his control slipping. He had maintained control of his horse during battle many times, but this was different. He had never faced a foe like this, and he had never done so while trying to hold onto a passenger. Katrina was struggling to stay in her seat, causing him to become unbalanced. When the wraith came at them again, Athena reared up. Katrina could not hold on and they both fell off, hitting the ground with a thud. Unable to stop in its tracks so quickly, the phantom kept riding past them when they fell.

When Ichabod looked over at Katrina, she was lying on the ground with her eyes closed. He crawled over to her and pulled her into him, urging her to wake. He stroked her face, watching the phantom turn around and double back on them again. She opened her eyes, and he kissed her quickly.

"Go hide in the woods. I'll come get you."

Katrina clung to him, shaking her head, her eyes wide with fear. "Please don't go. That thing will kill you."

"You must go. Run, now. And whatever happens, remember how much I love you. You shall always have my heart."

"I love you, Ichabod."

Katrina kissed him, then got to her feet, running towards the woods. She made it to the edge, then stopped to turn around and watch what was happening. She could not bear to leave Ichabod behind, even though she knew there was nothing she could do to help him.

Ichabod stood then, grabbing up his sword and letting Katrina go as he remounted his horse. He got atop her in time to face off with the other rider again. Their swords clashed once again, but this time, the horses were not in full gallops. They grappled with each other for a time, each thrusting and dodging. Ichabod landed a blow as his sword drove deep into the belly of the phantom, but it did nothing to stop it. He pulled back, separating himself from his foe as he regrouped, a thick black substance oozing along the blade of his sword. If his pistols had done nothing to stop the creature and his sword thrust into its belly did not even cause it pause, how would he ever defeat his opponent?

Ichabod circled Athena around in time to see the rider going after Katrina. The specter sheathed his sword and was almost upon her when Ichabod yelled, "Katrina, run," and charged at him again, drawing the phantom's attention away from Katrina.

The wraith turned back around to face Ichabod, drawing his sword and charging him once again. The ground was horribly uneven, and they had little room to maneuver between the river and the trees. The horses clashed before their riders could, each rearing up and lashing out at one another. When Ichabod's horse hit the ground again, she hit an uneven patch of ground, causing her to stumble. Ichabod struggled to maintain control while Athena struggled to regain her footing beneath her. The ground was soft this close to the river, and she was unable to recover. The soft dirt gave way beneath her front hooves, causing Athena to crumple over the edge of the riverbank. She rolled down towards the water, Ichabod still in the saddle. He tried to break free, but his foot caught in the stirrup.

As they landed at the edge of the river, Ichabod finally managed to crawl free from Athena. Though, he did not recover as quickly as his horse. Where she promptly righted herself, he tried to stand but was disoriented from the fall and a sharp pain shot through his leg. It was certainly broken. The riverbank was covered in rocks, leaves, and other detritus. He grabbed a branch on a nearby log, trying to pull himself up as the phantom dismounted from his own horse on the bank above him. He was walking toward Ichabod, sword drawn. Ichabod looked around desperately for his own sword, but it was still up on the riverbank behind the phantom. Before he could make a plan, the specter was upon him. Ichabod grabbed a large branch, using it as a club the best he could. He tried to bludgeon his way to freedom, but none of his blows made any difference, much as his sword and pistols had failed to. Ichabod was stepping away as the phantom thrust his sword, but he was not quick enough. The sword made contact, slashing his belly. If he had not twisted at the last second, it would have pierced him, likely killing him. He heard Katrina scream as he stumbled backwards. He tripped over the log he had used to pull himself upright, causing it to loosen from its spot on the riverbank. Falling back into the water, the log came in after him. Ichabod quickly found himself in deep waters being pulled downriver by the current. He scrambled to grab ahold of the log and stay afloat.

With the fog not as thick there, Ichabod had a clear view of the scene he left behind. Katrina rushed toward the riverbank, trying to find him. He tried to yell to her but was already too far away for her to hear him. He could see her desperation to find him in the inky blackness of the water and get him help. While searching for Ichabod, she did not see the phantom approach behind her. She must have not heard the noise until it was too late. Katrina turned her head in time to see him swoop down and reach for her. The last think Ichabod saw was her screaming as the specter scooped her up and put her on his saddle, face down like a sack of flour.

When he saw the specter ride off with her, he realized that it had only been trying to kill him, not her. He hoped he could trust that meant that she would somehow be safe. Though, what the specter wanted with Katrina, he could not fathom.

Ichabod struggled to hold onto the log as the current pulled him further downriver. He was fully in the middle of the water now, nowhere near the bank. The water was moving so fast that he did not have the strength to pull himself toward the shore. It was all he could do to stay afloat. He was in pain and had failed to best the specter. His leg would need to heal, as would his side where the sword had slashed him open. Right now, he had no other choice than to go wherever the water took him while trying to stay afloat and stay alive.

37

Modern Day

"You want to use Izzy as bait?" Simon asked, his voice pitched high. "Absolutely not."

Tamara met them at the manor as soon as they got back into town on Friday morning. It felt strange to be back there. The police had long since cleared out, and Alex's blood had been washed away by the rain. It looked as though nothing had happened. They knew the truth, though. Now, Tamara was explaining her plan to draw out the Hessian and break the curse.

Isadora's hand went to her hip and one eyebrow raised up. Simon knew that look, but he did not care. He was not putting her life in danger any more than it already was.

"It's not your choice," he heard her say.

It was exactly what he had been expecting.

"You can't do this, Iz. You saw what happened the last time. This isn't a game."

"No. It's not. It's real life. *My* life. And I want it back."

Since hearing that Tamara had a plan, Isadora had begun to hope. She knew people she loved would still continue to leave her; that would never change. But she had hope that at least they might be able to return her life to some semblance of normal, something without a maniac trying to kill her or drive her to despair from lack of sleep. The nightmares had continued in Brooklyn, and she knew now that Tamara was right about them. Even if she left town, the Hessian would still be able to follow her in her dreams. After not having slept in weeks, she knew she could not live like that forever. Eventually, the nightmares would kill her without the Horseman being physically present. "We have to try."

"She won't be in any real danger, Sugar," Tamara said. "I was watching the other night. The Horseman only showed up after Izzy stepped outside, off the porch, but he never tried to come up onto the porch while she was there. If the verse in Irving's journal holds any truth in it, the Hessian cannot come inside the house. Perhaps the porch is an extension of that. And we can have you waiting in the car, ready to whisk her away if things get too hairy."

"It's too risky." Simon shook his head. "We can't further endanger her life based on the possibility that a fiction-writer's notes have some factual merit to them. Or that curses and magic are real. No."

Simon turned and strolled out the back door, letting it slam shut behind him. He stood on the porch, breathing in the cool air. He leaned over, his hands on the railing. When he heard the door squeak behind him, he did not look up. He knew it was Isadora and he knew why she followed him out.

"I won't change my mind," he said without turning to look at her.

Without a word, Isadora sidled up next to him. She put a hand over the top of his. She thought things were going to be awkward between them after his declaration, and for a brief moment, they were. But they quickly fell back into old habits. They had been friends far too long for anything to come between them.

They stood there together in the quiet for a moment.

Finally, she said in a calm, even voice, "That's fine. I don't expect you to change your mind, but I'm doing this. I have to try something, and this isn't your problem. You'll be safer far away from it and knowing you're safe will get me through it."

Simon hung his head, his shoulder drooping. She knew exactly how to get him to change his mind. Without looking at her, he threw her words from the previous day back at her.

"I can't lose you, Iz."

"Do you seriously still think that it's someone in a costume?" she asked, ignoring his statement.

She had thought of almost nothing else since the night Alex was killed. She had seen the bullet impacts with her own eyes but seeing the photo that Tamara had taken had erased any doubt that she had been seeing things that night.

"I've never been one to believe in ghosts, Izzy."

"How else do you explain what happened? You saw the same things I did. Those bullets hit both the man and the horse with no effect. The horse was obviously not wearing body armor and judging by the blackness oozing out of him where the bullets hit him, the man was not wearing any either. What else could it have been if not supernatural?"

Simon stood upright, turning to look at her, his hands falling to his sides. "I don't know," he admitted.

"I don't believe in the supernatural either, Simon, but I have no other explanation." She was facing him, her arms folded across her chest. "Maybe we need to believe in order to defeat this thing. If Tamara is right, then maybe we can end this. I want to trust her. I want to give this a chance."

Simon wanted to reach out and touch her. Things were not awkward between them, but they were not the same as they used to be. There was a barrier between them now. He was not even certain it had anything to do with what had transpired at the park. It had been going up for days before that. Ever since Alex…

"Okay, Izzy. I'll do it. I'll believe in this for you."

"I'm not asking you to help. In fact, I don't want you anywhere near this."

"And I don't want *you* anywhere near it. I won't let you do it without me."

After arguing whether or not Simon would be involved, Isadora finally relented. They went back inside, where Tamara was sitting at the kitchen table, studying the pages in front of her. She had a photocopy of Irving's diary with his notes on what he saw and heard that night. On another sheet of paper, she had a list of items she would need for the ritual they would perform. She was double-checking the items on the list, trying to determine if she had forgotten anything. Hearing the door, she looked up from the pages as they walked in.

"What'd y'all decide? Are we doing this?"

Isadora looked over at Simon one more time, half expecting him to say no, but also half hoping he would. To her surprise, he asked, "What *exactly* are we doing?"

He looked back at Isadora who smiled at him. "And when are we doing it?" she added.

"Well, I should think you'd want to do it as soon as possible. How 'bout tonight?" Tamara asked.

Isadora was taken aback. "Tonight? But it's Halloween."

"And a full moon," Tamara added. "But more importantly, it's the start of Samhain. It's the best time to perform magic, Sugar. It'll make it more powerful."

"What's sow-in?" Simon asked, pronouncing the strange word as she had.

"It's the night when the veil between worlds is the thinnest. Time loses all meaning allowing the past, present, and future to all become one and the dead to walk amongst the living."

They accepted her answer with no argument. They were beyond that now. If Isadora was ever to be rid of this threat, she had to put her trust in Tamara Petit-Blanc. Still, Isadora hesitated. She wanted to wait and do it later, but when would it ever be a good time for this? She felt woefully unprepared but finally decided.

"I guess it's like ripping off a band aid. Let's do it."

She looked to Simon, and he nodded. Turning to Tamara, he asked, "What do we need?"

Tamara looked at her list and read off the items on it. "I have almost everything on the list. We'll keep Ichabod's memoir handy in case we need something of his but I don't think we will since you're here, Izzy. Your blood should be stronger than any physical object he came into contact with. I wish we had something that belonged to either the Hessian or the person who originally worked the spell. Our counter-spell would be much stronger if we did. Objects can retain a connection to a person they've come into contact with and influence them."

"We'll have to make do with what we have and hope it works," Isadora said, trying to be optimistic though she felt anything but.

₧₧ ₧₧

Under the circumstances, the last place Isadora wanted to find herself at dusk on Halloween was at a cemetery. Normally, she would have loved it, but not this year. Yet there they were. Simon kept watch as they stood around at the foot of a grave while Tamara asked permission of its occupant to take some of the soil there. Isadora found herself antsy as her anxiety increased, knowing it would be dark soon. She wanted to hurry and get out of there. Simon had suggested they go without her, but since she was the target of the curse, Tamara wanted her there as well. She would be asking permission next.

Looking at the name on the headstone, she said, "Katrina Martling, I'm here to collect dirt from your grave in order to release a curse unfairly placed upon my family. I ask your permission to remove it."

They did not know if Katrina Martling had anything to do with the original curse, but since she was the daughter of Eleanor Brush, they wanted to try obtaining the soil from her grave. If she was somehow involved, perhaps she would want to reverse the curse her mother cast. It was a risk. They did not know if Katrina had asked her mother to cast the spell, but Tamara assured them that was not the case. Isadora took her word for it.

"How will we know if permission is granted?" Simon whispered.

Before Tamara could answer, a raven landed on the tombstone. Simon and Isadora exchanged speculative glances while Tamara smiled.

"Where would you prefer we collect the dirt from?" Tamara asked Katrina.

The raven cawed, leading Simon and Isadora to exchange another glance.

Tamara handed Isadora the trowel and she knelt down at the head of the grave where Tamara pointed. She cut out a small divot, placing the dirt into a bag that Tamara brought with her. Tamara watched the raven and when it flew away, she directed Isadora to stop digging. They then exchanged the bag of dirt with nine dimes which Isadora would leave behind as payment. Under Tamara's direction, she smoothed over the dirt she had disturbed, then placed the dimes on top of the smooth dirt before filling it in with some loose dirt and crushed leaves from around them. They thanked Katrina for her generosity and quickly left, heading back to the house.

"Explain to me what the graveyard dirt is for," Simon asked as they drove back.

"It's called goopher dust," Tamara replied. "It attracts the spirit of the dead to the target. In this case, Izzy. Typically, it's used to cause serious harm to a person, either injuring or killing them. Irving's notes mentioned Eleanor using dirt in her original spell. Of course, we can't rely on that too heavily, but it's entirely possible she used goopher dust. Based on his notes, my guess is that she used her own blood and possibly Ichabod's to direct the curse while using the goopher dust to relay her intentions."

"Why did we have to wait until this close to dark to collect it?" Isadora asked. Her eyes remained focused outside as she watched the sky become darker. They would make it back to the house before it was fully dark, but she really did not want to be outside right now.

"Sunrise and midnight are normally the most potent times for spellwork, but dusk on Samhain is even more potent."

Back at the house, Isadora worked with Tamara as she prepped and anointed the thick candles she brought. They would be used to focus their energy, enhancing the spiritual work they were about to do. Anointing them would enhance their power. Pulling a black candle and a clear crystal sharpened to a point from her bag of supplies, she handed them to Isadora.

"Use the quartz to etch the name 'Eleanor' into the side of the candle. Then carve the word 'break' at the base."

When she finished, Tamara took the candle, handing her a purple one.

"Now, carve your name at the base of that one. The colors affect the vibration emitted from the candles and purple and black are both used to remove a curse." Tamara explained as much as she could about the process to Isadora as they went because she knew she would be curious.

With the candles carved, Tamara then handed Isadora a vial containing an oil she called 'jinx oil.' She was to anoint each candle by holding them one at a time in her non-dominant hand with the wick pointed away from her. Rubbing the oil into the candle from the base to the wick, she was to visualize the curse being drawn away from her and the oil washing her clean and casting off the bad energy of the curse. Despite feeling a little ridiculous doing it, she tried to focus on the task, visualizing the curse being broken as Tamara had instructed.

"We have a few minutes now," Tamara said when Isadora finished with the candles. "I'll finish setting this up if you want to prepare yourself for tonight."

They had already set up a low table to be used as an altar on the front porch that now awaited the items they would use during the ritual. Tamara would work from the altar which she now outfit with a cloth, ceramic bowls, and various black crystals that she had informed Isadora were onyx, obsidian, black granite, and black tourmaline. They were all useful in repelling evil. Each of the items used in the altar had been smudged with sage, as was the table and the entire front porch prior to them leaving for the cemetery. Tamara now set out myrrh incense for protection then moved on to crush pine bark then elm leaves and twigs with a mortar and pestle, placing the powder of each into separate bowls. In another bowl, she placed garlic and onion peels along with a black feather that she found left behind at the graveyard when the raven had flown away. Burning the skins and the feather all together would cast out dark spirits while burning the pine bark and the elm should reverse the original spell. She would work each one individually, see if it worked, then move onto the next. She had several others lined up ready to go if none of these worked. Not knowing the specific details of the original curse, she was not certain which spell was going to be the most effective now and she wanted to be prepared to try several different ones. At the edge of the altar, she laid out a decorative knife that she would use to draw blood if she needed to work a stronger spell.

Isadora left Tamara to finish setting up the altar and went to the back porch for a few minutes to herself. Simon moved the car alongside the front porch, parking it so the passenger door was even with the steps. He left the keys in the ignition, left the door open, and came around to open the passenger door as well. He wanted as quick of an escape as possible if they needed it. After getting the car into position, he went in search of Isadora. He found her studying the photo of the Hessian on her phone that Tamara had taken the last time.

"I'm trying to normalize him," she said without looking up. She had heard Simon come out onto the porch and knew it was him even before he spoke or came into view. "I thought if I looked at the photo long enough, I might not be as afraid of him when I see him."

Simon sidled up beside her, rubbing her back. She leaned into his comforting presence, putting her head on his shoulder. He could not help himself from kissing the top of her head. His face lingered in her hair, and he closed his eyes, taking in her vanilla scent.

"You'll do great tonight."

"So will you," she said.

He was supposed to distract the Hessian and keep Isadora safe while Tamara worked the spell. All Isadora had to do was bring the Horseman to them and wait.

They stood together for a while, then Isadora straightened, pulling herself from his warm embrace. She kept her gaze on the yard that she had come to love, taking in the shadows and the sounds that were growing ever quieter. The full moon was still low in the sky, casting shadows across the lawn.

"I want you know how much it's meant to me to have had you in my life all these years." She looked down at her hands, now resting on the porch rail. "No matter what happens, I'll always hold you in my heart."

Simon turned to look at her. "You sound as though you're saying goodbye?"

"I want to be prepared for anything, Simon. With Alex," she nearly choked on his name, "it happened so quickly, I didn't get a chance to say or do anything. But I want you to know how important you are to me."

Despite what she had just said to him, she was very careful to not say that she loved him. She wanted to say it but could not bring herself to do so. If she somehow managed to survive the night, she did not want that hanging between them.

Simon took her hands in his, turning her to face him. She looked up at him briefly, then back down at the ground between them.

"Nothing's going to happen to me, Iz. I'm going to be fine. We know the Hessian only harms anyone who gets between him and his target, so as long as I'm careful, he won't hurt me."

It was not him she was worried about getting hurt, but she did not voice that. Simon already had enough reservations about this plan; she would not give him even more. But there was no way she was going to let the Hessian hurt Simon. She would put herself between them if she had to. He was after her and no one else would be hurt in her place. They had no idea if any of their attempts to break the curse would even work, but she had one last resort if it came to it; one that would ensure no one else would ever be harmed because of her and her family. If she could not break the curse, she would end it. If the Hessian obtained his goal, the curse would finally be over. As the last of Ichabod's descendants, the curse would finally die with her.

Isadora had thought she would have been more upset at the thought of possibly being killed, but instead, she felt a calm wash over her. With acceptance that this may be the only way to keep those she loved safe, she felt a sense of peace. She would fight, but if nothing else worked, she would do what she had to do.

38

Summer 1815

As the sun began to rise, a sloop was making its way down the river when the crew saw a man clinging to a log in the middle of the water. They came about and came to a stop alongside him. It took several men to drag the poor soul from the river.

"Is he alive?" someone asked.

He was not conscious, and he appeared to be in bad shape. His face was covered in bruises and cuts, and he had slashes across his arms and stomach. He was pale and cold to the touch, but there was a faint breath coming from him. They carried him below deck and laid him on a cot in the main cabin while calling for the ship's physician.

Briefly while the physician was examining him, the man regained consciousness, though he was far from coherent. He kept moaning, "Katrina."

The physician tended his wounds, covering them in honey and did what he could to make the man comfortable. The sloop continued on to New York City. When they arrived a couple days later, all they had managed to learn from the man was that he was Major Crane from the Third Artillery. He was taken to the hospital where they admitted him. His temperature was high and the slash across his abdomen had become infected. They were not sure he would survive through the end of the week, but they sent a message to the colonel of the artillery corps, informing him that one of his soldiers was there.

Ichabod was in and out of consciousness for several days. He had been vaguely aware of being pulled from the water, though he had no idea how long he had been in the river. After that, he remembered a lot of rocking, then being inside some sort of building. Everything came in fits and starts. Nothing made sense, but all he could think about was Katrina. Where was she? What had happened to her? One minute, he remembered seeing her dead, but then she would be alive. She was in the water with him, then she would slip under, just out of his reach. He would scream for her, but no sound came from his mouth. All he could see was the nose of a black horse with flames shooting out of its nostrils. Everything was cold, though his skin burned. Despite a horse breathing fire down on him, his teeth chattered, and he could not warm up. He was lost in a fog so heavy, everything around him was white. He desperately needed Katrina. If she were there, she would warm him. He called out for her, but she never came.

Ichabod saw a plethora of people whom he did not know. There were women in white aprons, clergymen, and other men who all talked while observing him. They applied something to his arms and stomach, wiped his brow, or made him drink broth, then left. The days stretched into a never-ending state of delirium.

After several weeks, Ichabod finally broke through the fog. Or at least he thought he did. He woke one morning to see his mother in a chair beside his bed. How could his mother possibly be there? Was she not in New Jersey? He must still be delirious to be seeing her there. He moaned and closed his eyes again, then he heard her voice calling his name.

"Ichabod? Son, are you awake? Can you hear me?"

Ichabod opened his eyes again, croaking out a greeting. "Are you really here, mother?"

His mother cried, and Ichabod realized she was grasping his hand.

Abigail Crane choked on her sobs as her relief at seeing him alive and awake poured out of her, but she was crying and talking so fast, Ichabod could not make sense of it. His entire body hurt. It was far too much effort to try and keep up with what his mother was saying. He closed his eyes and slept some more.

When he woke again, his mother was still there. When she saw that he was awake, she squeezed his hand before letting it go. She stood and walked away, then came back a minute later with a cup of something that she pressed to his lips. He barely tasted the warm broth as it slid past his lips and down his throat. He was still in an immense amount of pain, but at least his mother was much calmer this time. When he finished the drink, she set the cup down and asked how he felt. He merely moaned his response.

"Your color has mostly returned. That's a good sign." In a small voice, she said, "We did not think you would recover." She choked on a sob, but recomposed herself and continued, "If the ship's physician had not put honey on your wounds immediately after they pulled you from the water, you likely would not be with us. Of course, the doctors argued over it, but I know that's what saved your life. How long have I been putting honey on your cuts?"

"Where's Katrina?" was all Ichabod could manage. He did not want to think about honey or doctors and what they thought about what was the best treatment for wounds.

His mother shook her head. "Who's Katrina, son? You called for her often these last weeks, but no one knows who she is."

Ichabod gasped. "Weeks? How long have I been here?" He looked around briefly, and added, "And where, precisely am I?"

"You're in a hospital in New York City. You've been here near two months, maybe more. I'm not certain when they brought you in exactly. But don't you worry; your commanders have been notified. You've not been listed as a deserter."

Ichabod knew it should be a relief to him that at least he was not labeled as a deserter, but he was far more concerned with the fact that it had been two months, if not more, and apparently there had been no word from Katrina. Was she even alive?

His mother helpfully informed Ichabod of his injuries. "Along with the various smaller cuts and bruises on your face and arms, you had a large cut across your stomach and a broken leg. Your leg has progressed nicely and is almost healed, though your stomach is another matter. The physician said the wound became diseased and gave you blood rot."

Ichabod tried sitting up but found himself weak and dizzy. He fell back against the pillows and his mother jumped to his side to help him.

"I must leave here. I need to get back."

"You must rest, son. Your command knows you're here. There's nowhere you need to be at this moment, except in this bed."

Abigail mistook his desire to leave with a responsibility to the army. It was not. He was eager to learn of Katrina.

"I need paper and ink. Can you procure me those, mother?" If he could not go to her, he would send word. If she had escaped that phantom, she would likely be as desperate as he to hear news.

His mother nodded her head. "I will. But only if you rest."

"I'll not be going anywhere."

His leg was still wrapped, though it was not entirely immobilized, but it was the rest of his body that kept him from getting up regardless of how much he wanted to. He was far weaker than he ever would have cared to admit. He did not have the strength to even sit up on his own; there was no way he would be standing anytime soon.

Abigail returned with a portable writing desk with compartments which held paper, ink, quills, and a wax seal that was not personalized to an individual.

Ichabod immediately set to writing a letter to Katrina informing her that he was alive and recovering in a hospital in New York City. He informed her that he did not know how long he would be in there, but he would come for her as soon as he was released. When he finished, he folded and sealed the pages, adding the address of the Brush farm on the outside. He handed it to his mother and asked that she see it delivered.

With a letter en route to Katrina, Ichabod felt slightly less anxious. He was able to finally converse with his mother when she returned from posting the missive. They talked for a while, but he still tired easily and quickly found himself unable to keep his eyes open. His mother patted his hand and told him to sleep.

The next several days were spent much the same way. Ichabod tried to wait patiently for a reply from Katrina. He spent most of his time sleeping, but when he woke, he would visit with his mother. She would update him with the latest word from his brothers or her own affairs. Ichabod had last seen his brother William not all that long ago, and there had been little update from him since. He had reached Boston and taken command of the *Independence*, then sailed to Algiers in July, just as he had said when Ichabod last saw him. He had been doing well the last time he wrote to their mother. His other brother was still in Ohio, working as a judge and supporting his family.

It took weeks before Ichabod was able to sit up on his own. He had broken through the delirium and the fog, but his body was still fighting the blood rot. His physicians had informed him that he had been very near death. It would be a long road to recovery. It was difficult for Ichabod to sit still, but it helped that he did not have the physical strength to do otherwise.

The weeks quickly turned to months. Ichabod was visited by his colonel who came to see about his welfare.

"How are you feeling, son?"

"I'm on the mend, sir."

Ichabod had tried to sit up and salute when the man came in, but the colonel would not have it. The man took a chair beside Ichabod's mother and gave her a sympathetic expression.

"And how are you doing, Mrs. Crane? I imagine this can't be easy so soon after losing the general."

Abigail shook her head. "No, only a few weeks ago, I thought I would be burying Ichabod alongside his father. It's good to see him recovering."

"I never got to tell you how sorry I was to hear about William. He was a good man and a good mentor."

Colonel Moses Porter had served under Ichabod's father as a sergeant during the Revolutionary War, fighting with him in the Battle of Brandywine, where he earned his commission. He had known the family for decades. It was no surprise to him when two of the general's sons enlisted as well nor when one of them ended up as a captain under his command. He had been more than happy to recommend Ichabod for brevet major and wholeheartedly endorsed it when it had been suggested.

"He was. I appreciate your words."

Colonel Porter turned his attention back to Ichabod. "Do you want to tell me what happened? How did you end up here? Last we heard, you had a lame horse and were allowing it to rest someplace called Tarrytown. How is it you came to be fished out of the river and taken to a hospital in New York City, near dead?"

Ichabod shook his head. "I'm not entirely certain, sir," he began slowly. Ichabod carefully chose his words, knowing the colonel would not believe his story. He still was not certain *he* believed it. With his brow furrowed, he continued, sticking to the truth as much as possible while leaving out details.

"I was attacked along the riverbank and ended up in the water. My leg was broken in the scuffle, and I received other injuries. The current caught me and carried me away. If it hadn't been for the sloop stopping to pull me from the water, I likely would not have made it."

Abigail let out a small whimper at the picture Ichabod had painted. He had tried to censor his words, but he knew it was still a difficult thing for a mother to hear about her child. Moses squeezed her hand in comfort.

"What was the reason for the attack?"

Ichabod again censored himself, trying to keep his answers vague. "There was a misunderstanding, sir."

"Would this misunderstanding have a name? Or was it a misunderstanding over cards? Perhaps something else altogether?"

Ichabod sighed. He had to tread carefully. "The misunderstanding does have a name, sir; though I'm hesitant to speak it. This is a private matter; not one for which the army need be involved."

"As your friend, I respect that, Ichabod. As your commander, I certainly hope not. Is this going to be a problem in the future?"

"No, sir."

Moses nodded. "Good. Now, about your future. Will you be returning to us? How extensive are your injuries?"

"Nothing permanent, sir. The doctors assure me I shall make a full recovery. I plan to return to duty as soon as I am able."

"I would expect no less." The colonel pulled some papers from his pocket and handed them to Ichabod. "I thought I'd deliver your orders while I was here," he said at Ichabod's confused expression.

Ichabod smirked. "Is that not a little beneath your pay grade, sir?" he joked. Ichabod would not normally speak to a commanding officer that way, but this one was like family. He had known him almost his entire life.

Moses sighed. "Yes it is. Don't make me regret coming to visit you and seeing after your well-being."

Ichabod knew the man was teasing right back when his face broke out into a grin.

"Thank you for coming sir. It means a lot to me," he said in all seriousness.

Colonel Porter spoke with Ichabod's doctors and got their reassurance that he would make a full recovery and would be capable of returning to service as soon as he did, though they informed the colonel that he still had a long way to go before that could happen. Ichabod had been eager to resume his service. He hated being this idle for this long.

The colonel stayed and visited for a while, but before he left, he made sure to tell Ichabod, "You will be expected to report to duty as soon as you're released from the hospital." He pointed a finger at Ichabod and placed a stern expression on his face before adding, "With no detours. Is that understood, Major?"

If the tone of his voice had not given him away, the use of Ichabod's rank let him know that the colonel was giving him an order. This was not a request nor a suggestion from a family friend. He had no choice but to obey unless he wanted to be court martialed. He would not be able to go see Katrina as soon as he was released from the hospital as much as he wanted to.

"Yes, sir. Understood, sir."

Ichabod waited until the colonel left to open his new orders. He was to report to Fort Preble in Portland Harbor, Maine. The order had been dated August 10, 1815. That had been a long time ago.

Ichabod continued sending letters to the Brush farm, though he never got a reply. He had thought that if anything had happened to Katrina, then Caleb would at least inform him of it. Maybe Eleanor would have even informed him, if only to blame him. He certainly blamed himself. But there had been no word at all. He even tried sending word to the Van Tassel residence, but still, nothing. Ichabod wondered if the letters were even being delivered. Regardless, he continued to send them.

39

Modern Day

With a look at his watch, Simon squeezed her hands, then pulled Isadora into his arms one more time, holding onto her as tightly as he could.

"It's time," he said as he finally released her.

Tamara had informed them that they would begin when the hands of the clock were pointed at the six and the twelve. Since the sun was setting early now, that put them in full darkness at six o'clock so they would not have to wait until twelve thirty.

They went through the house to the front porch where Tamara was waiting. "Are we ready?"

With nods of agreement, the mood somber, Tamara lit the incense, then the black and purple candles as the clock struck six o'clock. Isadora squeezed Simon's hand one last time, walked down the stairs by herself, stepped off the porch, and waited between the porch and the car. She did not have long to wait. The insects around them suddenly became quiet and soon they heard the whinny of a horse not far off. It took all of Isadora's nerve to hold herself still at the bottom of the porch and not run back up to the safety of the house. Her heart was already racing, but when the Hessian came into view, it pounded furiously. Her legs felt momentarily frozen in place as horse and rider barreled down on her.

Getting ever closer, the Hessian drew his sword above his missing head, readying to strike. As she stood there in fear, the sound of Simon screaming for her to run brought Isadora back to the present. Eyes wide, she found her courage and ran back up the steps of the porch. Simon met her halfway as he had begun running after her. Spinning around, he followed her up the steps. At the top of the stairs, she bent at the waist, hands on her knees, as she caught her breath. She had not exerted herself much, but the fear she had felt left her breathless.

Behind them, Tamara was working her magic. Using the candles, she lit the elm powder, chanting an incantation. "Let the evil done against this family reverse itself. Break this curse and leave them in peace."

The plant matter lit with a burst and quickly burned itself out, but nothing happened. They waited a couple of minutes, and Tamara repeated the chant while lighting the pine bark. Having more oil in the bark than the elm powder, it burned more slowly but went out shortly. The Hessian was still at the bottom of the porch, pacing back and forth on his horse.

Apparently tired of waiting, the horse reared up and began kicking at the porch railings. It seemed as though he was more anxious to get to Isadora this time and finally be done with it. Isadora knew the feeling. Simon went to the back porch, telling Isadora to stay there. Tamara lit the feather with the onion and garlic skins, trying to cast out the dark spirit before them. Simon was back minutes later with an armful of rocks. They began throwing them at the Hessian in an attempt to get him to stop his horse from kicking at the porch while Tamara tried another spell, this time adding a few drops of her blood to it to increase the power.

With a solid kick, the porch railing splintered, sending shards of wood flying, and causing Isadora to scream and step back.

"Maybe if I can get his sword away from him, it'll work against him."

Simon ran down the steps and jumped into the car, starting it up. He reversed the car to get a little distance, then pressed his foot on the gas, lunging the car forward, charging at the Horseman as he did the last time they confronted him. The Hessian turned towards the car and urged his horse forward this time, as if playing a game of chicken. Neither of them flinched, but as Simon was about to make contact, the horse suddenly reared up, jumping onto the hood of the car as if flying. He kept going over the top of it, coming down to the ground behind it. He spun around again, running back to the front of the car and thrust his sword through the hood. The sword went right through the solid engine block as if it was butter, making the car stall. Despite the damage to the engine, the car stayed in motion a few minutes longer and before it stopped, it knocked the horse and his rider down as it had the last time they confronted him.

Simon jumped out of the car and grabbed at the sword, pulling as hard as he could while kicking at the body on the ground in front of him. While he did, he got a close-up look at the neck and saw that it most definitely was not a costume. In his shock, he paused long enough that the Hessian grabbed at him, pulling at his ankle. Simon tried getting away, but lost his balance, his arms going above his head. He was soon on the ground with the Horseman crawling after him, again reaching for Simon's foot.

Watching all of this from the porch, Isadora screamed and ran down to help. There was no way she was going to let the Hessian kill Simon as he had Alex. She reached the pair and began kicking at the Hessian while Simon tried to get away and stand.

Off the porch now, Isadora became the target as the Hessian immediately lost interest in Simon in order to go after her. The Hessian stood and reached her quickly, his hands going around her throat. While he choked her, Isadora's kickboxing classes flashed through her mind, and she began punching and kicking at him. Her blows landed with no effect. Up close, her eyes went to his neck where his head should have been. She could not tear her eyes away from the horror of it. With her eyes glued on the neck, she saw the top edges of his uniform were torn and ragged. Something niggled at her brain, but she could not reach it. The edges of her vision started to turn black.

Simon got to his feet, retrieved the sword, and turned to see the Hessian choking Isadora. Her face was red, and her legs were beginning to give out underneath her. His blood boiling, Simon came behind the Hessian and pushed the sword into him. He turned and twisted the sword inside the body as the tip poked out from his chest. The Hessian's hands fell from Isadora's throat, and she fell to the ground coughing and clutching her neck.

The Hessian turned around as if looking at Simon. He stood almost the same height as Simon, even though Simon was not a small man. Had the Horseman had a head, he would have towered over him. He swatted at Simon, pushing him down then reached up behind his back. He tried to grab the sword but could not reach the handle. He gave up trying for the handle and instead, grabbed the length of sword sticking out of his back by the blade and pulled it out. With a gaping hole in the middle of his torso, the black goo gushed out again, running down his stomach and back.

While the Hessian was pulling out the sword, Isadora and Simon ran back up onto the porch. They watched him remove the sword with wide eyes. When the Hessian started walking forward again, Isadora turned to Tamara to see what was taking so long.

"I don't know," she cried. "It should be working. It must not be powerful enough."

While Simon and Isadora had been fighting the Horseman, Tamara had tried every spell she could think of. She began by trying to remove the curse, went on to protection spells, then tried communicating with spirits, and even banishing evil. Reciting every psalm she could think of and using blood, candles, and goopher dust had not worked. She was just about out of ideas.

Suddenly, the Hessian began hurling flaming pumpkins which seemed to appear out of thin air at them on the porch. The trio watched in shock as the Horseman scooped his hand as if reaching for something on the ground and when he straightened, the pumpkin was there, in his hand. They all thought the pumpkins to be apparitions, but when they landed against the house and smashed into pieces, the all-too-real shards remained. One after another, they appeared and flew through the air at them while Simon and Isadora frantically tried to extinguish the flames. They were quickly losing the battle.

That niggling thought while the Hessian was choking Isadora continued whirling through her mind and she finally realized what it was.

"Keep him here! I'll be right back!"

She knew it was a long shot, but they had to try something new. Nothing else was working. Isadora ran inside the house, down the stairs and pulled frantically at the boxes in the basement. As she fled through the house, she could hear the Horseman outside trying to coax her back out as he continued throwing things at the house. She flung the boxes aside with no regard for what was inside them until she found the trunk she wanted. It did not take long since she had left it near the front of the pile so she could have an expert examine the contents. Opening the lid of the trunk she had marked 'Civil War clothes,' she dumped the contents unceremoniously onto the basement floor, then dropped to her knees, digging through the textiles until she found the small pouch embroidered with the initials 'EB.' Dumping the button into her hand, she ran back upstairs as quickly as she could, the thumping still coming from outside.

Isadora had no idea where the button had come from, but with everything else surrounding the manor house, the family, the story, and now the Hessian himself, it could not be a coincidence that the very demon she had fought was missing a button at the collar of his uniform while there just happened to be a Hessian uniform button from the same period in a pouch downstairs with Eleanor Brush's initials embroidered on it. The same pouch in which she had found the ring, also from the same era. Isadora hoped beyond hope that it was the same button that had once been attached to the Horseman's uniform. Even if it was, would it be enough?

Rushing to Tamara at the altar, she flung the button into a bowl, removed the poison ring from her finger, and added it to the bowl before grabbing the knife. She then slit her palm and let the blood drop onto the button and ring inside the bowl. She had been watching Tamara cast her spells and she let her own intuition guide her now.

While facing the Hessian, Isadora spoke from her heart, the words flowing from her. "Blessed be, thou creature made of flesh and blood. Hessian soldier trapped between two worlds, you are a fighter and a protector, but you have done your duty. Let the evil done against my blood come to an end. I thank you for your service to the family you have remained so faithful to, but now I discharge you from your service, warrior. Cross to the next world and be at rest."

While Isadora spoke her incantation, Tamara poured the goopher dust they collected from Katrina's grave into the bowl, mixing it with Isadora's blood and recited Psalms 54.

"Save me, O God, by thy name, and judge me by thy strength. Hear my prayer, O God; give ear to the words of my mouth. For strangers are risen up against me, and oppressors seek after my soul: they have not set God before them. Behold, God is mine helper: the Lord is with them that uphold my soul. He shall reward evil unto mine enemies: cut them off in thy truth. I will freely sacrifice unto thee: I will praise thy name, O Lord; for it is good. For he hath delivered me out of all trouble: and mine eye hath seen his desire upon mine enemies."

Simon tried keeping the pumpkins from reaching the women while they worked the spell. Suddenly, the pumpkins stopped coming at him. While keeping one eye on the Hessian, Simon took advantage of the pause to stomp on the remaining flames still burning on the porch.

They all watched as the Hessian turned away from the porch and threw himself back into the saddle atop his horse. Momentarily confused and unsure as to what was happening, they all stood and watched, unable to do anything else. They collectively held their breath to see what he would do next. Their pulses raced. Sweat rolled down their backs. With every attempt they had made to stop him, he had only kept coming at them. Thus far, their efforts had done nothing to change his course of action. Had they actually done it this time or was he going to come at them in a new attack? If he could manifest flaming pumpkins out of thin air, what else could he do?

To their astonishment, the Hessian did not resume his efforts. Instead, he turned his horse away from the house and began down the lane away from them. At the end of the drive, the horse and its rider turned back to face the group once again. The Hessian dropped his sword to the ground. The horse bowed down, one of its front legs bent, the other extended out in front of him. The rider mimicked his mount's posture, placing one hand on his stomach and extending the other out to the side while bending slightly at the waist atop the horse. Before their eyes, the black horse, his rider, and the sword all faded into nothingness, leaving behind only a puff of smoke.

Isadora could not explain the sense of peace that washed over her. It was as if the very air had changed, feeling somehow less oppressive. The Hessian had been bound by the curse as much as she had been. Now they were both free.

Hearing a sizzle behind them, they turned in time to see the button inside the bowl slowly catch fire. It was gradual at first, but once the flame caught, it exploded into a ball of fire, then went out just as quickly. When the smoke cleared, the button was gone, much as the Hessian had gone. Only the ring remained in the bowl, which had slid open at some point during their efforts, a small black spot now charring the center of the hidden compartment.

"Is it over? Did it work?" Simon asked, hesitantly. He was covered in dirt and soot and was bleeding from a few small cuts and scrapes. Isadora looked as bad as he did, but it could have been so much worse.

They all exchanged uneasy glances and Isadora came to a decision. "Only one way to find out."

She strode over to the stairs and walked down to the bottom. Slowly, she lifted one foot off the last step, placing it on the ground, then placed the other firmly beside it. Nothing happened. Isadora waited another few minutes, but there was no horse, no rider missing his head, and no flaming pumpkins coming at them. As she stood there, Simon right behind her ready to scoop her up at a second's notice, she realized she could hear the insects again. All of the sounds of the night were slowly coming back.

"I think it's over." Isadora spun around with a huge smile on her face and threw her arms around Simon. He laughed, lifting her up and spinning her around. Setting her back on her feet, he kissed her. In her excitement, she kissed him back.

When she pulled back, she was grinning widely. She caught sight of Tamara still up on the porch and ran to her, bringing her friend in for a celebratory hug as well. While the women rocked each other in their arms, Isadora thanked her over and over again.

40

Winter 1815

After months of convalescing, Ichabod was finally released from the hospital. Though he wanted nothing more than to go to Katrina, he had a duty. He had been ordered to his new station in Maine and reluctantly made his way there. Upon arrival, he found that his personal items that he had left behind in Sackets Harbor had been sent to the new duty station and were all waiting for him. This was a relief seeing as how he had lost a uniform, his sword, his horse, and many other personal effects to the Hudson River. At least now he had a uniform and a few items that he would not have to replace.

Winter was upon them quickly after his arrival in late October. He spent his days going through the motions when all he could think about was Katrina. It killed him that he did not even know if she was alive. He continued sending letters, updating his whereabouts, but he had little hope of receiving anything in return. The winter was even more bleak than the previous two had been. It was hard to believe it had only been two years ago that he had spent his winter mourning his friend Samuel. Now he was mourning Samuel's cousin and the love of his life.

By March, the weather was attempting to warm as spring tried to poke out from the gloom of winter. While the snow continued to fall, it also began to melt more quickly. It warmed up, if only slightly, but it was enough to begin traveling once again. Ichabod put in for a leave of absence and was granted a short one. He made his way to Tarrytown as quickly as he could. He booked passage aboard a ship bound for New York City, then aboard a fancy new steamship up the Hudson River to Tarrytown. It was his first time aboard a steamship, and he thought he would have enjoyed the experience, had he not been so eager to get to his destination.

When he finally stepped off the ship, Ichabod hired a carriage to take him to the Brush farm, telling the driver to make haste. As they sped along the streets through town, Ichabod looked out the window of the carriage. Something caught his eye as they passed several houses. He banged on the roof and told the driver to turn around and stop. The driver pulled the carriage to the side of the road and Ichabod began to step out of the carriage, wanting a better look. He had thought he had seen Katrina in a garden of one of the houses. How could that be, though? Had she moved away from the farm or was he mistaken, and it was someone else he saw? Perhaps she was only visiting someone in town? In his eagerness to see her, was he conjuring her image and projecting it onto someone else? The latter was more likely, but he needed to be sure. If Katrina had moved away from the farm, there was no chance Eleanor would tell him where to find her.

Ichabod held back slightly, watching, waiting for the young blonde woman to turn around. Before she did, he saw Brom walking out the front door of the house. He approached the woman who tried to stand but had some difficulty. Brom reached out a hand to help her to her feet. As soon as she was standing, Brom tilted her face up to his and planted a kiss on her lips. She had placed her hands on his chest while he kissed her. He pulled her in for a hug, wrapping his big arms around her. Ichabod's heart raced. Could that be his Katrina? Surely she would not have succumbed to Brom so quickly in Ichabod's absence?

The couple were talking, but they were too far away for Ichabod to hear what they were saying. The woman pointed down at the ground for her tools that she had left there when she stood. Brom bent to pick them up while she moved toward the house. She finally turned when she reached the door to look back at Brom and Ichabod gasped. It was indeed Katrina, but she was round with child, her hands resting on her belly protectively. Brom retrieved her tools and handed them to her, then reached out a hand to rest on her belly near hers. Katrina went inside the house and Ichabod was frozen in place. He could only stand there in shock. Brom followed Katrina inside but turned back when he heard the carriage driver's voice. He had asked Ichabod if he wished to continue, but Ichabod had not heard him. Brom, hearing the driver speak, followed the man's voice and saw Ichabod standing there beside the carriage and Ichabod knew the moment recognition hit him. The blacksmith tipped his hat to Ichabod and smirked. His satisfied smile was the last Ichabod saw of him as he walked back into the house after Katrina.

Ichabod felt as though his heart had been ripped from his chest. He did not know how long he stood there, but somehow, he managed to climb back into the carriage, telling the driver to return to the pier. Ichabod thought of all of the courses of action laid out before him, but it was obvious that Katrina had made her choice. Not only had she chosen Brom, she had apparently married him and was going to bear his child. Ichabod would never stand in the way of Katrina's happiness. He wished her well and let the carriage take him away from Tarrytown. There was nothing more for him there.

41

Modern Day

Isadora whistled as she walked through the farmer's market in Patriots Park. Nothing could spoil her mood this morning. The trio had stayed up late into the night celebrating. After cleaning up the pumpkin remnants, shards of splintered wood, and the altar from the porch, they had sat out there, enjoying the cool, peaceful night air. Isadora occasionally ran down the steps into the yard, for no other reason than because she could. She was still hesitant to believe it was fully over. She slowly ventured farther and farther away from the front steps and even ran all the way around the house a few times every couple of hours. After the third time, she decided it really was over. The lack of nightmares when she finally did get to bed only helped confirm this.

After doing her shopping, she dropped off a few of the items at the rental, then went back to the manor house. She called for a tow truck to clear the car away from the front lawn, then went down to the basement and straightened up the boxes she had thrown around the night before in search of the button. Picking up the old articles of clothing, she carefully set them back in the box they had been in, happy to see they appeared undamaged from her rough handling. She wondered how old they were and if there was a museum to which she could donate them.

Shortly after she came back upstairs, she heard the front door open. When she moved into the hallway, she saw Simon standing there.

"You didn't wake me before you left," he accused.

"I wanted to let you sleep. It was a late, strenuous night and you needed your rest."

Simon nodded. It felt as though there was a distance between them this morning again that he could not understand. "What about you? Did you get any sleep?"

Isadora smiled, though there was a hint of sadness in her eyes. "I did."

"No nightmares?"

"No nightmares."

Things had not been awkward between them after his declaration of love for her, yet for some reason, they were now. He was suddenly not sure what to say to her. For a moment, they both stood stiffly in the hallway, looking everywhere but at each other. There had been so much to focus on in the last few days, but now, it was as if there was a gulf between them.

"It's hard to believe I've only been here two weeks," Simon said, finally moving forward into the house. "What are we working on today? Are there more boxes to inventory?"

Isadora was torn. She wanted to accept his help and go back to the way things always were between them. She also wanted to run into his arms and tell him how much she loved him, basking in their feelings for one another. But she did neither of those things. Ultimately, she knew neither would last. The last days had shown her how much she loved it there and she did not want to go back to Utah. Since long distance relationships never lasted, and she would not ask him to move for her, there was no point in continuing. Even if he somehow moved to be with her, it would not matter. Relationships did not last even when they were not long distance. There was no winning when it came to relationships. It was best to end it now, once and for all. The longer she put it off, the harder it would be. She would miss him desperately, but it was for the best.

"Simon, you don't have to help me. You should go see your mother. We left rather abruptly, but I'm sure she'd like to spend more time with you before you go home."

Something about how she said that made him feel as though she was dismissing him. "She'll be fine," he said slowly. "I'd much rather spend the time with you. Things have been so crazy; we haven't really been able to talk or hang out without a billion distractions."

Isadora looked away, and Simon moved closer. She was quiet, and he knew there was something she was not saying.

"Iz? What's wrong? What is it you're not telling me?"

In a small voice, she managed to say, "I'm not going back to Utah, Simon."

Simon stopped in his tracks. He had suspected this might be the case when he first arrived, though he was not sure after everything that had happened with the Hessian. "Okay," he said, unsure what else he could say. He chose to ignore it for now and give himself time to think about how best to deal with it. He was not leaving for a while yet. Maybe he would think of something before he had to go.

"Well, I'm here for another two weeks. I can still help you out while I'm here."

Isadora finally looked at him, shaking her head. Tears burned her eyes, but she bit them back. "No. You should spend the time with your mother."

Simon's brows furrowed. "What does that mean?"

Isadora looked away again. She was wringing her hands, trying to find the words. "I can't do this, Simon. I can't spend the next two weeks with you, knowing you'll be going back to Utah while I stay here. It's better if you just go now."

Isadora would have to go back to pack up her office and home and get moved, but that would not take her long. She could do a quick trip, only long enough to clear everything out, and not see Simon while she was there.

Simon felt as though the ground had been pulled out from underneath him. He scoffed. "It's better? What are you saying? Are you trying to tell me we can't be friends anymore if we live in different states?"

Isadora went quiet again. There was so much she wanted to say, but it would betray her to say it. The last thing she wanted was to lose him, but if it was bound to happen eventually, she would rather get it over with so she could move on. She did not trust herself to speak.

"Damnit, Izzy. Is this because of what happened at Central Park?"

Isadora looked up at him, her brows knitted together. "No," she shook her head adamantly.

Simon did not believe her. "I know you don't feel the same way I do, but it's okay, Iz. I'm okay with that. It doesn't mean we can't still be friends. I promise I won't even try to kiss you again." He tried making his words sound like a joke, but they fell flat.

"It's not about that," she insisted. "I just can't do the long-distance thing. And if you're not going to be in my life at the end of your time here, why prolong it?"

Isadora heard the callousness of her words as they came out of her mouth and could not believe they were coming from her. It was as if someone else had taken control of her body and was speaking for her. It was for the best.

Simon nodded slowly. "Fine. If that's how you want it, Izzy. I'll be out of your life before you come home tonight."

Hearing the anger and hurt in his voice made her want to take it all back, but she could not do it. Isadora stood where she was, watching him spin on his heel and leave through the front door without looking back. She felt as though she was frozen in place once again, but this time, she was unable to do anything about it. When the door slammed shut behind Simon, Isadora collapsed onto the hallway floor and cried.

After her encounter with Simon, Isadora was no longer feeling as good as she had throughout the morning. She had been determined not to let anything spoil her mood but had not taken into account her own ability to do so. Staying at the manor, she found she was no longer in the mood to do much of anything. Once she finally got her crying under control, Isadora sat out on the back porch, overlooking the vast property. The lawn was still fairly green, but the trees were a rainbow of color. She stood and found herself wandering down the steps and out into the grass. Moving further into the property, she let herself wander aimlessly for hours, winding her way through the trees, moving slowly and carefully, watching every step she took. Making her way down to the creek, she sat by the water for a while where the tears came again. She let them flow until she thought there were no more tears left. It was then that she realized she had not even cried for Alex this much. It was not really a surprise. Simon had always meant so much more to her than Alex ever could have hoped for.

Isadora stayed at the manor that night, unable to bring herself to go back to the empty rental house. Simon had said he would be gone by the time she returned, and she knew that would be true. But she also knew that she would still be able to smell and feel his presence there. Going to the basement, she pulled an old blanket from one of the boxes and brought it upstairs, curling up underneath it on the sofa. Sitting there in the dark, she cried herself to sleep.

42

April 1816

Katrina gave birth to healthy baby girl. She cried the first time she held the baby in her arms. Not only was she filled with love and joy for the girl, but she was simultaneously filled with sadness and despair. As much as she loved the baby, she wished Ichabod had been there to see her born. How he would have loved their daughter. She knew he would have made a great father.

After she saw the phantom impale him with his sword, she had watched as Ichabod fell into the river. She tried to get to him, but it had all happened so fast. All she could do was watch as he dropped under the surface of the water, then resurface, only to drop below again. He could barely manage to hold onto the log he had been clutching and she knew if the water did not take him, the impalement would. Her heart broke as she watched him get taken away from her. Before he disappeared from sight, the specter grabbed her and threw her on his horse. She did not even care. She wanted to die. If Ichabod could not live, then why should she?

Katrina had hung over the demonic horse, watching the ground fly past. After a time, they came to a stop and Katrina was lifted once again and set on her feet. When she looked up, she saw her mother standing there in front of her. Her eyes went wide and her mouth fell open. Her mother actually nodded at the phantom before he climbed back on his horse and rode away. Katrina was speechless. Had her mother really been responsible for that demon coming after them and killing Ichabod?

Before she could speak, Eleanor grabbed her by the arm and pulled her into the house. "You will go to your room and stay there until I allow you to come out. If I have to fetch you again, you will not like the consequences. Do you understand me?"

Numb, Katrina could only nod.

"I trust you shall not be trying an escape again anytime soon?"

Katrina shook her head meekly.

"Good. Get upstairs."

Katrina was thankful for the time to herself when she returned to the farmhouse. Her mother had not locked the door again, but she also did not call Katrina to come out for a couple of days. By the time she finally did, Katrina was fully and completely numb. She no longer felt like this was her home. She was but a prisoner, a pawn for her mother to do with what she would. What was more was that Katrina did not even care. Without Ichabod, nothing mattered. There was nothing more her mother could even do to her that would ever be worse.

∾   ∿

As life resumed, Eleanor continued pushing Katrina to marry Brom. She still did not agree with it, but she also did not resist it. No longer having the energy to fight with her mother, she found that with Ichabod dead, it no longer mattered. Katrina would have to marry someone eventually, if only to get away from her mother. Was Brom such an awful choice? Still, she was not eager to make the match and put it off as long as she could.

When she began throwing up, Katrina thought she had come down with something. When it did not abate, she slowly came to the realization that she would not be able to put off marriage much longer. After doing some mental calculations, she realized that she might still be able to fool everyone into thinking the baby simply came early if she married right away.

There was no way she could bring a baby into this world on her own. How would she support a child by herself? Her family would be shamed, and people would stop doing business with her father. It would not surprise Katrina if her mother tried to harm the babe. Katrina would do what she could to protect it, even if it meant marrying Brom. At least her baby would be provided for and protected.

"I've had time to consider your proposal," Katrina said after church that Sunday. Her and Brom had been walking through the fields, Jacob following behind them.

Brom perked up, cocking his head towards her. "And?" he asked.

"I accept."

Brom cheered, lifting her up and spinning her around. When he placed her back on her feet, he leaned in to kiss her, but she placed a hand on his chest, stopping him.

"But only if we marry immediately. I do not want a big ado. After everything that has happened in the last year, I wish to do it quickly with our families there to witness it."

Brom was grinning as wide as he possibly could. He readily agreed to her terms.

They married a week later. Eleanor, Rebecca, and Weintie helped Katrina ready herself.

"Why the haste cousin?" Rebecca had asked.

Katrina shrugged. "It's not really hasty at all, is it, Rebecca? We've been skirting around this for years really. Now that I've finally made up my mind, it seems silly to wait any longer."

Avoiding her mother's stare while she gave Rebecca her answer, she had been watching her from the mirror. If the woman suspected anything, she could not tell.

Katrina dreaded the wedding night. She had not been looking forward to letting Brom into her bed. It had been bad enough letting him kiss her, but to share her body with him felt like a betrayal. When it came time to be with him, she shut her eyes and laid there, letting him do what he needed to do, all while she thought of her one night with Ichabod. Perhaps if she made herself as unenticing as possible, Brom would avoid her bed in the future. She tried to be as still as possible. She only needed to consummate the marriage and make Brom and everyone else think that the child was his.

It came as no surprise that Brom was nowhere near as patient and gentle with her as Ichabod had been. She was glad that this was not her first time. If it had been, her first time would have been far more painful. Ichabod had eased her in gently and took great care to lessen her pain. Brom had not even considered it. His ignorance worked to her advantage, though, as he never mentioned the fact that there was no blood, even though this was supposedly her first time. Either he did not know what to expect, or he did not care to look. She was not concerned about the why of it but was glad that it was the case.

As far as she could tell, her plan worked. No one ever vocalized any suspicions that the child was not Brom's. Though she 'came early,' everyone took it at face value that she was his. He doted on the baby and showed her off to everyone. Katrina had to admit, Brom was not as bad a husband as she had expected him to be. She did not love him and never thought she would, but he provided for her and her child. After their wedding night, he tried to be with her again, but he never forced her. When she told him no, he surprisingly accepted it. Maybe her performance had given him enough reason not to pursue her that aggressively.

Every time Katrina looked down at her baby, she was reminded of Ichabod. It still broke her heart to think of him, but she was grateful that at least she had a part of him to hold onto. She would never regret the night they spent together, nor giving herself to him. The memory would sustain her for a long time to come.

ℭ   ℭ

Summer 1816

Washington Irving was surprised to see a letter from his friend Brom Bones. He had been making his way through Wales, Scotland, England, Spain, and Germany and it took a while for mail to catch up to him. The letter was an announcement of his daughter's birth a few months prior, along with an update on what had happened since Washington had left Tarrytown the previous summer. He had left shortly after Ichabod had disappeared.

Washington was surprised to learn that Katrina had finally agreed to marry Brom after he left. Brom confided in him now that he had been overjoyed at first but had wondered at her abrupt change of heart. When she had announced shortly after their wedding that she was pregnant, he immediately suspected the reason for the decision. Eight months later, when the baby was born, his suspicions were confirmed. He was angry at first, but then he decided it did not matter since he was the one who had finally won Katrina.

Even if she did not love him, she was his. He could show her beauty to everyone.

In his letter, Brom also confided to Washington that Ichabod was still alive. They had all thought him dead or run away the previous summer. Katrina had spent several days in her room, but when she finally emerged, she had told Washington a tale that chilled his blood. She had not wanted everyone to think ill of Ichabod, so she told her story of what happened one foggy night on the banks of the Hudson River. Of course, no one believed her. However, Washington remembered Eleanor's bizarre behavior the night before the disappearance and thought perhaps it was possible.

Washington continued reading to find that Ichabod had actually returned to Tarrytown that spring. The man had not visited anyone. Instead, he saw a pregnant Katrina with Brom and had apparently "tucked tail and run again," too cowardly to face Brom again, the blacksmith had boasted. Washington knew better. He had seen both men after their previous encounter. Ichabod had fared far better than Brom and Washington had no doubt he could easily best the man again. He also saw how deeply he had cared for Katrina. It made no sense to him that Ichabod would simply leave without a word after seeing Katrina again. When she had finally shared her story, she had told

Washington of the contents of the letter he had helped deliver and he knew they had been trying to run away together when Ichabod was lost.

While Brom's letter was full of gloating and bravado, Washington simply could not make sense of it. If the babe was Ichabod's why would he not stay? Why would he not come back for her sooner? He could have come back immediately and tried taking Katrina away again. Had it been Washington, nothing would have stopped him. He missed his beloved so much. He would give anything to be with her again. How could Ichabod simply throw that away? He had never thought the man a coward before, but he certainly did now.

After finishing Brom's letter, Washington found his notebook and turned to the pages he had written the night he saw Eleanor outside in the small hours of the night. He recalled her strange ritual as he read her words on the page. *Hear me my Hessian hero…*

After watching her, he had been compelled to make note of her chant and the strange objects surrounding her. He had come back to his room and hastily jotted them all down on a blank page in his book. He had always had an interest in ghost stories, and he thought he might be able to use her chant in a story one day. Come to think on it, Katrina's tale of that night would certainly make a compelling story. He would not even have to make many changes as no one would ever believe it to be true. Certainly, no one that had heard Katrina tell it had believed her. An idea started forming in his mind and he began making more notes.

43

Modern Day

Isadora woke Sunday morning to Tamara shaking her shoulder. "What's wrong?" she asked in a panic.

"You tell me, Sugar. You're the one who slept on the couch of a cold empty house instead of your own bed inside a nice warm house."

Isadora groaned and sat up slowly. Her eyes were puffy and swollen and her head pounded. She almost felt hungover. "I thought I'd stay here since we exorcised the demons from the property." It was a lame excuse, even to her ears.

"Mm-hmm. And where did Mr. Diego stay?" With a hand on her hip, Tamara looked around the room as if he would come walking in any minute.

Isadora looked away. She was still trying to get her eyes to adjust and was having a hard time thinking quickly. Her brain felt foggy.

"He left. He's spending the rest of his visit in Brooklyn."

"Did y'all have a fight?"

"Not exactly."

"What, *'exactly'* does that mean?"

Isadora sighed. "It means that he's going back to Utah in a couple of weeks and I'm not. I've decided to stay here."

Isadora's brain was finally starting to work, and she did not want to talk about this. If she did, she might start crying again.

"What are you doing here anyway? How'd you know I was here?"

Tamara raised one eyebrow as she sat down on the sofa across from Isadora. "You're always here. I thought I'd come check on you. You seemed good yesterday morning when you texted, but then you went quiet. I wanted to make sure nothing happened. I stopped by the house but when no one answered, I came here."

Isadora knew she was referring to the Horseman. "Nothing happened. I was out in the yard after dark last night and it was all quiet. I think we can safely say he's really gone."

"Good to know," she nodded. "Now, what are we going to do with you, Chil'?"

Isadora needed a break; from the house and everything in it, from the village, and from anything related to Washington Irving, Ichabod Crane, or the story.

"Let's go explore farther upstate. I've never been to New York and so far I haven't managed to spend any time outside this area and a little bit of the city."

Tamara hesitated. "We could go see the finger lakes," she finally suggested. "You'd love them. They're four hours away though, so we'd have to get on the road now."

Isadora was not used to doing things like this on the spur of the moment. She was flexible, but not particularly spontaneous. The idea excited her, though and she jumped at it.

"Let's do it."

They took Tamara's car since Isadora's rental had been towed away the previous morning with a destroyed engine. When the tow truck driver had arrived and looked at it, he immediately asked what had happened. It looked as though something melted right through the middle of the engine block. She shrugged, telling him she had no idea what had happened. It was obvious he did not believe her, but it was not as though he would believe her if she had told him the truth. She had taken a rideshare to get around the previous morning and was planning on purchasing a car sometime that week, but she would do that when they got back. Nothing would be open on a Sunday anyways.

It had been a while since Isadora had been on a road trip with anyone. Well, anyone other than Simon, she corrected herself. Shaking off the thought, she focused on the moment. She enjoyed spending time with Tamara who was missing church in order to take this trip with her. They figured they could drive up, spend a couple of hours, then drive back that night. It would be a long day with a lot of hours sitting in the car, but it would be worth it.

Of course, the best of plans do not always work out. They made it to the finger lakes area, but before getting to Watkins Glen State Park, where they were headed, someone behind them did not see the light turn red and did not apply their brakes, plowing right into them. The rear of the car crumpled, and their car lurched forward. It was a good thing no one had been in front of them and there was little traffic in the intersection, otherwise they would have been pushed into another car.

After several hours of dealing with cops, paramedics, and doctors and being poked and prodded for concussions or internal injuries, the women were both exhausted. While they were still at the hospital, Tamara called her boss who told her to take the next week off to recover. The accident ended up being an unexpected gift. They took a rideshare to a nearby hotel and checked in. They had discussed going back home the next day, but figured since they were there, they may as well take advantage of it.

The first thing Isadora did every morning was check her phone for missed messages. There never were any. Simon had not called or texted, not that she blamed him. She knew he would respect her wishes, but it still hurt all the same. Eventually, she would drag herself out of bed and her and Tamara would explore the area, going to parks and seeing the beautiful lakes and waterfalls. They hiked every trail they could find and kayaked one of the lakes even though it was quite cold.

The time away was exactly what Isadora needed. Standing on the edge of a rock overlooking the water, she was finally able to let go of Alex. She had always known he was not someone she could see herself with for the long-term. He was too overbearing for her. When he first passed, she spent those days in Brooklyn romanticizing the brief relationship they had. She still blamed herself for his death, but at least she was able to see that he was not the perfect person she had built him up to be immediately after he was killed.

The trip was very healing for her, though she still had plenty of demons left inside to shake off. They made their way home at the end of the week and resumed their lives. Tamara went back to work and Isadora went back to the chaos of the work being done on the house. With Alex's death, everything that followed, then the impromptu trip to the finger lakes, she had postponed meeting with the upholsterer or looking at any of the mock-ups from the decorator. Now she got back to it all. She still had a handful of boxes to work through and several more rooms which needed wallpaper scraped away. Once those were done, there was plenty of other work that needed to be done.

"It's good to see you again, Izzy," Neil Lowry said when she finally returned to the house.

Since it had been the weekend when she had been there the few days over Halloween, she had not seen him in two weeks. At that point, Neil had most everything under control, but there were still items that occasionally popped up which needed her attention. They had kept in contact while she was away, and he had continued his work, but it was good to be back where she could see things in person before making a decision.

Isadora slowly began making decisions about how she wanted to decorate the massive house. It helped to know what she planned to do with the property, which she had decided while kayaking the finger lakes. Once she decided that she was definitely staying, she decided to open up the house as a bed and breakfast. She was going to put some of the items from the boxes on display in the parlor, showing a little bit of what life was like in the time the house was built, but the upstairs rooms would be rented out. The enormous room with the en suite vanity and bathroom as big as her bedroom in Utah would be the honeymoon suite.

Isadora talked with Neil, getting recommendations from him for an architect. He introduced her to one who helped her draw up plans to build a small house on the property where she would eventually reside. Initially, she would move into the big manor house, but once she started renting out rooms, she wanted her privacy. She could stay on the property, being close by without actually giving up her own personal space. The property was certainly large enough for it. This would also allow her to rent out the entire house if there was a need for it. While they were at it, she also worked with a landscaper to put in a dirt path around the property where she or her guests could run or go for a stroll without tripping on tree roots sticking up from the ground.

Everything was moving along steadily, and Isadora felt like they were making progress. At night, she returned to her rental. After a few nights of being there by herself, she began reading Ichabod's memoir. It began with his time in the marine corps, then moved onto his commission with the army for the War of 1812. He talked about the battles in which he had been, which Isadora ate up. She loved having the firsthand record of his life and wondered how she could incorporate it into her lecture. The thought made her question whether she would ever teach again. Was it really something she still wanted to do? She could look into the universities nearby, but she had not thought about it since being there at all. Maybe she would only run the bed and breakfast and do some writing to fill up her remaining time.

As Isadora read on towards the end of the war, she was surprised to see the name Van Tassel in Ichabod's book. She had never come across anything that tied him to the story in any way other than having been at Fort Pike at the same time as Irving. Even that was a loose tie as there was no evidence that they had ever met. She hungrily read on, learning that a young man named Samuel Van Tassel had served as his lieutenant but was killed during a battle on a farm along the Saint Lawrence River. They had been close friends and at the end of the war, Ichabod took a leave of absence to return some of his personal effects to his family in Tarrytown. Isadora could not believe what she read about his time between leaving Sackets Harbor and arriving in Maine at the end of the war. After all this time, here was the proof that he had been to Tarrytown and known Washington Irving after all. To think that this had been in her possession all these years, made her question why she had never looked through the box before. She could have used this when she had written her dissertation. Though, the information in this book changed everything about what they knew of the story. But then, was that not the case with the appearance of an actual Headless Horseman?

Isadora was excited to share her findings with Tamara and sought her out at work the next day. They sat during Tamara's lunch break, and she showed her the memoir, telling her what it said. Tamara was as excited as she had been.

"This is the missing piece. I knew there had to be more when I saw that letter to Irving from Brom."

Isadora's brows drew together. "What letter?"

"The letter I brought you weeks ago, Chil'. I couldn't bring the original, but I made a copy and gave it to you."

Isadora did not remember any such letter. "I'm pretty sure I would've remembered that."

"When did I bring it?" Tamara thought about it for a minute while tapping her chin with her finger, her long red fingernail filed to perfection. "Oh, it was the night we first saw the Hessian." She had been excited that she remembered, but as the words came out, so did the memories of that night and her inflection went from excited to dour. "It's no wonder you don't remember."

"I must have set it down without reading it. I'm sure it's still at the house somewhere. I'll have to look for it."

"Well, with all the extra fabric and paint samples and designs laying around, I'm not holding my breath that you'll be able to find it." Tamara stood. "Come with me."

They went into an office filled with books on shelves around the room and a desk taking up a large portion of the center of the room. Tamara went to a shelf that held books enclosed behind a locked glass. She put on a pair of cotton gloves, took out a set of keys, and pulled out a portfolio. Opening it up, she carefully flipped through the loose pages inside until she found the ones she was looking for. She scanned them quickly. Then after having Isadora put on a pair of gloves as well, she handed them to her. Isadora read the pages and gasped.

As she read, Isadora found herself sinking into the chair behind her without even looking at it. It was a good thing she had taken note of it before reading the letter.

"Katrina and Ichabod were lovers," she said in a stunned whisper. Ichabod had left that part out of his memoir.

Tamara nodded. "She was carrying his baby."

"But he left her." She was still reading and everything had not yet sunk in.

Tamara had read the letter weeks before and had plenty of time to process the information. Now, with Ichabod's account, she had a much fuller picture of the events. "Look at Ichabod's memoir. He couldn't get back to Katrina for months. By the time he was able to get back to her, she was already fully pregnant and married to Brom. He didn't know the baby was his. He must've thought she'd chosen Brom and was happy with him, carrying Brom's child."

"She probably thought Ichabod was dead," Isadora exclaimed. "If Eleanor Brush was Samuel's aunt, then she was a Van Tassel, which is where Irving got the name from. This whole time, the story was all based on factual events with only a few minor changes."

That was the most incredulous part of this whole situation. She supposed she should have known when they first encountered the Hessian, but Isadora had still been in denial. She had not made the connection that the rest of the story had any truth to it.

"But why would he write Ichabod as a cowardly school teacher? If he knew him, he would have known he was not a coward." Isadora was still connecting all the pieces.

"Washington Irving loved one woman his whole life. She died before they had a chance to be married and he never recovered from that," Tamara explained. "When he found out Ichabod was still alive, had gone to see Katrina, and just walked away from her, he probably thought Ichabod was the biggest coward in the world. Who walks away from love?"

On their trip upstate, Isadora had confessed to Tamara that she had sent Simon home and that they would likely never see each other again. She had also told her that he had kissed her in Central Park, but nothing could come of it. What she had not told her friend about was her own feelings for Simon or her fears of him leaving her if she opened herself up to him. But Tamara's words now made her wonder if the other woman did not already know. Given her expert intuition, she probably did. Were her words about Ichabod or Isadora? She was not sure, but her first thought now was of Simon. Excitement ran through her at the thought of sharing this new information with him and she could not wait to call him and tell him. Then she remembered that would not be happening. Was that really what she wanted?

For days after reading Ichabod's memoir and the letter from Abraham Martling to Irving, Isadora had played everything over repeatedly in her mind. She had still been going through the last of the boxes and found a stack of letters from various people through the ages. She scanned them all briefly, and the oldest one was dated 1863, but was not signed with a name. When she saw the word 'curse,' Isadora immediately dropped the rest of the bundle and read it eagerly.

My Dearest Leah,

> *I know you have reservations about Rachel's betrothed, but I implore you to not stand in their way. There is a curse on our family that I would not wish to ever see come to life again.*
>
> *When I was her age, I deeply loved a man who was not your father. We were to be wed, but mother did not approve of the matrimony. On the night we*

were to run away, we were met with a curse mother placed on him. My beloved was killed. Some weeks later, I found myself with child and was forced to marry the man you know as your father. Despite my situation, he cared for me and raised you as his own. I never loved him as I did the man who sired you. And I hated my mother until the end of her days.

I do not know if your grandmother's curse ended on the banks of the Hudson River that night, but for Rachel's sake, I do not wish to find out.

I would not see history repeat itself. Please give her your blessing.

Your loving mother

Isadora had read the letter over and over again. She wished for more information. Remembering the family bible, she ran to it and opened the cover to the list of names there. She found a Leah Martling directly under the line listing Katrina and Abraham. Leah must have been Eleanor's granddaughter, the daughter of Katrina and Ichabod, who was raised as Brom's daughter. Under her name was Rachel, with an Elizabeth underneath it dated 1864 as the birth year. They all had different last names, supporting what George Bachman had said about the property having been passed down through the eldest daughters. It all made sense, but Isadora was filled with a sense of validation, finally knowing with certainty that Eleanor had been the one to place the curse on Ichabod, calling up the Hessian. She wished she had found the letter before facing off with the Hessian. It also explained why Katrina had married Brom, though it broke Isadora's heart to know that the girl had never learned that Ichabod had still been alive. His memoir said he had convalesced for months and had been unable to go back for her. Would Katrina have waited for him had she known?

Was this to be her own fate as well? Would Isadora be doomed to spend the rest of her life apart from love? Was it too late for her as it had been for Ichabod and Katrina?

Isadora knew she needed to go back to Utah and close out her life there now that she had made the decision to stay in New York. She had been putting it off, using the manor as an excuse to avoid going back. Utah was filled with Simon. He had been part of her life almost the entire time she had lived there. She was not eager to go back and have to face that. But knowing what she knew now of Ichabod and Katrina's story, was that still what she wanted, never seeing Simon again? Time was running out for her to keep avoiding it. She needed to make a decision once and for all. Would she stick to the choice she had already made, or could she open up and let Simon love her? Had she already destroyed any chance with him? She was filled with questions for which she had no answers.

44

Modern Day

Isadora bundled up as she left the warmth of the airport. She took a shuttle to the home she had left two long months ago. It was beginning to get dark outside, but she could see all of the homes with their Christmas decorations starting to go up. Many would have already been decorated for a few weeks, but nearly as many were still being decorated. Though the calendar said winter was still weeks away, it had already arrived in Utah. Of course, it had already arrived in Sleepy Hollow as well. It had been snowing when she left, and now it was snowing there, more than halfway across the country.

It was almost strange to be back at her old home after being away for so long. Isadora had already come to think of Sleepy Hollow as home. She would only be in Utah long enough to pack up her things and arrange to have them moved to New York. The manor house was almost finished, but it was finished enough that she could start moving her things in. Everyone had done a great job on it and it looked authentic without being gaudy. She planned to stay in Utah for a couple of weeks to finish everything up and officially give her notice at the university. The dean was not going to be happy, but there was nothing she could do for that.

Isadora did not waste any time and began packing the first night after her arrival. Once her shuttle dropped her off, she had climbed into her car and went out to purchase moving boxes. She laughed to herself as she thought this had been her life for months now. Packing and unpacking; it seemed it was all she ever did. With the time change, she ended up going to bed early but was up early the next day as well.

With a full day ahead of her, she started by going to speak with the dean. Having already typed out a resignation letter, she wanted to deliver it in person. She took some boxes with her so she could pack up her office while she was there, and she would say goodbye to her colleagues while she was at it.

She was still jet lagged, but by the second day, she was starting to feel more like herself. Isadora began the day packing some more, and when she was ready for a break, she decided she had procrastinated long enough. Simon's house stood before her now and she found herself standing on his porch, trying to get up the courage to knock. She had never been more nervous to see him. Though he had been pissed when she last saw him, he had done exactly what she had asked of him. She had not heard from him since. How would he react to seeing her there now?

Digging deep down, she found her courage and knocked on Simon's door. When a woman answered, she was momentarily stunned into silence. The woman was a beautiful blonde with long, flowing hair and big hazel eyes. It took Isadora a moment to find her voice.

"I'm looking for Simon Diego?" She hated that it came out sounding like a question instead of a statement.

The beautiful woman smiled, and said, "Babe, there's someone at the door for you."

Babe? Had he already found a new girlfriend? It had only been a little over a month since Simon had declared his love for her, and he was supposed to have been in Brooklyn for two more weeks before returning to Utah. How long had he even known this woman? Was she some random person he picked up somewhere? Maybe this was a mistake. She could turn around and leave before Simon even made it to the door. Before she could think about it longer, Simon appeared at the door, wearing nothing but a pair of jeans. Her mouth dropped open and all Isadora could do was stare at him.

"Izzy? What are you doing here?" he asked, as stunned as she was.

"I…um… I…came to… pack up my things."

It took her a moment to get out a coherent thought. She pulled her eyes from his hard chest and looked at his handsome face. She was not sure it made it any easier to think. Her brain seemed to have shut off. Of course, she had seen him shirtless plenty of times but the implication of seeing him like this with the random blonde woman answering the door had left her flummoxed.

Simon frowned as he leaned on the edge of the door. "I thought you didn't want to see me anymore?"

There was an edge to his voice that she had heard many times over the years but never directed at her. It hurt. Isadora looked down, wringing her gloved hands.

"We found some more letters and I finally read Ichabod's memoir. Tamara and I think we know what happened now."

It was not the reason she had come, but now that she was standing there, faced with the reality that he had already moved on, her throat closed up and she could not tell him why she was really there. Simon did not say anything.

Isadora shrugged as nonchalantly as she could. "Anyway, I thought you'd want to know."

Against his better judgement, Simon found himself nodding and opening the door wider to let Isadora inside. They went into the living room where he introduced her to Vinnie then excused himself so he could go grab a sweater.

"That's an unusual name for a woman," Isadora observed.

Isadora did not want to look at this woman and looked around at the familiar home she had been to so many times. Were those boxes in the kitchen? There was only a sliver poking through the doorway, and she could not be sure. Simon was probably setting up his own Christmas decorations and had brought the boxes in from storage.

"It's short for Vignette. It's easier," the woman explained.

Of course it was. "That's a beautiful name. It sounds exotic."

Vinnie laughed. "It is. It's so exotic that no one can ever seem to pronounce it or spell it properly."

Isadora wanted to hate this woman, but she was perfectly pleasant. Simon came back fully dressed and sat beside Vinnie on the sofa while Isadora sat in the recliner across from them. Isadora was grateful that at least the woman was not hanging on him possessively.

"How did you two meet?"

Simon cut off Vinnie before she could answer. "What did you and Tamara find out?"

Isadora got the hint. He only wanted to hear what she had discovered, but nothing more. She deserved that.

Isadora told him about the findings in the letter and the memoir. She told him of the relationship between Katrina and Ichabod, Irving, and Brom and that Katrina had become pregnant with Ichabod's child.

"So, does that mean you're descended from Katrina and Ichabod? And what does that mean for the Hessian? If the house remained in the family for two centuries, how is it he only just rose again to attack you and no one else in your family?" he asked, leaning forward in his seat.

Vinnie got a confused look on her face. Simon had deliberately referred to the entity as the Hessian since it was less likely to be recognized than referring to it as the 'Horseman' or 'Headless Horseman.' But his reference to something attacking after two hundred years was hard to understand.

"No. We looked at the genealogy and the names in family bible. Combined with the findings from ancestry DNA, we think Mary Crosby was descended from Ichabod and Katrina's offspring. I'm only related to Ichabod, not Katrina. We know I came from

Charles who was the son of Charlotte and Ichabod. But Mary's name was not in that bible. I finally found the paperwork from the attorney laying out the provenance of the house. It tied her to the names that were in the bible. The last entry in it was her parents." He nodded and she continued. "Tamara thinks that the words Irving wrote in his notes about Eleanor were likely pretty close to what was really said. He also mentioned that Eleanor used her own blood and a cloth that looked to be bloodstained. She thinks that must have been something with Ichabod's blood on it. Given the words she spoke, she would have been asking the Hessian to protect her family, while cursing Ichabod, and subsequently his entire line. Since Mary and everyone else that the house was passed down to had Eleanor's blood in them as well as Ichabod's, they were always safe from him. Since I don't have Eleanor's blood, but only Ichabod's–"

"He came after you because you weren't protected even though you were both related," Simon finished for her, nodding.

She could not help the smile that broke out on her face. This felt more like the way things had always been between them. "Exactly. And it was probably cutting my ankle and the blood dripped into the earth that woke him."

"That makes sense." None of this made sense, but given what they had experienced, he could no longer dismiss the supernatural and the power of magic and curses.

A smile had crept across Simon's face until Vinnie asked, "What are you guys talking about?"

He turned to look at her, momentarily having forgotten she was even there. "The Headless Horseman. Have you heard the story?"

"Sure. I saw the movie when it came out years ago."

"Izzy did her dissertation on it, but she's been in Sleepy Hollow the last couple of months digging up new research." He sounded proud of her, but he deliberately kept his answer vague, implying that it was all about the story. It was not entirely a lie.

When the conversation turned to small talk, Isadora decided it was time to leave, unable to sit there watching Simon with his new girlfriend while they all made small talk. She had done that countless times over the years, but everything was different now. She could not bear it. Standing, she made her excuses and started heading for the door.

Simon followed her. She opened the door, and he reached above her head to hold it open. Turning, she said, "It was really good to see you."

He nodded, looking away. "Thanks for telling me what you found out."

Her eyes were burning as she fought back the tears and quickly turned away, half running towards her car. When she got to the car, she found Simon right behind her. When she tried to open the door, he reached past her and pushed it closed again. Isadora found herself trapped between him and her car. Neither of them spoke for a moment as they stood there staring at each other, Isadora's heart pounding in her chest. When a car drove past, Simon finally blinked.

"How long are you in town?"

"A couple weeks. Just long enough to get everything packed up and moved."

"You decided what to do with the house, then?"

Isadora filled him in on her plans, but she had a hard time getting excited about them now. Why had he followed her out there only to engage in more small talk? This was killing her. She wanted nothing more than to climb inside her car and drive away.

When he did not say anything further, Isadora pulled her door open and started climbing inside. Simon held it for her, not stopping her this time. Before closing it, he leaned in.

"Maybe we could get together again before you leave?"

He was afraid to ask and almost had not done so, but he could not stop the words from coming out of his mouth. Simon knew she did not want to spend time with him, but he still wanted more time with her. If one more day was all he could get, he would take it.

To his surprise, she said, "I'd like that."

He was even more surprised when she agreed to meet him to go skiing before she left. He stood then, closing the door. How fitting that their last time together would be doing the same thing they were doing when they met.

ജ   ൙

Isadora was a nervous wreck. She changed her clothes five times before leaving the house to meet Simon. He lived closer to the ski resort, so she would drive over to his place, and they would leave from there. She had no idea what to expect from this day. Would Vinnie be there? He had not said whether he was bringing her, and she had not asked.

They got up the mountain and spent a wonderful day on the slopes. Vinnie had not come, and it was only her and Simon, laughing like the old days. For one day, everything between them seemed to have melted away and they were easy with one another again. They stayed for dinner at one of the restaurants after they finished skiing, then headed back to Simon's place.

"Do you want to come inside?" he asked sheepishly as they climbed out of his car.

Isadora hesitated. She looked longingly at the house but knew she should not go inside. Slowly, she shook her head. "I should get back. I still have a lot of packing to do."

Simon nodded, all the joviality suddenly going out of him. He walked her to her car, gave her a lingering hug, then kissed her on the cheek and went inside without a word.

Isadora could not fight the tears this time. She climbed into her car and started the engine but sat there with her head on the steering wheel without moving. The tears were falling too hard to drive safely, and she let them fall. She was exactly like Ichabod. Before leaving New York, she had decided that she was going to tell Simon how she felt and open herself up to the possibility of love. Seeing him with Vinnie had kept her from doing that. Vinnie was a reminder that not only had Simon already moved on, proving her point that love did not last, but that Simon's life was there in Utah and hers was no longer there. He deserved someone who could make him happy and be there for him.

Isadora took her gloves off as she dug through her console looking for a tissue to wipe her eyes. When she did, Eleanor's poison ring she had found in the box with the button caught her attention. Staring at it for a long moment, she thought about everything that had happened in the last two months. She thought of what she had learned of Ichabod and Katrina and Eleanor. Ichabod and Katrina had lost out on love because of Eleanor and because Ichabod had not had the courage to stand up and take Katrina from Brom. She had sworn to herself that she was not going to be like Ichabod. Wiping her eyes, she drew in a deep breath and gathered her courage.

When Simon opened his door and saw Isadora standing there, her face red from crying, he immediately pulled her inside.

"What happened?" he asked, his voice filled with concern.

Isadora opened her mouth to speak but her throat closed up on her once again. "You mind if I grab a drink? I'm parched."

She followed him into the kitchen where she could see the stacks of boxes more clearly now. These were not Christmas decorations.

"What's with the boxes? Are you going somewhere?"

Simon looked over at the stack against the wall. "I'm moving."

She could not hide the shock as she almost choked on her water. "Where? When? How did this happen?"

Simon rubbed a hand at the back of his neck and sighed. "I'm leaving after the first of the year. My company has a lot branches and I'm transferring to another location."

"Where?" she demanded.

"I don't know yet. We're still working out the details. We've narrowed it down to a couple places, but the final decision hasn't been made yet."

"I don't understand, Simon. I thought you loved it here."

"I did. It's not the same anymore."

"Since when?" she asked softly.

Simon avoided her gaze. He had already laid himself open to this woman once. Now he felt like she could burn through him with a look.

"Simon?" she asked. Isadora set down her glass and walked closer to him. She tilted her head, so she was directly in his line of sight. "Since when is it not the same?"

Simon closed his eyes, taking in a breath. It was meant to fortify him, but she was so close, all he could smell was her vanilla scent and the breath had the inverse effect it was meant to have.

"Since you won't be here."

Isadora put her hand on his arm. Her touch burned his skin.

"What about Vinnie?"

It was not what she had meant to say, but once the words were out, she realized she needed to know. She wanted him to be happy. If this newest girlfriend did not make him happy, then she wanted to know.

Simon laughed. "What about Vinnie? Vinnie's a friend. I've known her for a long time."

Isadora jerked back at this information. Brows furrowed, she said, a little angrily, "I've never met her."

"You haven't met everyone in my life, Izzy. There was never a reason for you to meet her." Her hands crossed her chest as if in challenge, so he continued, "Vinnie and I hooked up once, but there was never anything between us. The sex is good, so we stayed in touch. When we have the itch and we're both single, we meet up sometimes. That's all it's ever been and she was never important enough to me for you to meet her."

Simon was not sure why he was telling Isadora this about Vinnie. Was he trying to hurt her or merely trying to be honest with her? Their relationship was over anyways, so did it even matter?

"When I saw Vinnie, I thought…" she began before freezing up again.

"What did you think, Iz?"

Isadora took a step back. She turned around for a minute, so she could gather herself. Simon had never hidden Vinnie from her. Now that he mentioned their history, she remembered hearing about her, just not her name. It was not like she had not had her own relationships like that over the years. Seeing her discarded water on the counter, she picked it up and took another drink. Setting the glass back down, she decided Vinnie did not matter.

"I've been in love with you for as long as I've known you, Simon Diego," she said quietly with her back to him. It was somehow easier to say if she was not looking directly at him, but she turned to face him now. The look on his face was an odd mixture of surprise, happiness, confusion, and hurt. She leaned against the counter, holding on for dear life. "I'm sorry I didn't tell you in New York. And I'm unbelievably sorry for what I said to you that last morning. I was afraid. Everything you said was true. I'm as much of a coward as Ichabod. I'm terrified to let anyone in. I'm afraid you'll leave me, and it'll rip my heart open, so I thought it would be easier if I left first. But it wasn't easier. And I came here to tell you that I wanted to be with you, but then I saw you with Vinnie and I got scared again."

The words had come out fast, as if they had taken on a life of their own and needed to get out before she changed her mind.

Simon stared at her, stunned.

"Say something," she whispered.

Without saying a word, he closed the distance between them and dropped his mouth onto hers, taking her into his arms. Her eyes closed and she let him invade her mouth, relishing the taste and feel of him. His kiss was urgent, pleading. He smelled good and tasted even better. Finally, he broke the kiss. Looking into her eyes, he searched for the truth of her words there and any indication that she might run again. When he was satisfied with what he saw, he said, "I love you, too, Iz."

She stretched up and kissed him again. "I don't want to lose you, Simon. These last few weeks have been hell."

"They have," he agreed with a chuckle, "but I'm not going anywhere ever again. You better be certain that this is what you want, because it's going to take a lot to get rid of me after this." He kissed her gently, then added, "And I'm never going to let you push me away again."

Putting his hands in hers, he pulled her into the living room and sat on the couch with her beside him. Brushing a hair away from her face, he asked, "How do we fix this? What do you want to do?"

Isadora hesitated. "I wasn't really sure when I came here. I don't need to work anymore. I can go anywhere you want to live. I can hire someone to manage the bed and breakfast once it's up and running and I can go anywhere."

"I thought you loved Sleepy Hollow?"

"I do, but as long as you're there, it doesn't matter where I am. I've spent my entire life moving from place to place, but it wasn't until these last few weeks that I realized it doesn't matter where I am. *You*, Simon; *you're* home. Without you, it doesn't matter where I am. It's just another place."

Simon pulled Isadora in for another kiss, holding her tightly against him. His heart swelled hearing her say that he was her home. It was an echo of his own feelings towards her.

"I love you, Simon. I don't care where we live, as long as we're together."

Simon's smile split his face. "I don't think I'll ever get tired of hearing that. I love you so much, Iz."

He kissed her again, slowly. He would never get tired of kissing her either. When he pulled back, he said, "My company has offices in New York City. It would be a bit of a commute anytime I had to go into the office, but since I do most of my work from home, that wouldn't happen often."

Isadora's head pulled back. "You'd move to back New York for me? I thought you didn't like it there? Isn't that why you left?"

"Sweetheart, I'd move anywhere for you," he said with a smile. Simon found he could not stop smiling. He had never been so happy. "I wasn't crazy about the idea of staying in Brooklyn forever, but Sleepy Hollow isn't Brooklyn."

"No, it certainly isn't," she laughed.

"Besides, it might be nice to live a little closer to the family. But being an hour away, I wouldn't have to see them every day," he said teasingly.

"I guess we both have a lot more packing to do."

"Packing can wait. Right now, I want to extend this moment as long as I can."

"I can do better than that," she said as she pulled him to his feet.

With her hand in his, Isadora guided Simon down the hall to his bedroom for the night they had both been waiting years to finally have; the night that would mark the start of their life together. With her confession, everything seemed to click into place, and she was finally ready to fully open herself up to someone, to Simon. Isadora was done holding back.

AUTHOR'S NOTE

This story is a mix of fiction with factual events and people. The inspiration for it is based on the fact that Ichabod Crane was a real person who may still have living descendants. Knowing this to the be the case, it was easy to put the pieces together. The research was quite fascinating as many of the pieces came together better than I could have planned. Washington Irving was in Sackets Harbor during the War of 1812, reportedly until 1814, then went to Europe in August of 1815. Ichabod Crane was stationed there during the war, then was transferred to Fort Preble in Portland Harbor, Maine on August 10, 1815. The army discharged men from service at the end of the war effective on the first of May that same year. It took several months to wind everything down and reissue orders to the men staying on. This allowed the perfect opportunity for this story to take place. There was a very small window in which the story could have taken place based on the real timeline of history, but a small window was all that was needed.

Isadora's entire lecture at the beginning of the book is based on real facts. All references to the Revolutionary War and the War of 1812 are also based on actual events. The raid on the Van Tassel farm, the Hessian trooper who lost his head to a cannonball and was buried by the Van Tassel family, and the capture and hanging of Major John André for espionage are all true with several references for each incident. Likewise, the expedition up the Saint Lawrence River and the battle of Crysler's farm are well-documented events. While the events were all real, many details were imagined for the story.

Ichabod Crane was an actual person who served first in the marine corps briefly, then in the army for the rest of his life and was the captain of one of the artillery boats leading the expeditionary forces up the Saint Lawrence. His actions at Crysler's farm had warranted him a promotion to brevet major in 1813. All references to his father, grandfather, brothers, wife, and sons are factual, as is the personal link to Colonel Moses Porter, though it is only speculation on my part that Moses had ever met the rest of the Crane family. He did serve with both Ichabod and his father, but he may or may not have had a personal relationship with the rest of the family.

Real names are used in the historical part of the story whenever possible. While the Van Tassels were a real family who were prevalent in the founding of Tarrytown, the characters in this story are a mix of real and imagined. Samuel Van Tassel is a character based solely on my imagination. All other Van Tassel Characters have been given names based on real people, but the characters are entirely fictional. The historical accounts of the raid on the farm during the Revolution refer to the owners as a Cornelius and Elizabeth Van Tassel and their children Cornelius Jr and the baby Leah. Eleanor and John being part of this family are fictional additions for the purpose of the story. There was a Lena Van Tassel born June 4, 1764, who married a Caleb Brush and had three sons: Joshua, Caleb, and Jacob. I used this family as the source for Eleanor and Katrina's family by adding Katrina to the family and changing Lena to Eleanor, though Lena was a common nickname for Eleanor and that may have actually been Lena's real name. Katrina's character is entirely made up for this story based on Washington Irving's original story, *The Legend of Sleepy Hollow*. There was a John and Weintie Van Tassel who were actually married April 17, 1771, and had four children: Harmon Van Tassel, Rebecca Van Tassel, Betsey Van Tassel, and Margaret Van Tassel. This is the family into which I inserted Samuel.

Abraham Martling was another real person and the references to him and to Brom Bones in Isadora's lecture are both based on facts. Of course, Washington Irving was a real person as well, but all character traits are made up. His travels, home, time in Tarrytown growing up, and the events surrounding his fiancé are all well-documented. Given how he felt about his betrothed, it is not a stretch to imagine him thinking someone a coward who allowed love to simply fall through their fingers.

There is no record that Ichabod Crane ever stepped foot in Tarrytown or that he ever met Washington Irving in person. Though, along with their connection to Sackets Harbor during the war, Ichabod served as lieutenant under Captain Stephen Decatur during his service in the marine corps. Decatur was a close friend of Washington Irving, the pair even having lived together for a time. It is possible that Irving and Crane may have met at some point through their respective associations with Decatur or that at the very least, Decatur had mentioned the name to Irving.

Ichabod married Charlotte A. Rainger on September 1, 1819, and had two sons with her. Contrary to the character in Irving's original story, he was reported to be tall and portly with a high sense of personal honor and sterling integrity. He maintained strict discipline in his command but befriended every officer under him. It is not difficult to imagine him befriending a lieutenant under his command. I hope I have done his memory justice.

All modern characters are entirely fictional and based on my imagination. However, most of the modern events in the Westchester region are based on real events. The Halloween celebrations in and around Sleepy Hollow are entirely worth attending. It is easy to see why Washington Irving was so drawn to the area.

ACKNOWLEDGEMENTS

Thanks to my parents who told me my whole life that I was descended from Ichabod Crane. Without that in my head, I never would have come up with the concept for this story.

A special thanks to my *Salem Sistas,* Kristy Carson and Cori Greenland. Without our trip and the preparation leading up to it, I'm not sure I would have thought of any of this.

A huge thanks to Jennifer Hornback, Lisa Lambert, Billy Romero, and David Sorum who all helped encourage me and gave me input to improve the story of Ichabod and Isadora. It would not be what it is without the contributions of each of you.